OMEGA

Steven Konkoly

Book Five in the Black Flagged Series

Copyright 2017 by Stribling Media. All rights reserved. Except as permitted under the U.S. Copyright Act of 1976, no part of this publication may be reproduced, distributed or transmitted in any form or by any means, or stored in a database or retrieval system, without the prior written permission of the author, except where permitted by law, or in the case of brief quotations embodied in critical articles or reviews. For information, contact stevekonkoly@striblingmedia.com.

Acknowledgments

To the usual suspects. You know who you are. A special shout-out goes to my editor, Felicia Sullivan, for saving me from myself on this one. She knows what I'm talking about. The same thank you goes out to Pauline Nolet and Stef McDaid, both of whom responded brilliantly to my rather short-fused notice.

Dedication

To my family, the heart and soul of my writing. I couldn't do this without their tireless support and love.

About Black Flagged Omega

THANK YOU for very patiently waiting for this book. I released Black Flagged VEKTOR (Book 4) in the summer of 2013, after deciding to take a short break from the series. I'd written four books back-to-back in two years and was starting to see the Black Flagged characters in my sleep. That short break turned into a long detour. Six books and several novellas, in two different series, to be exact. I really appreciate your loyalty and patience. I think you'll find OMEGA worth the wait.

I had a lot of time to ponder the fifth book, which I thought would be the last novel in the core series. I'm very pleased to let you know that there will be a sixth book. Halfway through OMEGA, I realized that the finale I had in mind for this story was worth a full novel, so you can expect book six within the next year or so. I don't want to give too much away, but the scope of the conspiracy unveiled in OMEGA is vast and devastating, unlike anything you may have read before.

On that note, I need to make a statement that I've never included in my books before OMEGA:

All characters and corporations or establishments appearing in this work are fictitious. Any resemblance to real persons, living or dead, is purely coincidental.

Why the disclaimer? You'll soon find out. Here's a little background and a hint. In 2012, I created a fictitious political movement for Black Flagged APEX, called True America. Some similarities in core beliefs between the Tea Party movement and True America existed, but my intention, as stated in APEX, was to create a third, viable party vying for political power. I had plans for True America later in the series. Fast-forward to the spring of

2016, when I finished the first third of OMEGA, in which True America shocks the establishment and wins the 2008 (series time) presidential election. You can probably see where this is headed.

"Truth is stranger than fiction, but because Fiction is obliged to stick to possibilities; Truth isn't" — *Mark Twain.*

Black Flagged OMEGA takes place in 2009, roughly two years after the events of Black Flagged VEKTOR.

***At the end of the book, I have also included a short story written about Daniel Petrovich's time as an undercover operative in Serbia.

Cast of Characters

UNITED STATES

CIA

Zane Abid – Deputy Director National Clandestine Service
Audra Bauer – Deputy Director, Counterproliferation Center
Karl Berg – Staff Operations Officer, National Clandestine Service
Erin Foley – NCS Liaison to Black Flag group.
Thomas Manning – Director, Counterproliferation Center
Richard Sanford (TA) – Director
Sandra Tillman – Director National Clandestine Service

FBI

Dana O'Reilly – Deputy Associate Executive Assistant Director
Ryan Sharpe – Associate Executive Assistant Director, National Security Branch

BLACK FLAGGED

Dihya Castillo – Black Flag, Middle Eastern Group
Scott Daly – Former U.S. Navy, SEAL. Black Flag Americas Group
Richard Farrington "Yuri" – Black Flag, Russian Group Leader
Aleem Fayed – Black Flag, Middle Eastern Group Leader
Erin Foley – Former CIA agent. Black Flag, Contract Associate
Timothy Graves – Black Flag, Electronic Warfare Team, U.S.
Ashraf Haddad – Black Flag, Middle Eastern Group
Jared Hoffman "Gosha" – Black Flag, Russian Group Sniper
Nikolai Mazurov – Former Black Flag Operative.
Enrique Melendez "Rico" – Black Flag, Americas Group
Jeffrey Munoz – Black Flag, Americas Group
Daniel Petrovich – Black Flag, Contract Associate
Jessica Petrovich – Black Flag, Contract Associate
Brigadier General Terrence Sanderson – Black Flag, Leader
Abraham Sayar – Black Flag, Middle Eastern Group

Department of Defense
General Frank Gordon – Commander, United States Special Operations Command

White House
Alan Crane – President of the United States (True America Party)
Nora Crawford – Secretary of State
Erik Glass – Secretary of Defense
Bob Kearney (Major General, U.S. Army retired) – Homeland Security Advisor
Beverly Stark – White House Chief of Staff
Gerald Simmons – White House Counterterrorism Director

Office of the Director of National Intelligence
Frederick Shelby – Principle Deputy Director of National Intelligence
Gary Vincent – Director of National Intelligence

RUSSIAN FEDERATION

Federation Security Service (FSB)
Arkady Baranov – Director, Center of Special Operations (CSN)
Maxim Greshnev – Chief Counterterrorism Director
Alexei Kaparov – Deputy Director, Bioweapons/Chemical Threat Assessment
Yuri Prerovsky – Federation Agent, Organized Crime Division

Foreign Intelligence Service (SVR)
Dmitry Ardankin – Director of Operations, Directorate S
Vadim Dragunov – Zaslon operative, Directorate S
Mihail Osin – Spetsnaz operative, Directorate S
Stefan Pushnoy – Director

OTHER

Ernesto Galenden – Wealthy Argentinian business tycoon supporting General Sanderson's Black Flag program
Srecko Hadzic – Former leader of the "Panthers," a Serbian ultra-nationalist paramilitary group associated with Slobodan Milosevic's regime
Darryl Jackson – Brown River Security Corporation executive
Mirko Jovic – Leader of "White Eagles," a rival paramilitary group
Dima Maksimov – Solntsevskaya Bratva, *Pakhan* (Leader)
Matvey Penkin – Solntsevskaya Bratva, *Avtoritjet* (Brigadier)
Anatoly Reznikov – Former scientist at Vektor Institute
Grigor Sokolov – Former GRU Spetsnaz. Bratva Security.

Prologue

United Nations Detention Unit
The Hague, Netherlands

Srecko Hadzic shuffled impatiently along the pea green linoleum floor toward his cell. He'd just finished another unsatisfying meal of unidentifiable meat, mashed potatoes, and soft green beans in the cafeteria. He craved a cigarette, but this pleasure would have to wait. He'd waited all day for this moment. After dinner, the detention unit's staff invariably left him alone until the first evening room check around 7:30.

His attorney had passed him a USB drive, which contained an encrypted digital file from his nephew. Srecko had received an email from Josif a few days earlier, confirming that "production of the documentary was complete," but he gave no indication of when the film would be delivered. The suspense had aggravated Srecko's heart palpitations as he anxiously awaited the video of Zorana Zekulic's gang rape and murder.

The thumb drive had arrived earlier today at his attorney's office in Amsterdam via DHL Overnight Delivery from Buenos Aires. A message from his nephew's email account apologized for the delay and provided a decryption key for the thumb drive. He tried not to skip back to his cell. The mood in the detention unit ranged from dour to utterly depressed, and he didn't want to raise anyone's suspicions, including his fellow prisoners. He wanted a solid hour or two to enjoy Zorana's last miserable moments on Earth. He wasn't sure how long the video lasted, but he intended to savor it over and over again, fast-forwarding to the good parts…unless they were all good parts. He really hoped Josif had edited the final cut.

He walked into his cell and closed the heavy metal door behind him, making sure to shut the observation hatch. They could open the peephole, but generally respected the detainees' privacy during daytime hours. He couldn't remember the last time one of the detention center guards had checked on him between dinner and the evening room check. Still, his computer monitor was fixed facing the door, so he would have to be careful. Unfortunately, he wouldn't be able to watch the video with his pants down. He'd save that for later, after he found his favorite scenes.

He walked through his room, which resembled a decently appointed college dorm. A spare bed with clean linens sat across from a wall-mounted desk unit housing his computer. A simple hard plastic-backed metal wire chair was pushed under the desk. He moved the chair back and sat in front of the desktop, eagerly pushing the thumb drive into the single USB port on the ancient machine.

The screen activated and he quickly navigated to the contents of the thumb drive, which contained one file. He removed a scrap of paper from a folder next to the computer and clicked on the file. He was immediately prompted for the decryption password. Once entered, Windows media manager launched, recognizing the file as an MPEG. When the MPEG launched, the status window indicated "20:17."

A little short, he thought.

He had expected more than twenty minutes; then again, a well-edited effort could be more rewarding than hours of drawn-out torture and drama. He clicked on the play button.

The video started with a panoramic view of a neatly arranged bedroom, eventually settling in on a stainless steel contraption that Srecko immediately recognized as some kind of restraining device. It looked extremely durable and sturdy, with thick straps affixed at several points along the suspension bars. He tried to envision how she would be strapped into this contraption. The video stayed focused on the device, teasing him. His nephew produced superior work. He glanced at his cell door and reconsidered his clothing options. No. He would wait.

The image faded, replaced with a close-up shot of a bloodied woman that he immediately recognized. She looked like she had been beaten and strangled for hours, her clothing and skin slick with blood. She stood there for a moment with a blank look on her face, like she had given up. He kind of wished that they hadn't skipped the beating part of her experience. Maybe Josif would use flashbacks to show this. From what he could tell, his nephew had quite an artistic talent.

The scene changed again and Zorana was strapped into the contraption, but something wasn't right. Why had Josif dressed her up in white coveralls? He saw Zorana struggle and twist to no avail, which eased Srecko back into his chair for a moment. The writhing stopped a few seconds later, and she lifted her head above the horizontal plane of her body. He violently launched the chair back against the bed and stood up with a disgustedly confused look on his face. *Josif* was strapped into the harness with duct tape across his mouth. What in the hell was wrong with his nephew? This was the person he had groomed to run the show while he was temporarily stuck in prison?

He suddenly understood what he was watching when Zorana Zekulic appeared and took a seat on the bed next to his nephew. She grinned madly at the camera and effortlessly twirled a wicked-looking black serrated knife in her right hand. He sat back down and gripped the sides of the chair, squeezing them as Zorana went to work on Josif. He forced himself to watch the rest of the video, feeding the rage that raised his blood pressure and heart rate to dangerous levels. Several minutes later, he watched helplessly as one of her accomplices summarily executed his nephew. Josif had still been strapped to the harness when the man sprayed his brains onto the bedroom wall.

Srecko twitched in the seat, wanting to rip the computer from the wall and smash it over the nearest prisoner's head. He wanted to kill everything in his path, using everything at his disposal. He was wheezing at this point, breathing through his mouth. This travesty of a video was almost finished. The digital time counter in the lower left corner of the screen showed less than ten seconds remaining. He stared at the screen as Zorana suddenly appeared, covered in blood and smiling like nothing had happened.

"Hope you enjoyed the video, Srecko. Josif didn't get to deliver his lines, but I do like the pattern his brains made on the wall. Very artistic. What do you see when you look at the splatter? Quick. First impression. A butterfly? A waterfall? Do you know what I see? I see a good start. You're next."

She kissed the camera lens, leaving a smudge that blurred the screen. A few seconds later, the video ended.

Srecko sat down in his chair and leaned his head back to stare at the ceiling. He ran his stumpy, mottled hands through his thick silver hair and closed his eyes. One thing was certain. He was going to kill that bitch and her traitorous husband in person. Josif had proposed a plan to get him out of here, which made more sense now than ever before. He'd spend every last penny…every last ounce of his energy, making sure they paid dearly for this.

He pulled a gnarled cigarette from the crumpled pack in his shirt pocket and gripped it between his lips. He didn't care if the cells were designated as nonsmoking. Not today. He searched around for matches, but found none. On shaky legs, he rose and searched his pockets, still finding no way to light the cigarette he desperately needed. He crushed the cigarette in his hand and threw it against the wall, fully intending to rip his room apart. Instead, he calmly walked toward the door, opting to ask nicely for a new matchbook from his captors. He would need to be on his best behavior to have any chance of getting out of here.

PART ONE

GRAY AREA

Chapter 1

Tverskoy District
Moscow, Russian Federation

Matvey Penkin looked away from the flat-screen monitor on his desk, directing his attention toward the open office door. A bulky man wearing an oversized suit appeared in the doorway, holding a satellite phone. Penkin nodded, and the man approached, reaching across the wide desk to place the phone in his waiting hand. Once the phone was in his grasp, the security guard quietly withdrew from the room, shutting the door behind him.

Penkin examined the orange, backlit LED screen on the device, not recognizing the number. Whoever was on the other end of the phone had decided against using one of the preassigned satellite phones assigned to their post. A call placed using one of those phones would immediately identify the caller. He checked the back of the phone before answering.

A three-letter code stenciled in white indicated the phone had been set up to receive calls from his territory or operations bosses in Southeast Asia. Given that the Solntsevskaya Bratva hadn't widely penetrated the area, he had a good idea where the call had originated. Penkin braced for bad news about his special project, strongly suspecting it would be more than another unanticipated delay.

"This better be important," said Penkin, breathing heavily into the receiver.

A digitally garbled, Russian-speaking voice answered, "Mr. Penkin, time is short, so I'll get right to the point."

"Who is this?" said Penkin.

"Never mind that," snapped the voice. "Your laboratory project in Goa will be destroyed within the hour."

"By who? You?"

"It doesn't matter who. All that matters is that it will happen, and no amount of warning or resistance at the site can prevent it. Your only hope of salvaging the project is to discreetly evacuate only key personnel—

immediately. I recommend using the river. The roads leading out are most certainly under surveillance."

Penkin rapidly assessed the information passed by the mystery caller, wondering how much he or she knew about the true nature of his organization's business at the site. The caller's purposeful use of the word *laboratory* combined with the fact that he had somehow coopted one of Penkin's encrypted satellite phones was unnerving to say the least.

"I need more than a cryptic warning from a garbled voice before I disassemble one of my operations," said Penkin.

"You don't have time to disassemble the operation, only to evacuate Dr. Reznikov and key biological samples," replied the voice.

Penkin sat speechless for a few moments, a surge of adrenaline energizing his nervous system.

"I see."

"I sincerely hope you do," said the voice. "It would be a shame to lose one of our national treasures."

The call disconnected, leaving Penkin puzzled.

Our national treasures?

Who the hell could this possibly be, and why the mystery? He muttered a curse, contemplating his next move. The answer stared him in the face. It was likely no coincidence that the call had been placed on this phone. He pressed and held "1" on the phone's touch pad, immediately dialing the first preset number. Better safe than sorry. A gravelly voice answered several rings later.

"Yes?"

"Stand by to authenticate identities," said Penkin, opening the bottom drawer of his desk.

"It's three in the goddamn morning, Matvey," the voice griped.

He removed a notebook from the drawer and opened it with one hand while talking. "I'm well aware of the time. Are you ready to authenticate?"

"Hold on," the voice grumbled, followed by a lengthy pause. "Go ahead."

Penkin read a ten-digit series of letters and numbers that would be matched on the other end to confirm his identity. A different alphanumeric set was recited back, completing the process. The code changed every month or after each use.

"Code authenticated," said Valery Zuyev, his most trusted Boyevik, or "warrior."

"Listen closely, Valery. I just received information suggesting that your site has been compromised. I need you to get Reznikov and the critical specimens out of there immediately. Be very discreet about your departure. The fewer people involved, the better. I'm told the roads may not be safe."

"Do we have a time frame?"

"Within the hour," said Penkin.

Zuyev didn't respond.

"Are you still there?"

"I'm here. Just thinking for a second," said Valery. "I have a river escape contingency designed for a small group. Essential security personnel only. We can be on the water within five minutes."

"Good. Put as much distance between the laboratory and Reznikov as possible in the next hour, and whatever you do, avoid all contact with our brotherhood contacts in Goa. I don't know who I can trust right now."

"That bad?"

"I don't know yet. Just get Reznikov out of there. We can't afford to lose him."

"I'll call you when we're clear," said Zuyev.

"Good luck," said Penkin.

Penkin put the phone down and rubbed his face with both hands. He could barely believe this was happening. His fate would be decided within the hour. Or had it already been decided? The only person outside of his own small network of trusted associates who knew anything substantive about the laboratory project in India was Dima Maksimov, head of the Solntsevskaya Bratva. If Maksimov was involved in any way with tonight's call, he was most assuredly a dead man.

Chapter 2

Dudhsagar River
Goa, India

The skiff plied sluggishly through the water, its electric motor humming steadily. Reznikov lifted his right elbow onto the top edge of the aluminum hull and let his hand slide into the lukewarm water. The seemingly insignificant movement caused the overloaded boat to wobble, prompting him to pull his hand out of the river.

"Keep your damn hands in the boat," Zuyev hissed.

Reznikov turned his head to respond, shifting his body at the same time, once again unbalancing the skiff. He froze in place, firmly gripping both sides. He'd never learned how to swim, and they'd left the project site too quickly to locate the lifejackets. Somehow, it had never occurred to any of his hosts to keep the jackets onboard the boat, the most logical location. That would have made too much sense for these idiots.

"Quit moving, or you'll dump us all over the side," Zuyev whispered forcefully.

Reznikov considered a retort, but let it go, instead bringing his hands into the boat to retrieve one of the flasks of vodka tucked into his safari vest. He took a secretive pull from the metal container, feeling his nerves steady as the blessed liquid warmed his stomach and worked its magic.

"Take one more drink and put that away," said Zuyev. "In case you haven't noticed, we're in the middle of an escape."

He'd noticed, all right. It was a little hard to ignore being pummeled out of a hangover-induced coma and dragged through the pitch-black jungle by two overmuscled goons. He still wasn't sure what was going on. They'd dumped him into a boat and taken off into the darkness without an explanation. Twenty minutes later, nobody had spoken a word until now. Reznikov drained half of the flask with the next swig, holding it above his shoulder for Zuyev. Surprisingly, the mafiya boss took him up on the offer.

Not a good sign at all.

"Things must be pretty bad," whispered Reznikov.

"Things could be better," Zuyev replied, handing the flask back empty.

Reznikov briefly considered the second flask, letting the thought go. There was no telling how long he might have to stretch his limited vodka supply out here. Plus, Zuyev would likely knock it out of his hand into the river. The skiff continued its slow, steady voyage along the riverbank, staying under the thick tree canopy that hung over the water. Bits and pieces of the clear night sky peeked through the foliage, occasionally exposing the brief flicker of a star or two.

A few minutes later, he felt the skiff ease into a turn. The pleasant breeze created by the boat's forward motion died quickly. His face started to bead with perspiration within seconds. He hoped a vehicle with functional air-conditioning awaited them. The prospect of sitting crammed between these sweaty beasts in the backseat of a sweltering car terrified him. Of course, he was assuming they were headed to a vehicle. For all he knew, they planned on hiking to safety. He really hoped that wasn't the case. It was bad enough sitting still in the sweltering heat. Trudging through a rainforest was another matter altogether. Zuyev whispered something Reznikov couldn't decipher into his headset.

"Are we there?" said Reznikov.

"Shhhh." A hand gently gripped his shoulder. "Listen."

Reznikov kept still. A deep rumble rose above the chirps and squeaks, drowning out the jungle's ambient noise. He didn't recognize the sound at first until the steady rumble morphed into the distinct, rhythmic thump of helicopter blades. The skiff's aluminum hull scraped against the soft bottom of the river, gently stopping the boat.

Helicopters thundered overhead, their powerful rotor wash shaking the tree canopy with a gale-force wind that dislodged the skiff from the riverbed. The violent disturbance ended as quickly as it started, leaving them adrift and showered with falling leaves. The high-pitched whine of the helicopters' engines rapidly faded, replaced by the outbound thump of the rotor blades. He never saw the machines, but knew intuitively that they were headed upriver toward the laboratory. And when they didn't find what they were looking for, they'd be back.

"Why aren't we moving?" said Reznikov.

"Keep quiet," whispered Zuyev. "We're making sure they don't have anyone on the river."

"Who exactly are we talking about?"

"Someone with military-grade helicopters at their disposal," said Zuyev.

"And you somehow knew about this?" Reznikov asked.

"Someone knew about it. My orders were to get you out of there."

"Where do we go from here?"

"We have two vehicles hidden further downriver. GPS indicates we're about ten minutes away."

A distant buzz penetrated the forest, echoing from the opposite side of the river. The buzz repeated, followed by the staccato sound of small-arms fire.

"Let's go," said Zuyev.

The skiff lurched forward, turning in a lazy circle to point in a direction Reznikov assumed was downriver. He honestly couldn't tell for sure. It was a moonless night, and the dense jungle swallowed everything around them. Without night vision, which they had conveniently neglected to provide him, he was effectively blind and completely dependent on his hosts, no doubt by design.

A fierce battle raged a few miles behind them as they continued downriver. The trees on the opposite side of the river lit up once from a sizable explosion. The gunfire had started to slacken by the time he felt the boat slow again. He hoped they had finally arrived at the vehicles. The soldiers in the helicopters had to be moments away from discovering that he had recently escaped. Reznikov had zero doubt that he was the primary objective of the raid, and once they discovered he was missing, they would start scouring the area.

"We need to get off the river," he said. "They probably spotted us with their thermal gear on the way in. They probably thought we were fishermen. I guarantee they won't make that mistake again."

"Take another drink and calm down," replied Zuyev. "We're almost there."

He didn't need another drink. He needed to get the fuck off this river before the helicopters returned. Ignoring Zuyev's comment, he lowered his head, resting it against his knees for the rest of the short transit.

"We're here," stated Zuyev.

Reznikov raised his head as they glided silently under a low-hanging branch that scraped the top of his head. When the skiff stopped, the man seated on the raised bench in front of him swung his legs over the side and splashed down in the water, holding the skiff steady.

"Over the side, Anatoly," said Zuyev, yanking him up by the back collar of his vest. "We don't have any time to waste."

Reznikov inched his way onto the empty bench behind him, careful not to fall overboard. Logically, he knew the water wasn't deep, but his lack of swimming ability kept him from making any sudden moves. Without warning, Zuyev pulled him over the side, dropping him in the shallow water. A moment of panic struck when he hit the water, quickly dissolving when his rear side came to rest on the bottom of the river.

"Quit splashing around like a fucking baby. You're in a foot of water," Zuyev snapped, eliciting muffled laughter from the other two men.

Reznikov struggled to his feet, now soaked from top to bottom thanks to that ass, Zuyev. When all of this business was finished, he would kill Zuyev. The man had treated him like shit since the Bratva rescued him from the hands of his American captors. Two long years moving from one third world shithole to another, "staying off the radar," as Zuyev was fond of saying.

After a few close calls with a relentless assassination team in South America, Zuyev brought him by ship to the west coast of India, where he'd spent the past year working in an isolated P4 biosafety laboratory built specifically for him. The Bratva had undoubtedly spent a fortune on the lab, both in terms of money and time, and all they had to show for it right now was a cooler full of virus samples and the genius who created them.

He could expect Zuyev to be in a particularly vicious mood after this, the brunt of which would be taken out on *him*. Yes. He'd make sure Zuyev died a miserable death, preferably at the hands of one of the viruses he paid Reznikov to create. He appreciated a sense of irony.

Reznikov slogged forward through the water, following the dark forms in front of him toward what he assumed was the riverbank. Zuyev and one of the other men manhandled him up the steep, five-foot bank, pushing him into the thick, untamed forest. He started to think they'd made a mistake when the foliage cleared, dumping them on a hard-packed dirt trail.

"Not much furth—" started Zuyev, his words replaced by a sickening gurgle.

To his left, a dark shape swiftly but silently materialized from the forest, instantly closing the distance to the mafiya guard directly in front of him. A crack broke the silence, a brief flash illuminating the suppressed pistol pressed against the guard's head. The man dropped to the trail at Reznikov's feet, landing with a heavy thump. He had no idea where the third security guy had gone.

Now he was truly fucked. Zuyev and two former Russian Spetsnaz taken down in the blink of an eye? A helicopter raid at three thirty in the morning? He was dealing with professionals, which meant one thing—a secure prison cell for the rest of his life.

"All clear," said a Russian voice behind him. "Start the truck."

The man put a gloved hand on his shoulder, causing him to flinch.

"Dr. Reznikov, we need to move immediately. It's not safe here," the dark figure said in Russian.

No kidding.

Grigor was missing, and he didn't need the half-witted mafiya guard deciding to kill him rather than let him fall into enemy hands.

"There's a third man in my group. He was first on the trail," whispered Reznikov. "I don't see him."

A car engine roared in the near distance.

"That's him starting the SUV. Grigor has been on our payroll for a while now."

Grigor was one of the ex-GRU Spetsnaz that had freed him from the CIA prison in Vermont. The Bratva had extended his contract, assigning him a job as one of Reznikov's primary bodyguards. The gruff asshole had followed him around like a shadow for close to three years, apparently waiting to sell him to the highest bidder. Was there no end to the double-crossing with these people?

"Where are we going?" asked Reznikov, resigned to his current fate with his new captors.

"Anywhere but here," said the man, pushing a piece of gear with straps into his hand. "Hold these up to your face for now; we'll get them strapped on later."

Reznikov raised the device in front of his head, placing the two green-glowing eyepieces to his face. The darkness transformed into a monochromatic green picture, revealing the true nature of his rescue. The man that had given him the goggles was dressed in military camouflage and armed with a suppressed shortbarreled AK-74. He wore a heavily laden tactical vest rigged with communications gear and bulging magazine pouches; night-vision goggles were strapped to his bearded face.

The absence of a helmet led Reznikov to believe the man was not part of the raid against the laboratory. Those soldiers would be covered head to toe in body armor. This guy looked like he had geared up for an extended jungle operation. He wasn't sure if this was a good or bad sign. The fact that they hadn't put a bullet in his head was a decent enough start.

He turned to face the second, similarly outfitted commando, who scanned the trail behind them with his rifle. Valery Zuyev lay at Reznikov's feet, blood pumping from the back of his neck onto the hardened mud. Zuyev's lifeless eyes stared past him, fixed skyward. Reznikov spit on his face.

"We need to go," said the commando, picking up the temperature-controlled specimen cooler dropped by Zuyev.

"Who are you? What is this?"

"You've been liberated, Dr. Reznikov. But if we're not on the road moving south within the next thirty seconds, that may well change. I don't hear any more shooting from the lab. It's only a matter of time before they realize you're gone."

"Liberated by whom?"

"People with deep pockets," the commando replied, nudging him forward. "That's all I know—or care to know."

"Be careful with that cooler," said Reznikov, remaining fixed in place.

"The cooler was our primary objective," said the commando. "I suggest you start moving. If you slow us down too much, I'll have to leave you behind like Zuyev. Risk versus reward. The faster you move, the less risk."

Reznikov shook his head. Sold like cattle to the highest bidder. He could figure it all out later, after finishing off his second flask.

Chapter 3

FSB Headquarters
Lubyanka Square, Moscow

Alexei Kaparov strained to view the live camera feed displayed on the operation center's main projection screen. An impenetrable crowd of senior agents and high-ranking bureaucrats gathered in a tight semicircle around the display wall, essentially blocking most of his view. Only a cattle prod at its highest setting could open a space between these piranhas.

Mercifully, he'd been ushered into the darkened, overcrowded room several minutes after the Alpha Group Spetsnaz team had gone to work on the suspected bioweapons laboratory site. The FSB higher-ups obviously didn't want him and the rest of the B team to see the special operations team's insertion. Thank the world for small miracles. He really didn't care at all to watch the operation unfold. Unwatchable shaky green images, heavy breathing, and gunfire didn't interest him in the least. The end result was all that really mattered, especially in this case.

Killing Reznikov would close a dark chapter in Russia's history, a chapter the government had rewritten several times over the past decade, the most creative revision foisted on the Russian people and the international community several months ago. He had to give them credit. They must have dusted off the best Communist-era propagandists to pull it off.

Instead of continuing to blame the astonishingly tragic situation in Monchegorsk on some kind of separatist uprising, which nobody believed from the outset, the government took the unprecedented step of admitting that the city's population had been deliberately infected with a bioweapon created at the Vektor Institute State Research Center for Virology and Biotechnology. With a caveat, of course.

That faux caveat being that Russian authorities were completely unaware that a rogue group of scientists had secretly restarted Biopreparat's banned bioweapons research and development program until it was too late to stop the tragedy. Of course, as soon as Russian Federation authorities discovered the illegal and clearly unauthorized program, they did what any responsible government would do under the circumstances. They destroyed it. History was rewritten, and with the United States government's complicit silence, the story was bought hook, line and sinker, for the good of everyone, especially Kaparov.

Prior to the historical rewrite, he'd found it increasingly difficult as the head of the Bioweapons and Chemical Threat Assessment Directorate to pretend that the number one threat to Russian Federation security didn't exist. He couldn't wait to hear the Alpha team's final confirmation that Reznikov was dead. A late night drink—or five—could be in order.

"I'm beginning to suspect the raid is a bust," said a vaguely familiar voice to his right.

Kaparov turned to face Maxim Greshnev, Chief Counter-Terrorism Director for the FSB, one of the last people he would have expected to find watching the operation with the rest of the riffraff.

"Good morning, Director," said Kaparov, instantly disappointed with himself for the robotic underling response.

"Nothing good about it," said Greshnev. "They've been through every building except for the one they managed to blow up and they still haven't located Reznikov. Take a guess what building went sky high?"

"The laboratory?"

"Of course," said Greshnev. "Because why the fuck would we be interested in a full inventory of Reznikov's work?"

"Look on the bright side, maybe they blew him up with the lab," said Kaparov.

Greshnev chuckled, a rare show of visible emotion from the man. "We could only be so lucky," he said, shaking his head.

Kaparov decided to ask a question he suspected would not be met with a straight answer. It wasn't every day that you had the ear of one of the most powerful men in the FSB.

"How reliable was the source?"

"We received a onetime anonymous tip," Greshnev replied.

"You get what you pay for," Kaparov commented.

Greshnev stifled a laugh. "Apparently the laboratory is located in western Goa."

"India?"

"The warm beaches of Goa attract Russian tourists year-round," said Greshnev. "Hundreds of thousands of tourists and a few thousand permanent residents. They call the area between Arambol and Morjim beaches 'Little Russia.'"

"No doubt the Solntsevskaya Bratva is well represented," said Kaparov, understanding the connection.

"It's a small outpost for the Bratva, completely off our radar until now."

"And we're sure he was there?"

"It was impossible to get anyone too close to the compound without tipping our hand, but relatively easy to ascertain that a sophisticated, medical-grade laboratory had been built in the middle of the jungle. It fit the profile, so here we are."

He considered Greshnev's revelation. Unless the director had lied about the anonymous nature of the tip, the information couldn't possibly have originated from a source inside the jungle compound. A guard assigned to the laboratory would have attached a significant price tag to their sudden shift in loyalties. Nobody took a risk like this without a sizable financial incentive, and the Russian government wasn't exactly known for handing out generous bounties to informants. Something didn't make sense.

"How detailed was the information provided?" asked Kaparov.

"Detailed enough," answered Greshnev, signaling that Kaparov's line of questioning about the source had come to an end.

"Americans?"

"Definitely not," answered Greshnev.

"You don't expect they'll find him, do you?"

"I had my doubts from the beginning," said Greshnev. "I'll make sure you receive a copy of the after-action report for this operation. I need a pair of cynical eyes sifting through the results."

"Am I that transparent?"

"Your cynicism is what I like about you, not to mention your experience. Take a hard look at the report and get back to me with your observations. I'll make sure Inga knows."

Inga Soyev, Greshnev's personal secretary, had earned the reputation as one of the most pitiless gatekeepers in Lubyanka's history. Nobody saw Greshnev without her approval.

"I'll see what I can dig up," said Kaparov, still not sure what to make of this bizarre meeting.

"Looks like they finally discovered my absence," said Greshnev. "Surprised it took the jackals so long."

A pack of agents craned their necks from side to side to find him, some abandoning their prime locations in front of the screen to reposition themselves closer to the director.

Jackals indeed.

Instead of stepping forward into the inner circle, Kaparov took a few steps backward and made room for the swarm. A few eyed him skeptically, or jealously—he couldn't tell in the soft blue glow of the tactical operations center. He truly didn't care one way or the other. Getting out of there was his number one priority. If he managed to sneak away within the next few minutes, he could be home in bed within the hour. Any longer and he might as well lie down on the floor in his office.

One of the support agents seated among several smaller monitors arranged at a spacious workstation next to the main screen made an announcement over the loudspeaker.

"Alpha team leader reports negative contact with primary objective. The team managed a quick pass through the undamaged part of the laboratory structure, finding no human remains. Secondary objective destroyed in the fire."

He assumed the secondary objective meant live virus samples. Greshnev shook his head, mumbling something to one of the men standing next to him as the report continued.

"The team needs to be airborne in two minutes. ELINT support has detected increased sensor activity and radio transmissions from the Indian Naval Air Station at Hansa. The team has shifted its focus to intelligence collection for the little time they have left."

"Has there been any indication of a local law enforcement response?" Greshnev responded immediately.

A few seconds passed before he received an answer.

"No response detected," said the agent.

"Pass along an urgent request to Director Baranov at CSN (Center of Special Operations). I strongly suggest they leave a discreet team behind, as discussed during the planning phase. There's one shitty little road leading to and from the facility, and we've had it under continuous surveillance. If the primary objective was indeed on-site at any time in the past forty-eight hours and somehow narrowly escaped this attack, he can't be far away."

"Understood, Director Greshnev," replied the agent.

The director glanced back at Kaparov, his look betraying the same skepticism that Kaparov himself felt. Something didn't add up here.

Chapter 4

White House Situation Room
Washington, D.C.

Frederick Shelby studied the faces of the men and women seated around the conference room table. He was far more interested in their reactions to the unsuccessful raid than the news itself. Shelby was still an outsider within this tight circle of power, a fact he couldn't afford to forget or ignore. He'd secured a seat at the highest stakes table in town because of a single instrumental act of loyalty to the True America party, but knew all too well that the chair could be yanked out from under him at any moment, regardless of the cards he held. Reading poker faces could be as critical to success inside the Beltway as competence, especially tonight.

The failure to capture or kill Anatoly Reznikov in tonight's raid would fall squarely in the CIA's lap, and as the director of National Intelligence's representative tonight, it would hit Shelby's lap first. He noted a baleful flash from General Frank Gordon, commander of United States Special Operations Command, but he'd expected as much. SOCCOM had lives directly on the line tonight, and the intelligence shared with them by Shelby turned out to be a bust. He expected them to be hot. No. His focus centered on the immediate members of the president's inner circle, the people that really mattered. The wrong word whispered in the right ear could be disastrous for Shelby.

He briefly turned his attention to the massive projection screen mounted to the front wall of the room. Live video feed from Operation RAINFOREST occupied the left half; a digital map displaying military symbols filled the right side. Four blue symbols clustered a hundred miles off the central western coast of India, each corresponding to one of the friendly units still in play. Within minutes, barring any unforeseen circumstances, only two blue circles would remain, their speed and direction data indicating a high-speed run due southwest, away from the coast.

The adjacent green-scale image showed the slowly approaching flight deck of a low-profile combat ship from one of the pilot's helmet-mounted cameras. One of the two hangar bays situated forward of the flight deck was open, swallowing the tail rotor of a recently landed helicopter. The image switched to the crew chief's helmet, revealing a secret that would never extend beyond the handful of men and women in this room or on board the helicopters.

RAINFOREST redefined the concept of "need to know." Not even the ships' commanding officers had been told what the stealth helicopters had ferried across the Indian coast or where they had stopped. Each Arleigh Burke destroyer had capably served as a two-billion-dollar taxi for one of the most classified military operations in recent U.S. history.

Shelby sensed a shift in the White House chief of staff's posture and took his eyes off the body-armor-clad soldiers seated inside the helicopter to meet her glare. Beverly Stark's words were quick to follow.

"Well, that was a bust."

He held back, knowing that nothing good would come out of his mouth for the next several seconds. Better to let someone else speak first.

"The operational pieces are undamaged and appear to have remained undetected," said General Gordon. "That's all that matters at this point."

President Alan Crane continued watching the helicopter on its final approach to the ship's flight deck. Without turning away from the screen, he directed a question at Shelby.

"Any new information from our friends in Moscow?"

Shelby scanned his laptop screen for any last second messages transmitted from the Defense Clandestine Service (NCS) Operations Center. A single-sentence post appeared moments before he responded.

"Interesting. The Russians left a skeleton team behind to try to pick up Reznikov's trail," said Shelby, typing a question for the DIA (Defense Intelligence Agency) team talking to Moscow.

"They did what?" said Gordon, furiously typing on his own laptop.

"Is that confirmed?" asked Beverly Stark.

Gordon looked up, nodding. "Confirmed. A three-man team from Gladiator-One stayed behind."

"How did we miss that?" asked President Crane. "More importantly, how the hell did it go unreported?"

"I'm trying to get to the bottom of that," Gordon replied.

"Please do," said Beverly Stark, turning to Shelby. "And *you* need to make it crystal clear to our Russian friends that this is unacceptable. There was no mention of purposefully leaving a team behind during any of the mission briefings. This leaves us exposed."

Shelby couldn't see how it left them exposed, but instead of addressing the obvious kneejerk question, he summarized the answer relayed by the DIA. "Intelligence strongly suggested that Reznikov was on site when—"

"I don't see how he could have escaped if that was the case," interrupted Gerald Simmons. "It's not like he had many options."

Shelby feigned a smile. He hated Simmons. For the life of him, he didn't understand how this smarmy little shit had landed the position of White House Counterterrorism director. Prior to the 2008 election, Simmons had played a relatively obscure role in the Pentagon as the assistant secretary for Special Operations and Low Intensity Conflict. Shelby had only run into this turd a few times prior to the 2008 election and remembered wanting to smash a computer over his head the last time they were together.

In fact, the meeting had taken place in this very room, during the failed raid on Sanderson's Argentina compound. Operation BOLD SCIMITAR. What a cluster fuck that had turned out to be. He wouldn't be surprised if Simmons brought it up, especially since Shelby had provided the initial intelligence for that operation. Guys like Simmons thrived on other people's failures.

With a strained game face, Shelby replied, "That's precisely why they insisted on leaving a team behind. With few exfiltration options available, the Alpha Group commander felt they stood a solid chance of either catching up with Reznikov or uncovering a solid lead regarding his next move."

"With the state's Indian armed forces on full alert," added Stark. "Not to mention every law enforcement asset in the area."

"The Russians left behind are no longer our concern," said Shelby.

"Except for the fact that we deposited them on Indian soil," stated the president.

"Nobody will ever know that, Mr. President. We've run through the scenarios—"

"Not this one," Stark cut in. "At no point did we discuss leaving a team behind to investigate."

"I'm sure they don't plan on lingering at the site," Shelby explained, starting to get annoyed.

What was done was done. Everyone in the room knew the risks going in. Ferrying Russian commandos into India to conduct a raid against a suspected bioweapons target was unheard of in the first place. Now they were squabbling about three Spetsnaz operators that could probably live off the land, remaining undetected for weeks? He hated this kind of shortsighted pettiness.

"The Russians know what they're doing," said General Gordon. "And I suspect the detachment they left behind is part of Spetsgruppa Charlie, or Smerch."

"Smerch? Sounds like something out of a James Bond movie," said Stark, eliciting a few stifled laughs.

"Service of Special Operations," said Shelby, who had made it a point to learn everything there was to know about Russian Special Operations (Spetsnaz) groups. "It's a relatively new group that specializes in the capture and transfer of high-profile mafiya or bandit leaders throughout Russia. If Reznikov or his handlers left a trail, they'll find it, and will stay out of sight."

General Gordon interrupted the conversation. "Gladiator-Two is secure on board USS *Mustin*. The taskforce is headed southwest at top speed. There's no indication that either the ships or helicopters have been detected by Indian sensors. I'd say we're free and clear."

The video feed next to the map changed to a black screen blinking the words *LINK LOST*.

"The helicopters flew over thousands of people and shot up several buildings just a few miles away from some reasonably populated towns," stated Nora Crawford, secretary of state. "I expect State to hear from the Indian embassy tomorrow, especially when they determine that the buildings are part of a laboratory facility."

"Surely not blaming us," said Erik Glass, secretary of Defense.

"Not directly, but I'll get the call nonetheless," said Crawford. "There's only one military capable of flying helicopters in and out of another country undetected."

"*Rumored* to be capable," said the secretary of Defense.

Crawford took a deep breath, exhaling before she replied, "I'd get these two warships back into their regular deployment schedules immediately. I guarantee that India's Research and Analysis Wing will be monitoring our ships' movements closely."

"They can watch our ships all they like," said Glass. "The USS *Mustin* is on its way to the Arabian Gulf from Japan. Part of a scheduled deployment.

And the USS *Howard* is on its way home to San Diego after an extended deployment. They'll adjust their speeds, supported by fuel tankers, to maintain their schedules after diverting close enough to Diego Garcia to launch the helicopters. The Navy has worked out the timing for a late night landing at the air base on the island."

"I want those birds out of sight and out of mind as quickly as possible," said General Gordon. "We have another mission brewing in the region that might necessitate their use."

"Strategic Airlift Command has two C-17 Globemasters waiting at Diego Garcia to fly your birds stateside. You'll have your helicopters within the next forty-eight hours," said Glass.

Beverly Stark shook her head. "I still can't believe we let the Russians see those helicopters."

Neither could Shelby, but he wasn't about to share that sentiment. The entire mission had been a compromise-turned-joint-effort between the United States and the Russian Federation. The Russians had precious, timely intelligence on a top-tier threat to both countries and the United States had the delivery platforms to pull off the raid. U.S. Special Operations Command offered to execute the mission on behalf of the Russians, but Moscow wanted confirmation that Reznikov had been terminated, not assurances, and that meant Russian boots on the ground during the mission.

"Trust but verify," they'd said. He didn't blame them for throwing Reagan's words back in their faces.

"Their interaction with the helicopters was minimal, as agreed," said Gordon. "On load. Off load. There's not much for them to see inside the helicopter, or outside for that matter."

"But now the Russians know we have them," said Stark. "Which means everyone will know soon enough. Seems like the Russians came out ahead on this one."

Gordon shrugged, blatantly offering the same sentiment Shelby fought to conceal. They'd been through this over and over again. The Russians hadn't faked the intelligence and gone through the motions of putting their own commandos in harm's way just to gain access to their latest generation stealth helicopters. Beverly Stark couldn't seem to get this particular conspiracy theory out of her head.

"So…where does this leave us with Reznikov?" asked the president.

"Back to square one if the trail goes cold," said Shelby. "The

Solntsevskaya Bratva has proven to be adept at hiding Reznikov."

"Then I guess we better offer Moscow our support in the matter," said President Crane. "Frederick, make the necessary arrangements with the National Reconnaissance Office to coordinate a real-time package."

"Understood, Mr. President. I'll coordinate with them immediately."

"Is there anything else?" asked President Crane, scanning the faces in the room.

Shelby gave him a quick shake of his head when their gazes met, taking his cue from the rest of the room.

"Then that's it for now."

The room cleared, leaving Shelby alone with General Gordon, who appeared to linger. He wasn't in the mood to deal with Gordon right now.

"Look at the bright side. At least the Russians didn't hijack one of the helicopters or purposely disable one," said Gordon.

The last part of his statement was a clear reminder of the failed operation to grab Sanderson two years ago. The only shot fired during the clandestine raid, a strategically placed .50-caliber sniper rifle bullet, shredded the tail rotor assembly of a Black Hawk helicopter that had landed inside Sanderson's compound, forcing the assault team to leave it behind on Argentinian soil. A fact used by Sanderson to buy a blanket immunity deal for the Black Flag organization. All sins of his past and present wiped away with a single bullet. The whole thing was a setup, and Shelby had provided the intelligence that led Gordon's people and the White House right down the primrose path. At least the general had waited until the president and his cronies had departed.

"You win some and you lose some in this game," said Shelby. "You've been around long enough to know that."

"So far you're batting zero when it comes to invading other countries," replied Gordon.

"I just provide the intelligence. You can always say no."

Gordon considered him for a moment, his caustic glare easing imperceptibly. "Not with people like Reznikov on the loose," said the general, leaving the room.

Shelby cracked a faint smile. "*Especially* not with people like Reznikov on the loose."

Chapter 5

Lockrum Bay, Anguilla

Jessica Petrovich stirred under the soft silk sheets, a warm breeze caressing her face. Her eyes opened to a red-orange sky beyond a wide, floor-to-ceiling glass sliding door. A scattered band of puffy, dark purple clouds floated above the red ocean, outlined by the fiery sunlight moments from breaching the horizon. She'd never get used to this view, or the life that came with it.

She yawned, stretching her hands above her head until they touched the headboard. Holding that stretch for a few seconds, she glanced at Daniel lying next to her. He appeared undisturbed by her movement or the light pouring into the room, but she knew better. Her husband woke to the slightest change in his sleeping environment; a survival instinct drilled so deeply into his psyche that she doubted it would ever slip away.

He'd probably been awake for several minutes now, waiting for her to rise naturally. Possibly all night with the balcony door open. If the intermittent breezes didn't keep him awake, the fact that an exterior door just a few dozen feet from their bed was wide open to intruders most certainly doomed his night of sleep. The pristine ocean air carried into the room by the calm late evening winds had lured her into bed with the best intentions of getting up and closing it a few minutes later. She vaguely remembered Daniel joining her in bed a little while later, nestling his warm body against hers. Nothing after that.

"You awake?" she whispered.

"Yep," he said immediately, keeping his eyes closed.

"Sorry. I should have shut the slider."

He met her glance with weary, half-open eyes and a warm smile. "I could have shut it before I lay down."

She playfully raised an eyebrow. "Why didn't you?"

"Because I love you," he replied, broadening his smile. "And I'm not afraid of the boogeyman."

Jessica kissed his lips and pressed her forehead against his. "It's not about being afraid. It's about being smart about our security."

"I know how much you enjoy the fresh air."

"And I love you even more for that," she said. "But it's not like I can enjoy it after I fall asleep."

"You were up at least three times last night, breathing in the ocean air," he said, kissing her.

"It is kind of nice," she admitted.

"By this point, I should be able to leave a door open and not worry about someone sneaking in and slitting my throat," said Daniel.

Jessica wasn't sure how to respond. The fact that he'd so bluntly brought it up was a significant step down a path she wanted him to follow. On the surface, Daniel always looked unaffected, rock solid to a fault, but nothing could be further from the truth. He had an exceptionally difficult time letting go of old habits. He was just far better at concealing and suppressing his emotions; a talent she'd never really mastered.

Unfortunately, Daniel's façade took a severe toll on both of them, hindering the kind of joint emotional progress needed to put enough distance between the past and present to escape or, at the very least, keep them from regressing.

They'd been close to escaping before, living a slightly forced version of the American dream in Maine, until General Sanderson crashed the party. Within the short span of twenty-four hours, the general had erased every gain they'd made after disappearing from Belgrade. Five years of healing, rebuilding, reprograming, forgetting, all flushed down the Black Flag toilet. They needed to make a clean break from the past this time, or they'd never break free. For the first time in a long while, she sensed that Daniel wanted it just as badly. The sooner they made their move, the better.

"I'm running the George Hill loop, then a quick swim in the bay," she said. "You up for the swim?"

"I might join you for the swim," he said. "Wake me up when you get back from the run."

All of that meant no, and it had nothing to do with getting a bad night of sleep. Daniel had stopped exercising regularly a few months ago, a really bad development. He needed rigorous physical exercise and constant distraction to keep his mind focused on the present. Without it, his mind turned inward. To dark places she had never managed to access. Places she had no interest in visiting.

Daniel had stood at the edge of the abyss at some point in Yugoslavia, staring into a vast darkness meant to swallow him. He'd made that much clear, without going into specifics. Bumping into her outside of a Belgrade nightclub had saved him from jumping into the blackness that had already consumed most of the Black Flag operatives assigned to the Balkans. She'd seen him like this a few times before, but never for this long. It was time to revisit an idea they had batted around a few months ago.

"Maybe you should get some more rest. I'll make us a nice breakfast when I'm done," she said, kissing his forehead.

She'd broach the topic over gourmet coffee and omelets.

"That sounds good," he said, burrowing his head into the pillow.

Jessica walked to the balcony and shut the slider, locking the door. A faint beep sounded from a compact digital tablet on Daniel's nightstand. The home's security system had registered the change in door status. A few minutes later, dressed in black triathlon shorts and a pink tri-top, she descended a wide, open-riser metal staircase to the gray marble foyer.

In the kitchen, she flipped the switch on the stainless steel espresso maker and downed a tall glass of cold water poured from a bottle-fed water dispenser. A double shot of espresso and a few glasses of spring water would fuel her five-mile run. She refilled the glass and left the kitchen, headed for the two-story bank of windows covering the eastern side of the villa's great room.

Bright orange rays of light reflected off the far wall, illuminating a collage of colorful Caribbean-inspired artwork. A deep blue Dubai leather sectional faced the window, flanked by two polished chrome arc lamps, encompassing the entirety of the great room's furniture. She walked deeper into the room, pausing to shield her eyes from the blazing horizon with her unoccupied hand. A few seconds later, the room dimmed as the bottom of the sun disappeared behind one of the low-lying cloud masses.

Jessica walked to the window and scanned Lockrum Bay. The tall bobbing mast of a blue-hulled sloop immediately caught her eye. A Hinckley Sou'wester 52 sat at a storm-reinforced mooring a few hundred yards offshore. Just the sight of it gave her hope. She'd come up with the idea a year ago, soon after insisting that they take sailing lessons and follow up with a two-week bareboat charter out of the British Virgin Islands. Daniel took to sailing like a natural, embracing its dynamic nature and the constant need for vigilance.

The two-week taste of sailboat life far exceeded Jessica's expectations. Not only did she feel far more relaxed and liberated than she could ever remember, but Daniel had caught the sailing fever. It had started with mojito-fueled conversations about what it would be like to freely sail around the Caribbean for a few months a year, and ended with the purchase of a rarely used sailboat built by one of the most reputable names in the business.

They'd cruised the islands for three months after the purchase, pausing to conduct some business for Sanderson in South America. Ugly business that nearly got all of them killed. Daniel hadn't been the same since. Something had shifted in the dark recesses of his mind, brought too close to the surface for his comfort. She needed to get him back on that boat—permanently.

Jessica took a sip of cold water and grinned. *La Ombra*, Italian for *ghost* or *shadow*, swayed gently in the bay. Ghost. Exactly what they would become once they sailed for the horizon and never looked back.

Chapter 6

Lockrum Bay, Anguilla

Daniel contemplated the warm remains of his espresso before downing it moments later. When his glance returned to the water's edge, Jessica had disappeared below the jagged rocks bordering the narrow strip of beach. She'd reemerge shortly, swimming through the light morning chop toward the sailboat moored in the cove. He couldn't wait to spring his surprise on Jessica.

From the moment she suggested sailing lessons out of Saint Martin, Daniel understood what she was after. Disappearing, or at least making it as difficult as possible for anyone, friend or foe, to find them. Relocating to another anonymous fortresslike house halfway around the world only solved part of their problem. They needed a new lifestyle. One that kept them challenged, with infinite possibilities, none of which required their current skillsets. Cruising the world fit that bill perfectly.

Never in the same place for longer than the weather dictated. Full freedom to choose the next destination. Rigorous at times. Inherently unavoidable but manageable elements of danger, both predictable and capricious. He had read hundreds of firsthand accounts about couples and families sailing the world, all reinforcing the unspoken decision Jessica and Daniel had reached by passionately embracing a series of extensive sailing lessons.

The next step had been obvious. They needed a boat capable of comfortable transoceanic passage, and if they were really going to do this, they would do it right. Extensive research pointed to several well-established boat builders, one that caught his eye immediately: a Maine-based boatyard renowned for building top-of-the-line, luxurious sailboats coveted around the world. While he was likely initially drawn to the Hinckley line of yachts by the link to Maine, where he and Jessica had first tried to build a normal life, the matter was settled by the discovery of a gently used Hinckley Sou'wester 52 for sale in the British Virgin Islands.

As a newly minted sailing couple, they were in well over their heads with the fifty-two-foot vessel. They'd fared better than either of them had expected during their three-month shakedown cruise, but island hopping across the Caribbean was hardly the final test for what they had in mind.

Daniel chuckled at the thought. Just a few months ago, he'd spent the better part of two days tied to a chair in a Montevideo slum, praying that Jessica was still alive after their mission tanked. Now he was worried about sailing a luxury yacht to points unknown. He'd gladly trade the former burden for the latter. If reefing the sails in the face of stormy weather or navigating a treacherous pass was life's new stress, he could live with that. He was pretty sure Jessica wouldn't have a problem making that transition either. It *had* been her idea, after all. She just didn't know how quickly he intended to make it a reality.

Their days on Anguilla were numbered, quite possibly in the single digits if she literally and figuratively was on board with his plan to sweep her away from a life that had grown comfortably toxic to their relationship, and their survival.

Jessica reappeared in the water, her arms cutting through the surf toward *La Ombra*. Her recently acquired habit of swimming to the boat every morning after a long run had forced him to modify the original plan. He'd quit running with her in the morning to see if he could break the new routine, but he only seemed to reinforce it. She'd swim out every day, sometimes twice, trying to lure him out of his "funk," as she described it. He couldn't possibly load the boat with the supplies without her knowing, and he wanted everything to be a complete surprise. Not an easy feat when you were married to a covert operative easily your better.

For all he knew, Jessica had already unraveled his plot, though he sincerely doubted it. From what he could tell, she was completely unaware of his scheme, more focused on his "deteriorating state of mind." He'd led her down that rabbit hole after the disastrous Montevideo operation, hoping the intense ordeal would be a believable trigger point for him to start seriously weighing the risks of their line of work against the rewards.

They'd talked about this at length in the past, but *the life* was hardwired into them. It was not as easy to leave behind as they had originally thought, especially when they were rarely more than a phone call away from the next job. Even more so when the man sending you the work was a relentless, undeniably talented spin doctor. All the more reason to dump every means of communication and put a few thousand miles of blue water behind them. Sanderson's reach was extensive, but it didn't include an anchorage in French Polynesia or Fiji. He hoped. The sooner they left, the better.

Watching Jessica swim effortlessly toward the yacht bobbing in the cove, he decided to make the call that would activate his plan. They'd enjoy a sunset dinner at their favorite seaside restaurant, and Daniel would propose all over again. Instead of a ring, he'd present her with a fully provisioned boat, ready to sweep them away from *the life* and usher in a new era.

Chapter 7

CIA Headquarters
McLean, Virginia

Karl Berg leaned back in his seat and checked his watch, once again finding himself unable to answer the same question that had troubled him for the vast majority of the year. Why the hell was he still here? He'd routinely worked excessively long office hours during his two-decade stretch at headquarters, never complaining. The work had always absorbed him, and in his own way he'd thrived on it, turning even the most mundane assignments into gold.

He'd pieced together the significance of Reznikov's sudden reappearance on the world scene while holding down a chair in what most of his colleagues considered to be an end-of-the-line lateral transfer out of the National Clandestine Service (NCS). A few months later, after the controversial but successful clandestine raid against Vektor Institute, he was back in the game, promoted to deputy director of the Special Operations Group (SOG) within the Special Activities Division (SAD).

The dirty word *retirement* faded into the distance during the incredible year and a half that followed. As promised by Thomas Manning, then director of NCS, Berg was promoted at the start of 2008 to director of the Special Operations Group, taking over for Jeffrey McConnell, who took over the entire Special Activities Division. There was serious talk about Manning taking over as associate deputy director of the CIA, and of Audra Bauer, Berg's longtime friend and guardian angel, sliding into Manning's position as director of NCS.

Life was good until late 2008, when Alan Crane became the first third-party candidate in history to win a U.S. presidential election. True America had pulled off an epic, seemingly impossible win, and nobody saw it coming, because the most critical pieces of the plan to achieve victory had taken place deep inside the beltway's Stygian nether-regions. Without a shadow of a doubt, deals had been struck between the most corruptible and sycophantic power brokers, a secret cabal that simultaneously orchestrated the implosion of a major political party and the swift ascendancy of a grassroots movement that few of the political elite took seriously.

Speculation and conspiracy theory ruled the day when the incumbent president, who was favored to comfortably win the election, was toppled nearly overnight by coordinated revelations that his administration had delayed warning the public about the true extent of the Zulu virus threat against the United States in the spring of 2007.

Several citizens of Morris County, New Jersey, died from drinking virus-infected water. Other leaks followed, clearly designed to question the administration's knowledge and handling of the events leading to the entire situation surrounding the Zulu virus's arrival on U.S. soil. Immigration policies were attacked, foreign policy decisions questioned. Hints were dropped suggesting U.S. involvement in an incident outside of Novosibirsk, Russia. The timing couldn't have been worse for an administration that had grown complacent with a comfortable double-digit lead in the polls entering October. A dangerous complacency unquestionably fostered by key White House advisors and D.C. insiders complicit in the conspiracy.

The conspirators were relatively easy to identify in most cases. Anyone that landed in a key role within the administration that hadn't previously been part of the True America entourage was immediately a suspect in Berg's mind. This particularly applied to anyone that had served in the previous administration. Similarly, any of the presidentially appointed cabinet members deserved a close examination. Most of them did not pass the initial sniff test.

Jacob Remy's nomination as secretary of Homeland Security was the most notoriously questionable appointment in Berg's opinion, and the public's. Having served under the previous president as chief of staff, logic dictated he had been made privy to the disgraced administration's most closely held secrets. Apparently the deal he made with Crane's White House outweighed reason or any sense of justice. James Quinn remained in the position of National Security advisor, requiring no political maneuvering, a quiet but telling gesture by Crane's True America administration. The list grew daily as new announcements made the headlines.

Some of the conspirators managed to remain in the shadows, but Berg had spent a career connecting hard-to-see dots. He'd predicted the uncharacteristically ruthless, career-breaking shake-up at the CIA long before anyone else. It started with an appointment that didn't raise any eyebrows at first. As customary between outgoing and incoming administrations, the CIA remained untouched for a few months after Crane took office, keeping the U.S. intelligence-gathering apparatus working full steam during a period of significant change. In fact, consensus among top CIA officials suggested a longer delay for replacement appointments, because the upset election had left the United States, the House, and Senate locked in a power struggle. True America candidates had taken enough seats to make things difficult for the two parties that had dominated politics for two centuries.

With those battle lines still being drawn, the administration pushed through the less controversial nominations first. One attracted Berg's attention immediately. Frederick Shelby, director of the FBI, was nominated and unanimously appointed to the position of principal deputy director of National Intelligence. This move signaled the beginning of the end for the CIA's current leadership. The True America fix was in, and it went far deeper than Berg ever imagined.

The final investigative report detailing the events surrounding the June 2007 coordinated bioterrorism plot against the United States had meticulously and conclusively separated the link between the rogue True America spin-off group, led by disgruntled founders Jackson Greely and Lee Harding, and the mainstream True America movement sweeping its way to the White House. Once Shelby was nominated for the post at DNI, Berg held little doubt that the director of the FBI had purposely steered the investigation clear of any potentially messy connection in exchange for an even bigger seat at the table. If Shelby could be co-opted by True America, there was little hope that the rest of the intelligence community's senior leadership positions hadn't been predetermined by backroom deals and dirty handshakes.

As the Senate and House finally settled into a functionally cooperative state by late spring of 2009, the intelligence community's leadership was gutted, replaced by the men and women who had sold their souls at some point over the past few years to True America. Within days of Richard Sanford's appointment as director of the CIA, anyone with past connections to Zulu virus operations or General Sanderson's Black Flag team was demoted. *Realigned* was the corporate euphemism used to describe the changes.

Manning and Bauer were dropped into the Counterproliferation

Division, as director and deputy director, still in solid leadership positions commensurate with their experience level, but the message was clear: their careers would go no further. Both of them had embraced their new assignment with enthusiasm, not that they really had a choice. As rising stars within the CIA, they were younger than most of their peers and still had several years to go until they reached the minimum retirement age of fifty-five. Neither was in a position to leave, unlike Berg, who could have elected to take his retirement package and walked out of headquarters on the same day. He had more than enough vacation days saved to bridge the gap between notification and out-processing.

Instead of skipping out overnight, Berg decided that the wiser—and safer—course of action was to stick around long enough to convince his new overlords that he didn't pose a threat, but more importantly, to ascertain the danger to his own safety. Such a cleverly engineered political coup left Berg skeptical of the FBI's supposed efforts to pry deeper into the connection between Greely and Harding's fanatics and the scheming cabal of political operatives calling the shots behind True America's red, white, and blue façade.

He wasn't the only person stranded outside of True America's juggernaut with information that could call into question their truly miraculous ascension to power. If the wrong people started dying of heart attacks during their daily jogs, he would vanish into thin air. Maybe he'd take Sanderson up on the offer to put his services to use in a sunnier climate. The idea didn't sound half bad, even without the specter of a threat against him.

Reassigned within NCIS to a generic staff operations officer position with nobody reporting to him, he hadn't handled anything overly significant or controversial since sitting behind his new desk in a godforsaken cubicle. He hadn't been part of the cubicle culture at headquarters in sixteen years. Berg had been effectively retired by the new power brokers at the CIA, both marginalized and demeaned, in the obvious hope that he'd take his retirement and leave.

Berg had no intention of caving to these pressures or going anywhere until it suited him. It could be tomorrow if Sanderson was willing to import a whirlpool hot tub and a few other luxuries to the forest compound in Argentina, or it could be two years from now. That call was his alone to make.

He reached for the computer mouse on his desk with the intention of shutting down his workstation, but decided to give his email inbox another scan. Not because he thought an exciting case had been delivered late in the day, but more out of habit. The second email from the top, sent fifteen minutes ago, instantly piqued his attention. The message was a notification that he had a TOP SECRET/SENSITIVE COMPARTMENTED INFORMATION (TS/SCI) classified message waiting on a separate, secured message system.

Interesting.

He couldn't remember the last time he had received one of those. Whatever waited for him was guaranteed to be anything but low profile.

His finger hesitated over the mouse, ready to click the link provided in the email. It really had been a while. If his memory served correctly, he had been required to access the classified server through a completely separate program on his desktop. The link didn't feel right, but he hadn't received a message like this in a long time, and so much of the CIA's technology had changed over the past few years. He thought about asking someone, but he hated to draw any attention to himself. The email inbox was intranet based. The email in question couldn't have originated outside of the secure CIA server.

Berg had convinced himself of this by the time the link launched the secure message interface he recognized from the past. After typing a string of personalized alphanumeric codes and the twenty-six-key passcode provided in the notification email, the system granted him access to the message.

The subject line read SERAPH/AUTOMATED.

Now *that* was more than just interesting. SERAPH had been Nicole Erak's codename.

Nicole Erak, a name that always resurfaced bittersweet memories. She was also known as Zorana Zekulic while operating undercover throughout Europe. She was presently known as Jessica Petrovich, the woman who had pulled off the disappearing act of a lifetime, fooling everyone.

In 2005, after learning that SERAPH was still alive, he'd set several automated search patterns to scan online and paper news outlets for keywords related to all of her known aliases and relatives, along with the names of various people she'd likely pissed off in Serbia prior to vanishing, and that list was long. He'd done this as an off-the-books favor at her request, in case any of the ugly men or women on that list decided to travel to the United States for revenge. If one of her nieces or her mother suddenly disappeared, Nicole…Jessica would get some advance notice. What she might do with that notice was never explored.

Berg was glad he'd checked his email, until he read past the subject line. Now he needed a stiff drink. Jessica's mother had been admitted to hospice care at Palos Hills Community Hospital. The message contained no additional links or references that might explain how Vesna Erak ended up there. He clicked the only link provided, finding a screenshot of the story published in the digital version of a local newspaper. He found few details about her illness in the piece. The author was far more interested in describing "the decade-long cloud of tragedy that hung over the Erak family." Berg knew the story all too well. He'd monitored the parents' situation closely after handlers in Serbia reported her missing in late April 1999.

Vesna filed for a divorce a few months after their daughter's unexplained disappearance in Europe. As far as either of her parents knew, Nicole Erak had vanished outside of Prague during a planned two-week backpacking trip across Czechoslovakia. Amidst resurfaced whispers of past sexual abuse against his daughter and wife, Dejan Erak, family patriarch and prominent member of the Serbian community, blew his brains out before the divorce proceedings and rumors gained critical momentum. Vesna had a nervous breakdown shortly after the suicide, spending the next year in and out of psychiatric hospitals.

The article described the awful matter in excruciating detail, which didn't sit well with Berg. Yet it wasn't the content that raised his hackles. It was the fact that the article had been written in the first place. The article felt personal, like someone with a real grudge against the Eraks had either written or encouraged the story. Or—Palos Hills was a boring-as-shit suburb, and the Eraks' continued string of misfortunes was big news. The story of a lifetime for a jaded, part-time journalist at the local paper.

Berg took a deep breath, releasing it slowly. The safest course of action was to delete the message and pretend he'd never seen it, on the off chance that the article had been designed to lure her out of hiding and she actually decided to visit her estranged mother. The individual odds against either of these scenarios were long. The probability of both scenarios combining to enable an attack on Jessica had to be nearly nonexistent, especially given Srecko Hadzic's untimely death earlier in the year. He'd been the most likely and capable prime mover of revenge against the Petroviches prior to his spectacular demise.

Whether Hadzic was assassinated by fellow detainees who were worried that he was on the verge of cutting an immunity deal or accidentally killed in a botched rescue attempt remained the only point of speculation in the investigation surrounding his death. Berg wanted to believe his own people assassinated him, the irony inescapable; however, evidence suggested otherwise.

Most investigators opined that the explosive charge detonated underneath the armored United Nations Detention Unit transport van had been too small to guarantee the immediate death of the vehicle's occupants and had more likely been used to disable the vehicle, and a team had been assigned to break into the van and grab Hadzic. By sheer chance, the explosion simultaneously breached the van's bottom armor and blasted the contents of the gas tank into the passenger cabin, instantly engulfing Srecko Hadzic and three United Nations security officers in superheated flames. Little remained inside the scorched and twisted van chassis beyond a few blackened skeletons held loosely upright by the metal frame of their seats.

When news of Hadzic's death arrived, Berg had felt smugly satisfied.

Good riddance.

One of humankind's worst had burned to death, maybe a little too quickly from what he could tell by the video streaming out of The Hague. The ghastly, smoldering skeletons looked far too at peace in the context of the inferno that had taken them. A few weeks later, after DNA extracted from the bone marrow of one of the skeletons confirmed Hadzic's death, he raced to inform Jessica that Hadzic no longer posed a threat. He'd felt relieved for her and, interestingly enough, himself.

Verification of Hadzic's death meant one less danger in the world for the woman he'd thrown to the wolves. When it came to Nicole Erak, aka Jessica Petrovich, Berg was ruled by guilt. Against his better judgment or, better stated, in collusion with blinding arrogance, he'd pushed an exceptionally talented CIA recruit with identified emotional baggage into a high-risk, pressure-cooker assignment. Regardless of her ultimate betrayal of the agency, he felt personally responsible for the downward mental spiral that led her there. Infiltrating Hadzic's Panthers had shattered the young woman he'd trained, replacing her with a hardened, remorseless wretch.

He'd never forgive himself for what happened to her, which was why he struggled with the information in front of him. He really should delete the message, but the thought of unilaterally making the decision to deprive her of the last chance to see her mother didn't sit well with him.

"Fuck it," he muttered. "She can figure this out."

He'd send her a text, passing along what he knew when and if she returned the call. There was no guarantee she would respond. General Sanderson seemed to think the Petroviches were on the verge of disappearing for good. Berg hoped so. As useful and effective as they had been in the past and could continue to be in the future, their luck would run out sooner than later. Thinking of Sanderson gave him an idea. If he could arrange a little insurance policy, he'd feel far better about the situation.

Chapter 8

Long Bay, Anguilla

Daniel eyed the sunset beyond the natural rock jetty that formed the western end of the long white sand strip of beach in front of their table. Jessica caught his glance and stole a quick look over her shoulder before lifting her mojito from the table for a long sip.

"Should I be worried?" she asked.

"Uh…no," Daniel said, stalling for words and coming up with something completely unconvincing. "I just feel bad that you're not enjoying the sunset."

"Okay…" she said, eyeing him suspiciously. "It's not like we don't see the sunset every night."

His eyes darted to the western horizon again. Where the hell was the boat? He'd drawn out the evening as long as possible, paying the wait staff for a leisurely service pace that redefined the concept of "island time." He'd even arranged for the kitchen to inform Daniel of a faux mistake with Jessica's order, resulting in a twenty-minute delay while both of their meals were prepared freshly, to their satisfaction. He needed every spare minute he could muster.

The crew he'd hired needed a minimum of two hours to outfit the boat and deliver it to the shallow waters in front of the restaurant. When he'd last checked with them, roughly forty minutes ago, they'd assured him that everything was still on schedule. The boat should have arrived fifteen minutes ago. Daniel considered excusing himself for *another* bathroom break to check in with the crew when the top of a sailboat mast appeared over the rocky outcropping.

He smiled at Jessica and turned his head toward the kitchen entrance, where a member of the wait staff stood unobtrusively to the side, pretending to busy himself at one of the server stations. Daniel nodded at the man, who moved swiftly toward the bar.

"Now you have me worried," said Jessica, looking in the direction of the bar.

La Ombra's bow emerged from behind the rocks, the dark blue-hulled sailboat motoring swiftly through the calm reddish-orange reflected water. Daniel stared a little too long at the boat, drawing Jessica's attention.

"Is that our boat?" she asked, squinting at the shape moving across the setting sun.

Their waiter materialized with a stainless steel ice bucket tilted in its bamboo stand to reveal an open bottle of champagne. While the waiter arranged the bucket next to the table, another server slid two champagne flutes onto the white-linen-topped table. Jessica looked convincingly flummoxed, which convinced Daniel that his scheme had gone undetected until moments ago. She downed most of her remaining mojito and placed the sweating glass on the table away from the champagne flutes.

"What are you up to?" said Jessica, half smiling.

"I'm proposing," he said, mouthing, "Thank you," to the waiter, who quickly disappeared.

"We're already married, if I remember correctly."

"Don't worry, I'm not doing one of those re-proposal things."

"I'm not opposed to the concept," said Jessica, her attention focused on the sailboat anchoring offshore.

"I'm proposing something better," he said, sliding the chilled bottle out of the ice bucket.

After filling each glass halfway and replacing the bottle, he raised one of the champagne flutes, holding it halfway across the table. Before Jessica could grab the other glass, her smartphone buzzed on the seat next to her, the screen illuminating the chair back in the declining light. They rarely received calls, which was why he wasn't surprised or bothered when she interrupted his ceremony to check the phone. Given their past and present line of work, both of their phones remained close at hand at all times. A call from Sanderson or one of their intelligence contacts could mean the difference between life and death if a last minute threat was detected.

Jessica looked bothered. "Berg wants me to call him immediately. Says it's urgent."

"As in life-threatening urgent?"

She shrugged and then read the message. "Urgent that you call me immediately."

The message didn't sound immediately life threatening, but its nebulous quality made Daniel nervous. Better safe than sorry.

"The champagne is chilled, the boat is anchored, and I'm not going anywhere. Let's see what the mysterious Mr. Berg wants."

"You're the mystery man tonight, with champagne and boats suddenly appearing out of nowhere," she said, placing the phone on the table.

"I think you'll like what I have to propose," he said.

"Hold that thought."

Jessica pressed her phone's screen and raised the device to her ear. Daniel listened to the one-sided conversation, trying to piece it together from her responses. He didn't have much success. Jessica's side of the conversation remained mostly confined to one- or two-word questions. *When? Where? How long? Threat assessment?* A staccato series of questions rattled off without the slightest betrayal of emotion. When she placed the phone on the table, he truly had no idea what had transpired between Berg and his wife. He knew it hadn't been good; the solemn look on her face reinforced that assessment.

"What's going on?" he asked, placing his champagne glass on the table.

Jessica took her time answering, downing the glass of champagne in front of her first. Definitely not a good call.

"My mother is in a hospice," she said, eyeing his glass of champagne.

Tonight is going to be rough, he thought, pushing his glass toward her.

She accepted the gesture, draining the bubbly spirit.

Very rough.

Vesna Erak was a delicate subject on a good day, a nervous-breakdown-provoking topic the remaining three hundred and sixty-four days of the year. Something told him today would not be the good day.

"Why?" he asked, mimicking the brief interrogation style she used on Berg.

It sounded like an impersonal question, but he knew from experience that this was the safest way to communicate with her when she was like this.

"I don't know. Berg received a secure automated message alert linking to a local newspaper article."

"Is it real?"

"The article?"

"All of it," he stated. They could never be too careful.

"I'll confirm it with the hospital," she said, staring at the empty glass in her hand.

Her attention suddenly shifted to the water. A fiberglass-hulled, rigid inflatable boat plied through the smooth cove toward the beach in front of the restaurant. The two-person crew that had delivered *La Ombra* would pull the dinghy onto the sand, leaving it for Jessica and Daniel.

"You had something big planned for tonight," she said sullenly.

"The boat is stocked for a long-distance voyage. I planned on sailing you out of here tonight to the destination of your choice."

Jessica's eyes glistened, her face remaining neutral. She looked at the boat for a few seconds, turning back with an uncertain look. He could tell that she wanted to say something but couldn't form the words.

"Tonight's proposal has no expiration date," he said. "If you want to visit your mother—"

"I don't *want* to visit her," she blurted, grabbing the chilled champagne bottle.

He was convinced she intended to drink right from the bottle.

"But I owe it to her," she whispered, setting the wet bottle on the table next to the glasses. "I can give her closure. At least let her die at peace with herself. I should have done this years ago."

"You've done a lot for her over the years."

"I made sure she lived a comfortable life," said Jessica. "Anonymously."

"She knows it's you," he said. "She has to know you've forgiven her."

"I should have told her myself years ago. She deserved better from me."

Daniel had to tread lightly here. Despite the fact that she had anonymously set up a trust to take care of her mother, Jessica harbored a deep, long-standing resentment against Vesna Erak for failing to protect her from the serial abuse suffered at the hands of her father. Unleashing that bitterness put her in a bad place.

"She understood," he said, reaching across the table for her hand. When she let him take it, he knew she was still in control. "If you want to visit her, you should do it," he added.

"I think I need to see her," she said, taking a sip of champagne.

"I'll make the arrangements and do a little digging. Just to be safe."

She nodded. "Thank you, Danny. When I get back, we'll sail out of here and never look back."

"When *we* get back," said Daniel, hoping she had misspoken.

"I need to do this alone."

Daniel didn't push the issue, but he had no intention of letting her travel to the United States, to open one of the darkest chapters of her life—alone.

Chapter 9

FSB Headquarters
Lubyanka Square, Moscow

Alexei Kaparov laid the classified intelligence report on his desk, digesting the information. He'd skimmed through the bulk of the report, not wishing to rehash what was already known. Alpha Group, outfitted in protective biohazard gear, had swept the facility and the immediate grounds, finding no trace of Reznikov. Parts of the laboratory had been "rendered inaccessible" during the raid, a polite way of saying *irresponsibly destroyed and burned to the ground*. This precluded a full search of the buildings most likely to house Reznikov, leaving the strike force unable to confirm Reznikov's death or escape.

Strong circumstantial evidence gathered before and after the ground assault suggested that Reznikov had escaped. A close review of the thermal imaging and night-vision video captured by one of the helicopter's sensor pods suggested that the raid force had flown over a small boat on the final inbound leg of their attack. Faint thermal blooms, mostly obscured by jungle canopy, corresponded to the distinctively pointy shape of a boat's bow. Even at this late hour, a fisherman or poacher on the river wouldn't draw much suspicion, but the fact that the boat's occupants had made a considerable effort to hide themselves from aerial detection suggested something different.

While the theory was far from conclusive, it led the three-man Service of Special Operations (Spetsgruppa C) team to an interesting discovery. Roughly a mile downriver from where the boat had been first detected, commandos discovered a motorized aluminum skiff pulled onto the southern riverbank and tied to a tree. Not far from the river, in the thick brush next to a barely used walking path, they discovered two bodies covered by a heavy thermal-protective blanket. Neither turned out to be

Reznikov, and the corpses' identities generated more questions than answers.

One of the men turned out to be an ex-GRU Spetsnaz sergeant named Gennady Ageykin. Outside of a spotty service record, not much was known about Ageykin beyond his suspected association with a mercenary outfit that routinely performed security duties for wealthy oligarch types based outside of Russia. The mercenary group also held a sinister reputation for accepting less than legitimate assignments. At face value, a dead ex-GRU mercenary found a few miles away from the laboratory wasn't a significant discovery. However, discovering Valery Zuyev, one of the Solntsevskaya Bratva's top crime lieutenants, with his throat slashed in the same location? What did the American commercial say? *Priceless.*

According to recently shared U.S. intelligence reports, Valery Zuyev had been involved tangentially and directly to the Reznikov fiasco from the beginning. He was first identified by U.S. forces in the spring of 2007, as "Viktor," senior ranking Bratva member in Novosibirsk at the time of the Vektor Institute raid. Kaparov found it amusing that the report cleverly slid past the likely fact that the source of this information originated from the team that used Zuyev's resources to destroy the Vektor bioweapons facility. Not to mention the trail of carnage left behind by the team during their escape to the Kazakhstan border. Several armored vehicles destroyed, two helicopters shot out of the sky, and a few dozen Russian Federation soldiers killed. *Minor details when both sides had reasons to sweep the fallout from that day under the rug.*

Following the Vektor attack, Zuyev travelled to Argentina and Bolivia several times from Moscow over the course of the next year, raising Russian and American suspicions that he was paying close attention to the Bratva's most recently acquired prized possession, Anatoly Reznikov. Kaparov had to roll his eyes at yet another glaring omission conveniently left out of the joint intelligence report. Nobody appeared to question or explain how Reznikov fell into Bratva hands in the first place!

Once again, not a surprise given the questionable circumstances surrounding the scientist's disappearance and the numerous Russian and American lives lost in the bloody tug-of-war to capture him. Absurdly, Kaparov was probably the only person in the service of the Russian Federation who knew the full story. He couldn't imagine any circumstance under which the Americans would disclose the details of Reznikov's brief stint in captivity on U.S. soil, or the brutal attack by the Bratva-sponsored mercenaries that freed him. No. The story moved on, both sides burying their secrets while independently keeping a close eye on South America.

In 2008, the strategy nearly paid off—for the Americans. Zuyev surfaced unexpectedly in Montevideo, disappearing north into Uruguay's highlands and returning a few days later with a much larger than usual security entourage. The significant departure from his normal routine attracted the CIA's attention, resulting in a botched attempt by Berg's private army to grab the scientist. Neither Zuyev nor Reznikov had been seen since, until the Russian Foreign Intelligence Agency (SVR) received an anonymous tip two weeks ago, indicating that Zuyev and Reznikov were hiding in a remote jungle location in Goa, India. Satellite imagery confirmed the presence of several unusual structures at the reported site, triggering the raid.

This was where the report once again went cloudy, unlike his memory. He distinctly remembered hearing one of the agents in the operations center tell Greshnev that the team needed to be "airborne" in two minutes. Kaparov wasn't an expert on his country's military capabilities, but he was pretty sure the Russian Federation didn't have the ability to launch a helicopter raid in the vicinity of Goa, India. He didn't even need to look at a map to know a land-based operation was physically impossible. A sea-based mission? He highly doubted it. The nearest accessible naval base was at Vladivostok, at least several thousand kilometers away, and the Russians had no way to refuel a ship that far from port.

If the Russians didn't launch the helicopters, then who did? The answer was obvious, but Kaparov had no intention of broadcasting his guess. He'd been shuffled into the tactical operations center after the Alpha team debarked the helicopters, and shuffled out before they headed to the extraction site. Given a glimpse of the big game as a professional courtesy, in the new spirit of "cooperation" stinking up headquarters. Whatever. He didn't give a shit how they got there. They didn't get Reznikov, and that was the only thing that mattered. As long as Reznikov continued to draw oxygen, the world was a vastly more dangerous place.

So now what?

Kaparov read through the preliminary conclusions attached to the report, nodding with indifferent agreement. Yes. Yes. A monkey could have connected these dots. Obviously, someone snatched Reznikov close to the boat, which meant someone had known precisely when and where to grab him. The Russian team on the ground observed that the aluminum skiff had seating for three passengers, leaving Reznikov as the sole survivor. A wooden shedlike structure large enough to house an SUV had been found several hundred meters away near a rough jeep trail. Despite the pounding rain that hit the area the day after the raid, the team was able to find recent tire tracks on a few of the rises in the trail, headed south. No boot prints were found near the shed due to the rain.

The prevailing theory at this point was that Reznikov took advantage of the darkness and confusion to kill his Bratva escort and escape. He'd stabbed Zuyev in the throat with a hidden knife and then shot Ageykin in the head with Zuyev's pistol. On the surface, the theory made sense. Goa wouldn't be the first time that the scientist had pulled a fast one on his captors. Three Al Qaeda operatives had been found shot to death near a suspected makeshift bioweapons laboratory site in Semipalatinsk, Kazakhstan, a few weeks before Reznikov infected Monchegorsk's water supply with the Zulu virus.

Kaparov squinted at the page, feeling the urge to break his recent pledge to quit smoking in his office. Something about the theory felt uninspired, like the investigative work routinely submitted by the younger generation of agents seated right outside his office door. So easily offended by cigarette smoke and foul language, quick to jump to conclusions based on "facts," so they could turn in a shitty report and snag a seat on the Metro for their long rides to the suburbs. There was more to this story than an opportunistic escape. Reznikov wouldn't have lasted more than a few hours on his own in that jungle. Even if he had found the stashed vehicle—in the dark, in a panic, on his own—where would he have gone? No. He had help. Three seats in a boat did not limit a boat to three people.

Another person in play expanded the field of theories. The third guard could have seized the opportunity at the last moment to steal Reznikov for himself and sell him to the highest bidder. Presumably, they had stopped at a preplanned location, which included the stashed vehicle, which would have been known to the security detail. Or even better, the third guard could have dropped the anonymous tip, triggering the raid and the preplanned river escape. But how would he know when to expect the raid? And what if the raid had included a river element?

His mind drifted back to the Reznikov theory. Maybe he'd struck a deal with a Bratva guard or one of the far less loyal Russian mercenaries. Either way, it meant Reznikov had help, and figuring out who helped him was their only hope of finding the rogue bioweapons scientist. Kaparov had an idea, but it was a long shot. Of course, his scheme would require some discreet assistance.

Chapter 10

FSB Headquarters
Lubyanka Square, Moscow

Yuri Prerovsky studied the floor-to-ceiling flowchart that covered most of the wall outside his office. Comprised of color headshot photos with brief captions, the chart visually outlined the known connections between the different leaders and groups within the Solntsevskaya Bratva criminal gang. Three rows of loosely arranged folding chairs sat empty behind him, waiting for tomorrow morning's division update, when his boss would unveil one of the biggest changes to the Solntsevskaya's leadership roster in the past several years.

Valery Zuyev's long absence from the Moscow scene had just become permanent, erasing any continued speculation. Of course, Prerovsky would have to play dumb, like he had several minutes ago when his immediate boss told him to remove Zuyev from the wall. Nobody within the Organized Crime (OC) Division knew the real story behind Zuyev's sudden retirement. Center of Special Operations agents yanked information from his OC bosses without providing any context why they needed it. Standard operating procedure within the Federation Security Services. CSN operated in near complete secrecy, grabbing whatever it wanted without explanation, with the express approval of the director.

Despite the widespread disdain generated by CSN's "grab and go" authority, Prerovsky appreciated the high level of secrecy. Arkady Baranov's Center of Special Operations maintained a reputation for being incorruptible; a claim no other division within the greater Federation Security Services framework could make. Stringent background checks and surprise polygraph examinations ensured the highest recruit quality possible, but the key to CSN's continued success in fighting off corruption had more to do with geography than the quality of its people.

In 2004, Baranov moved all of CSN, save a handpicked headquarters liaison group, from the Lubyanka complex in Moscow, relocating to a close campus southeast of Moscow. The overwhelming majority of new CSN personnel trained and lived in the vast facility, which resembled a university setting. Close to ninety percent of CSN agents continued to live in the enclave long after initial training. At any given time, many of them were deployed as teams to different regions of the Federation and beyond.

The very nature of their work kept them from the static routines and lifestyles that made most FSB agents vulnerable to the street-level targeting of organized crime recruiters. When you had a family to support and protect, it was difficult to turn down the profitable offers made by the Bratva recruiters, especially when they started showing up at your children's school to help them cross the street or carry their backpacks.

It was estimated that close to five percent of FSB agents at headquarters and in field offices throughout the Federation had some type of regular contact with an organized crime handler. The high percentage made it nearly impossible for the greater Organized Crime Division to secretly plan and execute high-profile busts against the different crime groups, so mid to lower ranking division personnel collected data on the different groups through stakeouts, informants, daily surveillance, and electronic surveillance, and the assistant deputy directors assessed the data to recommend impactful operations to CSN leadership. It was the best the FSB could manage over the past several years.

Prerovsky sensed someone in the room and turned around to find Alexei Kaparov staring wryly back at him, holding two large Starbucks cups.

"Don't let me interrupt your deep thinking," said Kaparov. "I can come back once you've figured out who disappeared from the wall. Unless you want a hint."

"They let you out of your cage?"

"From time to time I'm set free to roam the building," said Kaparov, approaching him with one of the coffees extended.

Prerovsky cracked a sly smile, ruining any pretext of not wanting to know why Kaparov was plying him with his favorite coffee. He checked his watch, thankful that Kaparov had waited until after six to pay him a visit. No doubt by design. Kaparov always came armed with Starbucks coffee when he wanted something. A quick glance around confirmed they were alone for the moment. Most of the division had left for the day, and he was the last assistant deputy director on the division floor. As the junior AD, he'd been tasked with making the changes to the flowchart for tomorrow morning's briefing.

After Prerovsky accepted the coffee, the two shook hands vigorously for a moment; then Kaparov pointed at the empty position in the chart.

"It will be interesting to see who fills that void," he remarked.

"Possibly nobody. Bratva business has carried on as usual in Moscow during his extended absence. They're shifting more and more to a decentralized organization. A year from now, I'm not even sure we'll have a chart that resembles the typical top-down pyramid shape," said Prerovsky, glancing around to confirm they were still alone. "I assume you didn't come by to talk about the current state of Moscow organized crime?"

"Am I that transparent?"

"The coffees give you away every time. I only wish I could be there to see you struggle with the rush-hour crowds to fork over your hard-earned money. No gift card this time?" said Prerovsky.

"I'm saving for retirement," said Kaparov. "Do you mind if we step inside your office?"

Now he was intrigued. Kaparov knew more about Zuyev's recent activities than anyone in his office, including Prerovsky. If anyone knew why Zuyev had been scratched from the lineup, it would be his former boss.

"Of course. Step inside my humble abode," he said, motioning to the door next to the chart.

When Kaparov stepped inside, he shut the door.

"What's up?"

"Did you get the background on Zuyev's untimely departure from the land of the living?" asked Kaparov.

"No. I was just told to remove him from the chart," said Prerovsky, signaling for Kaparov to take a seat. "Please. Can I interest you in something stronger than an overpriced coffee?"

"Now who's prying whom for information?" said Kaparov, nodding his approval.

Prerovsky reached down and opened the lowest drawer of his desk, digging far back to retrieve an unopened bottle of Russian Standard and two shot glasses.

"The good stuff!" said Kaparov. "You spare no expense."

"I've saved this for a worthy occasion, but tonight will suffice," said Prerovsky.

"Very funny. I'm sure it won't hold a candle to my usual poison."

"It's all poison in the end," stated Prerovsky, twisting open the cap. "I assume you know the real story behind Zuyev's demise? And I presume it has something to do with a former Russian scientist?"

"You presume well," said Kaparov, accepting a full glass. "To what shall we toast?"

"To keeping our jobs," stated Prerovsky.

"And staying out of prison," Kaparov added, clinking Prerovsky's glass. "I'm too old for that, and you're too young."

"I'll drink to that," said the younger agent, downing his glass with a grimace.

He didn't care how smooth they claimed the good stuff was, it still burned going down when it wasn't mixed with juice or soda. Kaparov swallowed the liquid without a reaction.

"I could get into real trouble drinking this," said Kaparov. "I barely noticed it."

"If you didn't notice, I would suggest a temporary halt to drinking," said Prerovsky.

"Since we both know that's off the table, I'll stick with the stuff that burns," said Kaparov, sliding his glass across the desk. "After another sample of the good life."

They raised their refilled glasses.

"To killing Reznikov," said Kaparov.

Prerovsky's eyes darted to the door. The scientist's name was in the open, no longer one of the Federation's dirtiest secrets, but that didn't mean they were safe to throw it around casually, especially in the wrong context.

"Don't worry. I shut it tight," said Kaparov. "Unless the walls have ears around here."

"If they did, I'd already be in prison, or dead."

"You and me both," Kaparov said.

"To killing Reznikov," said Prerovsky.

He screwed the top on the bottle and started to collect the glasses. "How can I help make our wish come true?"

"Nothing as dramatic as before," said Kaparov. He opened his worn black suit jacket and removed a thumb drive from the left breast pocket, placing it on the desk.

"A CSN raid barely missed him, or so it is assumed. Based on the evidence gathered, it appears that he initially escaped in a boat, accompanied by two men. They found the boat tied to a tree a few miles downriver from the site…and two bodies off a nearby trail. One with a gunshot wound to the head, the other with a stab wound to the throat. Care to guess their names?"

The warm flush in his face had been replaced by a cold tightening, the mellow vodka buzz gone.

"I'd be willing to bet my next paycheck that one of them was Zuyev," said Prerovsky, reconsidering the bottle.

"I see your powers of deduction have not been dulled in organized crime," said Kaparov. "Zuyev got the stab wound, and an ex-GRU mercenary named Gennady Ageykin took a bullet to the side of his head. They think Reznikov took advantage of the confusion and turned the tables on his captors."

Prerovsky raised an eyebrow. "Really?"

"My thoughts exactly. Possible, but unlikely, which is why I've come to you," said Kaparov, tapping the thumb drive. "I have a list of names, with known or assumed profile data, of everyone identified by CSN during and after the raid. Twenty-three IDs for twenty-five bodies. That number includes Zuyev and Ageykin."

"Why the discrepancy?" said Prerovsky.

"Apparently, they blew up the laboratory during the raid. The bodies were burned beyond recognition."

Prerovsky involuntarily chuckled. Kaparov just stared at him, smiling wryly.

"They really blew up the most obvious place to find him?"

Kaparov nodded, shaking his head in mockery.

"Holy mother. Heads must have rolled for that. How do they know one of the bodies wasn't Reznikov?"

"The assault team first engaged the two men outside of the laboratory, forcing them inside. Based on a number of factors, they concluded the men had specialized combat training."

"He would have been fighting for his life," said Prerovsky. "In the heat of the moment, at night, I don't see how they could be so positive about that assessment."

"The assault team collected DNA samples," said Kaparov. "They eliminated Reznikov as a match for the toasted bodies."

"I don't want to know how they managed that," said Prerovsky.

"You really don't," stated Kaparov. "I picture a bag of thumbs being shipped in dry ice back to Moscow."

Prerovsky grimaced. "Thanks for the image. So we know Reznikov wasn't among the dead on the riverbank trail or at the primary assault site."

"Correct."

"If Zuyev was there, Reznikov was there. Any reason to assume differently?"

Kaparov shook his head.

"And you don't think Reznikov killed Zuyev and an ex-GRU type by himself?"

His former boss continued to shake his head. "Doubtful."

Prerovsky understood what Kaparov wanted, but it would be a stretch to make a connection. The older agent seemed to read his troubled look.

"You'll find a second file on this thumb drive. An overseas friend of mine provided some surprisingly clear, professionally catalogued video still footage of faces that I need you to run against your database. My gut tells me this was an inside job. Someone close to Zuyev had a hand in this. Someone that knows a lot about Reznikov."

Prerovsky reached across the desk and took the thumb drive. "I can't do this on my computer. The databases and facial recognition system is locked down in our SCIV (Sensitive Compartmentalized Information Vault)."

"I presume associate deputy directors have access?" said Kaparov.

"Yeah, and I have to log in to the system to use it, leaving a trace."

"I can't imagine anyone getting upset over an ambitious young agent assembling a list of Zuyev's known or presumed associates immediately after being notified that Zuyev was dead. There's bound to be a shake-up in the Bratva's hierarchy. You might even score some points for getting ahead of the inevitable power struggle," said Kaparov, pausing for a moment. "You should also run a list of all former government or military Spetsnaz mercenaries known to work with the Solntsevskaya Bratva, particularly Zuyev or Matvey Penkin, his immediate boss."

"You really don't like me, do you?"

"You'll be fine," Kaparov said smoothly.

"Easy for you to say. You're not the one sitting in the SCIV after hours, researching one of the top Bratva bosses in Moscow. That kind of shit gets noticed around here, and I don't feel like attracting the wrong kind of attention."

"You might make a few of the other assistant deputies jealous, but I'm sure you can handle it," said Kaparov.

"I'm not talking about here. I mean out there," said Prerovsky, gesturing toward the window behind him. "I don't need to be on the mafiya's radar."

As soon as Prerovsky finished the statement, he realized his mistake. Kaparov had already formed that mildly smug look he'd come to simultaneously admire and loathe during his years working with the older agent. Prerovsky shook his head with a defeated smile.

"Any more than I already am by working in the organized crime division. I'll see what I can do."

Prerovsky squeezed his eyes shut and pinched the bridge of his nose. He knew he was going to regret this somehow, but if it helped rid the world of Reznikov, it was worth the risk. When he opened his eyes, Kaparov had already opened the bottle.

"To killing Reznikov," he said, taking a long swig before handing it over.

"To killing him for good this time," Prerovsky agreed, accepting the bottle.

Chapter 11

CIA Headquarters
McLean, Virginia

A phone rang from the direction of Berg's cubicle, drawing his attention away from the start of his post-lunch pilgrimage to the campus coffee shop. It could wait. Probably wasn't his phone anyway. He started walking toward the stairwell again, stopping a few steps later. He didn't get a lot of calls these days, and the insistent ringtone beckoned him.

"Coffee can wait a few minutes," he muttered, returning to his cubicle. He dropped into his worn chair and grabbed the handset, glancing at the caller ID. Shit. He needed to be somewhere else to take this call. Somewhere a lot more private. Preferably out of the building.

"Give me ten minutes and call me back on my cell phone, unless this can wait until tomorrow."

Kaparov grunted. "I just left the office."

It was eight o'clock at night in Moscow. Something was up.

"That important?"

"Could be. Ten minutes." He hung up.

He thought about using one of the secure communications rooms, but dropped the idea. He'd have to swipe his access card to enter the bank of soundproof telephone booths, leaving a public record. It was better to retrieve his cell phone and take a walk outside, where he was free to place a call.

With a few seconds to spare, he had negotiated the byzantine process required to get out of the building. He walked briskly toward the tree-lined, grassy area blocking the nearest parking lot. Without a doubt, his sudden departure generated some kind of report to the regime stooges assigned to keep an eye on him. At least they couldn't eavesdrop on his conversation, or maybe they could. The phone in his front trouser pocket buzzed against his thigh. A quick check of the caller ID once again gave him a chill. Taking this call would only lead to trouble. He couldn't wait.

"To what do I owe the pleasure?" Berg said in his best Russian.

"Let's stick with your native language. No offense, but I speak better English today than you ever spoke Russian."

"Fair enough. How is life treating you, my friend?"

"Let's skip the pleasantries this time. It's cold out, and I'd like to get home in one piece."

"Don't you carry a pistol?"

"I lock it up in my office as a suicide prevention measure," said Kaparov.

"Do I need to call the Federation Security Service's suicide hotline on your behalf?"

"Please don't. They might encourage me," said Kaparov. "Anyway. Remember that mutual acquaintance of ours? The one that keeps getting away?"

"Yes. Did he surface?" asked Berg.

"You tell me."

"What is that supposed to mean?"

"Exactly what it sounded like it was supposed to mean," Kaparov retorted.

Now Berg was more concerned than intrigued. At first he thought the Russian was fishing for information, but now it sounded like he had good reason to suspect that the Americans, or possibly Sanderson's people, might have new information regarding Reznikov.

It wasn't Sanderson. He was fairly sure of that. Not one hundred percent, but close enough. Sanderson's assets hadn't been used for a number of months now, a trend that was unlikely to change in light of the Beltway's regime change.

Berg also had good reason to doubt the CIA had run an operation. He still had a few deeply placed friends in the Special Activities Division. If the CIA had been tasked with a mission to kill or capture Reznikov, SAD would have been involved, and word would have reached him by now. If the operation was military, he couldn't say one way or the other unless the Pentagon tapped the CIA for help.

He hated being this far out of the game.

"I have nothing new on my end regarding our acquaintance," said Berg, composing himself. "What leads you to conclude we were involved?"

"A lifetime spent reading between the lines and the fact that we don't have the land-based or naval capability to launch a helicopter raid into India. Here's the quick version of what I know."

Berg listened as the Russian hastily described the operation, which had miraculously failed to capture Reznikov. They couldn't even be sure he hadn't escaped with any of his gruesome work because they torched the laboratory. And now the scientist was either on his own or sold to the highest bidder. Neither scenario boded well.

At best, it reset the clock on the next bioterror attack. At worst…he didn't want to think about the worst-case scenario.

"So what does this leave us with?" asked Berg, sensing there was more.

"Very little," stated Kaparov.

"But something?"

"Grigor Sokolov."

Berg recognized the name immediately. Sokolov had been part of the mercenary team that snatched Reznikov out of "retirement" in Vermont. Several high-resolution digital cameras had caught his ugly face during the raid. A year or so later, video surveillance footage acquired by Sanderson's people put him next to Reznikov during the failed attempt to neutralize the scientist in Uruguay. Sokolov had been part of the scientist's personal security detail from the start. He'd expect to find Sokolov's body at the site, but it did little more than reinforce the likelihood that Reznikov had been there moments before the Russians raided the laboratory.

"He's not much good to us dead."

"Did I say he was dead?" asked Kaparov, pausing before continuing. "He's missing."

"He could have been burned up in the lab," Berg suggested.

"I don't think so. Sokolov and Ageykin have been close to Reznikov from the beginning. They're plank owners, part of the original crew that stole him right out from under your nose. The rest died in Uruguay."

"No need to get personal," said Berg.

"Sorry. I get a little animated when I think about how all of this could have been avoided."

Berg let it go. No point in reminding his friend that Reznikov was a Russian Federation-sponsored product of an illegal bioweapons program. He knew it better than anyone.

"So you think Sokolov betrayed the Bratva?" Berg asked.

"It's a theory."

"Sounds like your only theory," replied Berg.

"It's the only theory that makes sense to me. Reznikov didn't get the drop on two seasoned mercenaries and Zuyev. No fucking way."

"I guess the big question is who owns Reznikov, or does he own himself?" asked Berg. "Could he have bribed Sokolov somehow? Maybe convince him there's a bigger payoff if he sets him free?"

"Big question, indeed. Gut instinct tells me Sokolov either reached out on his own or was approached. These mercenaries deal in real money, not promises of wild payoffs by crazy scientists. Hard money turned Sokolov, and lots of it. The Bratva isn't overly forgiving of traitors. We're talking the kind of money that can fund a very expensive, permanent disappearing act."

Berg couldn't argue too deeply with Kaparov's prevailing theory. Even if Reznikov somehow turned the tables on his captors and escaped on his own, who had provided the intelligence for the raid? Certainly not Reznikov. He had no way to control the most important variable in that plan—how to avoid the military unit sent to capture or kill him. Reznikov was without a doubt mentally deranged, but he wasn't stupid. Far from it. A few well-placed smart bombs could have landed at any time, turning him into human confetti.

It wasn't Reznikov, which only left them with the Sokolov angle. A narrow angle no matter how you looked at it. And that was just the beginning of the bad news.

"Who knows about Sokolov on your end?" he asked.

"Me and one other person I trust with my life. I suggest you keep it that way on your end. The timing of Reznikov's escape suggests a leak somewhere. Can't be too careful."

"Then we discreetly look for Sokolov while everyone else shakes the trees for Reznikov."

"Agreed. And when we find him, we let your special friends handle it."

"I'll put them on alert. If Sokolov is out there, he's guaranteed to screw up. The guy spent the last two years in hiding. Put some money in his hands, and he'll draw attention. If he's still travelling with Reznikov, the chance is tripled."

"My thoughts precisely. Keep me updated," said Kaparov.

"I will. Good to hear from you again."

"Uh-huh," said Kaparov. "One last thing."

"Sure. What is it?"

"Why are you talking outside?"

"Do you have me under surveillance or something?"

He didn't reply, forcing Berg to answer the question.

"They've redecorated the place, and I don't exactly fit with the new décor."

"Maybe I should have asked that question at the start of our conversation."

"I'm just being ultracautious," Berg said.

"I appreciate the courtesy," said Kaparov then hung up abruptly.

Shit. Berg couldn't tell by the Russian's tone if that was the last he'd hear from him. Like himself, Kaparov had too much to lose, and it wouldn't take much to unravel his ties to everything that had transpired two years ago. If the roles were reversed, he'd strongly weigh the risks of making contact again. In a way, Berg's situation wasn't all that different. If the wrong person linked his sudden interest in Sokolov to the rogue bioweapons scientist, he'd quickly find out what this new administration was capable of. Regardless of the risk, he had to do something. Getting rid of Reznikov was his cross to bear.

Chapter 12

CIA Headquarters
McLean, Virginia

Karl Berg paused in front of a partially opened door, reading the nameplate on the wall next to him. *Audra Bauer—Deputy Director, Counterproliferation Division.* He'd walked directly from his call with Kaparov to her office, afraid that he might lose the nerve to approach her if he waited too long. They were still good friends despite the unspoken strain of their recent demotions, but Berg felt tentative about bringing her this new information.

It fit right in her wheelhouse at Counterproliferation, but Sandra Tillman, the new NCS director, or someone even higher up the chain of command, had no doubt given Bauer the same message as Berg: Forget Reznikov ever happened. Forget anything connected with Reznikov ever happened. The new administration didn't like connections to their sordid past, which was exactly how he intended to pitch his plan to Bauer.

He knocked on the door frame and peeked inside, catching her glance.

"Get in here," she said, standing up at her desk with a warm smile.

So far, so good, he thought, stepping inside her office for the first time.

"May I close the door?" he asked.

Her smile faintly waned; then she nodded. "I thought this might be a friendly visit. Long time no see, Karl."

He pushed the door shut before answering. "It's a long overdue visit. Sorry, Audra."

She motioned for him to take a seat in one of two comfortable-looking, modernist accent chairs bordering a white marble coffee table. The office was half the size of her previous space, but she'd done her usual job turning it into an art-museum-quality space.

"I see you haven't lost your decorating touch," he commented, sitting in the pristine black leather chair contraption.

Bauer joined him at the table. "I suppose your office is still filled with unopened boxes from the move?"

"Cubicle. Not much room for collectibles."

"Sorry. I didn't know," she said. "I should have, but I haven't exactly been anyone's best friend lately. I wish you had told me this. I could have done something."

"Things are uneasy enough around here. The last thing either of us needs is to draw any undue attention. I can ride this out in a cubicle."

"Ride out the current administration? That's one hell of a protracted ride," she said.

"No. I won't be around that long. I'm waiting for the right moment. Letting myself fly under the radar for a few months, maybe a year, long enough to show them I can play by the rules."

"And that's why you popped into my office out of the blue and shut the door before saying hello? Flying under the radar?" she asked, raising an eyebrow.

Berg leaned across the table, lowering his voice. "This is big. At least it could be big. Especially for your division."

"If it has to do with Reznikov, I'm not interested."

"Hear me out," Berg pressed.

"I'm not interested, Karl. I'd like to have something to show for my years of service here other than a punitive letter of reprimand that will magically follow me while I hunt for another job," she said.

"Let me explain, and if your answer is still no, I won't bring it up again," said Berg.

"Why don't you take this up the chain if it's that important?"

"Because I'm radioactive, Audra. They put me in a fucking cubicle, where I sit around all day reviewing bullshit reports about nothing," he said. "I can't bring this to anyone but you."

"Fuck," she muttered, leaning back in her chair and shaking her head. "Karl, this better be good. If I walk this up to Manning—"

"You won't have to get him involved," said Berg.

"Excuse me? Manning is my boss. That's kind of how it works," she snapped.

"I know. Sorry. I'm not explaining myself," said Berg. "The information I received is a long shot at best, and it's only tangentially connected to Reznikov. His name doesn't even need to come up. Seriously."

"I'm listening," she said, eyeing him skeptically.

Berg spent the next few minutes bringing her up to speed, substituting "very high value target" for Reznikov. She nodded imperceptibly throughout his briefing, never interrupting. When he finished, she sat like a stone, her eyes fixed on the table in front of them for an uncomfortable period of time. Berg barely breathed, afraid to move or make a noise. She hadn't outright refused yet, giving him a tiny glimmer of hope.

"Sokolov is the key," she said.

"Reznikov is on everyone's watch list, but nobody is looking for Sokolov. We generated a profile for him connected to the Vermont disaster, but that wasn't widely distributed," said Berg.

"It wasn't distributed at all, beyond you. I made sure of it," she said. "My hope was that we might wrap this up quietly at some point."

"Then Sokolov doesn't exist outside of a tight, private circle. We stand a good chance of accomplishing your goal. Can you discreetly add him to the counterproliferation watch list?"

She nodded. "I can add him without drawing any attention. Another Russian mercenary mixed up in the chemical weapons trade."

Berg rubbed the stubble on his face. He'd stopped shaving every morning a few months ago. A kind of subtle protest, more like a resignation to his current fate. Either way, he felt overly conscious of it in front of her. Embarrassed might be a better word.

"I'll reach out to Ryan Sharpe at the FBI. He's pretty high up in their National Security Branch. I might be able to convince him to add Sokolov to the Interpol watch list in addition to whatever broader identification resources they can influence. Worth a shot, and I don't see any way that would come back to haunt us. That about covers it."

"Nice try. There's still the matter of what happens if Sokolov pops up," said Audra.

"I'll take care of that. One phone call. No exposure," said Berg. "If we all get lucky and our high-value target is with Sokolov, they'll send us pictures, fingerprints, DNA samples, whatever is necessary to put this ugly chapter to rest."

"No severed heads, please," said Audra, referring to Daniel Petrovich's unconventional method of providing the first Zulu virus samples examined by U.S. bioweapons scientists.

"If they want to deliver his severed head, who am I to say no?" said Berg, eliciting a faint smile from Bauer.

She stood up without warning and took a deep breath. "I'm not expecting much. Someone with deep pockets bankrolled his escape. I'd be shocked if Sokolov, or Reznikov for that matter, fucked up that badly. That said…"

Berg nodded. "Reznikov is a loose cannon, and they've both been stuck in one shithole after another guarding him," he said. "I expect them to turn up sooner than later."

"Precisely," she said, grinning like he always remembered. "Good to see they haven't crushed your spirit, Karl."

"They tried, but it's going to take more than a cubicle to keep me down," he said, winking.

"The entire intelligence community was gutted a few months ago. I don't know if things will ever be the same around here."

"I wish I could tell you that this is business as usual, but True America's Beltway sweep is unprecedented. This is my seventh administration in thirty plus years, and…" he said, considering his next words carefully, "a storm is brewing unlike anything we've seen before."

She studied him for a few moments before responding. "There's nothing we can do about it. The game has changed."

"Hopefully I'll be gone when it fully reveals itself," said Berg. "Somewhere warm."

"Argentina?"

"Not likely," he replied. "Unless I spot a black van parked in front of my town house."

"If you do, let me know. I'll probably have one parked on my street too," she said. "I'll add Sokolov to the watch lists. Maybe we'll get lucky."

"I appreciate you doing this for me. I'd like to retire knowing that psychopath is permanently off the market."

"Don't torture yourself over this. You didn't create that monster," she said.

"But he escaped on my watch," said Berg.

"Thirty trained CIA guards were also on watch that day, and it didn't make a difference," she said. "What are you doing to keep yourself busy these days? Getting out of the house enough?"

"Sounds like our visit just turned into a psych eval." Berg chuckled.

"You're the one that keeps dredging up the past, constantly beating yourself up," said Bauer.

"Funny," said Berg, standing up.

"Karl, we all took a big hit earlier in the year. It hasn't been easy."

"I'm fine. Really. As a matter of fact, I'm meeting Darryl Jackson for dinner and cocktails tomorrow night," he said.

"All right. Please say hi for me, and thank him again for his help in the past," said Bauer.

"I'll be sure to pass none of that along. His left eye twitches whenever he hears the letters C-I-A."

Bauer laughed, moving around the table to shake his hand. "I'll keep you posted. Good seeing you."

"Good seeing you too. I grab coffee down at the Starbucks most days around 1:30 PM. I probably shouldn't make a habit of visiting your office."

"Radioactive?"

"Positively glowing," he said, showing himself out.

Berg avoided eye contact with the busy collection of analysts and CIA officers swarming in and out of the cubicle farms occupying the Counterproliferation Division's middle ground. Reaching the stairwell unmolested, but presumably not unnoticed, he stopped to collect his thoughts. There really was nothing else to do at this point. He'd return to his desk and continue to mindlessly tackle an email inbox full of mundane tasks, all the while keeping his fingers crossed. But before he returned to his cubicle, a leisurely stop at the on-site Starbucks was in order.

Chapter 13

SVR Headquarters, Yasanevo Suburb
Moscow, Russian Federation

Dmitry Ardankin unconsciously fidgeted in his chair. He only noticed when the stoic secretary behind the oversized antique desk raised her eyes, keeping them fixed on him until he remained perfectly still for a few seconds. He hated that woman, though not for any rational or personally justifiable reason. Just the fact that she made him feel so uncomfortable every time he sat here was reason enough. And now she had stilled him with nothing more than a mildly annoyed stare.

Fuck you and the Metro card you rode in on, he thought, recrossing his legs in defiance of her disapproving look. He had good reason to squirm.

Director Pushnoy had never made him wait this long before. Not because Ardankin commanded Directorate S, one of the most secretive directorates within the Foreign Intelligence Service (SVR), but because he religiously kept to his schedule, especially the regularly scheduled meetings with the service's deputy directors. No doubt thanks to the emotionless machine standing guard over the entrance to his office, and his attention.

He resisted glancing at his watch again. The time didn't matter. The last time he checked, the appointment was twenty-three minutes past due. That was all he needed to know. Uncharacteristically late. He wondered if the director's secretary had notified the other deputy directors of the delay, or was he the last deputy scheduled for each day? He had no idea. He'd never once seen another person waiting for the director when his previous appointments had ended.

Ardankin sensed a shift in the secretary's posture. "The director will see you now."

After closing the door behind him, he walked through a darkened privacy vestibule into the director's spacious office, freezing in place. For the first time in five years, he wasn't alone for his regularly scheduled morning meeting. Worse than that, he didn't recognize the man seated in one of the chairs at the oval mahogany table with Pushnoy. At least the mystery guest didn't look comfortable. If he'd looked at home sitting with the director, Ardankin would be worried. Not that he wasn't a little unnerved to be sharing his allotted time with a total stranger. This couldn't be good.

"Dmitry, please," said the director, motioning for him to join them at the table.

Stefan Pushnoy remained seated as he approached, but the angular-faced stranger started to stand, which was immediately stopped by a casual glance from the director. Already halfway out of the chair by the time he caught Pushnoy's silent order, Ardankin got a quick look at the man as he sank slowly back into his seat.

One thing was clear: the guy was not comfortable in a suit. Nor was the suit comfortable on him. Stretched tight across his chest and broad shoulders, the jacket strained when he sat down again, its cuffs pulled back to expose a few inches of the white dress shirt covering his arms. This was the first time the man had worn a suit in years—if ever. If forced to guess, Ardankin would say the guy was former or current Spetsnaz.

"Dmitry, this is Colonel Levkin with the Main Intelligence Agency's Special Operations Command. He knows full well who you are," said the director.

"Colonel," said Ardankin, nodding at the GRU officer.

"I'm honored to be here," said Levkin, extending a hand across the table.

Ardankin reached across the table to shake Levkin's hand, anticipating a bone-crushing grip that never materialized. When his hand was safely out of the colonel's grasp, he stated the obvious.

"I wasn't aware that the GRU had a Special Operations Command."

"They don't," said Pushnoy. "Not yet, at least. We'll get to that in a minute."

Once Ardankin was seated, Pushnoy opened the same briefing folder he always used for their morning appointment, squinting at its contents. Two additional folders, with different markings, sat beneath it—taunting him. The bulky man seated across from him had a similar folder.

"What is your assessment of the operation in Goa?" asked Pushnoy.

Ardankin fought the urge to glance at the newcomer, but his eyes betrayed him.

"Colonel Levkin is aware of that situation," said the director.

"Compromised," Ardankin replied.

"Indeed," said Pushnoy.

"My directorate's regional asset was unaware of the laboratory. The Bratva managed to keep it exceptionally quiet," said Ardankin.

"Until they didn't," said Pushnoy, closing the file. "Someone inside the Bratva turned."

"Turned to who?"

"Nothing your people need to worry about right now. We didn't even know the Bratva owned Reznikov until a few days ago."

"Or how he came into their possession. We all know who had him last," said Ardankin.

"All part of the absurd charade both of our countries have been playing for the past two years," Pushnoy said, pushing one of the new folders in his direction. "This came across my desk yesterday. Take a few minutes to look it over."

Ardankin drank in the details. The information was compelling and well worth immediate investigation, but it raised red flags. Lots of warnings. When he finished reading the documents, he looked up, his face once again betraying him.

"I can't help acknowledge the coincidence," Pushnoy remarked.

"Two intelligence coups within a week?" said Ardankin. "And loosely related? Do we know the source?"

"The data arrived electronically."

"And anonymously, I presume. Just like the Reznikov tip-off?" said Ardankin, wondering if his skeptical tone had crossed the line.

Pushnoy displayed a rare smirk. "Everything will be vetted before a move is considered."

Interesting. He neither confirmed nor denied whether the information had arrived anonymously.

"It appears to me that a move has already been considered," said Ardankin, nodding at Colonel Levkin. "Have we submitted satellite reconnaissance requests to the Space Directorate? This intelligence is outdated."

"Cosmic Intelligence Directorate," said Pushnoy. "I've authorized the colonel to request satellite imagery."

"I still can't bring myself to say *cosmic*. Why in hell they would choose that name is beyond me," said Ardankin.

Colonel Levkin chuckled. "I'll submit the request immediately. We should have enough imagery to make an initial assessment within forty-eight hours."

Ardankin considered another wry comment, but decided he'd already used up his monthly quota. Frankly, he was surprised Pushnoy hadn't shut him down in front of the colonel. The director had never been one to hold back. Instead, he took the safest route.

"How can Directorate S be of service?"

"Colonel Levkin has been temporarily assigned to Directorate S, along with his new command, Spetsgruppa Omega."

"Omega?" said Ardankin. "I assume the final letter of the Greek alphabet was chosen for its significance, not because the Russian Federation has plans for ten additional Spetsnaz groups?"

"The last. The end. The ultimate," said Levkin.

"Levkin has handpicked the best special operators from the GRU's Spetsnaz ranks to form an experimental unit," started Pushnoy. "Colonel, why don't you elaborate, as briefly as you can."

"I've been tasked to create a company-sized, rapid-response force capable of carrying out emergency missions around the globe, Deputy Director," said Levkin.

"No offense, Colonel, but isn't that role currently fulfilled by our Federation Security Service's Spetsgruppas?" Ardankin asked.

"You're not mistaken, sir," said Levkin, pausing as if to choose his words carefully. "The joint chiefs and the Main Intelligence Agency recently convinced the defense minister that we needed the same capability in each military district, without the usual bureaucratic delay."

"Or the bureaucratic oversight, I imagine," said Ardankin.

Levkin hesitated to agree.

"No need to play coy here, Colonel," said Pushnoy.

"Very well, Director," said Levkin. "Yes, the generals are tired of *requesting* assets for special operations missions outside of the traditional combat zones. Frankly, the current use of Federation Security Service personnel outside of the Russian Federation territory is bizarre."

"And embarrassing?" said Ardankin.

Levkin grinned. "There's plenty of that sentiment at the top as well."

"I don't have all day," sighed the director. "Here's how this is going to work. We'll approach the task from two directions. Dmitry, I want a team watching Ernesto Galenden day and night. If the satellite imagery requested by Colonel Levkin shows the location indicated in the file to be abandoned, we will need to have a private talk with Galenden."

"Easy enough," said Ardankin.

He purposefully didn't expand upon his directorate's capabilities. He imagined the colonel had a fairly accurate concept of Directorate S's mission and generic capabilities, but rumors had a way of inflating or deflating the truth, each scenario benefiting his Directorate, depending on the circumstance. In Colonel Levkin's case, he preferred that the GRU officer overestimated. Legend among your countrymen never hurt.

"Colonel, my only hesitation, actually more a concern, lies purely in the numbers," said Pushnoy.

"I'm not going to overestimate my unit's capabilities," said Levkin. "If this group is as skilled as you indicate and they presently occupy the position designated in this report, the numbers are not in our favor. Not without military-grade air and ground support."

"How many men do you have in Omega?" asked Ardankin.

"I have two direct action platoons comprised of twenty men each," Levkin said after a moment of hesitation. "Plus a special-purpose weapons team of twelve, which can be integrated with the direct action platoons as required."

Members of this American mercenary unit had driven straight into what should have been a turkey shoot for his directorate's Zaslon operatives. Not only did the smaller force of Americans drive away with Anatoly Reznikov, the Zaslon team's target, but they also massacred every last Russian operative. Eight of the deadliest Spetsnaz officers in the Russian Federation's arsenal lay dead on a Stockholm street. Killed within seconds of the Americans' arrival.

Ardankin shook his head. "It won't be enough. Not on their turf. Not without absolute surprise, which is unlikely to be achievable against these people."

"Then what do you propose?" asked Pushnoy.

The question caught Ardankin off guard. He wanted to say *let sleeping dogs lie*. The American mystery unit had been quiet since the raid on Vektor Institute. Clearly Pushnoy didn't feel the same way, or was he under pressure from above to make this work? The train of thought led to an idea. Probably a long shot, but it was the only hope of pulling this off.

"Colonel, if I'm off base tactically, please don't hesitate to say so," he said, continuing after Levkin nodded. "We stack the numbers in our favor by drawing them out of their lair?"

"It still leaves us with the same problem, just spreads it out," said Levkin.

Pushnoy leaned back in his chair with an approving look. "You mean to suggest we go after Sanderson himself when he's least protected."

"Cut off the head of the snake," whispered Levkin.

"And burn the framework of his operation to the ground, ensuring it can't be used against the Russian Federation any time in the near future," said Ardankin.

"How will we lure his people away?" asked Levkin. "I assume a string of firecrackers down the road won't do the trick."

"It might have to," said Ardankin, turning to the director. "Unless the email containing all of this wonderfully convenient information included a return address."

Pushnoy neither blinked nor changed his facial expression, which meant he had the man's undivided attention and that his earlier assumption about the anonymity of the information was correct.

"With all due respect, Director, if they want us to do their dirty work, the least they can do is set the stage. Sanderson will need a convincing reason to deploy the bulk of his people. I hear that a certain high-profile bioweapons scientist is on the loose again."

The director stared at him with piercing ice-blue eyes, the faintest hint of a grin on his face as he stood up. "This goes without saying, but the two of you will not be seen with each other outside of this office. Figure out a way to coordinate efforts."

"Understood, Director," said Ardankin. "I'm sure we can work something out."

Colonel Levkin stood at attention, echoing his statement.

"Colonel, you are dismissed. Report directly to Ardankin from this point forward. My secretary will provide you with a secure briefcase for that folder. I can't stress enough the confidentiality of its contents."

"With my life, Director," said Levkin. "Thank you for this opportunity."

"Don't thank me yet," said Pushnoy, motioning for him to leave.

When his secretary closed the door, the director addressed Ardankin less formally, a surprise to him.

"We move cautiously on this. One misstep and we have a disaster on our hands."

"I agree, sir," said Ardankin. "I have just the man for the job."

"Osin?"

"He has the most experience with Sanderson's people."

"Not many live to share that experience," said Pushnoy.

"That's why he's so valuable. I have no doubt he will be eager to nail Sanderson's coffin shut."

Chapter 14

Neuquén Province
Argentina

General Terrence Sanderson stood on the deck of the timber lodge he had once called headquarters, and drew deeply on a Cuban cigar. He'd missed this place. The Black Flag program rose to full strength from the ashes here, forging men and women of the highest caliber for the dirtiest unacknowledged missions the United States had to offer. Now the valley compound served as temporary lodging for long-range reconnaissance and scout-sniper training. They didn't spend much time in the valley that sheltered the complex before heading out into the massive expanse of land leading right into foothills of the Andes Mountains. The less time spent here, the better.

He'd rubbed too many people the wrong way during the painful process of rebooting the program to trust the sanctity of deals signed and sealed under the old guard. Immunity didn't protect you from a payload of ground-vaporizing two-thousand-pound smart bombs released from a B-2 stealth bomber. The coordinates to this location were likely in the wrong hands already, which was why part of any training exercise based out of the former headquarters started with a three-day infiltration and surveillance operation to ensure the location was safe.

Electronic sweeps confirmed that no electronic signals emanated from the buildings or surrounding valley, which would have indicated the surreptitious installation of remote surveillance equipment. Most of the Black Flag operatives were familiar with the use of portable radio frequency detectors and handheld spectrum analyzers. Since background electromagnetic noise was nearly nonexistent in the isolated valley, detecting a hidden signal, no matter how cleverly disguised or transmitted, should be a fairly simple prospect. To be on the safe side, he always brought a member of the program's dedicated electronic warfare along to oversee the analysis.

An array of portable sensors stood guard over the compound during their brief stay, watching the sky and the forest for emissions indicating a potential threat. Of course, a smart bomb didn't advertise its arrival. You were there one minute, gone the next, which was why he was meticulous about countersurveillance during their short stays.

After checking his watch, he pulled a sturdy-looking satellite phone from one of his jacket pockets. He was about to break one of his own rules and accept an incoming satellite call, only because the originator had been insistent and they were less than thirty minutes from leaving the site. He counted the seconds, reaching "two" before it buzzed.

"It's been a while, stranger," Sanderson answered.

"Well, it's been a while since I've had anything for you," said Karl Berg.

"Been a while since anyone has given us anything," said Sanderson. "Frankly, it makes me nervous."

"You and me both," said Berg. "I was counting the hours to retirement, until I got a call from a friend in Moscow. I might have a mission for you."

The line went quiet for a few moments.

"I'm not in the mood for theatrics, Karl. What do you have?"

"I forgot what a pleasure it is to talk to you," said Berg. "We got a possible hit on Reznikov. A Special Forces raid against a hidden laboratory on the west coast of India missed him by minutes, and my friend strongly suspects that one of the ex-GRU mercenaries assigned to guard Reznikov arranged for the convenient last minute absence from the site."

"Russian Special Forces?"

"Possibly a joint U.S.-Russian operation," Berg replied. "But that's purely speculative based on my friend's assessment."

"Any way you can confirm it?" asked Sanderson.

"The CIA wasn't directly involved. I'd know if that was the case. Audra Bauer would definitely know."

"Maybe she's trying to protect you—from yourself," said Sanderson. "Sniffing around for Reznikov is likely to draw the wrong kind of attention."

"I'm willing to make some noise to catch Reznikov."

Sanderson understood where he was coming from, which was why he admired Berg. *Tolerated* might be a better term. The general's disdain for intelligence professionals was nearly pathological. Berg had been the first intelligence officer to gain his trust in decades. Sanderson sensed a firm commitment to their shared nation, linked by a willingness to take extraordinary and, if necessary, unsavory steps to safeguarding it. Berg understood what it took to protect America under the new rules shaped by global terror organizations and the states that sponsored them. And apparently he hadn't lost his enthusiasm for upending those rules.

"What are we looking at?" Sanderson asked.

"It's kind of a long shot, but if this mercenary turns up, he could lead us directly to Reznikov. That's where you come in. This will be a short-fused mission."

"I can pre-stage a team for immediate takeoff from Buenos Aires or possibly one of the regional airports. That would be our best bet. We have a few discreet jet services on retainer that can transport a lightly armed team. My guess is we could be in the air within an hour of notification. Give me twelve hours to get everything in place."

"Perfect. With that kind of response time, it might even be possible to nail them in the same place. My best guess is that they have been attached at the hip since Vermont. Video surveillance of that mess identified the mercenary. Same with Uruguay. If that's the case—"

"They'll be looking to blow off some steam," Sanderson cut in.

"That's what I'm thinking. They'll want to discreetly spend some money. A double-cross deal like this cost someone a pretty penny."

"That was my next question," said Sanderson. "Any idea who funded and presumably orchestrated Reznikov's escape? Sounds like they had help on the ground. I'm trying to picture a single mercenary dragging that sorry sack of shit around the jungle, and it's not happening."

"That's the big mystery," said Berg. "My guess is someone connected to the Russian Foreign Intelligence Service. From what my source in Moscow can tell, the raid against the laboratory was real. Someone on the inside tipped them off at the last minute."

"It almost sounds like the raid provided a necessary distraction," Sanderson suggested.

"I was thinking the same thing."

"One hell of a risky gamble. Nearly impossible to control all of the variables."

"Right. But given the isolation of the facility, this may have been the only viable option to snatch Reznikov without making it blatantly obvious," said Berg.

"The Bratva will figure this out eventually. They have people on the inside too."

"Maybe. Maybe not. If they have someone deep enough in the Federal Security Service to relay access to all of the evidence gathered and reported by the strike team, I think they'll assume the Russian government sent a covert team to grab Reznikov, to permanently disappear the guy."

"Or put him back to work," Sanderson said.

"Don't say that," said Berg. "Please."

"You have to consider the possibility that this was an inside job disguised to look like an outside job. If that's the case, he's probably deep underground inside Siberia."

"All we can hope to do right now is work with the scant intelligence we've been given," said Berg.

"I'll stack the deck with the largest team I can fit on a jet in case we're looking at a complicated mission."

"I guarantee it will be complicated."

"You know what I mean," said Sanderson. "It's easier to scale back than scale up."

"I got you," said Berg. "I'll keep you updated from my end. Let me know when everything is in place."

"Copy that," said the general. "Good to hear from you, Karl. I was worried you might have retired without inviting me to your farewell party."

"Funny. I won't get so much as a pat on the back when I leave."

"Word of advice?"

"Do I have a choice?"

"Whenever you decide to leave, do it quietly. And watch your back."

"I plan to have you watching my back."

"Only if you've signed on the dotted line," Sanderson said. "You'd like it down here."

"Not sure how much use I could be," said Berg.

"You'd be surprised. Times change. Administrations change. A person's value can fluctuate, but their potential remains the same. Given the right circumstances, you'll be worth your weight in gold again."

"Thanks for the pep talk."

"Just trying to say that you're always welcome around here," said Sanderson.

"Let's hope I'm not forced to take you up on the offer. Let me know when everything is in place," said Berg, disconnecting the call.

Sanderson lowered the phone and took a few puffs on his Montecristo No. 2. He wasn't thrilled by the lack of details passed by Berg. The CIA officer had been generous with information in the past, which led him to believe that the mission was a long shot at best, even if they miraculously caught a sniff of Reznikov. Even more troubling was Berg's subtle air of desperation.

He understood Berg's position well. The Black Flag organization had lain dormant under the new administration, and Sanderson was eager to get back in the game. A fine line existed between eagerness and desperation. An often-imperceptible line, mostly marked by patience—a quality rigorously honed by Sanderson during his years in exile. He sensed that Berg might have drifted over the line to a dangerous place, where judgment lapsed and good men and women were senselessly killed. He'd have to carefully evaluate the intelligence provided to support whatever mission eventually materialized. They'd come too far to throw caution to the wind.

The Black Flag program had enjoyed a productive two years after their controversial but silently celebrated destruction of the Russian bioweapons program at Vektor Institute. A few months before the raid, they had also played a critical role in unraveling and stopping the bioweapons plot perpetrated by True America-aligned extremists. The mainstream True America political movement successfully disavowed any connection to the fanatics, but Sanderson had no doubt his organization's involvement in the fiasco was the primary reason why his program had remained dormant for the past several months. It also validated his decision to relocate the headquarters and scatter his teams. Sanderson and his operatives represented an untidy loose end for the True American administration.

A small group of operatives approached the darkened porch from the direction of a waiting convoy of SUVs. He could identify them by their general bearing and movements. Richard Farrington carried himself fully upright and moved assertively. The soldier was afraid of nothing, but not out of a misplaced sense of bravado. He was confident in his own competency and the proficiency of his colleagues, which extended to the surveillance teams that had ensured the valley's security and continued to watch as they packed up to depart.

Trailing several feet behind, Jared Hoffman's shadowy form lurked over Farrington's shoulder. To the casual observer, the two would appear to exude the same air of sureness, but Sanderson could recognize the stark difference between them, night or day. Trained primarily as a sniper,

Hoffman couldn't help distrusting the security of his surroundings. When you spent hours observing unaware targets through a scope at great distances, you never quite shook that subtle, paranoid feeling that you could be in the same crosshairs anywhere and at any time.

He walked upright like Farrington, but his movements were stiff, less fluid, almost like he was tensed for action. Out of habit, he frequently scanned his surroundings for telltale signs that he was being glassed. Usually mistakes: a flash of sunlight reflected off an unprotected scope lens, an out-of-place open window, movement in the distance. Anything that might give away a sniper or provide him with the fraction of a second he needed to throw himself to the ground. He'd already glanced around twice since meeting Farrington behind the rear vehicle, despite the sheer blackness of the night. Some habits died hard. Others made it harder to die. Hoffman's habit definitely fell into the latter category.

"Gentlemen," said Sanderson, "we ready to roll?"

"Affirmative," said Farrington, stopping a few feet in front of the porch steps. "Need us to lock up behind you?"

"I took care of it," said Sanderson. "How did Castillo fare in the hills?"

Hoffman stepped into the open next to Farrington. "She's ready to take on the new role. A-team level. I can still shoot better, but she's sneaky as shit."

Sanderson joined them on the soft ground. "What do you think?"

"She's more than paid her dues. If she can work a sniper rifle half as good as Jared claims—"

"It's a verified claim. Petrovich built the foundation; Melendez put up the framework and put all the finishing touches in place. She can shoot," said Hoffman.

"Then that settles it," said Farrington. "She's on the primary assault team unless the mission requires a homogenous Caucasian unit for infiltration purposes."

"If that's the case, I'd be happy to fill in," said Hoffman. "I could use a few days in Finland or Norway. Frankly, I'd be happy to go anywhere outside of the usual shitholes we've seen."

"I'd be glad to see one of those shitholes again," said Farrington. "Anything good come from your call?"

"I'm not sure. Sounds like a long shot, whatever it turns out to be," said Sanderson. "And I doubt we'll be sent anywhere to your liking, Jared."

"At this point, I think the team would take anything," said Jared.

"Myself included. I'd even consider stepping foot in Russia again."

"You and I are permanently off the Russia list," said Farrington.

"Moscow's most wanted." Hoffman chuckled.

Sanderson placed a hand on Farrington's shoulder. "If this pans out and the target in question emerges in Russia, we might not have a choice."

"Jesus," Hoffman breathed. "Reznikov?"

"Yes. Our ever-elusive friend has once again flown his coop. We're still not sure who sprang him this time, but the Russkies haven't been crossed off the list of suspects."

"If the Russians grabbed him, he's probably a slurry of lye at this point," said Farrington.

"I'd like to think so," Sanderson said, "but he'd be an invaluable asset to a bioweapons program, and the Russians don't have the best track record of complying with the international Biological Weapons Convention."

"Fucking Russians," muttered Hoffman.

"The CIA has no idea who nabbed him. They just know that he vanished under suspicious circumstances, minutes before a joint U.S.-Russian Special Forces raid against a covert laboratory."

"Yep. My money is on the Russians," said Hoffman.

"I wish I could say I'd take that bet," stated Sanderson. "Let's move out. I want to hit the ground running when we get back to the compound. We have twelve hours to position a rapid-response team in Buenos Aires."

"What's the size of the strike package?" Farrington asked.

"As many as we can stuff into one of the larger Dassault Falcons or an extended-range Gulf Stream," said Sanderson.

"Then we better move it out," said Farrington after quickly glancing at his watch. "This is going to be tight."

Chapter 15

FBI Headquarters
Washington, D.C.

Ryan Sharpe replaced the handset on his encrypted desk phone and shook his head, mumbling a distant obscenity. Something was brewing at the CIA, and it gave him an uneasy feeling. He'd just taken an unexpected call from the former director of the FBI, Frederick Shelby, who personally requested his help arranging the international version of an "all-points bulletin" for a Russian national. Shelby wanted Ryan to go beyond the usual broad coordination with Interpol and liaison directly with Europol and the major players on each continent, focusing on countries with the most extensive and expansive law enforcement networks.

The request itself wasn't unusual, though requests like these usually reached the FBI's National Security Branch through a specific process designed to automatically screen for potential or known conflicts of interest with ongoing FBI investigations. What struck him as unusual was the fact that Sharpe had already vetted the individual in question late yesterday afternoon, based on an identical request by Karl Berg at the CIA. Sharpe couldn't know for sure, since efforts at his own organization were often mistakenly duplicated, but he got the distinct impression that neither Shelby nor Berg was aware of each other's activity. This feeling convinced him to take a second look at the individual under scrutiny to be certain that he hadn't overlooked anything.

Since taking on the role of associate executive assistant director of the FBI's National Security Branch, a substantial promotion fast-tracked by Shelby just over a year ago, Sharpe had refocused a significant portion of the branch's resources to the detection, tracking, and prevention of emerging weapons of mass destruction (WMD) threats, foreign and domestic. After the attempted bioweapons attack two years ago by homegrown terrorists, he'd sworn never to let a similar catastrophe get that close to the United States again. He owed it to the men and women under his command who were murdered and injured in the cowardly bomb attack against the National Counterterrorism Center.

Neither Berg nor Shelby had expanded upon their reasons for the request, but with Berg involved, Sharpe's spider sense tingled. Add Shelby's personal request to the mix, and his hair was standing on end. Another look was warranted. If they weren't going to connect the dots for him, he'd put his best people to work on it. They never failed to produce results.

Sharpe navigated through a series of menus on his computer screen to arrive at the electronic dossier for Grigor Sokolov. Unfortunately, it wasn't an extensive file. Not only that, it told a familiar story. Nothing stood out. Like most of the for-hire Russian mercenaries and mafiya enforcers, Sokolov was a former noncommissioned officer in the GRU Spetsnaz during the late Soviet era. Drastic military spending cuts and the targeted political dismissal dumped thousands of Russian Special Forces soldiers on the job market, with few skills to offer beyond murder, sabotage, and mayhem—a perfect fit for a number of unsavory corporations and organizations rising to power in the post-communist industrial market.

The scant details of Sokolov's post-GRU career didn't raise an eyebrow. He'd dropped off the radar in 2008, his last documented link to a four-man crew that rather uniquely specialized in direct action rather than the usual high-risk security detail work taken by mercenaries. That was the only thing that remotely stood out. He led a team that gained a reputation for kidnapping, assassination, and sabotage. Exactly what he had been trained to do by the Soviet military.

Sharpe scanned the information one more time, focusing on the dates. 2008 was the only connection he could make, and that was shaky at best. Sokolov disappeared the same year True America extremists tried to poison Congress and thousands of innocent Americans. Not much to go on there. Intelligence sources couldn't pinpoint a narrow time frame for his disappearance. He'd popped up a few times a year, with no detectable regularity, loosely tied to a murder or crime by a foreign federal law enforcement agency. His file went cold in 2008 and had stayed cold. Until now.

He drummed his fingers on the desk next to the keyboard, then marked the electronic file for distribution to Dana O'Reilly, his deputy assistant director. He typed a quick email to O'Reilly and waited. A few seconds passed then a quick rap on the closed door announced her presence.

"Come in!" he called.

She appeared in the doorway. "What's up?"

"Shut the door and grab a seat," he said, turning his screen to face the empty chair at the side of his desk.

He rolled his chair a few feet to the right so they could view the screen together. Sharpe no longer paused or winced internally when he looked at her, a monumental task given the long, twisting scar that ran from her chin to her left ear. It was unfair to pretend not to notice, on top of the fact that it was virtually impossible. Nobody in the office or headquarters was immune. She was a hero, if not somewhat of a legend in the FBI, but none of that erased the angry red scar and the awkward moments that followed her around day after day, hour after hour.

"This guy looks worse than I do," O'Reilly commented.

Sharpe was once again caught off guard by her self-deprecating humor. Sokolov had a scar running from one ear to the other, the obvious victim of a botched throat slitting.

"You need to get used to it. Helps me get through the day," she said, an underlying tone of sadness hanging on the statement.

The scar wasn't her only reminder of that fateful day. Eric Hesterman's massive frame had absorbed enough of the blast to keep her alive, but she'd been close enough to the explosion to suffer severe internal and external injuries. She'd spent the better part of a year recovering, the prospect of her return to the FBI never a sure thing.

A barely noticeable limp and a subtle but perpetually pained look stood as a testament to the fight she had won to get back to work. Sharpe didn't hesitate to bring her on board as his deputy. He didn't do it because he felt sorry for her. He did it because she had been one of the finest special agents he'd ever worked with—and she would have been Frank Mendoza's first pick. The thought of Frank always stopped him in his tracks.

"I'm trying, Dana."

"You're doing better than most," she replied. "Who is this guy?"

"Grigor Sokolov. Ex-GRU turned mercenary," stated Sharpe, sitting back in his chair.

"Why are we looking at this guy?"

"Because within the span of twenty-four hours, I've received two requests to add this guy to our watch list, along with Interpol, Europol, and any other national law enforcement agency that will play ball with us."

"Intriguing."

"Wait until you hear who made the requests," said Sharpe, pausing for a moment. "Karl Berg and Frederick Shelby."

O'Reilly's eyes widened a fraction. "I'd like to change my original assessment to disturbing."

"Let the record reflect that this is highly disturbing," said Sharpe. "And just when you thought it couldn't get stranger, I'm pretty sure the requests were independent, as in not coordinated or purposefully duplicative."

"Interesting."

"Something's up," said Sharpe, "and I need you to get to the bottom of it. There's not much to work with, but you've performed some miracles in the past."

"I'll start digging."

"Discreetly, please," said Sharpe. "The walls have ears nowadays, and I don't need this to get back to Shelby."

"I'm glad you said something," she stated, looking serious. "I was going to put the entire branch to work on this."

A sly smile slowly materialized on her face, reminding Sharpe that he was in the presence of a world-renowned smart-ass.

"That's not funny," said Sharpe, shaking his head with a grin.

"Yes, it is."

"Maybe," he admitted.

He rolled his chair back to the center of the desk while she studied the file on the screen.

"I've sent you what I have on this guy," he said. "Gut instinct tells me he's mixed up in something big."

"How big?"

"I have no idea, but he hasn't been linked to a crime since 2008. Prior to that, he was an Interpol regular. Never anything big, but busy enough. Suddenly he's the focus of Berg and Shelby?"

"Berg's involvement stands out," said O'Reilly. "From the little I know of him."

"Right. And if my read of the situation is correct, he's not working with Shelby on this, which is what scares me the most."

"What makes you say that?"

"Just a feeling," Sharpe said. "Berg was demoted when True America swept in, while Shelby was put on the fast track to becoming our country's top intelligence community director. Two polar opposites in pursuit of the insignificant. That's what scares me. There's more to this than meets the eye."

"Then let's pull back the curtain a bit," said O'Reilly.

"Discreetly," Sharpe reiterated.

She grinned. "Of course."

PART TWO:

BLACKLIST

Chapter 16

Chicago, Illinois

Daniel squeezed Jessica's hand as the Learjet crossed the boundary between Lake Michigan and Chicago's northern suburbs. The jet had approached the airport from the east, passing a few miles north of the iconic Chicago skyline. Through his window, the sprawling tangle of high-rise buildings slowly drifted aft. It wasn't the prettiest city from the sky, or the ground for that matter. He recalled the familiar sight from his younger days, prior to meeting Sanderson, though he couldn't recall the last time he had landed at O'Hare. Seemed like a lifetime ago.

A quick glance across the aisle through Jessica's window had brought a few back into sharp focus. The familiar shape of Northwestern University's Lakefill expansion was visible beyond the aircraft's sleek wing, further north along Lakeshore. The two of them had spent hundreds of hours on the lakefront together, walking, jogging, and picnicking, among other less public activities. The three years he had spent with her there had been the best.

Jessica continued to gaze absently out the window, her mind preoccupied with her mother. When another gentle squeeze didn't soften her thousand-yard stare, he let it go for now. She had more than enough on her mind. Enough to ensure that he'd be their only reliable set of eyes and ears once the flight landed. He leaned his head back against the plush leather headrest and closed his eyes for the few remaining minutes of the flight, reviewing the plan.

They'd chosen to land at O'Hare instead of a more private jetport in the Chicago area to give them the best chance of arriving discreetly and keeping their visit anonymous. If Jessica's mother's illness was a ruse, the most obvious and easy-to-watch point of arrival would be one of the numerous smaller airports that catered to private or chartered jets. O'Hare International Airport was a different story altogether.

With hundreds of private flights arriving daily from destinations spanning the globe, O'Hare provided them the best chance to disappear into the Chicagoland area. Even a sophisticated and extensive government surveillance operation would find it difficult to locate and track the Petroviches once they disembarked the aircraft.

They had cleared customs at New Orleans International Airport, paying cash on the spot for a luxury sedan to drive them to Lafayette Regional Airport, where a second Learjet awaited them. The lengthy ride gave them ample time to determine if they had been followed out of New Orleans. They were alone from what either of them could tell, though U.S. authorities were no doubt aware of their arrival.

They used their own passports to enter the country, a calculated risk under the circumstances, but one designed to keep their most recently acquired counterfeit identities intact. If things went sideways on them in Chicago, they would flee the country using a leftover set of U.S. passports and identification from a few years ago. Once out of the U.S., they would switch to freshly minted Spanish papers, granting them visa-free access to nearly every nation they could possibly reach by sailboat. The trick would be getting back to their boat in Anguilla. Of course, they could always buy another boat. There was no shortage of cruising sailboats on the market.

A bump of mild turbulence brought Jessica's hand across the aisle to his. Daniel met her glance and was treated to an apprehensive smile. Better than no smile. She'd remained detached, almost trancelike since learning about her mother's condition, and coming to grips with a reluctant but irresistible desire to seek closure. From start to finish, he knew this would be a rocky trip on every level for her. Another round of turbulence underscored the thought, and her hand tightened around his wrist.

Twenty minutes later, after a featherlight landing, their aircraft taxied into position in front of a modern glass and steel building. GLOBAL AVIATION's terminal handled three-quarters of O'Hare's private flight arrivals, making it an ideal choice for their disappearing act.

"Ready?" he asked, standing up in the tight cabin.

"Yeah," Jessica replied.

He offered her a hand, helping her out of her seat.

"It's not too late," said Daniel. "We can be back in the air within the hour."

"I wish I could," she said, a strained look on her face. "But I can't."

He nodded, knowing not to push any further. She was resolved to put this part of her life to rest, even if her mannerisms suggested that Chicago was the last place on Earth she wanted to be. His only mission at this point was to get her back to the airport by tomorrow morning to board the jet that would return them to Anguilla and the new life she so desperately needed. Nothing about the next eighteen hours would be easy.

"I know," he said, kissing her gently on the forehead.

Daniel turned toward the cockpit, holding her hand. The dark-haired copilot stood next to the forward exit door, peering through its small oval window. Through the forward-most passenger window he caught a glimpse of the black canvas-covered structure that would shield them from the public eye and any surveillance teams closely watching flight arrivals. A silver SUV arrived a few moments later, pulling next to the tarmac end of the ramp.

"We're almost ready," said the copilot. "They're connecting the walkway to your vehicle for maximum privacy."

"Thank you," replied Daniel, edging forward down the tight aisle.

While the pilot released the door handle, Daniel removed a hard-case carry-on piece from the storage compartment next to the door.

"I can take your bags to the vehicle," offered the pilot.

"We can manage," said Daniel.

He placed Jessica's suitcase next to his, then pulled two thick rubber-banded rolls of cash from an interior coat pocket. When the copilot turned his attention back to the Petroviches, Daniel handed him one of the rolls.

"A token of our appreciation for a smooth flight," stated Daniel. "And your continued discretion with regard to the protection of our identities."

The man smiled, accepting the money. "It's not every day we get to transport such a striking blond-haired, blue-eyed couple. Nordic royalty from what I would guess."

"Sounds good to me," said Daniel.

He leaned through the cockpit door to deliver the second money roll, the pilot preempting him.

"Dolph Lundgren and Brigitte Nielsen lookalikes," said the pilot.

"I don't expect anyone to ask questions," said Daniel, pressing the money into his hand. "But you never know."

"It wouldn't be the first time we've dealt with celebrity reporters," said the pilot. "Or private investigators."

"We appreciate the discretion," said Daniel. "And I meant the part about the smooth flight. Barely felt the landing."

"Between you and me, these birds pretty much fly themselves. I'm just here in case something goes wrong."

"I won't tell a soul," Daniel said, gripping his suitcase. "Ready, Jessica?"

"Ready as I'll ever be."

He stepped through the exit hatch, taking the short stairway to the tarmac. The canvas and translucent plastic tunnel extended about fifteen feet beyond the jet, connecting seamlessly to the SUV that would drive them out of the airport. Their driver, a squat, middle-aged Latino man in a black suit, ushered them into the vehicle and closed the rear passenger door, then disappeared through a flap in the canvas with their suitcases.

Less than thirty seconds after their feet had touched the runway, the powerful vehicle passed through a manned security station that separated the public world from the private aircraft tarmac. Their driver was efficient and practiced. It was a shame they had to ditch him so quickly.

"Where to, sir?" asked the driver.

"Main terminal parking. I'll guide you when we get there," said Daniel, tapping his shoulder with a money roll. "Sorry, but this pickup was more of a security precaution than anything."

"No need to apologize, sir," said the driver, briefly turning his head to see the money. "We're good. You're all paid up for the day."

"My treat," said Daniel. "I insist."

The driver reached over his shoulder and took the roll of cash, placing it somewhere out of sight. "Thank you," he said with a subtle hint of regret, possibly disappointment.

Daniel pegged him as ex-military. Someone that didn't require a tip or bonus to put any extra effort into a job or assignment. A professional. The SUV eased right onto Bessie Coleman Drive and picked up speed, heading toward the main terminal in the distance. Jessica lifted a black briefcase from her foot well and placed it in her lap while Daniel scanned the road behind them. The private terminal access road beyond the security gate remained clear as they continued down the four-lane road. He didn't expect to detect any possible surveillance this quickly, but it never hurt to look.

Satisfied that they hadn't been followed directly out of the private terminal or joined on the road from a nearby parking area, he glanced at the open briefcase in his wife's lap. He caught a glimpse of a compact pistol as she refastened a hidden compartment cover. Jessica looked at him and nodded, indicating that everything they'd requested was present. She removed two sets of rental car keys and a notecard containing a few letters and numbers before shutting the briefcase. Daniel went back to watching the road behind them.

Jessica leaned toward the driver. "Terminal One departures. United."

"Copy that, ma'am."

Definitely ex-military.

One of Sanderson's people? Someone neither Jessica nor he had met? That would be an interesting twist and not completely out of the realm of possibilities. Sanderson had reached out to them after Karl Berg's phone call, to talk them out of going. Failing that, he offered to coordinate the logistics for the trip and provide personal protective equipment upon arrival in Chicago. They'd taken him up on the offer since neither of them had the kind of contacts needed to procure firearms that quickly, and because Sanderson footed the bill for the flights.

He dismissed the idea as fast as it materialized. Sanderson had also orchestrated the next part of their countersurveillance maneuver, which entailed ditching the driver entirely. Daniel didn't care either way. If Sanderson wanted to keep an eye on them, there wasn't much they could do about it, and there were far worse things in the world than having Black Flag operatives watching their backs.

Jessica held the notecard where he could see it.

Vehicles in main garage hourly parking across from terminal one. Kia—row B and Nissan—row G. Good luck and watch your back. Call Ramon—your driver—for pickup from hotel on way out. He's not one of ours, in case you're curious.

"Ramon?" said Daniel.

"Yes, sir?"

"Looks like we'll be using your services on the way back to the airport."

"I'm happy to hear that, sir," said Ramon.

"Why do I get the feeling you already knew it?"

"I've arranged a sedan through a cooperating agency for the return trip. Wanted to change things up. I'll still be your driver."

"That's good to know," said Daniel.

"Any particular reason?" said Jessica.

Daniel gave her a quizzical look.

"Unique skillset, ma'am," said Ramon.

"Sounds familiar," muttered Jessica, squeezing Daniel's hand.

The driver glanced into the rearview mirror, briefly making eye contact with Daniel. A look of acknowledgment passed between the two of them. The guy was definitely Sanderson material, and it was no coincidence that he had been chosen to drive them. To the general's credit, he maintained an extensive list of loyal and capable people around the world. The man had that kind of effect on people, a sort of infectious attraction that you could never fully shake. He couldn't even begin to guess how Ramon had come under Sanderson's spell.

After taking another long look at the road behind them, he kissed Jessica on the side of her mouth. She smiled flatly, taking a deep, but quiet inhale. Her stomach inflated and deflated slowly, a breathing relaxation technique she had mastered over the years. Not that he thought it would help her right now.

"Everything's going to be fine," he whispered, instantly regretting the clichéd statement.

"Don't."

Message received. In a way, he was glad they would take separate cars to Palos Hills. The closer they got to the source of her rage, the worse it would get. Daniel stole a glance at his watch. Seventeen hours and forty-seven minutes until they could officially start a new chapter in their life.

A lot could go wrong in eighteen hours.

Chapter 17

O'Hare International Airport
Chicago, Illinois

Jessica pulled her carry-on suitcase into the restroom on the departure level and maneuvered it into the nearest open stall. She laid the red luggage piece flat across the toilet seat, quickly opening it to expose a smaller black carry-on bag fitted snugly inside. She removed a compact pistol and two spare magazines from her oversized red leather handbag and transferred the items to a zippered compartment on the outside of the nested bag.

After separating the two pieces of luggage, she removed her stylish black jacket and hung it on the back of the door. A few moments later, she left her old suitcase in the stall, closing the door behind her, and headed for the exit. She slowed in front of the mirrors to adjust the wig she had retrieved from the original carry-on suitcase. She could use a lipstick refresh too, but decided against it. A quick turnaround in the bathroom was more important right now. On her way past the paper towel dispenser, she pushed the handbag into the stainless steel trash bin, retaining a black clutch purse that had been hidden with the wig.

Less than ten seconds after Jessica entered the restroom, she walked out with cropped red hair, black luggage, and a trendy white blouse. Not exactly the most radical transformation, but hopefully enough to temporarily throw off anyone that had hustled into the terminal after them.

She followed the signs for the baggage level, which took her toward a distant escalator. A casual look toward the bucket seats in front of the terminal's floor-to-ceiling windows eased her fears. Daniel rubbed his right eye with the back of his hand, their prearranged signal that he hadn't detected any surveillance.

Jessica kept going, never pausing to look back. Daniel would wait for her phone call before heading for his car. By that time, Jessica would be on the road to Palos Hills, most likely stuck in afternoon traffic. She remembered how brutal the congestion could be in the areas around the city, especially near the airport. The thirty-mile drive could take an hour and a half at this time of day. All the better. She was in no hurry to get to the hospital.

She walked through an automatic door near the center of the baggage carousel pickup area, immediately choking on diesel fumes. She'd forgotten how nasty the air was on the arrivals level. A dozen or more buses and airport shuttles sat idling at any given time in front of the exits. More passed through every minute to discharge exhaust into the concrete and pavement hell beneath the arrival lanes constructed above. Dark. Dirty. Smelly. Airport planners had managed to make a traveler's first taste of Chicago a shitty one.

Taking shallow breaths, Jessica hustled to the pedestrian crosswalk and crossed two wide rows of uneven traffic to emerge into the sunlight. She stopped to fiddle with her suitcase, taking the moment to scan the people she could observe in the shadows underneath the overpass. Nearly everybody hauled luggage. Nobody stood out.

Once inside the garage, she quickly analyzed the signage and headed in the direction of row G. A silver Nissan Sentra with Wisconsin license plates finally responded to her repeated press of the key fob. With her suitcase situated on the front seat and the zippered pocket containing her pistol opened, Jessica backed out of the space and followed the signs to the exit. She stopped the car several feet in front of the automated pay gate, mumbling curses. No. It was too late to turn back, and it would be the cowardly thing to do. Her mother deserved her forgiveness, and Jessica wanted to give it.

"You will fucking do this," she whispered, easing her foot off the brake.

Ten minutes later, after paying for three hours of parking with a preloaded credit card, she sat in bumper-to-bumper traffic, pointing south on Interstate 294. She called Daniel to report a seemingly uneventful departure from the airport.

"Coast is clear?" he asked.

"Couldn't say," she said. "I'm at the American Airlines counter, booking a flight back to Anguilla."

A long pause ensued. "You sound like you're in a car."

"Parked on the expressway," she said. "I didn't detect anyone paying attention to me on the way out."

"I think we arrived undetected," said Daniel.

He didn't bring up the obvious, which she appreciated. It was one of his best qualities. Never making her feel worse about a situation, particularly one she'd created for herself.

"Arriving clean was never the real challenge," she said.

"We'll be just as cautious at the hospital," he said. "By this time tomorrow, we'll be over the Gulf of Mexico."

"I hope so," she said, not sure why she threw that at him.

He didn't take the unintentional bait. "I found a tapas restaurant in Oak Brook. We could both use a bite to eat. A drink wouldn't hurt either."

"I'm not really hungry. Or thirsty."

Her statement didn't reflect the truth. It was more like the warped perception of how she *thought* she should be feeling. She could eat her way through an Old Country Buffet right now, heat-lamp-preserved food and all.

"Well, I'm kind of starving, so if you don't mind, I'd like to eat something before we roll into Palos Hills," said Daniel. "Plus we need to kill some time outside of town. It doesn't start getting dark until around seven."

"That's fine," she said.

"Get off at Cermak, headed west. Take a right on Spring Road. El Tapareya is in Le Meridien."

"The restaurant is in a hotel?"

"I didn't think you'd care. Not being hungry and all."

"Just saying."

"I was eyeballing a nearby Long John Silver's, if you want to know the truth," Daniel cracked.

"Hush puppies and French fries. You know the way to this girl's heart," she said.

"Trust me on the tapas."

"I could go either way, honestly," she said, half meaning it.

"Your choice," he said.

"Cermak then Spring Road. I'll grab a table."

"Facing the door, please."

"That goes without saying."

She needed to get him off the phone. Their conversation would dance around the edge of nothingness, a never-ending banter tinged with anxiety and framed by the gravity of her approaching reunion. Fuck that. She was better off tapping her fingers on the steering wheel and creeping along in traffic with her thoughts for the next hour. On top of that, they each needed to pay attention to their surroundings. Close attention. One slipup could cost them everything.

Part of her hoped the whole thing was a setup, and it was sprung before they got to the hospital. That would be the easy way out for her. Fight and win, no holds barred, just like she'd been trained. But this wasn't a trap in the traditional sense. She was most certainly trapped, but not by any of the enemies they'd made in the past. No. The worst enemy possible had cornered Jessica. The one guaranteed to fuck up everything. Her guilt. And there was absolutely no way she was getting out of this one.

She'd let this enemy convince her to make a potentially dangerous trip, right on the cusp of sailing away from her shattered past. Her battle with this adversary ended tonight. She heard Daniel's voice, but didn't catch what he said.

"Sorry. What was that?"

"I said I'll let you go," said Daniel. "Stay alert, and let me know when you get there."

"I will," she said. "And…thank you."

"Just doing my job."

"Sometimes you do it frighteningly well."

"That's because we're a good match. Catch you in an hour or so."

Jessica eased her car forward with the mass of traffic, the hope of a breakthrough short-lived. After stopping, she craned her head back and scanned the windshields behind her in a mostly useless gesture. It would be nearly impossible to spot a tail in this mess and not likely worth the effort. Unless someone wanted her dead, badly, she was as safe here as anywhere.

Safe. A relative term for people with their kind of background and history. Even at their home in Anguilla she never felt completely safe. That was the underlying problem with their life. One she hoped to permanently leave behind when they sailed away on *La Ombra*. She just needed to keep her shit together for a few more hours. By this time tomorrow night, she could be on their boat, making final preparations to put an entire ocean between the past and a new future.

Chapter 18

Palos Hills Community Hospital
Palos Hills, Illinois

Daniel examined the reflective sign on the left corner of the intersection, which read "main entrance." Unfortunately, that would be their only option for tonight's visit. There would be no forged keycards and identification cards allowing them to enter more discreetly. They would walk through the visitor entrance to the hospital as Daniel and Jessica Petrovich, until they reached her mother's room, where she would have to identify herself as Nicole Erak, daughter of a dying woman.

He slowed for the turn across the empty intersection, his car's headlights drowning out the subtle lights highlighting a wide *Welcome To Palos Community Hospital* sign. Once past the bright sign, he caught a glimpse of a tall illuminated building between the thick stand of evenly spaced trees lining the right side of the road.

Research on the Internet gave him little useful information about the facility. Images of the exterior and interior suggested it had undergone extensive renovations at some point recently. A few buildings had been added, mainly outpatient surgery and physician office facilities. His best guess was that the hospice rooms would be located in the main patient building, which towered over the rest of the hospital.

Security inside the place would be a mess. He couldn't think of any effective way to sweep the areas they'd need to move through, clearing a path for Jessica in advance. The best he could do was observe the areas outside the entrance for any obvious snatch-and-grab teams. Anyone wishing to do Jessica and him harm faced the same complications inside. There was no way to go about business inconspicuously unless your plan was to kill and you really didn't give a shit about keeping it covert. A distinct possibility in this case.

Daniel had no intention of letting his guard down outside or inside the building. Their greatest ally would be time. The sooner they got in and out, the better, and that would solely depend on Jessica. He hated to admit it, but part of him hoped Vesna Erak was incommunicative or unresponsive at this point. Jessica could spend some time in the room "talking" to her mother, and they could get the hell out of here within the hour. Quicker possibly. Or would that just make matters worse for Jessica?

He knew the best outcome would be for his wife to spend as much time as she needed to clear the air and say goodbye to her mother. All he had to do was keep her safe. As his car cleared the trees, the main entrance appeared, directly across from a three-story parking garage.

"Shit," he muttered.

Google Earth hadn't shown a parking garage, which changed his plan. He was no longer dealing with a straight line-of-sight surveillance situation across a parking lot. He'd need to accompany Jessica the entire way instead of hanging back to watch the surroundings. Too many nooks and crannies in a parking garage to ensure her safety. He dialed her phone.

"What's up?" she answered.

"There's a massive parking garage instead of a parking lot. I'd feel better about this if we walked into the hospital together. We can put some space between us once we're inside. I'm going to pull into the drop-off area in front of the main entrance and wait for you to get here. Pull up behind me and we'll find adjacent spaces in the garage."

"I guess we should have driven together after all," she said.

"It would appear so," replied Daniel. "I don't see any other parking options, either…hold on."

The kit provided by Sanderson included handicap placards, so there might still be some hope. He scanned the area around the entrance for handicap parking spaces, finding a few rows of cars in a small lot located directly in front of the garage. They might be able to station at least one of the cars as close as possible to the building in case they needed to make a quick exit. No such luck.

"Never mind," he said. "I thought we might be able to use a handicap space."

"It'll be fine. I'm about five minutes out," she said.

"I might take a look inside the lobby before you get here."

"Not a bad idea," said Jessica.

He disconnected the call and eased into one of several unoccupied patient pickup spaces under a wide, two-story-high roof sheltering the entrance. The moment he stopped the car, an older gentleman dressed in pressed khaki pants and a red sweater vest over a white collared shirt emerged through one of the main entrance doors and ambled toward him. Daniel met him on the other side of the car, halfway to the door.

"You can't park here, sir," stated the man.

Daniel read the plastic name tag pinned to the vest.

"My apologies, Tom," he said. "I'm supposed to grab my sister-in-law here and drive her home. My wife's mother is in one of the hospice rooms, and everyone is in from out of town. I'm doing what I can to get people back and forth. Do you mind if I leave the car here while I have a look around the lobby?"

"As long as you don't linger," said the venerable parking sentry.

"I'll be gone in a minute or so," said Daniel. "Thank you."

The man didn't change expression, clearly unimpressed by his promise. He'd undoubtedly heard every excuse in the book at this point.

"I'll be right back."

"We tow," warned the man.

"I don't doubt it."

Daniel pressed the blue handicap access button plate on the thick metal post in front of one of the automatic doors. By the time he reached the entry, the door had opened far enough for him to slide into a glass-enclosed, three-story atrium. The lobby looked more like something you'd find inside fancy tech start-up headquarters than a community hospital, which made his job easier. He had clear sightlines to all of the seating areas scattered throughout the space.

Pretending to search for his sister-in-law, he was able to cross the few people seated in the lobby off his running list of obvious lookouts. No police either, or any discernible security sensors like a metal detector or X-ray machine. Not that he had expected to find that kind of security in Palos Hills. He might find a cop at the emergency entrance on the opposite side of the hospital. Not that it really mattered. His pistol was concealed, and there was no reason to search him. He sensed a presence behind him.

Instinct told him it was Tom, but it could be anyone. Well-practiced and perfected skills beat instinct any day in this business. Not that his current skill level met either description at the moment. Covert operations field craft involved highly perishable skills, their easy expiration directly related to an abysmally low survival rate. He turned his head slightly, confirming the red vest. He hated living like this. They couldn't get back to the sailboat quickly enough.

"Do you see her?" asked the man.

The guy was relentless, which Daniel decided might work to his advantage.

"I don't see her," said Daniel. "She's supposedly been here a while. Like almost an hour."

The man took a quick look around, shaking his head.

"I'm going on five hours here, and I haven't seen anyone hanging out in the main lobby for that long."

"Maybe hidden back in the café?" said Daniel, looking in that direction.

"Café closed at six thirty. That group just sat down a few minutes ago to grab their kids a snack from one of the accessible vending machines," said the man. "She might be waiting in the hospice wing. They have a comfortable lounge for family there."

Tom had the lobby locked down tight. Anyone lingering here would have drawn his attention long ago.

"Maybe she went back up to the hospice floor. Let me move my car, and I'll get this all sorted out," said Daniel. "I know she didn't walk home. At least I hope she didn't. Right?"

The man nodded, feigning a smile. All business. Daniel returned to his car in time to take a call from Jessica.

"I'm turning onto the main entrance road," she said.

"I'll meet you at the parking garage entrance. The lobby is clear."

"I can't wait," said Jessica.

She sounded distinctly different than a few minutes ago. In fact, she sounded remarkably like she had in Belgrade during their final days in that mess. The closer she got to seeing her mother, the worse this would get. The trick was keeping her from a complete breakdown, and if anything had the potential to trigger one, this was it.

Daniel pulled the car out of the drop-off zone and waited at the top of the drive for Jessica. He prayed for a short visit, fully aware that it would be a long night no matter what.

Chapter 19

Palos Hills Community Hospital
Palos Hills, Illinois

Jessica rode the elevator up to the fourth floor, single-mindedly focused on one thing: not freaking out. Actually, she was more concentrated on not showing any outward signs that she was on the verge of breaking down. Daniel's concerned glances and sympathetic smiles indicated she wasn't doing a good job. Or maybe she was. She had no idea. All she knew for sure was that she would see her mother in a few minutes, and the thought terrified her.

It shouldn't. If anything, this moment should be one of those cathartic, transcendent kind of moments that alter the course of your life, but she wasn't interpreting her body's response that way. She knew exactly what it felt like to have a nervous breakdown. She'd spent the better part of a year downing Xanax like Tic Tacs to little avail in Serbia. And another year after that convinced that the new life she was building with Daniel would come crashing down at a moment's notice.

"Fuck. This shouldn't be so hard," she murmured, barely aware that she had spoken out loud.

Yeah. She wasn't doing a good job at concealing this at all.

"Sorry," she said.

"About what?"

"This."

"You've endured worse," said Daniel. "Way worse. Don't lose sight of that."

His words didn't make a dent in the field of nervous energy that radiated from her chest. She was nearly shaking from it, like an adrenaline boost, except this neurochemical reaction wasn't helping her in any way she could interpret. It was drawing her inward, where she could least afford to be. For all practical purposes, they were in enemy territory, and she was dead weight. No. She was worse than dead weight. More like a zombie.

When the elevator door opened, Daniel stepped into the lobby and glanced around, nodding for her to exit when he saw it was safe. A backlit sign on the wall pointed them in the direction of the room block used for hospice care. Rooms 440–459. Elevator C would have delivered them closest to the rooms, but Daniel insisted they use a different elevator as long as the areas connected. She would have taken the shortest route. The most obvious route.

She hesitated for a moment, desperately wanting to return to the lobby. Daniel placed his hand against the inner door, making sure it didn't shut. He kept his eyes in the hallway, waiting for her to move or stay put. It didn't matter to him one way or the other. Right now, he served as her bodyguard and not much more than that. He wasn't her husband, lover, or best friend. Daniel was her only protection from a potential attack or trap.

Jessica stepped out of the elevator and immediately felt dizzy. She didn't stumble, but it must have been clear from her face, because Daniel looked worried.

"I'm good," she said, starting to walk.

A firm grip on her shoulder stopped Jessica in place.

"Wrong way," he said, giving her a funny look.

"What?"

"You need to get this out of your system," he said.

It was an odd thing for him to say, especially after successfully tiptoeing around her for nearly two days.

She shook her head. "I'm sorry. What?"

"You need to find the nearest bathroom and reboot your system," he said.

That was right! Danny remembered. As a deep cover CIA operative in Serbia, she occasionally induced vomiting before a nerve-racking mission or field operation, particularly if she felt like she was losing the battle with anxiety. Initially admitting that to her handler had put her under close scrutiny.

Excessive anxiety was viewed as a liability. The CIA's behavioral health division maintained that a certain degree of anxiety was beneficial to the job. It tended to keep operatives on their toes—and alive—but they didn't like the kind that led to mistakes, which ultimately led back to the agency. A few months after confiding in her handler, she was ordered out of the field. An order she refused, because she'd reunited with Daniel, and they'd hatched a plan to walk away from it all. Together. With a lot of money. They were on the cusp of escaping again. This time for good. The thought made her smile, and she felt oddly better.

"I can hold your hair for you," said Daniel.

"I'm wearing a wig," she reminded him.

"I didn't say I would go into the bathroom with you," he said. "I can hold your hair in the hallway."

"Such a gentleman," she said, seeing an illuminated bathroom placard down the hallway.

He gripped both of her shoulders and stared into her eyes with determined love and seemingly infinite compassion.

"You're going to be fine. I know that's the last thing you want to hear, but—"

"No. I need to hear that," she said. "*We're* going to be fine, as soon as I get to that bathroom."

Chapter 20

Palos Hills Community Hospital
Palos Hills, Illinois

Daniel situated his far more lucid-looking wife on a deep, brown leather couch in the hospice lobby and made his way to the caregiver station. A tall intense-looking man with glasses looked up from his computer monitor as he neared, the screen reflecting in his wire-rimmed glasses.

"Can I help you find someone?" asked the man.

"Yes," said Daniel. "My wife is here to see her mother, Vesna Erak."

The man started typing on his keyboard. "Just a second. Ms. Erak hasn't received any visitors since arriving in hospice. I need to see if—no, she hasn't placed any restrictions on visitation. You're welcome to stay as long as you need. We're pretty well appointed here, as you can probably tell. Family members can order from the hospital's twenty-four-hour menu. Anything you need, don't hesitate to let me know. I'm here until eight in the morning. My name is Dave. Your wife's mother is in room 451. Would you like me to show you the way?"

"Thank you, Dave. That's all right," said Daniel, glancing over his left shoulder in what he assumed was the direction of the hospice rooms.

It was the only hallway open to the generously furnished and empty lobby. The hospital had gone out of its way to make the hospice area as soothing and comfortable as possible for grieving families. The walls were painted a warm color and the lighting was softened compared to the patient hallways they'd travelled to get here from the distant elevator. The institutional feel had been erased, a far cry from the room his mother had died in. Not that he ever saw her alive in that room. She'd been delivered to the funeral home by the time he managed to get back from Japan. Car crashes didn't wait for your ship to pull back into port.

"All of the rooms are down this hallway, right?"

"Correct. 451 is on the left side, about halfway down," said the attendant.

"May I ask you an odd question?"

Dave slid his chair to the left of the monitor and looked at Daniel over his glasses. "Yes?"

"My wife hasn't been back to this area in a long time," said Daniel. "A lot of that has to do with an ill-tempered ex-fiancé connected to some unsavory Serbian gentlemen. Organized crime, she thinks, though he's never been formally linked. Anyway, this guy has gone out of his way to harass my wife in a number of different states. We live in Baja, Mexico, now, if that gives you any indication of the degree of hassle he's given her. This won't be a long visit for that very reason."

Dave looked absolutely enthralled by his tale, barely blinking.

"There's obviously a sizable Serbian community in the surrounding towns, so it wouldn't be unusual for Serbian Americans to visit the floor, but have you seen any men in their mid-thirties that might fit the bill? Perhaps someone visited her mother and left quickly or hung around here waiting? Someone asking questions?"

The man shook his head slowly. "I'm not the only person that works this station, but we always log activity, even information requests. Nobody has visited her or asked about her. I can't speak for the other attendants, but nobody comes up here unless they have a relative or friend in one of those rooms. Hospice gives people the creeps."

"You aren't kidding," said Daniel. "All right. If you don't mind, I'd like to check out the room first. I know it sounds crazy, but—"

"That's fine."

"I might glance into the other rooms from the hallway, just to be sure."

"I don't have a problem with that, as long as you stay out of the other rooms."

"How many rooms are occupied?"

"About half," Dave said.

"Last crazy question. Is the room directly in front of hers occupied?"

The man looked uncomfortable with the question.

"I know it sounds paranoid, but these people have given us hell over the past several years."

"The woman across the hallway is asleep. Her family left about an hour ago. She sleeps soundly through the night."

"Serbian?"

"Hispanic. And nobody has entered her room since they left."

"Final question. Not a crazy one."

"Your questions are fine," said the man, looking relieved.

"Does her record say what happened? Why she was put in ICU in the first place? We didn't get any details. A friend of my wife's got in touch with us a few days ago. She didn't have any information."

"You'd have to ask the doctor that admitted her or Ms. Erak herself. Patient confidentiality. Once they come through these doors, we keep them comfortable according to the plan they have in place. I can tell you that she's on palliative care, which means…that's pretty much it," he said. "Sorry."

"I understand," said Daniel. "Thank you."

Daniel returned to Jessica, who looked a little less composed than when he left her. He needed to get this moving along. She was starting to slide backward.

"I'm going to take a quick look around. Make sure we don't have any surprises. Be back in a minute. Are you good here?"

"I'm fine," she said.

"Okay." He leaned over to kiss her forehead.

The plan was simple. Walk up and down the hallway, looking into each room. He'd briefly enter Vesna's room, checking the bathroom and any possible hiding spots. It was the best he could do under the circumstances. Once Jessica was inside the room, he'd move one of the chairs where he could watch the hallway and wait for Jessica to emerge.

He could generally guess which rooms were occupied by the lighting scheme or the obvious presence of family members. Each room contained a couch that was visible from the hallway and a comfortable-looking chair, though he suspected the rooms likely contained more furniture that could be moved closer to the bed. Room 451 had a solitary light on somewhere deep in the space, probably on a table next to Vesna's bed. He kept going to the end of the hallway. Nothing stood out from what he could tell, and he now had a good sense of which rooms held patients and posed less of a threat. Someone would have to go through a ton of trouble to hijack an occupied room. He filed the information away for later. All of the rooms were well within his center-mass pistol-shooting capability, the majority of the rooms an easy headshot. The problem would be the time needed to make the shot if someone darted out of nearby room. He'd have to borrow Jessica's handbag to conceal his pistol in a quickly accessible location. There was no way he could draw from the concealed holster on his right hip.

The only other thing that kind of bothered him was the service elevator located at the end of the hallway. Generally, it was an odd location for an elevator, which he suspected had been selected specifically for the hospice floor. Patients put in these rooms always left the same way. The elevator's remote placement spared anyone resting in the lounge from an early funeral procession. From a security perspective, it represented a significant danger.

The elevator was a wild card. He and Jessica could be under remote surveillance right now, a sizable team waiting in the basement for the right moment to take the elevator to the fourth floor. Daniel would have no warning, just a sudden rush of men from the end of the hallway, which he'd meet with rapid, accurate gunfire. Once Jessica's gun joined the fight, they could neutralize the threat and withdraw. The more he thought about it, the elevator was his only real concern at this point.

Now for room 451, just in case. He stepped lightly inside the room, finding the bathroom where he expected it. Like nearly every hotel room, it was right next to the entrance. He pushed the bathroom door open slowly, finding its hinges surprisingly quiet. A quick check confirmed it didn't hold a hidden assailant. Backtracking out of the dark bathroom, he faced the rest of the room. Almost tiptoeing at this point, he approached the corner wall of the bathroom, which gave the bed privacy from the hallway.

Daniel peeked around the corner, observing any remaining hiding places. The room was clear. He glanced up at Vesna, expecting her to be asleep, but instead finding her eyes wide, locked onto his own. Shit. He barely recognized her. Actually, he didn't at all. She looked moments from death. Grayish-yellow, a look beyond exhaustion. The face of someone trying to will themselves to die because they're too physically weak to end it with their own hands.

Staring into her eyes, he felt an overwhelming compassion for the woman, despite his brief history with her. He'd met her twice, under rushed and strained circumstances, one of them overtly hostile when he had to rescue Jessica, then Nicole, from a family dinner turned violent. He'd wanted nothing to do with her family after that, which had suited her fine. She didn't seem to want anything to do with them either.

He nodded at her, and she formed a thin smile.

"Nicole came to see you," he whispered.

Her smile broadened for a moment, then waned, as if the simple effort of using her facial muscles was too much to bear. This was going to be hell on Jessica, but there was no going back. His words had sealed that.

When he returned to the lobby, Jessica sat on the edge of the couch, waiting. She stood and walked over to meet him.

"Did you see her?" she asked, glancing nervously toward her mother's room.

"I did."

"And?"

"Are you sure you want to do this?"

"I have to do this," said Jessica.

"The room's clear," he said. "As far as I can tell, the floor is clear. There's a service elevator at the end of the hallway that makes me a little nervous. I'm going to move a chair where I can watch the entire corridor. If anything happens out here, I'll yell 'left' or 'right,' and you'll know which direction to scan for targets. I need your handbag to keep my pistol immediately accessible."

She handed him the bag, her hands shaky. "I can't believe I'm like this," said Jessica. "I'd rather be in a knife fight."

"A knife fight sounds wonderful right about now," he said. "Not with you, though."

She stifled a quick laugh.

"Take your time," said Daniel. "Regardless of what happens inside, you close this chapter in your life by walking through that door."

Jessica's eyes moistened.

"Get on with it before you change your mind," he said, and briefly touched his lips to hers.

She nodded and turned around, slowly making her way to the room. He waited until she was inside before going to work on the furniture.

"Mind if I move this chair where I can keep an eye on the hallway?" he said to the attendant.

"You're really serious about this, aren't you?"

"Can't be too careful," said Daniel.

"Go ahead."

He grabbed one of the cushioned chairs surrounding a wide, circular coffee table and positioned it where he could see the entire width of the hallway. He also had a peripheral view of the main elevator lobby across from the attendant, and the double doors leading to the rest of the fourth floor. While lowering into the chair, he removed his concealed pistol from its holder and tucked it into Jessica's handbag with one swift motion, nobody the wiser. He set the bag next to his right thigh and placed his hand inside, making sure he could draw the pistol without it catching. All he could do now was wait.

Chapter 21

Palos Hills Community Hospital
Palos Hills, Illinois

Jessica paused in front of the bathroom. She could see the outline of her mother's legs under a familiar patchwork quilt toward the foot of the bed. Her mom had made that for the family room couch when Jessica was in elementary school. She remembered the day she proudly unfolded it like it was yesterday. A flood of memories followed. Good ones. She had expected the opposite. Instead of the anger and betrayal she'd anticipated, she felt a bittersweet nostalgia. She could do this. A few more steps brought more of her mother's body into focus. Another step and she'd be face-to-face with her mother for the first time since she left for Langley.

"Nikki?" said a gravelly voice. "Is that really you?"

She took the final step. Any trace of the anger she'd harbored for years drained away permanently. Jessica knew it was gone. Regret filled that void, replace by a warmth toward her mother that she didn't think could be rekindled.

"Mom," said Jessica, unsure what to do.

"Come here, sweetie," said her mom, struggling to raise her arms to beckon her.

Jessica rushed to the side of her bed and hugged her gently, careful with her frail body. Vesna's arms barely managed to apply any pressure to the embrace. Jessica kept the side of her face pressed lightly against her mother's, crying uncontrollably while holding her.

"I'm sorry, Mama," she sobbed. "So sorry."

Her mother patted her back. "You have nothing to be sorry about, sweet one," whispered Vesna. "I'm the one that's sorry. I always understood. You took good care of me."

"I didn't take care of you, Mama," whimpered Jessica.

"Nonsense," said Vesna, in a firm voice.

Jessica pulled away from her, staring into surprisingly resolute eyes. They appeared to be the only part of her that was still alive, sunken deeply in darkened sockets. What the hell had happened to her?

"Look where I am. And where I've been. You've taken good care of me, my angel. More than I had any right to expect."

"I should have taken you away from this place," said Jessica. "Things would have been different."

"I'm right where I was always meant to be. You must believe that."

Jessica leaned in again, holding her mom as close as possible. She'd seen and smelled death in its most sickening and violent forms before, but something about this was far worse. The stale air, the near absolute absence of any vibrant color, a feeling of complete depletion.

"I love you, Mama," she barely managed to say between sobs.

"I love you too, my angel," said Vesna, keeping her close.

After a few minutes, Jessica pulled one of the chairs closer to the bed and held her mother's hand.

"How did this happen?" Jessica asked.

"Nobody knows," her mother answered. "Organ failure. Pain all over. It started a few months ago, coming in waves, and just kept getting worse and worse. None of the tests showed anything."

"You don't have cancer?"

"They couldn't find anything."

Something stirred in Jessica. None of what her mom said made sense. It sounded like she'd been poisoned.

Vesna squeezed her hand. "Let's not talk about it. It doesn't matter anymore. I'm just so happy to see you. This is like a dream come true. Maybe I'm already in Heaven."

"Don't talk like that, Mama."

"Promise me something," said her mom.

"Sure. What?"

"When you walk out of here, you don't look back. Ever. You go off and live a good life with that young man," said her mom. "I remember him from the last time I ever saw you. He had the devil in his eyes that night. Like he could kill a man."

"He almost *did* kill a man that night."

"Let's not talk about it," said Vesna, her eyes looking glassy and distant. "I'm just so happy to see you one last time."

"I should have come sooner."

"I'm glad you didn't. You deserved to get out of here. A lot of your friends didn't."

If only her mother knew where she had ended up. That was the irony of it all. Jessica had traded one nightmare for another and, in all likelihood, would have been better off staying. There was no psychiatrist's couch for the things she'd seen and done after "escaping" Palos Hills.

Jessica started to respond when she heard the sound of an elevator chime.

Chapter 22

Palos Hills Community Hospital
Palos Hills, Illinois

Daniel sat up in his chair when the elevator chimed. A quick glance to his right told him it didn't come from the elevator lobby. Neither of the indicator lights next to the doors had illuminated. He turned his head a little further to catch the hospice attendant's eye.

"Service elevator," said the man.

"You expecting anyone?" asked Daniel, tightening his grip on the pistol.

A bright green plastic laundry cart emerged from the service elevator, pushed by a man wearing maroon hospital scrubs.

"That's just Kevin. He takes away dirty towels or sheets left in bathroom hampers. He comes by once a shift."

Daniel confirmed that Kevin was the only person to get off the elevator. The attendant raised his hand to acknowledge the man's arrival. The gesture was returned in kind by the man maneuvering the cart into the center of the hallway.

"You're sure that's Kevin?"

"He's been on the night shift for close to a year," said the attendant, pushing his glasses higher on his nose.

"Does he go in all of the rooms?" Daniel asked, keeping his eyes locked on the man in scrubs.

"He has a list of the occupied or recently vacated rooms. I send it to janitorial services through the computer. Sometimes he forgets it, though," he said. "Kev, you got the list?" he called.

"Got it, man!" replied the guy, lifting a sheet of paper out of a tray attached to the cart. "I'm already pretty full, so I might need to make two trips."

"Tell him to skip 451 and the room across the hall," said Daniel.

"Dude, you need to seriously take it easy. Unless Kevin's your wife's ex-boyfriend, there's no problem here. You're acting like there's some kind of international cartel out to get her."

You have no idea.

Despite this initial thought, the attendant's last sentence somehow eased Daniel's tension. He was indeed being ridiculous. The line between healthy caution and morbid paranoia could be a fine one in this business, but he wasn't vetting a meet-up location with a clandestine field contact. He was sitting in an upscale hospital outside of Chicago, waiting for his wife to finish visiting her terminally ill mother. He didn't trust the U.S. government to honor his immunity deal, especially the new administration, but if they'd really wanted him in custody, there wasn't much he could do except get on that sailboat and vanish.

"You good, man?" the attendant queried.

Daniel eased his grip on the pistol. "As long as you know this guy."

"I see him every night. You can go hang out down by her room if it would make you feel better."

Not a bad idea. Daniel started to get up.

"Just don't bother Kevin or I'll have to call security."

He sank back into the cushions. There was no way he *wasn't* going to bother Kevin if he got up, and the last thing he needed was a run-in with hospital security or, even worse, a police officer.

"That's okay," said Daniel, turning his head toward the attendant for a moment. "Sorry if I'm making you nervous."

"I totally get it. Just trying to keep things low-key around here."

"You're doing a good job."

Daniel took a deep breath and exhaled slowly, bringing his surface-level tension down a notch. He checked his watch, dismayed by how little time had passed since Jessica entered her mother's room. On the bright side, it was enough time to convince him that the visit wasn't going to end in disaster.

Chapter 23

Palos Hills Community Hospital
Palos Hills, Illinois

Dragan Ilic shifted uncomfortably in the cramped laundry cart, his knees nearly touching his cheeks. When the cart bumped across the lip of the elevator door, the hard plastic base of the cart jarred his tailbone. He should have put one of the towels under his ass before climbing inside. Better yet, he should never have agreed to this insane plan. How the fuck was he going to pull this off without both of them in the same room?

He craned his neck as far forward as possible without pulling a muscle and squinted through the two-inch-diameter hole that had been drilled into the front of the cart. Even worse, Marko Resja, or whoever the fuck he really was, had a clear sightline down the hallway. The son of a bitch had moved a chair to the edge of the lounge and was staring right at him!

"How are we doing up there?" he said softly, but loudly enough for Kevin Shaw to hear.

"Everything is normal. Just like it always is," said Shaw. "Just like I said."

"It better be, for your family's sake."

"I guarantee you it will be fine," hissed the man, in a tone Dragan didn't care for. "As long as you don't keep talking."

"You better watch your tone," said Dragan. "I alone determine what happens to that little girl of yours. Don't forget that."

"I won't," said the man in a defeated voice. "Is the plan still the same? I see a guy watching us."

"The plan is that you do exactly what I say, when I say it. Service the rooms as normal."

"Understood."

Srecko had a few guys "babysitting" the man's wife and daughter. If all went as planned, the man's family would be released within the hour. Unfortunately, he'd never see his family again. Dragan needed to make a slight adjustment to the plan in order to ensure a clean getaway from the hospital. With Resja watching the hallway like a hawk, he couldn't take the chance that Shaw might make a noise and draw the trained operative's attention.

The original plan had been to take them both down in the old woman's room. Kill Resja with a suppressed pistol and Taser "the whore," then knock her out with a strong sedative for the return trip. Things would go down differently.

The whore. He had to laugh. Srecko had called her by no other name since he'd been hired to work on this job. Not even during the detailed briefings leading up to tonight. He'd warned Dragan repeatedly that she was lethal and that he wanted her delivered alive. He wouldn't get paid a penny beyond the down payment if he killed her or allowed her to kill herself.

"Do not underestimate this one," Srecko had echoed, over and over again.

The woman intrigued him. From the limited number of newspaper clippings Dragan had found hidden in a shoebox, he'd learned surprisingly little about Nicole Erak, "the whore," that had arranged the upscale town house on her mother's behalf. She'd been one of those varsity athlete, National Honor Society types, got into a good college, graduated with honors, then essentially disappeared—at least from her mother's life.

He'd found no pictures or evidence of a father. How she'd ended up in Belgrade, infiltrating Srecko's Panthers, remained a complete mystery. If any clues had been kept in the house, he would have found them. He'd spent the better part of the past two months as Vesna's daytime caregiver at the town house. Ironic considering the fact that he had been the one to prick her skin at the nearby Jewel-Osco grocery store with a tiny drop of dimethylmercury, guaranteeing her rapid, but controlled decline.

Framed photos of Nicole alone or with her mother adorned the mantel and nightstand at the town house, all of them taken long ago. The daughter had been a seriously hot piece of ass back then. She'd looked pretty damn good in the dossier Srecko had given him too. Dragan seriously hoped Srecko let him take part in the rumored festivities planned for the woman. He might even consider discounting the job to get a backstage pass. Why not? It wasn't every day you got to be part of a snuff film. And a patriotic one at that! Nicole Erak had apparently played a major role in the downfall of Srecko Hadzic's Panthers, one of the cornerstones of Serbia's Nationalist movement.

Dragan bumped against the sides of the cart as his hostage went about the business of removing and replacing the towels and linens left in each bathroom. As discussed prior to exiting the elevator, he was to drag the cart at least halfway into each room to conduct his business. The front of the cart had been modified to swing open so he could slip out undetected and load Erak's unconscious body into the bin. A false top had been installed three-quarters of the way up the interior of the cart, layered with used towels. Anyone casually inspecting the contents would see a nearly full bin full of dirty laundry. Anyone pushing the inspection any further would get a hollow-point bullet to the face.

Smaller holes had been drilled into the sides of the cart, allowing him to see in either hallway direction when the cart was parked inside each door. Marko Resja appeared to remain alert in the lobby, never taking his eyes off the cart. He'd have to be extremely careful in the final stages of this operation. Any slipup would undoubtedly lead to a messy situation. He was convinced that he could deal with Resja if necessary, but he had little confidence in his ability to take out Resja and silence the attendant simultaneously from this range. Dragan cursed the moment he refused the offer of a suppressed, compact rifle. With that type of weapon, he could Taser "the whore" and quickly hit both Resja and the attendant with headshots and be long gone before somebody raised the alarm. Based on his hostage's assurances, the place was a mausoleum at night. Figuratively *and* literally. Everyone here was on death's doorstep, including Resja and Nicole Erak.

After a few more minutes of rumbling through the hallway, he heard a distinct sound: triple knocking against the back of the cart near his head. After a long pause, the triple knock sounded again. Their next stop was the room across from 451. He acknowledged the notification with a double knock. Now for the moment of truth.

The cart turned and stopped, the interior darkening when Kevin repositioned himself in front of the cart to pull it into the room. Four knocks indicated they were safely in position within the room. Dragan felt along the left, front side of the cart and released two latches. He slowly opened the door and peered into the dark room. Half of Kevin's body was visible, outlined by the illumination from a night-light in the bathroom.

"It's all clear," the man whispered in a barely audible voice.

Dragan twisted his head at a nearly impossible angle to press his left eye against the hole drilled into the back of the cart. He wasn't taking any chances with Kevin. People did crazy things under pressure. Across the hallway, the couch and chairs visible from his point of view remained empty. He could still make this work.

"Hold the cart," said Dragan.

When Kevin's hand firmly grasped the horizontal handle along the rim, Dragan slowly and carefully inched his way out of the cramped hold and onto the carpeted floor. He sat there for a few seconds, listening intently. He then reached into the cart, quietly removing a duffel bag.

"Get inside the bathtub and lay down. Shut the shower curtain," whispered Dragan.

The man complied, disappearing into the bathroom. When Dragan heard the shower curtain ruffle and the plastic tub creak under Kevin's weight, he unzipped the bag and withdrew a suppressed pistol. He pushed the bag onto the bathroom tile and crawled into the softly lit space, standing up once he was completely inside. Equipped for handicap use, the bathroom was spacious, allowing him to shut the door without getting too close to the bathtub. He needed the door shut. The sound of a suppressed pistol, no matter how quiet, would be immediately recognizable to a trained operative.

"You okay in there?" he asked quietly.

"I think so," said the man. "Hey, there's a solid stainless steel handle in here. It might be easier just to tie me up in here."

Dragan opened the shower curtain a quarter of the way with his left hand, keeping the pistol concealed behind his right thigh. The handle would have indeed served his purposes well if the plan hadn't changed so drastically. He raised the pistol and aimed it at the man's forehead, pressing the trigger before the guy could react. A single hole appeared above the eyebrows and his body went slack. The subsonic 9mm hollow-point projectile had obviously done its job. There was no need to fire a second bullet. He closed the curtain and knelt next to the tub, removing a black wig and a pair of thick-rimmed, nonprescription glasses from the bag.

After a few seconds of adjustment in the mirror, he closely enough resembled the man lying dead in the bathtub. The disguise wasn't perfect by a long shot, but at the distance between here and the lobby, he should be able to go about his business without drawing any scrutiny.

Dragan opened the bathroom door and placed his duffel bag on top of the dirty towels, shoving it far enough down to remain undetected. He reached inside the bag and removed a Taser and a gray auto-injector syringe, placing them on the tray attached to the cart handle.

He pushed the cart into the hallway, avoiding eye contact with Resja or the attendant. Halfway across, Dragan swung the cart around so he could pull it into the room instead of push it. This was where it got a bit tricky. He stepped through the open doorway and started to bring the cart with him.

"Hello?" said an alert female voice, followed by movement.

Dragan gripped the Taser in the cart, keeping his back toward the room. He turned his head in time to see a redhead with tightly cropped hair appear at the foot of the bed. Her right hand was hidden behind her right hip, most likely gripping a pistol. He wasn't going to win this quick-draw match.

"I'm so sorry," he said. "There's rarely anyone here at this hour. I should have checked with the desk. I even saw someone sitting in the lobby. I'm so stupid. Sorry to have interrupted you."

The woman's tense posture eased, but her hand didn't come away from the concealed weapon.

"Can I help you?" she said sternly.

"I'm just collecting dirty towels. I can come back later," Dragan said in a wimpy, deferential voice.

"It's fine. He comes in every night," said a weak voice from somewhere deeper in the room. "He's a nice fellow."

Her arm shifted forward, just slightly. Still not enough for him to take a chance with the Taser. He'd been warned about her.

"It'll only take a few seconds, but I don't mind coming back," he said. "I'm on shift all night."

She put her hands on her hips, which sealed her fate.

"That's fine. Just do it qui—"

Dragan turned his body, simultaneously extending the hand gripping the Taser. The woman reacted swiftly, her hand slipping behind her hip, but fifty thousand volts of electricity prevented her from taking any further action. She dropped to her knees, momentarily fighting the Taser's effects before tipping over onto the floor, her back arched and limbs locked into place.

Keeping the Taser in his right hand, he grabbed the auto-injector syringe and approached her twitching body. A quick jab to one of her legs delivered the sedative. All he had to do at this point was wait several seconds for the strong dose to take full effect. This left him just enough time to take care of the old woman. He glanced in Vesna Erak's direction, catching her horrified look. She raised her head off the pillow, trying to form words. Nothing escaped her lips beyond a continuous, low-volume gasp.

He stepped past Nicole Erak, placed a hand over Vesna's mouth, and stabbed her twice in the Adam's apple with the business end of the auto-injector. It was messy work, better suited for a knife, but it did the job. Her head immediately lowered to the pillow, a weak gurgling sound sputtering from her lips.

Turning his attention back to the target, Dragan disengaged the Taser. When Erak's body relaxed, he kicked her sharply in the side of the rib cage, eliciting no reaction. She was out cold. Less than ten seconds later, he pushed the fully loaded cart into the hallway.

Chapter 24

Palos Hills Community Hospital
Palos Hills, Illinois

Daniel kept a close watch on the man that pushed the cart into the center of the hallway. The guy had taken a little longer in room 451 than the one across the hall, but he'd heard Jessica's voice, so he assumed his wife had briefly interrogated him. The man turned briefly to give the attendant a wave.

"I'm full. Be right back," he said, pushing the cart to the end of the hallway.

The man pressed the elevator button and moved behind the cart, immediately pushing it into the elevator carriage. Daniel squinted almost imperceptibly, feeling that something was off. He hadn't heard a chime, and the guy hadn't paused for a moment before maneuvering into the elevator, almost like the door had already been open. But why would he press the button? Shit. He'd only do that to try to maintain some semblance of normal procedure—to keep Daniel from instantly reacting.

He burst out of his seat, holding Jessica's purse, and sprinted toward the end of the hallway. By the time he reached the elevator, the brushed steel doors had been closed for a number of seconds, the hum and whir of the elevator machinery audible through the thick barrier. Responding out of desperate instinct, he tried to pry the doors open with his hand, just as quickly abandoning the futile attempt. An insistent voice from the opposite end of the hallway momentarily distracted him. The attendant had finally gotten off his ass and was heading in his direction—and he didn't look happy. Fuck. He didn't need any complications right now. Processing the information on hand, he made a few decisions and headed swiftly toward the attendant.

"Dave, I think they took my wife in the laundry cart!"

The man shook his head, continuing to approach. "Dude, nobody kidnapped your wife."

"Check the room," said Daniel. "Just do that for me."

The guy broke into a lazy jog, clearly wanting to get to the room before Daniel. "I'll check the room, but I need you to stand clear," said the man, pointing a finger at him. "Then I need you out of here. Back in the main lobby. Security will walk you down."

Daniel nodded, slowing his pace. "Thank you. Sorry to be like this, but we have reasons to be cautious."

"Yeah. I bet you do," said the man, pausing in front of room 451. "Stay right there, or security will do more than just walk you out of here."

Daniel stopped several feet from the room, nodding his understanding. "Hurry."

The man shook his head and rolled his eyes, stepping into the room. The instant he disappeared, Daniel drew the pistol out of the handbag and slung the bag's handles over his shoulder, slipping into position right next to the door.

"Son of a bitch," muttered the attendant, a touch of confusion in his voice.

Leading with the pistol, Daniel entered the room, finding the attendant fumbling with the handheld radio attached to his belt.

"Stop what you're doing and raise your hands," said Daniel.

The man let the radio hang half connected to his belt and put his hands up. "What the fuck is going on here?"

"What floor does Kevin take to offload his cart?"

"What?"

"You heard me," said Daniel.

"S-two. Second subfloor."

"Can I get there from the stairwell?"

The attendant thought about it for a little too long. "David, I need an answer right away," said Daniel, shifting his aim to the man's head.

The guy turned his head and lowered his hands in front of his face, a fairly natural reaction for untrained civilians when a firearm is pointed at their face.

"Jesus! You don't have to point that at me," he said, suddenly blurting an answer. "You can get there, but you'll need an access card to open the door. My card doesn't open any of the sublevel doors. Swear to God!"

Daniel snatched the radio off his belt with enough force to break the plastic clip barely keeping it in place.

"Sit on the couch and don't move," Daniel hissed, sliding next to Vesna's bed to reach the nightstand.

The gruesome sight didn't distract him. Daniel was single-mindedly focused on taking the steps necessary to save Jessica, and Vesna Erak's dead body didn't weigh into that equation. Every fraction of a second counted now. He ripped the phone on the nightstand out of its connection and tossed it on the other side of the bed. A quick scan of the room on his way out didn't reveal an intercom system.

"I'm going to shut this door. If it opens and I'm still here, you're a dead man. Understood?" he said, keeping the pistol aimed at David's head.

The man nodded emphatically. "Understood."

Daniel closed the door behind him and took off for the lobby. He could shoot his way through the sublevel door if necessary, or take a card from someone on the way down. One way or the other, he was getting through that door. He hadn't gone more than a few steps when the service elevator chimed.

Coming to finish me off? Big mistake.

He reversed direction and bolted for the end of the hallway, diving into position on the floor in front of the doors as they started to open. Steadying his aim from a prone position, the doors slowly peeled back, revealing the blue cart.

What the fuck?

"Daniel?" said a familiar voice from the elevator car. "It's me, Munoz. We don't have time to fuck around."

Munoz? Sure as hell sounded like him. Sanderson must have sent a team to keep an eye on them. Fucking Sanderson!

"Show yourself," said Daniel.

A head slowly appeared from the right side of the elevator, confirming Munoz's identity. He was dressed in the same type of maroon hospital scrubs the kidnapper had worn. Daniel hopped to his feet and rushed into the elevator, frantically digging through the blood-splattered towels and linens. He looked up at Munoz while still tossing the cart.

"Where is she?"

"She's out cold in a hidden compartment underneath the towels," said Munoz, pressing S2 on the elevator panel. "Vitals are strong. She's fine."

"How the fuck do you get this open?"

Munoz grabbed his shoulder, forcefully pushing him back. "I need you to focus here. Jessica is going to be unconscious for a while. We'll make sure she's safe."

Daniel knocked Munoz's arm away and knelt next to the cart, examining the plastic bin as the elevator doors closed.

"There's a plastic latch on the front right corner," said Munoz.

He immediately located the latch and pulled it upward, releasing the door. Jessica lay crumpled inside, her head lolling on the base of the container. He placed his hand on her neck and felt for a pulse, finding it quickly. Slow but steady, definitely sedated. The elevator started to descend.

"We need to get her somewhere safe until she's conscious. Then I'm flying her out of here," said Daniel. "I assume you're staying somewhere off the books?"

"We have a bigger problem," said Munoz.

"I don't care about your bigger problems," said Daniel. "I have a plan to get her away from all of these problems. It was a mistake coming here."

"You definitely fucked up," said Munoz. "Almost got her killed."

"Fuck you," said Daniel, then he muttered, "And thank you."

"Thank you?" said Munoz with an amused look. "Sanderson was right. You *are* going soft."

Daniel rubbed his face and took a deep breath, trying to compose himself. He'd almost lost her. How careless and stupid. To get this close to escaping their previous lives and fuck it up so stunningly. Sanderson was right. He *was* getting soft, and it was time to walk away for good. Either he'd get them killed, or she'd get them killed, sooner or later. They'd had too many close calls lately. The only way their departure on *La Ombra* could have been timed better was if it had happened two weeks ago. They'd planned to permanently cut every communications tie to anyone in their past.

"You there?" Munoz prodded.

"Just thinking."

"Well, here's something to think about. Srecko Hadzic is alive and well, not too far away from here."

"Hadzic? He died in a botched rescue attempt. I thought that was confirmed?" said Daniel, closing the hidden door.

"Apparently not," said Munoz, pausing to listen to his earpiece.

Daniel shut the latch on the cart and stood up, studying the longtime Black Flag operative. Munoz's face was a storybook of scars, the most recent addition visible on his forehead, just below his dense hairline. They'd both had close calls in Uruguay. Sanderson nearly lost the two remaining graduates of the first Black Flag class in the same operation. The operative responded to whatever message he'd received.

"We're almost to S-two," said Munoz, listening again.

"Copy," he replied, hitting S3.

"Change of plans?"

"Always. Melendez found the van."

"What are we dealing with here?" said Daniel.

"Our electronic surveillance team picked up some encrypted transmissions piggybacking the in-hospital signal-boosting system. They were able to pinpoint the location to the second subfloor, near this elevator. Melendez and I have been stashed in a closet on S-one for the past hour, waiting for the two of you to arrive."

"GPS trackers on the cars at the airport?" said Daniel.

"And one sewn into the briefcase," said Munoz. "We eliminated a two-man team waiting with a stretcher and body bag by the elevator on S-two just as the elevator started its return journey. The guy that pushed the cart onto one of the elevators never saw it coming. We weren't sure if they had more men roaming around, so I pushed the cart back in and came straight back to you. Melendez located a van with a single driver waiting in the loading bay."

"How do you know this is Hadzic?"

"We don't, but the electronics team has already identified the guy that kidnapped Jessica as Dragan Ilic. He's a Serbian-born contract killer, based out of New Jersey, with suspected ties to Serbian nationalists released by the tribunal. It's only an assumption, but a fair one at this point."

"Jessica and I made a lot of enemies there at the end. This could be anyone," said Daniel.

Munoz pulled a smartphone from one of his pants pockets and showed Daniel the screen. "Recognize that?"

Daniel did. He had a faded version of it high on his right arm. A black panther head, the symbol of Srecko Hadzic's infamous paramilitary group. If Hadzic was alive, he and Jessica would never be safe. Daniel had to end this tonight, once and for all.

"How much time do we have to put together a plan?" he asked.

"Little to none. Text messages going back and forth between phones indicate that Jessica is expected shortly."

"Then we shouldn't keep them waiting," said Daniel. "How many operatives do we have for the operation?"

"You, me, and Melendez, plus the two electronics wizards."

"Jesus," muttered Daniel.

"I suspect He's gonna steer clear of this one," said Munoz as the elevator came to a stop at its destination.

Chapter 25

Crestwood Industrial Park
Crestwood, Illinois

Srecko Hadzic paced the concrete floor, drawing deeply on a cigarette. He wasn't supposed to smoke them after the heart attack and had mostly given them up, but tonight he desperately needed his old friend nicotine. He was minutes away from fulfilling a long overdue promise made to himself and his precious nephew, Josif, who was so callously slaughtered by that viper of a whore.

He only wished the other traitor could be here to bear witness, but it had been deemed too risky to try to grab them both. That was fine by him. The traitor would get a bullet to the head like any traitor deserved, and the whore would get what a whore deserved. He was well supplied with heart medications and his little blue pills, everything he needed to make sure he could savor the next few days, and not only as a satisfied observer. No. Srecko planned to take this woman over and over again, cutting her eyelids open if necessary to make sure she had to endure his face on top of her.

"How long?" he demanded.

One of the men seated on a folding chair thumbed a message on his phone and waited a few seconds for a reply.

"About five minutes out."

"And the whore is still alive?"

He sensed a flicker of insubordination, possibly a quickly halted eye roll, before the man sent another message. This newest breed of Panthers was pathetic compared to the dedicated and skilled men he'd commanded during the Yugoslav Wars. Few of these punks would have been worthy of consideration in the old Panthers, but like the old saying went, "beggars can't be choosers."

In Srecko's situation, the phrase pretty much fit him literally. He'd come close to spending the last of the money he'd managed to keep hidden from the war crimes tribunal, paying for his escape and putting together this operation. The lust for revenge was only a small part of why he'd gone to such careful and expensive lengths to capture the whore.

The Petroviches, as they now called themselves, had stolen close to one hundred and thirty million dollars from Srecko's European accounts before they lit the spark that started a bloody civil war between the Panthers and Mirko Jovic's Eagles, a war that essentially destroyed both groups and accelerated the fall of Milosevic's regime. He was hell-bent on retrieving what was left of that money and had even convinced an old colleague to come out of hiding just for the occasion.

Mirko Jovic had disappeared during the brutal month of fighting between the Panthers and Eagles, rumored to have been killed in a coup attempt within the Eagles. Srecko had little reason to doubt the rumor, since his own paramilitary organization had come apart at the seams, factions turning on factions. Srecko held on to the bitter end, surviving the bloodbath, but Jovic had been the smarter of the two. While the rest of them clung desperately to their empires, while NATO bombers pounded the regular Yugoslavian forces into submission, he'd fled the country, taking his money with him.

Despite escaping with his life and money, Jovic still had an axe to grind with the whore and Marko Resja. Once again, a most literal interpretation. Jovic's youngest daughter had been found beheaded in a Belgrade ditch on the outskirts of the city, supposedly last seen in the company of Zorana Zekulic. Srecko had always assumed that Marko Resja had killed both of them, only delivering Zorana's head to him in that duffel bag. Years later in prison, when he discovered that Zorana had been in league with Resja all along, it suddenly made sense. They'd hacked Jovic's daughter's head off and passed it off as Zorana's!

After his escape from the Hague Detention Unit, he got in touch with Jovic through an intermediary and negotiated a sit-down meeting to explain the depth of the deception that had led to the war between them. Srecko hadn't done this out of a need to mend fences, he'd done it to raise capital for this operation and to recruit one of the most ruthless torturers in recent history. Jovic had a talent that made him indispensable to Milosevic. He could make anyone talk.

Srecko held up his hands. "Well? Are you going to answer me?"

"He's still typing," said the soldier.

"I'm not paying him to type a fucking novel!" yelled Srecko. "Dial his number and give me the damn phone."

The man pressed a button and handed him the phone. Srecko put the phone to his ear.

"Hello? Is she still alive or what? I'm not paying you to deliver a cadaver. I can buy a sex doll for about a thousand times less than your fee."

"You're really going to regret saying that," replied a gravelly voice in Serbian.

For a brief moment, he thought Dragan had gone rogue, suspecting that the hit man had somehow discovered the value of Srecko's remaining fortune and decided to extort more money out of him. He always assumed that a conspiracy or double-cross was in the works and that everyone was out to get him. That was how he stayed one step ahead of these jackals. A fleeting thought, the memory of that voice hit him like a sledgehammer. Dragan had somehow failed. He dropped the cigarette.

Srecko cleared his throat. "Marko?"

The men around him stiffened, looking to him for guidance. A few preemptively stood, readying their weapons. Mirko Jovic sat in the corner of the warehouse office, apparently unmoved by the mention of the name.

"In the flesh. Well, I'm not there yet, but I'm getting close. Your guys really shouldn't put important locations in their navigation systems. It's almost too easy."

Srecko motioned with his empty hand for the men to leave, pressing the phone against his chest to muffle any sound.

"Something went wrong at the hospital. We're out of here," Srecko whispered to Obrad, the man in charge of his security detail.

"We'll be out of here in thirty seconds," said Obrad, turning to the men.

As his crew piled out of the office, he glanced toward Jovic, who remained unmoved in the corner, sipping what had to be the tenth coffee made with the Krups machine he'd insisted Srecko provide.

"Are you coming or what?" said Srecko.

One of Jovic's security guards started to get up, but the former paramilitary leader put a hand on the guard's shoulder.

"I'll take my chances in here," said Jovic.

"You'll die in here," said Srecko, rushing to the office door. "He's coming."

"He might already be here," said Jovic.

The statement stopped Srecko in his tracks. He gave Jovic's comment a quick thought, glancing between the dozen men running for the vehicles inside the warehouse and the three men seated in the office. He'd take his chances with the larger group. He put the phone back up to his ear.

"Hello? Did you have another heart attack?" Marko Resja taunted.

"Fuck you!" he spat into the phone. "I'll fucking kill you and that whore no matter what it takes. You'll never be safe!"

"Don't get your heart all worked up, Srecko. I wasn't all that impressed with that hospital," said Resja. "Speaking of unimpressed, where did you find that joke, Dragan? I hope you didn't give him a down payment. I don't think you can afford to throw money away like that."

Srecko threw the phone against the warehouse floor, scattering plastic pieces in several directions.

"Three vehicles. All SUVs. Four men to a vehicle. You're with me in the middle vehicle!" he yelled to his security chief, the last sentence fading to a grunt as the pain in his chest became unbearable.

While Obrad organized the men, Srecko dug under his collar and pulled a gold chain necklace out of his shirt. He feverishly worked the cylindrical gold pill fob hanging from the chain until he'd retrieved one of the nitroglycerine pills he kept for chest pain emergencies. The rest of the pills fell to the floor. He only needed one! With a trembling hand, he forced the pill into his mouth, under his tongue. Unable to draw more than a short gasp of air, he stood frozen several feet from the loaded vehicles.

Obrad rushed over and escorted him into the backseat of the middle SUV while the tall warehouse door slowly opened. His breathing had eased by the time the line of vehicles had reached the sliding gate fifty yards in front of the warehouse. The effects of the nitroglycerine were finally kicking in.

"Get us as far the fuck away from here as possible," he ordered.

The wide, reinforced chain-link gate ambled along its track, seemingly making little progress.

"As soon as they can fit through, they go," he barked, not wanting to spend a single moment longer than necessary in the open.

Obrad relayed the order, and the first SUV edged closer to the gate.

Chapter 26

Crestwood Industrial Park
Crestwood, Illinois

Daniel lay as flat as he could manage behind the motor unit opening the chain-link gate. The long, six-inch-high concrete platform holding the motor in place gave his legs just enough concealment to remain unseen. He hoped. As the trucks' headlights swept the fence line and the gate and tendrils of bright light poked through the motor housing, he felt entirely exposed. When the gate rumbled to life and he could see right into the driver's side window of the first SUV, there was no question about it. He was exposed. Staying hidden for several more seconds was critical to their hastily assembled plan.

Munoz was hidden in a patch of scrub next to the fence, twenty yards on the other side of the gate, outside of the facility. Ideally he would be inside the fence line to engage the rear vehicle, but their surveillance team didn't have enough time to analyze the warehouse's electronic security signature. A few wireless motion or disturbance detectors hidden along the perimeter could trash the element of surprise. They had their hands full with something more important and impactful.

The team had hijacked the remote control signal for the gate motor, and Petrovich had reached through the gate and snipped the wires powering the automatic motion sensor inside. Under normal circumstances, when the vehicles pulled up to the gate from the inside, the gate would automatically open. Access from the outside required a paired remote control. According to the techs, control of the gate was solely in their hands. Of course, none of this could be tested prior to the vehicles' arrival, but it seemed to have worked. Unless he'd cut the wrong wires and the motion sensor was still operational.

Even if the trick didn't work, it wouldn't matter. They could pound the trucks with bullets and sniper fire until everything was quiet. He'd lose the opportunity to return Srecko to prison, where he'd most certainly be held without possibility of release, but that was a price he was more than willing to pay. Just knowing he was gone would be satisfaction enough.

He watched the gate roll slowly past the stones he had set in the road. When the rollers passed the second of four rocks, he triggered his radio.

"Stand by to engage," he whispered.

No response followed. They had checked and rechecked the communications just prior to the warehouse door opening. He was passing information to Melendez, who lay on top of the warehouse a hundred or so yards beyond Daniel. The rollers passed the third rock.

"Stand by. Stand by." The rollers reached the fourth rock, where he'd calculated the vehicles would be able to squeeze through. "Fire!"

The lead vehicle lurched through the opening in the gate, and Daniel pressed the suppressed MP-7's trigger, sending several 4.6mm bullets through the driver's window. Before he could fire again, a supersonic crack snapped overhead, Melendez's bullet hopefully taking out the driver of the second SUV. Daniel's second burst peppered the rear driver's side window and upper door. The SUV continued past the gate, the driver's foot stuck on the accelerator. He'd anticipated this possibility.

"Munoz, switch targets with Melendez."

The entire motor housing unit shook next to him as the second SUV lurched to a stop halfway through the gate. The surveillance team had reversed the gate in time to catch the second vehicle's rear driver's side door, halting its forward motion and pressing it against the opposite gate post. The door dented inward with the continuing pressure, trapping the rear passengers. Daniel fired a quick burst through the already shattered driver's window at the head of a man yelling in the front passenger seat, instantly silencing him.

Staccato bursts of suppressed gunfire echoed across the road from Munoz's position, repeatedly striking the unobserved side of the lead vehicle with hollow, metallic thumps until it finally slowed.

"Melendez?" Daniel said.

"I got one more fucker playing hide-and-seek behind the last vehicle."

"Munoz?"

"All quiet in the lead vehicle," Munoz replied. *"I have some frantic movement in the backseat of the middle truck. Watch yourself. I don't have a good angle on them."*

Neither did Daniel, and he wasn't keen on raising his head above the motor unit. He reloaded the MP-7 and waited for the standoff at the rear vehicle to play out. Srecko wasn't going anywhere. A supersonic crack was followed by a report.

"Rear vehicle neutralized. Want me to put a round through the back of Srecko's SUV?"

"That would be kind of you," said Daniel, still flinching when the bullet passed several feet above him, shattering the SUV's cargo compartment window.

"Srecko!" said Daniel.

Gunfire erupted from the backseat, bullets pinging off the fence and motor. Daniel pressed himself into the hard dirt until the fusillade ended.

"I can see right into the backseat now. Srecko is leaned up against the passenger-side door, grasping his chest. There's one other guy in back with him, staying low. Probably reloading."

"Can you hit the gunman low through the door?" Daniel asked.

"Bravo units, this is control. I have multiple 911 calls reporting gunfire coming from the Crestwood Industrial Park. Average response time for this department is five minutes and thirty-three seconds. We'll need another minute or two to get clear of the area. Not a lot of traffic around here at night."

"Copy that, control. Good job on the gate, by the way," said Daniel. "Munoz, hit the backseat with a full mag. Melendez, confirm the results."

Munoz's MP-7 chattered first, followed by Daniel's, each of them methodically firing short burst after short burst into the rear passenger area. Sixty bullets—total overkill for the situation.

"They're gone," said Melendez. *"Heading toward primary pickup."*

"Let's get out of here," said Daniel, picking himself off the ground.

He ran cautiously past the lead SUV, seeing four heads lolling at unnatural angles. The surveillance team's passenger van appeared in the distance, driving toward the warehouse used by Melendez. Daniel slowed long enough for Munoz to catch up, and they took off for the van.

Chapter 27

Crestwood Industrial Park
Crestwood, Illinois

Mirko Jovic stayed seated inside the office until the gunfire ended with a dramatic crescendo. Srecko's final stand.

"Should we go, Mr. Jovic?" asked one of his security men.

"Give it a minute to be sure," said Jovic. "I suggest you grab a cup of coffee and a few of those snack bars they have stashed in the cabinets."

"Coffee?"

"My guess is we're not driving out of here," said Jovic. "It's going to be a long night on foot getting back to the hotel."

"I'll start scouting a location to cut the fence behind the warehouse," offered the guard. "We have a pair of bolt cutters in the truck."

"Patience, Goran. You can't reach the truck without exposing yourself to that vast wide open. We leave when the sirens start. Whoever's out there will be gone by then."

"Of course, Mr. Jovic," said the guard, settling back into his seat.

"I'm serious about the coffee and snack bars," said Jovic. "The hotel is several miles from here and we're not stopping until we get there. Not even for your beloved Long John Silver's or Wendy's."

"Really?"

"Really," said Jovic, mildly annoyed. "Why do you need to eat again, anyway?"

"I don't know. Bored."

"Good. Let's hope this stays boring," said Jovic. "If it stays that way until we get back to the hotel, I'll treat us to Denny's. It's open twenty-four hours."

The prospect of Denny's seemed to cheer up his sullen crew. He understood why they were disappointed. He felt the same way, though for a different reason. While the guards were justifiably let down by the loss of the sex toy they had so eagerly awaited, something far more important had just slipped through Jovic's fingers. A rare and likely once-in-a-lifetime chance to exact revenge against the snake that had lured his precious Mira into that murderer's trap. The thought of what had happened to his daughter dropped a crushing weight of sadness on him. And anger. The Styrofoam cup trembled in his hand.

Jovic pounded the last of the lukewarm coffee and set the cup on the floor. He considered taking the cup and his fingerprints with him, but there was no point. There was no way he could wipe down every surface he might have touched in here. Fucking Srecko. He should have known the guy would fuck this up. The fat slob was a shell of the man he used to be. At least he'd served one final purpose.

The faint whistling sound of a faraway siren arose.

"I think it's time," said Jovic.

While his men rushed to the remaining SUV to retrieve the gear they would need to cut their way out of the perimeter, Jovic walked slowly to the warehouse door, peeking outside. The volume of bullet holes in Srecko's convoy indicated that Resja hadn't been alone. This had been the work of a highly trained and well-coordinated team, not something their target had thrown together at the last second. There was more to Resja these days than met the eye. Something Srecko had failed to discover, and he'd died horribly because of it.

The dim red glow of distant taillights penetrated the darkness between rows of warehouse buildings. Resja and company, no doubt. His fists clenched. So damn close! He took a deep breath and exhaled, releasing his hands. Maybe there was hope. If that idiot Srecko could find the Petroviches, so could he. The sirens grew louder, their echoes bouncing off the surrounding warehouses. The taillights disappeared, and Jovic turned to his men. They had a long night ahead of them.

Chapter 28

Georgetown
Washington, D.C.

Karl Berg savored the last bite of the short ribs swirled in butternut squash puree. Perfect every time. He set his fork down on the bottom right corner of the plate next to the knife, tidily arranging them in the 11 o'clock position. He was officially done with the main course.

"You're eating like somebody's chasing you."

Darryl Jackson cut into his halibut with a fork, a slight faux pas in a restaurant like this, and swirled the detached piece around in the sauce on his plate before eating it.

"A hard habit to break," said Berg, purposely leaning back in his chair and sipping a glass of red wine. "Is that better?"

"It's a start. You've been making me nervous the whole meal," said Jackson. "Makes me think twice about eating out in public with you."

"Even if I'm paying?"

"Especially if you're paying," said Jackson. "I have two kids in college. If you're footing the bill for a two-hundred-dollar bottle of Ceretto Barolo, I don't want to feel like we need to chug straight from the bottle to finish it. I get whatever they serve at Applebee's, if I'm not drinking it at home. Did I mention I have kids in college?"

"It may have come up a few hundred times," said Berg, taking a generous sip of the exquisite wine. He felt himself loosen a little.

"See? Doesn't that feel better?" said Jackson, cutting another piece of fish.

Berg's eyes diverted to the plate. A third of his fish still remained. They'd be here all night.

"That's right," said Jackson, smiling. "You better settle in with that glass of wine. My ass isn't going anywhere fast."

"You're on a business trip. You don't have anywhere to go."

"Bingo. That's the concept you need to start embracing. When you have nowhere to be and nobody telling you what to do, you need to be able to stop and smell the proverbial roses or it's going to be a long-ass retirement. How's that going, by the way? You've been awfully quiet about it."

"I'm waiting for the right time," said Berg.

"Uh-huh," replied Jackson with a raised eyebrow.

Berg looked around again.

"Can you please stop doing that?" said Jackson. "You do know they have more sophisticated methods of eavesdropping these days. The old hand to the ear right when you're about to say something important method went out of style a few hundred years ago."

"Very funny," said Berg.

"It's bad enough I have to put up with your daily check-ins."

"I just want to make sure they know I'm not a threat before I leave."

"Who? The new idiots in charge of this town?" said Jackson, keeping his voice the same volume.

Berg couldn't stop himself from starting to scan the room.

"You're doing it again. Trust me. You're not the only CIA employee to retire with some serious secrets lodged up there," said Jackson, pointing his fork at Berg's head. "Have any of your former retired colleagues vanished or died unexplainably?"

Berg shook his head. "Not that I can think of."

"Exactly. They're all professors at colleges. Working for think tanks. Advising corporations. All kinds of cushy stuff. Some of them might even be sitting on their asses, retired. Imagine that," said Jackson, holding the last piece of his dinner up with his fork. "All you have to do is follow your own advice. Keep your head down, don't make any waves, slowly fade into the background."

Berg feigned a smile, nodding stiffly, then taking another long pull of the velvety-smooth wine. Jackson studied him while taking the last bites of his meal. The rapidly expanding warmth of the wine did little to ease his underlying tension. His friend of many years shook his head almost imperceptibly.

Busted.

"You fucked it up, didn't you?" said Jackson.

"I might have been passed some information I couldn't ignore," Berg admitted.

Jackson put his hand on the bottle of wine. "Should I tip this back right now? I hate to see it go to waste if the restaurant is about to blow up."

Berg laughed softly. "I don't think it's that bad."

Their waiter appeared, offering to pour the wine for Jackson, who graciously released his grip on the bottle and let the waiter fill his glass.

"Are you sure? You look a little—let me rephrase that—*a lot* out of sorts," said Jackson. "I was just busting your chops earlier, thinking it was retirement nerves. How bad is this? Really."

"It's something our new overlords would prefer to remain buried. But the information could seriously help them throw some more dirt on that certain something."

"Then this is a good thing. Maybe get you bumped up a retirement tier or two as a thank you," said Jackson, holding up his glass for a toast.

"I'd be happy to get out of there without a bull's-eye painted on my back," said Berg.

"Well, it doesn't sound like something you need to worry about."

"Maybe not from that angle. The information itself is another story."

"I assume it's highly classified and completely inappropriate to share in public, especially over an expensive wine, which you're ruining."

"I apologize for the dour mood. Here's to you having enough money to retire after paying for college," said Berg, clinking his glass.

"I'll drink to that," said Jackson.

They declined dessert, earning a momentary look of confusion from the waiter. The prix fixe meal included dessert. They opted for a fine cognac instead, instantly redeeming themselves in the establishment's eyes, particularly at thirty dollars a glass. After another twenty minutes or so of purposefully, and sometimes awkwardly, avoiding the topic of their jobs, Berg paid the bill without looking at it. He didn't trust his eyes not to freeze on the total, and the last thing he wanted to do was make his friend uncomfortable. The iconic Georgetown restaurant wasn't the most expensive in town, but it gave the Michelin-star establishments a run for their money. His money. He treated himself at least once a week to an exquisite meal, an expense he could afford without kids in college.

They'd walked halfway to Darryl's car, parked just past Thirty-Fifth Street on Prospect, when Berg realized they'd left the bottle of Barolo at the restaurant. Despite Jackson's protests over not having paid for the wine, he'd convinced his friend to take the rest of the bottle back to his hotel.

"I forgot the wine," said Berg. "I'll be right back."

"Don't go back and get it on my behalf," said Jackson.

One way or the other, he was leaving it with Jackson. Money really wasn't an issue for Berg, but the thought of leaving fifty dollars of wine behind didn't sit well with him.

"You're not getting out of taking the wine," Berg insisted.

Jackson held up his hands. "I wasn't trying. You don't have to twist my arm too tightly. I'll pull the car up. See you in a few."

"Yep," said Berg, turning on the red brick sidewalk and heading back toward the restaurant.

The streets were quiet, mostly Georgetown students moving from friends' apartments or returning from happy hour at one of several dozen bars or nightclubs within easy walking distance of the university. The closer to the weekend, the more hectic and chaotic the streets would get. He reached Thirty-Sixth Street, the restaurant's entrance visible just past an annoyingly oversized black Suburban blocking his way. The SUV stayed in place, the driver's silhouette barely visible through the tinted glass. He waited a few moments, deciding to walk behind the vehicle.

Some self-important asshole in the back was no doubt distracting the driver. Even the most modest homes in Georgetown often housed diplomats, politicians, or generationally wealthy families. None of whom cared the slightest about a man on a mission to retrieve fifty dollars' worth of Italian wine.

The Suburban's rear cargo doors sprang open, unleashing a blur of darkly dressed figures wearing ski masks. Before Berg could react, a hood was jammed over his head, turning his view pitch black. He pulled fruitlessly hard against the strong hands gripping his arms. A quick sideward jab from his right foot connected with something solid, producing a snap and an agonized groan. The grip on his right arm instantly tightened, his attacker's weight pulling Berg toward the street.

Berg's body locked in place, an incredible pain radiating from his stomach. The pain continued, along with an inability to voluntarily move. All he could do was fall to his knees. When his knees hit the pavement, he was lifted and pulled into the back of the Suburban by multiple hands. He heard the doors slam shut and somebody yell, "Let's go!" The Suburban lurched forward.

Despite the residual pain and the oversized man literally sitting on him in the rear cargo compartment, he had enough mental clarity to determine that they had turned left, heading in Darryl's direction. Berg genuinely hoped he hadn't inadvertently killed his friend by inviting him to dinner.

"What about the other one?" said a voice.

"Negative. Get us out of here. I guarantee we had a witness or two," replied a voice from the front of the SUV.

A few seconds later, the team leader spoke again.

"Scorpion, this is Stinger. Grab successful. Primary target undamaged. No collateral business."

Undamaged?

He didn't like the sound of being delivered undamaged. That implied someone else wanted to damage him.

"Possible street-level, passerby detection. No cameras in vicinity."

Jesus. How long had they been watching and waiting for the perfect opportunity? He couldn't have set it up better for them unless he'd opened one of the rear passenger doors and invited himself inside.

"Copy that. We're about thirty minutes out," said the voice.

Thirty minutes until his status would most likely change from undamaged to damaged. Very damaged. He hoped Jackson acted fast. His friend had nearly died laughing when Berg explained the details of the insurance policy he had arranged. The laughing stopped when he explained the steps and passed along the information Jackson needed if he disappeared.

Berg wasn't sure if he stopped laughing because he took it seriously, or he'd written Berg off as clinically paranoid. Either way, he prayed that Jackson hadn't tossed the information in the trash. Karl Berg hadn't been grabbed for a stern "talking to" by True America goons. He was ultimately headed for permanent retirement, in a crematorium, plastic tub of acid, or tied to a block of concrete in the middle of the Chesapeake Bay. In his contorted, pretzel-like position, he managed to inch one of his hands along his right shin. It was all in Jackson's hands now.

Chapter 29

Georgetown
Washington, D.C.

Darryl Jackson squeezed between his front bumper and a minivan that hadn't been there when he parked the car with Berg.

"Goddamn. Get any closer?" he muttered, remembering the vast space separating the minivan and the car in front of it.

A black Suburban zoomed past, headed east on the tight street at an extremely unsafe speed.

"It's not the interstate, you fucking idiot," he said a little louder.

Jackson looked around the minivan to make sure the first SUV wasn't part of some VIP convoy. Especially the diplomats. They wouldn't even stop if they hit you. They'd drive to the embassy and dial it in ten minutes later. No harm, no foul. Diplomatic immunity. Satisfied that the streets were safe, he got in his car and spent the next minute inching backward and forward between the minivan and the car parked uncomfortably close behind him. Berg was probably swigging from the bottle at this point.

He arrived at the corner of Prospect and Thirty-Sixth Street, assuming Berg would be waiting for him on the side of the street. A quick look around killed that thought. A few students walked past the restaurant entrance on Thirty-Sixth, turning west on Prospect, toward the university. Jackson eased the car through the intersection slowly, still not seeing Berg. His friend was probably still inside, dealing with the wine. He parked between the no-parking sign and corner of Thirty-Sixth, far enough into the pedestrian crosswalk for Berg to see him if he emerged from the restaurant, and waited.

Jackson considered himself to be a patient man, but when three minutes passed and Berg didn't appear, he started to get impatient. Karl knew a lot of people in this town, and it wasn't unlike him to get distracted by an acquaintance, particularly a lady friend. In fact, it wouldn't surprise him in the least to find Karl inside, chatting it up with someone and generously sharing the rest of the bottle. Tonight wasn't going to be that night. He still had to drop Karl off at his apartment and check in to the hotel.

He left the car double-parked and headed into the restaurant, where the hostess immediately approached him with the corked bottle of Barolo.

"I thought you might be back," she said, holding it out for him. "It's a wonderful bottle."

"It is," he barely uttered, searching the restaurant for Karl.

"Is everything all right?" asked the hostess.

He absently took the bottle. "My friend didn't come back inside?"

"I've been here since the two of you left. By the time the bottle reached me, I didn't see either of you on the street. I went outside to check. Sorry."

"No. That's…uh, that's fine. Do you mind holding onto this while I check the men's room? Just in case. He was supposed to have grabbed the wine and waited outside."

"Sure. No problem."

The bathroom was empty, and he returned to the hostess with a bad scenario developing in his head.

"Didn't find him?"

He shook his head. "You didn't happen to see a black government-looking Suburban around a few minutes ago, did you?"

"Absolutely. It sat at the stop sign for a little longer than usual. I thought it might be some kind of VIP drop-in. I even looked through the reservation book to see if I could create a table, just in case."

Jackson stood in front of the hostess stand and looked at the street. "You couldn't see the entire vehicle. Right?"

"Just the front, really."

They took him. Those motherfuckers had actually grabbed him off a public street, in front of a restaurant. Karl must have been onto something bigger than he guessed. He started for the door.

"Sir? Your wine," said the hostess.

Jackson didn't reply. He hustled down the sidewalk and got into his car, opening the dashboard and removing a concealable holster. He released his Sig Sauer P228 from the holster and placed it on the front passenger seat along with two spare magazines. The pistol was far from legal in the District of Columbia, but so was snatching people off the street. He shifted the car into drive and continued west on Prospect Street until he found a parking spot just past the "Welcome to Georgetown University" sign.

He grabbed the pistol and spare magazines and got out of the car, quickly concealing them on his way toward the campus. He needed to make a call, and he couldn't make it from his car. They might have bugged it. In fact, he wasn't sure it was a good idea to use it until he could sweep it for electronics. He'd have to do that from the tow lot. Without a parking sticker, the car wouldn't last the night parked on campus.

With that in mind, he returned to the vehicle to get the concealable holster. No reason to raise any alarms with the D.C. police. They had a tendency to take unauthorized firearms seriously in this town and would be on the lookout for him by morning. Jackson couldn't afford to be stopped at this point. His friend's life depended on it.

Chapter 30

Downers Grove, Illinois

Daniel pulled the covers past Jessica's shoulders and kissed her on the forehead. Whatever they had given her had been potent, delivered by an auto-injector. He found the nasty wound it had inflicted on her right thigh. This hadn't been a little EpiPen. Something far more serious, like the kind of injectors used in the military-issued Mark I kits to counter the effects of a nerve gas attack. The thick needle had been powerful enough to penetrate her jeans.

He had no idea how long she'd be out, but he wanted to be the first face Jessica saw when she opened her eyes. She'd likely seen her mother stabbed right in front of her, unable to stop the man or make a sound to help her. He had no idea what kind of mental state she'd be in when she woke, but he assumed it would not be a good one. He needed to be there to hold her, make sure she knew everything was safe.

Once she was ambulatory, he would contact the private jet company and expedite their departure, no matter what the price. They had a number of jets on standby in the area, and he wanted be on one capable of a nonstop flight to Anguilla as soon as possible. He kissed her again and stepped out of the room, leaving the door open wide enough to hear if she called out. Not that he planned on being out of her sight for long.

The bedroom hallway led directly into the dining room, where Anish Gupta and Timothy Graves, long-standing members of the team's electronics warfare branch, sat next to each other at the dining room table, their open laptops illuminating their faces. The usual array of wires, power cords, black boxes, and other gear cluttered the table. Daniel once again marveled at the electronic miracles they could work with that mess.

He felt oddly comfortable having them here. Their type of warfare might as well be magic spells and potions as far as he was concerned.

Daniel was far from a technophobe, having been extensively trained in the use of commercial and military-grade encryption devices, communications gear, and electronic field gear, but he was just an end user. Guys like Graves and Gupta stood on the cutting edge of technology, creating the gear and carving out the cyber advantages that gave people like Daniel and Sanderson an edge. It was easy to take them for granted.

Nights like this reminded him how critical they could be to the success of an operation, not that he needed reminding with these two. He'd heard the stories about Uruguay. Graves had done more than type at a keyboard that day. Daniel leaned on the table with both hands, careful not to disturb any of their gear.

"Thank you."

"Any time," Graves said. "Good to see you again."

"We have to stop meeting like this, Daniel," Gupta added.

Graves looked at his counterpart.

"What? I've been waiting, like, a year to say that. It's funny," said Gupta.

"Don't quit your day job. The delivery is way off."

Daniel found himself laughing at and with them. The two made the oddest pair, but it worked brilliantly.

Graves inclined his head toward the bedroom door. "How is she?"

"I can't find any serious physical trauma beyond the injector site and the Taser probe holes. She has a nasty bruise on her ribs, probably from a kick, but nothing to stop her from getting on a plane and flying out of here first thing."

"You just got here," said Gupta, winking at Petrovich.

Graves groaned and shook his head. "See what I mean? Way off."

"I think your friend there is fucking with you," said Daniel. "Sorry to dime you out, Anish, but you shouldn't take advantage of your elders."

"He *is* old. I've told him that," said Gupta. "Glad to hear Jessica is all right. The two of you gave us one helluva fucking scare."

"Thanks again. Seriously," said Daniel. "That Serbian guy was good. Snatched Jessica right out from under me."

"That didn't sound right," said Gupta.

Graves lightly hit the back of Gupta's head. "What's wrong with you?"

"He's fine. I still have a sense of humor," said Daniel. "I'm going to check in with the other wonder duo."

"Can you tell Munoz junior to take a break? I got this covered," said Gupta.

"What do you mean?"

"You'll see," said Graves, pushing his chair back. "I need one of those delicious-smelling coffees."

He found Munoz at the kitchen table, doing exactly what he expected—drinking coffee, presumably one of his own brands by the toasty aroma. Melendez stood by the couch in the TV room, peeking through the edge of the curtains.

"I thought we had cameras doing that job," said Daniel.

"I've seen these mofo's hack enough cameras to keep me awake twenty-four seven," Melendez replied.

Gupta yelled from the dining room, "We take active countermeasures to keep that from happening."

"And they take countermeasures to counter your countermeasures. It's a never-ending cycle of electronic cluster-fuckery, and I don't understand any of it."

"That's your real problem with it," said Gupta.

"I think you can stand down," said Daniel, looking to Graves for support.

Graves nodded. "He really does have it locked down."

Melendez relented, drifting toward the kitchen table.

"Fresh pot of the good stuff," said Munoz, motioning toward the simple coffee maker on the counter. "Best I could do with the paper filter."

"What's Sanderson's take on this?" asked Daniel.

"He's concerned," Munoz answered.

"Still? Does he know something we don't?"

He was getting out of there as soon as Jessica started coming around. Munoz could read it on his face.

"We're safe here. The town house isn't connected to Sanderson in any way. Airbnb."

"Air what?"

"Airbnb. It's an online service where people turn their homes into hotels," said Graves.

"Never heard of it," said Daniel.

"You need to get out more," said Munoz.

"If this is what *getting out* gets me, I'm happy hiding out for the rest of my years."

"I'm just messing with you," said Munoz. "Our only concern here is a nosy neighbor."

"The windowless van in the driveway isn't exactly inconspicuous," said Daniel.

"That's why we didn't bring it to the industrial park," said Graves. "We had it near the hospital, but not close enough to draw any connection."

"We'll be out of here soon anyway," said Munoz.

"Back to my original question," said Daniel. "What's bugging Sanderson?"

"The fact that Hadzic managed to orchestrate and conceal his escape, continued to elude authorities for the better part of a year, only to emerge in the United States as the ringleader of an elaborate kidnapping attempt."

Daniel nodded. "It does boggle the mind."

"He doesn't think money alone would be enough to pull it off," said Munoz.

"State sponsored?"

"That's what he's thinking."

"Russia," said Melendez.

"Sanderson's program has certainly dealt them a few serious blows over the past few years, and your remarkable resemblance to Marko Resja, made public by the war crimes tribunal, wouldn't be a stretch to connect."

"Why go through the trouble of using Hadzic?"

"Deniability. Impact." Munoz shrugged. "Let's be honest, the Russians undoubtedly have some unsavory characters available for brutal and sadistic work, but Hadzic would have taken it to the next level. Sanderson is convinced it was the Russians, going for the heart and soul of the Black Flag organization."

"Sounds a little melodramatic."

"If Hadzic's plan had succeeded, think of the impact," said Munoz. "Seriously, give it some thought relative to the program."

Daniel hadn't thought about it like that. He'd justifiably been focused on Jessica and himself. If Hadzic had pulled off his twisted plan and created a video even a fraction as graphic as the one Jessica had made of Srecko's nephew's demise…just the thought of it made him sick. The impact would have sent shockwaves through Sanderson's ranks. An unmistakable message. Fuck with Mother Russia again, and you're next. The ultimate anti-recruitment video.

"So now what?" said Daniel. "I'm one flight away from disappearing for good."

"On *La Ombra*?" said Munoz.

Daniel tried his best not to react.

"Don't worry. Sanderson is pretty sure your secret remains intact. If the Russians knew where to find you, they could have sent Hadzic straight to Anguilla. It would have been a lot easier to grab you on a deserted stretch of Route One coming back from one of your favorite places on the northwest coast. Probably could have set up shop at your house on Lockrum Bay."

"Fucking Sanderson," Daniel growled.

Munoz started to open his mouth, but stopped, pausing for a few seconds before proceeding. "I don't need to say what I was about to say."

"I know," said Daniel. "Thank you. All of you. If it wasn't for Sanderson's close interest in my well-being and your high give-a-shit level, things would have turned out very differently for us."

"I might have substituted give-a-shit for dedicated professionalism," said Munoz, cracking a grin.

"Fuck you, Jeff. You get what you get."

"Don't get upset. Works for me," said Munoz. "Grab a cup of my world-famous coffee."

"I didn't realize you had a piece of the world market," said Melendez.

"I've shipped it to Canada."

Daniel laughed along with them, but his mind was on Jessica and the long journey ahead of them. The more he pondered Sanderson's suspicions about the Russians' involvement in this fiasco, the more he wanted to get on with his plan to take *La Ombra* through the Panama Canal and into the wide-open Pacific. The possibilities felt endless, their anonymity nearly guaranteed. A second, darker path appeared to Daniel, steering him in the direction of the puppet masters responsible for sending Hadzic to rape and murder his wife. Nothing good would come from that path, but he saw it anyway, and it held a frightening appeal.

Chapter 31

Salta Province
Argentina

Sanderson stood alone in the worn hillside lodge, stoking a dying fire. He'd probably be up most of the night, waiting for the final word from Munoz. The general's suspicion had been right about Jessica's mother. More like an instinct. Mostly self-preservation. He simply couldn't afford the numerous risks presented by the capture of either Petrovich, or the emotional burden of consigning them to the kind of fate their long list of enemies would impose.

Daniel and Jessica stood on the precipice of escaping the past, a rare triumph in this business. Few walked away, and not because they were trapped. Most stayed because it was in their blood, part of their programming long before they ever turned up at a military recruiter's office, Langley, or wherever their formal training started. They were different. Some far more than others, and the Petroviches were no exception.

Jessica hadn't been recruited because she spoke Serbian and studied international relations at a top university. A seasoned recruiter had seen something more. An unquantifiable quality that set her apart from thousands of college students graduating the same year. She was indisputably hardwired for this kind of work and had embraced it openly.

Her husband was a slightly different story. Same hardwired affinity, with an annoying, but ultimately useful twist. Daniel's pathological aversion to authority nearly disqualified him from the original Black Flag program. The program evaluation survey he unwittingly completed while on active duty in the Navy suggested he was a troublemaker. The fitness reports filed by the commanding officer of his ship confirmed it.

Petrovich hadn't assimilated into the regular Navy for one simple reason: he couldn't stand authority, an aspect of his personality somehow missed while he was in the Naval Reserve Officers Training Corp

(NROTC) at Northwestern University. The fact that he had come from a Serbian home and spoke fluent Serbian made his file hard to throw away without a one-on-one interview.

Sanderson was sold on Petrovich within the first few minutes of the meeting. It had nothing to do with his answers. He just had a quality about him that the general trusted would be right for the program. His instinct had been richly rewarded. Without question, Daniel had turned out to be the pinnacle of the program's success, even though he could be an insufferable pain in the ass most of the time.

His satellite phone on the table behind him chirped and buzzed. He hoped to hear that Jessica was awake and the Petroviches could be moved to the airport shortly. He was anxious to get the rest of the team out of the country. If the Russians were ultimately behind Hadzic's revenge plot, there was no telling what else his Commie friends might have set in motion. It was better to corral the troops and wait. Maybe dig for some answers through Karl Berg, though he strongly suspected Karl had been effectively cut out of the loop at the CIA.

Sanderson didn't recognize the number displayed on the phone. Interesting.

"Hello. With whom do I have the pleasure of speaking?" he said, taking the call.

"Stand by to authenticate your identity. Kilo-bravo-echo-victor identifier," said an unfamiliar voice.

Very interesting.

"Wait one," said Sanderson, pulling an encrypted mobile phone from one of his cargo pockets. He quickly found what he needed under the contact "Karl Berg Emergency Verification."

"I authenticate sierra-bravo-two-niner-eight-seven-delta-romeo-four."

"Copy your last," said the voice. *"I authenticate delta-fife-tree-echo-one."*

"It's a pleasure to finally speak with you, Mr. Jackson, though I suspect this will not be under pleasant circumstances."

"You got that straight, and you can call me Darryl," Jackson said. "Karl Berg was abducted about forty minutes ago."

"Shit," was all Sanderson could manage.

Berg and the Petroviches on the same night? He'd been right. Something big was going down.

"Shit is right. I'm on foot right now, making sure none of these fools are following me," said Jackson. "You don't sound surprised."

"Something similar almost happened to an operative closely linked to a few of Karl Berg's past operations."

"I don't want to know any of the details," said Jackson. "The less I know, the better."

"You supplied the hardware for a number of those operations."

"Son of a bitch," muttered Jackson.

"What exactly happened, Darryl?"

"I had dinner with Karl at a restaurant in Georgetown. He went back to the restaurant to get a bottle of wine I forgot to take with me, and by the time I drove down the street to pick him up, he was gone. He never made it into the restaurant. The only clue I have is a big-ass black Suburban sitting at the stop sign right around the same time. Same vehicle nearly ran me over speeding out of the area."

"You're absolutely sure he didn't pull a disappearing act?" said Sanderson. "He was working on something you might say was slightly on, but mostly off the books."

"No way he would pull something like that on me. He knows you'd be the first person I called if he didn't check in."

"Check in?"

"Yeah. He emails, texts, and leaves me a daily coded message every fucking day. I thought he was nuts. You didn't know about the check-ins?"

"No. I just have some emergency verification codes," said Sanderson. "How long has he been doing this?"

"Ever since those lunatics took over Washington," said Jackson. "You really don't know more than those codes?"

"That's it. I'm not even sure how I can help in this situation," said Sanderson. "I hate to say it, but he's gone, Darryl."

"Not exactly."

"What do you mean?"

"Karl took out a little insurance policy when True America swept into town," said Jackson.

"I don't think True America has anything to do with his abduction."

"Karl certainly seemed convinced they might pull something like this. What's your theory?"

"The other kidnapping attempt I mentioned was stopped dead in its tracks, and we most definitively linked it to a Serbian crime syndicate, but I think the whole thing was orchestrated and funded by the Russians. This operative worked closely with Berg to give Moscow a serious black eye.

This is not a coincidence."

"I don't know if that makes me feel more paranoid or less than I already am," said Jackson.

"He was smart to put together an insurance policy, but it won't do him any good. Threatening to leak classified information about the full scope of True America's involvement in that mess is like pointing your gun at the wrong target."

"Who said anything about information?" said Jackson. "Berg took out a different kind of policy, and he explained exactly how you would cash it in."

"Something tells me this is going to sound crazy."

"You have no fucking idea," said Jackson.

Chapter 32

Downers Grove, Illinois

Daniel had barely drifted to sleep, holding Jessica, when he heard footsteps coming down the carpeted hallway. He rolled onto his back and snatched the pistol from the nightstand, returning to his original position with the pistol hidden behind his leg.

"Daniel," someone whispered from the hallway, "you awake? We need you in here right away. Karl Berg has been kidnapped."

"I'll be right there."

He was half-tempted to open the bedroom window and disappear with Jessica. Daniel wasn't sure how far he'd get in the suburbs carrying an unconscious woman over his shoulder with a pistol tucked into his pants, but it had to beat sticking around here. He muttered a few curses and got out of bed, taking a few moments to steel himself for a tough decision.

Graves and Gupta had already started packing up their electronics mess when he reached the dining room. Munoz and Melendez sat across from each other at the kitchen table, a small teleconference device between them.

"He's here," said Munoz.

"*About time,*" Sanderson's voice came over the phone's speaker. "*We thought you had fallen back asleep.*"

"I'm not sticking around, if that's what you're going to suggest."

"*You're not gonna get very far alone with an unconscious woman,*" said Sanderson.

"You must be reading my mind," said Daniel. "I'll have my good friends drop me off at the jet park terminal. They have sleeper couches in private rooms for the privileged class."

"*The team doesn't have time for that kind of detour. They need to be in the Washington, D.C., area as quickly as that van can deliver them, or Karl Berg dies. Along with any hope of getting to the bottom of these kidnappings.*"

"You know where Berg is being held?" Daniel asked.

"*Not yet.*"

"We both know how this works. Unless you know something I don't, Karl Berg is gone."

"It's my job to know more than you, Daniel," said Sanderson. *"More than you think I know. We have a window of opportunity to find Berg."*

"And that window will be closed by the time we drive from here to D.C."

"Actually, if the team left within the next fifteen minutes and drove straight through the night, you could arrive two hours before the window opens. With traffic, it will be a lot tighter."

"Or we might not make it. We're obviously not talking about an assault window," said Daniel.

"Yes and no. You might not believe what I'm about to tell you, but I've been assured that it's true. Karl Berg had a transmitter implanted in his leg a few months ago."

"He had a GPS tracker implanted in his leg?" said Daniel. "That's like the size of a cell phone."

"They have smaller versions, but that's not what he used," said Sanderson. *"The device implanted in his leg is cutting-edge industrial espionage technology. It transmits a virus that specifically targets Wi-Fi receptors, co-opting the Wi-Fi enabled phone or computer. The applications for this kind of device are limitless, but Berg chose one function. Location flagging. The virus will continuously update and upload the infected devices' locations to a website accessible by our team."*

"What if they're underground or in a remote location?" said Munoz.

"I'm told it doesn't matter. It'll send undetectable calls. Geo-locate by known IP addresses. Daisy-chain with other wireless devices. Like everything, I'm sure this thing has its limitations, but if he's anywhere within a twenty-mile radius of D.C., odds are good that we're going to locate him. Then it's a matter of doing what we do best."

"Just us?" said Munoz.

"No. I'm gathering a small flock for this one. You'll have Daly, Mazurov, Foley, and Sayar, plus Darryl Jackson. He's ex-military, but not an operator. Jackson is the one that brought this to my attention, and he's good friends with Berg. You treat him like one of the family."

Timothy Graves joined the conversation. "General, it's Graves. Tell me a little more about this window. Why can't I log into the website now and find him? Your operatives are excellent, but the F.B.I's Hostage Rescue Team isn't shabby, and they could probably kick in some doors in a few hours instead of half a day."

"I asked the same question, but Berg has thought this through," said Sanderson. *"He set a fourteen-hour delay for a couple of reasons. First, he figured they would move*

him around a few times if they intended to interrogate him, so he wanted the signal to activate at his final location."

"Fourteen hours?" said Melendez. "Break out the SCUBA gear. He'll be at the bottom of Chesapeake by then."

"Possible. The other reason is related to battery life."

"That shouldn't be an issue if a device is hijacked," said Graves. "Unless…"

"You've probably figured it out. If this is a state-sponsored operation, the attackers will likely possess devices with automated virus scan capability and shifting encryption protocols. There's a distinct possibility the devices will repeatedly purge the infection, requiring the transmitter to regularly reengage the device. We're talking a small transmitter, with limited battery power. Berg wanted a rescue team in place and ready to go when it started transmitting."

"Then we're burning precious time," said Munoz. "We can hash this out on the road."

"I'll put you in touch with Jackson once you're mobile," said Sanderson.

"And I'll send you a postcard from the Pacific," said Daniel.

An uncomfortable pause ensued, broken by Sanderson.

"You're gonna turn your back on Karl Berg?"

"My number one priority is taking care of Jessica," he said, pausing for what he knew would be a controversial statement. "And I don't owe Karl anything."

"I wonder what Jessica might say?"

"Well, considering the last thing she saw was her mother murdered right in front of her, I'm willing to bet she'd like to get on a plane and get the fuck out of here. Karl Berg will be the least of her priorities."

"Daniel, you can't run from this."

"That sounds like a line from a shitty movie," said Daniel.

"You know it's true. One attack I can write off, though Srecko Hadzic's stunt is a damn hard sell as a self-orchestrated incident. Now Berg is snatched off the street in front of a popular Georgetown restaurant? Trust me. This is just the beginning unless we drive a stake through this thing's heart right now."

"Then why are we still talking about this?" said a tired female voice, turning all of their heads toward the dining room entrance.

Jessica stood with one of her arms draped over Timothy Graves's shoulder. Graves held her steady as she trudged on unsteady legs toward one of the empty chairs. Daniel rushed over and helped her into the seat.

"How are you, Jess?" he asked, looking into her barely focused eyes.

"I feel like throwing up," she said, catapulting Melendez into action.

He placed the kitchen trash bin next to her in time to catch whatever she still had in her stomach from dinner. Jessica heaved a few more times, then sat up and took several deep breaths. Daniel knelt behind the chair, holding her tightly. Her body trembled in his grip.

"I think you should lie back down," he whispered in her ear. "I can have us on a direct private flight in a few hours."

"We're not leaving until this is finished," she said in a low voice. "Russians? Is that who we're dealing with?"

"Jessica, I can't tell you how relieved I am to hear your voice," said Sanderson. *"And yes, evidence strongly suggests the Russians are behind this."*

"Evidence?" said Daniel. "You don't even have circumstantial evidence! More like a theory."

"It's a moot point. Neither attack is an isolated incident, and we have an opportunity to identify the source. Unless you can revive Srecko Hadzic from the dead and reconstruct the circumstances surrounding his escape."

"We weren't given that opportunity," said Daniel.

"Then we need to make the best of this opportunity," said Sanderson. *"And while I'm certain the team could handle this without you, I'd feel much better if you were directly involved. No offense, Jeff, but he's better at the direct-action stuff. Even in his slightly deteriorated state."*

"There was never any question about it," said Munoz, shaking his head with a smile.

"Jessica?" started Sanderson. *"Do I really need to say any more? We need both of you on this one. If this whole transmitter thing turns out to be a bust, you're on a flight within the hour."*

"Let's get this show on the road," said Jessica.

"Are you absolutely sure?" Daniel asked. "This could turn out to be a deep rabbit hole."

"We never climbed out of the first one," she said. "Karl has always looked out for me."

Daniel pressed his head into hers and held it there for a few seconds.

"All right. We're in."

Chapter 33

Oakton, Virginia

Karl Berg sat in the pitch darkness on a sturdy wooden chair, his hands tightly bound to its back and his ankles to its thick legs. He guessed the chair was somehow bolted to the wood-planked floor, since his earlier attempts to budge the chair had absolutely no effect. A concentrated earthy smell dominated the air. Dirt and mildew—his favorite combination. From the light cast by his captors' flashlights when his hood had been removed, he'd noticed thick, rough-hewn wooden girders running parallel across the planked ceiling. The shafts of light played across a few vertical wood beams connected to the girders.

His best guess was that he sat in a farmhouse cellar in Maryland or Virginia, not too far from the D.C. Metro area. The trip hadn't lasted long enough, and his captors had been in a hurry to reach this destination. They'd grabbed him off a public street, which always carried a risk. A random witness could call in the abduction, putting the police on alert. Anything was possible in a crowded city, so they'd expedited his journey to a prepared location.

Judging by his surroundings, Berg assumed this would be his final destination. The end of the road. Hopefully they'd start his interrogation with a long period of isolation to "deprive the senses and disorient" before moving on to less subtle methods. Fourteen hours ideally. His prospects were dashed moments later when a light spilled down a crudely framed staircase built along what appeared to be an ancient fieldstone wall. He was most definitely in an old farmhouse—with no Wi-Fi. Even the cellular service might be spotty out here.

Three men descended the stairs and approached, one of them activating a lightbulb between the stairs and his chair. The man let go of the string attached to the bulb socket and shook his head. None of their faces were concealed, a foreboding sign in this line of work.

"We have a lot of ground to cover, Karl."

"Berg or Mr. Berg, please. Until we're properly introduced."

The man lashed out at him with a fist, connecting with his left cheek. The blow knocked his head back violently, straining his stiffened neck muscles.

"Don't fuck around, Karl. I'm sorry. Mr. Berg."

He got a better look at the man. Mid to early thirties. Athletic, but not overly muscular build straining his untucked, button-down long-sleeved shirt. Clean shaven. Closely trimmed hair—not buzz cut, but the sideburns had been taken too high. A former military guy that hadn't quite figured out how not to look military. The other two looked the same. All three wore thigh holsters over deep brown or khaki cargo pants. High-end, subdued-tone hiking boots. Their look screamed paramilitary contractor.

"Just trying to keep things civil," said Karl, forcing a smile.

One of the men chuckled. "Well, that's completely up to you."

"That's usually the way this works," said Berg.

"Good. Sounds like we've come to an understanding. You answer our questions and we keep things civil."

"That depends on the questions," said Berg.

The guy hit him again, a vicious downward punch striking his other cheek. A blast of pain rocked his head, blurring his vision for several seconds until he could focus again.

"You answer all of the questions," said his captor. "Without any bullshit, and to my complete satisfaction."

Berg considered his response and decided to go with the most painful option. "You really don't have a clue how this works," he said, shaking his head and grinning.

The man cocked a fist and fired it at Berg's face, catching the top of his quickly lowered head instead. Bones cracked, and the man stumbled back with a scream. Berg stared at him as he clutched his broken hand, the man's face a mix of anger and agony.

"Fuck him up good, but make sure he can talk," the guy said, wincing in pain. "I'll be back."

"Motrin and ice for now, but you'll need to get that looked at by a professional soon," said Berg.

"What the fuck did you just say?"

"Just trying to be civil," Berg said with a wink.

He never saw the blow that hit his stomach, knocking the wind out of him. It was going to be a long thirteen hours or so.

Chapter 34

Rockville, Maryland

Jessica dragged herself out of the van and walked stiffly toward one of the ground-floor rooms the team had grabbed. The early arriving members of the team had struggled to find vacant adjoining rooms in a proper motel with exterior doors, near D.C., settling for a location a lot less centralized than they'd hoped. Berg could be anywhere outside of the Beltway. For all they knew, he was five states away. It was all a mystery that they would resolve in a few minutes.

She reached the second-floor overhang in front of the hotel door and took a moment to stretch her legs and back. The effects of the sedative or tranquilizer, whatever those fucks had used on her, still had a grip on her. She had a splitting headache and still felt a little wobbly. Daniel opened the door before she could knock.

"Spying on me?" she asked.

"Trying. They're all set up. Less than a minute until showtime."

"I hope this works and he's not on a container ship in the Atlantic, headed for Russia."

"There's always that possibility," he said, ushering her inside.

The team had rearranged the furniture, pushing the double beds together and moving a table next to the narrow desk just beyond the foot of the beds, which served as the tech team's workstation. A low dresser sat next to the desk, strewn with most of the mess she'd seen in the dining room at the Chicago area location. Graves was busy connecting wires while Gupta sat in the only chair, watching his laptop screen intently.

Munoz and Melendez sat at the foot of the bed, looking over Gupta's shoulder, while a woman Jessica had never seen before splashed water on her face from the vanity sink in the back of the room. She had to be Erin Foley. The woman caught her glance in the mirror and nodded. Jessica returned the gesture.

A few more steps and she could see partially into the adjoining room. Sayar, who she'd worked with before, unpacked the team's gear with two unfamiliar men. It wasn't hard to guess who was who. Mazurov, a Black Flag graduate from Sanderson's original program, had to be about Daniel's age, pushing forty, except he didn't look like he'd stayed in the same top physical condition. The other guy didn't look a day over thirty and was built like an Olympic swimmer. Had to be Daly, a recently recruited SEAL.

They emptied the nylon bags methodically, placing everything on the opposite bed. Weapons, body-armor vests, communications gear, grenades. The kind of stuff you didn't want housekeeping to walk in on. A tall, annoyed-looking black guy appeared next to the bed, straightening out the gear and mumbling curse words. Jackson. She remembered him from the mission to stop True America. He'd begrudgingly delivered a cache of weapons that had made all the difference in that operation.

Daniel sat on the bed next to Munoz.

"Lie down or something," said Daniel. "You still look a little unsteady on your feet."

"I can manage to sit up," she said, leaning over to speak quietly. "How is Sayar doing? I was a little surprised to find out he was still around."

"This whole crew is kind of a patchwork, outside of Munoz and Melendez."

"Finally. A compliment," said Munoz.

"Don't get ahead of yourself," said Daniel, inching away from the eavesdropper.

"I have no idea what Foley has been doing. Sanderson thought he could bring her on board full-time, but the Russian Foreign Intelligence Service put a sizable bounty on her head after the Vektor raid, confirmed by the agency. Foley quit the CIA and dropped off the radar. Sanderson has kept in touch, but hasn't been able to convince her to leave the U.S. I don't blame her. She's probably only here because of Berg."

"How was she involved with Vektor?"

"She took out the Iranian scientist working on the bioweapons program at Vektor, along with his bodyguard. She also managed to steal the keycard that got them into the facility. She's good, from what I'm told."

"Mazurov? He looks a little—"

"Rusty?"

"That's one way to put it," she said.

Mazurov worked with the new Russian group operatives on an

occasional paid-contract basis for Sanderson. He'd spent close to ten years as a sleeper agent in Moscow, teaching school of all things. He played a part in something big around the time of the Vektor raid, but even Sanderson wouldn't say what he did."

"That leaves Daly, who just left the SEALs. He'll be sharp, but he hasn't trained with Sanderson's people."

"And then there's me," said Jessica. "This is like the Bad News Bears."

"I heard that," whispered Munoz. "You don't have to worry. We'll do the heavy lifting, like always."

"Funny," said Daniel.

Gupta sat up in the chair and started typing furiously.

"You got something?" asked Munoz, leaning forward to see.

"Fucking A. It worked," Gupta crowed. "I'm getting three independent signals, all clustered in the same location…in Oakton, Virginia. Let me synch this to a better map."

A satellite image of the area appeared, zooming down to street level. Gupta pulled the image back far enough for them to get the lay of the land. Foley rushed over, wiping her face with a towel.

"Looks like an uncrowded mix of one-acre lots, tighter subdivisions. Some land here and there. Target location is off Hunter Mill Road in an area with a lot of trees and not many roads."

"Zoom in on the signals again," Munoz requested.

All three signals were co-located within some kind of structure mostly obscured by trees. A home was visible between the hidden structure and Hunter Mill Road. Gupta centered the screen on the home without anyone asking.

"Do you think that's visible from the road?" asked Daniel.

"I don't know. It's a good tenth of a mile from the road. The target building is a hundred yards past that."

"I bet the target building is an old barn," said Foley. "This is a big lot compared to the rest, especially for a town this close to D.C. Not part of the subdivision around it. The original owners probably sold most of their land, but kept this one and a small parcel, which is why they kept the barn."

"That's quite an analysis," said Daniel.

"I grew up on a small farm in Connecticut. That's exactly what my parents did. They get crazy offers all the time because of the barn. Stockbrokers and hedge fund managers wanting to feel all country-like," she said, smirking.

"What kind of signals are we getting?" asked Graves.

"Cell phone. One had Wi-Fi enabled. The virus must have called the other phones and daisy-chained," said Gupta. "This is fucking brilliant technology."

"Is the system interactive?" asked Graves. "Can you ask it to daisy-chain with other devices?"

"I'm not seeing an interface, and I get the impression we're not hacking into this system any time soon."

"Probably not," said Graves.

"I guarantee we're dealing with more than three hostiles," said Munoz. "It would be nice it if gave us more."

"That's not its job, but I think we might get what we we're looking for. The virus clearly felt the need to hijack three phones," Graves explained.

Jessica shook her head. "You're talking about it like it's alive."

"In a technology sense, it *is* alive, or smart," said Graves. "It hijacked three phones, presumably to ensure continuity of signal. It had one, then decided to spread, but it didn't go any further. It mapped the closest three devices, probably some kind of parameter set by the programmer. I bet if one of our hostiles gets too far away from Berg, the virus will daisy-chain to someone closer, maintaining the three closest points. It might morph strategies altogether and expand to more than three."

"I guess we have another decision to make," said Munoz.

"What's that?" said Daniel.

"Do we wait until dark, or hit them in broad daylight?"

"It's already been fourteen hours," said Foley. "The chances of finding him alive grow slimmer by the minute."

"We don't have the right night-vision gear to make the best of the darkness," said Daly, standing in the doorway between rooms. "I counted two sets of goggles and one unmounted scope. No dual-beam lasers mounted to the rifles. Two of us can walk around in the dark, but that's about the extent of it. If we're up against professionals that plan on sticking around through the night, they'll have all the right gear."

"Nobody's forcing you to use any of the gear," remarked Jackson from the other room. "I'm sure that Spyderco knife clipped to your belt will be a real force multiplier combined with your bare hands."

"I'm not complaining," said Daly. "We can work with this."

"Then that's it," said Munoz. "Let's start moving toward the target. Graves and Gupta, I want you mobile and as close to this location as possible. Sayar and Mazurov will provide security. Start looking for a suitable drop-off point along one of the roads behind the property. It doesn't have to be perfect, we just need a few seconds to slip into the woods."

"Got it," said Graves.

The room erupted in a beehive of activity, everyone but Graves and Gupta moving into the other room to kit up. Jessica followed Daniel toward the door, but was stopped by Munoz.

"Jess, you have to sit this one out."

"I'm not leaving her alone," said Daniel.

"Then I guess you're not coming along either," said Munoz. "We can manage."

"I'm fine, Danny," said Jessica. "Seriously. Get Berg and get back in one piece. I'm not going anywhere."

Daniel stared at her, obviously torn about the decision.

"Let me rephrase this. I will forever think less of you if you don't go with them," she said firmly. "We owe this to him. He's stuck his neck out for us before."

He paused for a long time, a neutral look on his face. "I'm doing this for you," he said after the long silence. "Nobody else. And when I get back, we're out of here. You need some serious downtime."

"Thank you," she said. "This is the right thing to do."

"No, it isn't, but it's what I'm gonna do. For you," he said, disappearing into the other room.

Munoz grabbed her arm. "I won't let anything happen to him."

Despite the fact that Munoz's statement was one hundred percent, pre-mission pep-talk bullshit, it somehow made her feel better. She felt safe with these people. It was the one thing she would miss about this life.

Chapter 35

Oakton, Virginia

Daniel lay between two trees on the northern border of the gap between the farmhouse and the barn. He'd been here for close to thirty minutes, scanning the property with his binoculars for mobile sentries, finding none. Melendez had reported the same from the southern side. The woods were clear to the east. The entire team had confirmed that on the way in.

Graves had found a cul-de-sac connected to a trail that abutted the far eastern edge of the property. Jackson dropped them off at the trailhead and met the van in the parking lot of the Unitarian Universalist Congregation of Fairfax less than a quarter of a mile away. They'd lucked out with that spot. Berg was being held in the middle of an affluent D.C. suburb, where windowless vans parked on the side of the road tended to draw attention.

The western part of the property looked clean from Daniel's position. Their only blind spot was the farmhouse's front porch, a reasonable place to expect a sentry. Back far enough away from the road to avoid detection, with a commanding view of the only passable vehicle approach. A second sentry had emerged from the sliding glass door at the rear of the house and stepped out onto the sprawling covered deck to smoke a cigarette. He'd gone back inside as soon as he was finished.

That brought the likely total to six; five confirmed. The virus had behaved precisely like Graves had predicted. One of the original three targets had left the barn and gone inside the house, "infecting" another member of the team. It hadn't been the man they observed smoking. The signal remained stationary inside the house when he'd passed along the observation. They now had three in the barn, two in the house, and one possibly on the front porch. All in all, a manageable number.

Security was minimal at the site, but he guessed the property's present occupants hadn't anticipated any kind of external threat. Why would they? Oakton, Virginia, was Anytown, U.S.A., if you had a sizeable bankroll. This place looked as sleepy and boring as a well-manicured suburb could get. They'd probably changed vehicles to something more family friendly on the way here and pulled in without raising an eyebrow. The house was owned by a corporation that Graves and Gupta would thoroughly investigate later.

"*Overwatch report,*" he heard through his ear mic.

Melendez reported all clear. Daniel took a final look around without the aid of binoculars.

"Oscar Two clear."

"*Copy,*" said Munoz. "*No change to the plan. Initiating assault. Three. Two. One. Assault team moving.*"

Daniel limited his field of vision to the house, watching the structure over his scope. Any movement in the windows or doors would draw his undivided, scope-magnified attention. His job was to keep Munoz and his assault team undistracted from the team's primary mission—securing Karl Berg. He didn't envy Munoz's job. They were headed into the unknown, the numbers stacked even. Three on three. The presence of a hostage tipped the scales against them. They had to be careful where they sent their bullets. Their adversaries would have no such concerns.

He caught a brush of movement in the far second-story window of the farmhouse. The assault team had been made. Maybe security was a little tighter than they'd guessed.

"*Southwest corner. Oscar One engaging,*" said Melendez.

A man with a rifle hopped over the front porch banister and landed with a thud in the grass on Daniel's side of the house. This group didn't waste time.

"Oscar Two has a target heading front to back, north side of the house," said Daniel, shifting his rifle in the man's direction.

He wasn't in a big hurry. The scenario had played out in his head dozens of times since he'd arrived in the sniper's nest. Repeated snaps echoed across the open backyard, followed by the sound of breaking glass and splintering wood. Melendez wasn't taking any chances with the potential shooter in the far window.

Daniel stopped his scope's crosshairs on the southeast corner of the house, about five feet above ground level. The gunman from the front porch appeared in the scope, stopping at the corner to peek into the backyard. The suppressed Mk 12 Special Purpose Rifle (SPR) bit into Daniel's shoulder; a mottled red splotch exploding onto the white clapboard siding next to the man's head.

He shifted his crosshairs to the center of the back door and started to apply pressure to the two-stage trigger. When the door opened less than a second later, he eased the trigger the rest of the way, sending an Mk 262, match-grade bullet toward the empty space. A body rushed into the void and collided with the bullet, instantly toppling to the deck under a fine red mist.

"Oscar Two has one tango down southeast corner, ground level, and one tango down at the back door."

"Oscar One has one tango down far southwest window, second level. Confirming three total," reported Melendez. *"Continuing over watch."*

"Oscar Two continuing over watch."

"Alpha team breaching," said Munoz.

Now for the hard part—waiting for the rest of the team to do their job. A sharp crack sounded from the vicinity of the barn, followed a few seconds later by a long burst of gunfire erupting inside the barn. Three rapid, back-to-back gunshots answered the burst, and things got quiet. Their job had just gotten infinitely more complicated.

Chapter 36

Oakton, Virginia

Munoz simultaneously detonated the three charges spaced evenly against the barn's locked side door, knocking it off its hinges. He pushed the door out of the way and burst into the sunlit space, panning rapidly from left to right with his M4 carbine while hugging the wall to the left of the door. An extended burst of gunfire exploded from the depths of the barn in his peripheral vision. He centered his EOTech sight center mass on a man partially visible on the opposite side of the barn and fired twice. A third bullet fired from one of Munoz's teammates struck the gunman's head, snapping it backward. The body dropped below the floor, indicating the possibility of a staircase.

A quick glance to his right revealed a pair of motionless, contorted legs protruding into the barn from the outside. Daly covered the staircase while Munoz backtracked a few steps and peeked through the door. Foley's head was canted sideways, her eyes staring vacantly at nothing—a red dot visible just below her right eye. A ballistic helmet wouldn't have made a difference.

"One tango down. Hostage is located below ground level. Alpha Three is down," said Munoz.

He moved forward, searching the barn for a second shooter while Daly focused on what appeared to be a rectangular staircase-sized opening flanked by open trapdoors. Munoz signaled for Daly to stop. Any closer and someone in the basement could take a shallow-angled shot at them. He had a few other concerns too, having to do with the floor beneath them. It was solid earth, but he suspected that would transition to wood planks at some point closer to the suspected stairwell. If the planks weren't tightly laid, it might be possible for the two remaining hostiles to track their approach using the natural sunlight entering through the windows.

Munoz took a moment to analyze the situation. The opening was about fifteen feet away from the front of the barn, leaving him with the impression that it was the farm's original root cellar. The subterranean space probably started at the hole and extended to the front of the barn. It gave him a slightly clearer concept of his engagement zone.

A few more hand signals revealed his updated plan. Munoz lowered to the floor and slithered to the left of the opening, making sure he stayed below any possible sightlines into the cellar. He stayed on hard ground the entire time, confirming his suspicion about the room below. When he descended the stairs, the threat axis would be limited to a one-hundred-eighty-degree arc. Not exactly a narrow field, but it could be worse. He also had to worry about someone hiding under the stairs.

A double nod set everything in motion. Daly lobbed a flash-bang grenade into the cellar while Munoz scrambled across the dirt floor toward the top of the stairs. When the flash-bang grenade immediately sailed back out of the wood-framed opening, headed back toward Daly, Munoz rolled off his back into a prone position at the top of the stairs and triggered his rifle-mounted flashlight.

The powerful light exposed a man with a submachine gun at the bottom of the stairs, who instinctively raised a hand to block the light. The first bullet from Munoz's rifle passed through the man's palm, striking him in the face. Two more bullets hit him in the neck and upper chest, knocking him backward. Munoz rolled away, narrowly missing a long fusillade of bullets splintering the wood floor where he had just lain.

"Hostile down. One hostile remaining," said Munoz.

With one shooter left and the angle of hostile fire established, Daly edged past the inert grenade he had thrown as a decoy and tossed a live flash-bang into the darkness below. Munoz added a second. When the first grenade detonated, Munoz lifted himself into a crouch at the top of the stairs, feeling a quick tap on his shoulder that indicated Daly was in position for the assault. The second blast jarred them into action.

Munoz and Daly rushed down the stairs in staggered formation, hopping to the right when they were clear of the ceiling. They triggered their lights and sought cover behind the closest support beams, searching for the last target through the thick cloud of freshly disturbed dust. A burst of gunfire erupted, the bullets smacking into the thick support beam in front of Munoz and peppering the staircase.

A bullet grazed his left leg and tugged at the right shoulder of his ballistic vest. Daly crouched behind his beam, pressing his hand into his thigh. When the bullets stopped flying, Munoz raised his rifle and scanned in the direction of the gunfire, fully aware he might take a bullet to the face. The rifle light was a bullet magnet, but it was the only way to penetrate the darkness and dust scattered by the flash-bang grenades.

He immediately located Berg secured to a chair toward the back of the cellar. A form shifted behind the CIA officer's naked body, the last hostile using his hostage as a shield to reload. Berg's face was bloodied and bruised. Multiple lacerations crisscrossed his chest and thighs. Mercifully, his manhood appeared undamaged. Berg squinted, confirming that he was still alive.

"Hostile is using Berg as shield," he said into the radio.

The former SEAL glanced in his direction, and Munoz gave him a quick hand signal. Daly nodded, then straightened up, pointing his rifle toward Berg. The CIA officer responded to the focused LED lights, turning his head.

"Withdraw your men immediately, or I'll kill him!" yelled the man hiding behind Berg.

Munoz and Daly remained silent, focused on their rifle sights.

"Backup is a few minutes out! You don't have time to think this over," said the man. "I already got what I needed out of him. You withdraw now, and Mr. Berg gets dropped off at the nearest ER. You have my word."

No response. Munoz took most of the pressure off his rifle's two-stage trigger. He could see an inch of the guy's head behind Berg's, which wasn't enough.

"Are you fucking crazy? You're going to get yourselves and Berg killed. That's not your mission!" the guy yelled. "If my backup gets here before you stand down, there's no deal."

A long pause ensued before their target raised his head a few inches above Berg's right shoulder. Two small holes appeared in the top of his forehead and Munoz rushed forward. He passed Berg, pausing to fire two bullets into the hostile's inert body.

"Hostile down," he said. "Berg is alive, but needs immediate medical attention. We'll need a vehicle on-site for extraction. Possible hostile backup en route."

"Juliet one copies, en route for pickup," said Jackson. *"Great work, gentlemen."*

"Echo team staying put," said Graves. *"I need to divert local law enforcement responding to reports of gunfire. They don't have an address, but they'll be crawling all over the area shortly."*

"Oscar One, set up sniper position facing Hunter Mill Road. Oscar

Two, clear the house. I don't want any surprises."

By the time he finished issuing the final orders, Daly had freed Berg from the chair.

"I want pictures of these guys, Scott. Grab their phones too. I'll take care of Berg," said Munoz. "Pass that along to Oscar Two."

He found Berg's clothes in a pile next to the chair, taking the time to dress him in his pants, stuffing his phone and wallet into a cargo pocket.

"We need to warn Audra Bauer," croaked Berg.

"Who's Audra Bauer?" said Munoz.

"CIA. She's in danger."

"We'll work on that once we get out of here."

"Call her now," Berg insisted.

"I need to move you ASAP," said Munoz, lifting him off the chair. "How far away is Bauer?"

"CIA. Langley."

"She's in the safest place she can be right now," said Munoz. "You ready to move?"

Berg nodded, grunting in pain as Munoz and Daly helped him out of the barn. Berg started to protest when they reached the barn's side door, Foley's body blocking their way.

"We need to keep moving," said Munoz.

Daly pulled her out of the way and lifted her lifeless body onto his shoulders.

"Leave her," said Munoz. "We don't have the time."

"No," growled Berg, not a hint of compromise in his voice.

Munoz relented, not sure how they were going to deal with a dead body. Berg represented enough of a challenge. Fortunately, one of their vehicles was essentially windowless.

"Echo team, we're going to need to make a transfer in the church parking lot," said Munoz.

"Copy that," said Graves.

"And as soon as you get the cops off our back, I need you to find us some private lodging and a doctor willing to make a house call. Berg is in bad shape."

"What's Alpha Three's status?" said Jackson.

"KIA."

Munoz had a strong feeling she wouldn't be the last. Something was way off with all of this.

PART THREE:

BLACK MAGIC

Chapter 37

Vienna, Virginia

Jackson couldn't hear what the doctor was saying through the closed French doors, but the young physician treating Karl Berg had behaved justifiably nervous upon first meeting his patient. Berg's wounds, while superficial, were extensive. Dozens of shallow cuts, evenly spaced and methodically applied to the front of his torso and legs, could not be explained away by a simple accident, or a complicated one. It was obvious that the wounds were intentionally inflicted, and Jackson would be skeptical too about the purpose of the private medical care he'd been summoned to provide.

The doctor stood up from the chair next to the brown leather couch and shook Berg's hand, sharing a few more words. Probably asking for the tenth time if Berg wanted him to call the police. The physician feigned a smile and made his way to the doors. Jackson got up from the chair he'd dragged into the hallway outside of the study.

"So what's the verdict?" he asked.

The physician glanced nervously around the spacious home.

"The man you just treated saved my life a number of years ago. I owe him everything. On top of that, he's my best friend. I know this doesn't look good, but trust me when I say that my friend is now in good hands. A few hours ago, that obviously wasn't the case."

"I don't want to know any of the details," said the doctor.

"All the better," said Jackson. "What are we looking at?"

"The patient needs rest, obviously. You need to keep him well hydrated and nutritionally satisfied."

"Yeah, yeah. That sounds like advice for a nursing home resident. Move on to the important stuff."

The doctor frowned. "Well, unfortunately, you're going to need to *treat* him like a nursing home resident for a week or two, maybe longer. Most of the cuts will heal on their own, with constant supervision. You'll need to clean them a few times per day, replace the gauze and tape. Watch for signs of infection. I left a bottle with some strong antibiotics that he should start taking immediately. Follow the instructions. I stitched a few of the deeper wounds. Same rules apply. The big thing here is that he needs to remain completely immobile until the shallow cuts scab over. I counted seventy-six separate wounds. I suspect a few of the deeper ones that I stitched could count twice, since there's evidence of repetitive injury."

"What does that mean?" said Jackson, pretty sure he had a good idea.

"I'd rather not speculate out loud," said the doctor. "Bottom line, he needs to stay still unless you want me to stitch up the remaining seventy wounds."

"I think we'd rather avoid that," said Jackson. "He's been through enough."

"That's an understatement. You have my secure email address. I'd prefer you use that if you have additional questions or concerns. Call this number," he said, producing a card with nothing but a phone number, "if you need me to visit before our next scheduled appointment."

"When do you need to come back?"

"I'd like to check on him in two days."

"Same time?"

"I'll be here. Email if there's a change to that plan," said the doctor.

"Thank you. I appreciate your timely response and discreet service."

The doctor smiled politely and walked to the front door. Jackson followed him onto the wide, wraparound porch, catching a glimpse of Melendez near the property's inner gate. The primary gate stood a quarter of a mile away, concealed by the thick woods surrounding the estate. Melendez opened the gate manually for the doctor's convertible Mercedes, securing it after him. Jackson waved, drawing a nod from the operative, who disappeared into the foliage with his sniper rifle. Back inside the spacious home he found Munoz in the entrance hallway.

"Berg was concerned about someone named Audra Bauer. She works at Langley, so I told him she's safe for now," said Munoz, checking his watch. "It's getting close to four o'clock. If she's somehow linked to Berg in all of this, she'll be next."

Jackson saw Berg motioning for him. "Speak of the devil."

"How are you feeling, my friend?" asked Jackson, approaching the couch.

"Like I have a thousand paper cuts," said Berg, through swollen lips.

"Seventy-six to be precise," said Jackson, eliciting a short laugh that looked like it hurt Berg more than helped. "Sorry, man. What can I get you? The place is stocked."

"I'll take that bottle of Barolo if it's still around," said Berg, causing himself to laugh and wince.

"Maybe we should knock off the jokes," Jackson suggested.

"I concur," said Berg, looking past Jackson to Munoz. "We need to warn Audra Bauer, a deputy director with the CIA. She was instrumental to stopping Reznikov in 2007, so she's one of us. She has to be in danger, especially now. Where are we?"

"We're safe," said Munoz. "This is one of a dozen or more properties in the D.C. area owned by Ernesto Galenden through his various international corporations. Sanderson called in a favor."

"Why do you think the Russians are after Bauer?" asked Jackson.

"Russians? Who said this was the Russians?" said Berg, trying to sit up.

"The doctor said you need to lie still, as in perfectly still, or you'll start leaking like a sieve again," said Jackson. "Did you hear what happened with the Petroviches?"

"Jesus," said Berg. "I knew something was off with that. I'm the one that asked Sanderson to keep an eye on them."

"That turned out to be a good call, possibly one that saved your life too. Srecko Hadzic came close to kidnapping Jessica in the hospital. Munoz and a small team managed to turn the tables on that. Hadzic is dead."

"Hadzic?" said Berg, looking utterly perplexed. "That's not poss—shit. How is that possible?"

"It's not, really. Unless you have some serious backing," said Munoz. "That's why Sanderson thinks this is a Russian job."

"The guys that took me weren't Russian," said Berg. "Military contractors, if I had to guess."

"There's some pretty sketchy groups out there. Could be a team hired out by the Russians through a proxy," said Jackson.

"To kidnap and torture a CIA officer?" said Berg. "How far down have some of these paramilitary contractor companies fallen?"

He ignored the obvious implication about Brown River. They'd been the first serious security contractor company to win major Department of Defense and State Department contracts, growing at a nearly unstoppable pace after 9/11. By the time other former military and security entrepreneurs jumped on the bandwagon and started to form similar companies, most of the available talent was taken. The rest of the companies fell between decent and crappy on the quality spectrum. Even Brown River had its quality inconsistencies from time to time.

"I don't mean to sound insensitive, Karl, but—"

"When has that ever stopped you?"

"It hasn't," said Jackson, deciding not to sugarcoat his question. "What the fuck did they want from you?"

"They wanted the name of my source in Moscow."

"Sounds like the Russians," said Munoz.

"They've had two years to pull this off," said Berg. "Now, all of a sudden, barely a few days after I'm passed new information from my informant, Moscow decides this is important? And they wanted to know everything I knew about Reznikov? I smell a rat, and it's not a Russian one."

"How do the Petroviches figure into this?" asked Munoz. "It looks like Jessica's mother was poisoned. Something that takes months to kill, like dimethylmercury."

"I don't know," said Berg, closing his eyes. They shot open a second later. "When did she get put into hospice?"

"Four days ago," Munoz replied.

"Right. And a local reporter decides out of the blue that it's big news and creates a whole story around her dad's sordid past. It felt contrived enough for me to warn Sanderson. Now it feels calculated, like everything else going on."

"You sound like the general," said Munoz. "Except he's convinced this is the Russians cleaning up loose ends related to Vektor."

"Somebody's cleaning up loose ends. I'm just not convinced it's the Russians. Our current administration also has a vested interest in permanently erasing any link to Reznikov."

"It sounds like we need to secure Bauer until this can be sorted," said Munoz. "Does she have family?"

"A husband that works in Tyson's Corner at a government think tank. Grown kids on the West Coast."

"Daniel is bringing Jessica back here. Maybe we should divert him to pick up Bauer's husband, so we can take that leverage out of the immediate equation."

Berg nodded. "I know David Bauer well enough. I'll give him a call. You have my phone?"

"Our tech team downloaded your contact list, call history, all that shit, well before we made our way here. I have a satellite phone for you and a tablet with all that information," said Jackson. "Your friends here don't take any chances."

"That's why I had you contact them," said Berg. "Nobody else could have pulled this off."

Munoz looked puzzled. "Why not have Ms. Bauer call her own husband?"

"Because I want to test a theory. If I'm wrong, this is the Russians, and we can all rest easy."

"Rest easy?" Jackson echoed.

"Yeah," said Berg. "Because if I'm right, we are most truly fucked."

Chapter 38

Falls Church, Virginia

Audra Bauer drove southwest on Lee Highway, approaching the Interstate 66 overpass. She'd left significantly later than usual from The George Bush Center for Intelligence, per Karl Berg's instructions. Late enough to take advantage of the fading sunlight on the way to their rendezvous if she detected she had picked up a tail. The other benefit was the traffic. While the roads in and around this area were always busy, they wouldn't be constrictive. Berg had insisted that this was important, once again, in case she needed to take evasive action.

She didn't know what to think of Karl's late afternoon call, heavy on wild conspiracy theories about the Russians and light on any verifiable facts or evidence. She'd almost hung up on him and called the Protective Services Division to arrange a Surveillance and Intervention team escort for herself. But Karl had used a long ago established code word toward the end of their conversation that meant her life was in immediate danger. He might have sounded unhinged, single-mindedly focused on the Russians again, but she didn't believe he'd play that card for any reason other than its intended purpose.

Now she was on the way to meet him at her favorite coffee shop in Falls Church, though she suspected he had different plans for the final location of their rendezvous. He'd told her to park in back and enter through the rear entrance. Bauer figured he'd intercept her in the parking lot and drive her somewhere else, in case she'd picked up a tail. She still wasn't one hundred percent convinced she'd go with him. It would all depend on how he looked and acted. She carried a stun gun and pepper spray in her coat pockets just in case he didn't take no for an answer.

Traffic on Lee Highway, a local two-lane state route, lightened significantly after the Interstate 66 exchange, the beltway artery grabbing late commuters headed to distant western D.C. suburbs. Glancing in her rearview mirror, she noted a few pairs of headlights following her into the heart of Falls Church.

Bauer intended to turn on East Columbia Street, a few blocks up, and drive around the neighborhoods, just to be certain she hadn't been followed. East Columbia Street was at the next stoplight, which she could see was green and had been green for a short while. She'd try to time her approach to run the light just as it transitioned from yellow to red.

As her car neared the intersection, it looked like the timing would work out. The light turned yellow just before she reached the point on the road where it opened into a left-turn-only lane. When the light immediately went from yellow to red, she pounded her fist on the wheel. The lights in the downtown area were erratic at best. It didn't matter. She'd still take a little trip through the neighborhoods, emerging on Broad Street.

Bauer triggered her car's turn signal and eased into the turn lane, rolling to a stop at the intersection. A black Town Car sedan with tinted windows pulled up to the light next to her two lanes over, next to the curb. Not an unusual sight at all in the D.C. area. She stared at the dark sedan for a few seconds, then returned her attention to the intersection. Catching her eye for a moment, a late model, oversized SUV started to turn onto North Washington Street from the direction she intended to take. She glanced up at the light, then back at the SUV, noticing that it had stopped right next to her car. Her right hand shot into her coat pocket. The rear passenger door was open; two men wearing ski masks were rushing her car.

Chapter 39

Falls Church, Virginia

Melendez watched the intersection through the second-floor corner window of the vacant, unleased building next to North Washington Street, on the opposite side of the westbound lanes. His earpiece crackled.

"This is echo one. Bauer is pulling up to Columbia. I need to cut the light short."

"Oscar One ready," said Melendez.

"Oscar Two on the way."

Oscar Two was composed of Sayar and Petrovich, who had parked in the far north reaches of an expansive parking lot across North Washington Street. They'd start moving through the lot, ready to run street-level interference if a threat emerged that Melendez couldn't handle. They had no idea if Bauer had been followed.

"Alpha One pulling into position."

Munoz was in charge of Alpha One, the team that would grab Bauer from her car. With Mazurov driving, Daly would assist with the transfer. It wouldn't take much to unravel this op. They were stretched precariously thin. A silver, four-door BMV sedan approached the intersection, slowing for the red light initiated by Graves and Gupta.

"Alpha One moving."

Melendez rapidly scanned the thin westbound traffic, focusing his attention on the black Town Car that pulled up to the light, two lanes over. A white SUV entered his field of view, screeching to a halt next to Bauer's sedan. He settled into the suppressed M110's fixed stock and pressed his right eye into the 4X ACOG sight, centering the green reticle on the Town Car's rear driver's side door, which sprang open moments later.

A single 7.62mm armor-piercing round struck the man that started to emerge from the car, knocking him back inside. Melendez methodically and rapidly fired tightly spaced groupings of bullets at the vehicle's most likely points of occupancy. The driver's window shattered last, the most obvious and immobile occupant taking the last rounds in the magazine. He reloaded, never taking his eyes off the Town Car. Sounds of a pitched struggle between Audra Bauer and Alpha One reached the second-story window.

Tires screeched to the east, momentarily pulling his attention away from the bullet-riddled sedan. An SUV lurched onto North Washington Street, pointing in Alpha One's direction.

"This is Alpha One. Engaging SUV headed toward the transfer point. Alpha Two, confirm black Town Car at intersection is neutralized," said Melendez, swinging his rifle in the direction of the new threat.

Melendez centered the reticle on the driver's side of the windshield and pressed the trigger three times as flashes of gunfire erupted from multiple points along the incoming SUV.

Shit.

He canted the rifle forty-five degrees and acquired the vehicle with the side-mounted unmagnified reflex sight, intent on suppressing the gunfire. Keeping the sight's red dot centered on the racing SUV, he repeatedly pressed the trigger until his thirty-round magazine ran dry.

Chapter 40

Falls Church, Virginia

Munoz's body locked in pain, the familiar static discharge sound of a stun gun filling the air. Bauer didn't waste the moment, pivoting under him and judo flipping his stunned body to the street. He landed hard, a sharp kick to the side launching him into the BMW's rear tire. The stun gun sounded again and he flinched, anticipating another dose of high-voltage agony. When it didn't come, he sprang upward, fully expecting to rescue Daly from a similar beat down.

Instead, Daly had managed to turn the tables on the stun-gun ninja. The SEAL had her arm bent in an awkward angle over her shoulder, the stun gun zapping her own collarbone area, but she still resisted. Her feet pushed back against the side of the SUV, preventing Daly from pushing her inside, despite the high-voltage snap, crackle, and pop.

Munoz quickly closed the gap, hell-bent on knocking one of her legs loose so they could stuff her inside. They didn't have time to explain this to her. Another threat was inbound. Gunfire exploded from the approaching SUV, drowning out the steady, suppressed fire from Melendez's rifle above them. Bullets snapped through the air and thunked into the adjacent vehicles. They really needed to get off the street.

A bullet shattered the window next to Daly and Bauer, miraculously missing their entangled mass. Bauer dropped her legs in response, and Munoz barreled forward, knocking her into the SUV. He sat on her until Daly opened the door on the opposite side a few seconds later and hauled her the rest of the way in. He closed the door and tapped Mazurov on the shoulder, yelling for him to get moving.

With Bauer still struggling in both of their grips, the SUV raced east on North Washington Street, sailing past the inbound threat without taking any fire. Warm spring air rushed through the empty window next to him. Melendez had done his job well. He always did.

"Get off me!" screamed Bauer, squirming underneath them.

"Any time now, David!" Munoz yelled.

A terrified face appeared between the front seats. "Audra! It's me."

She stopped struggling for a moment, resuming with even more ferocity. "You fucking animals!" she screeched. "He has nothing to do with this!"

"Audra! Everything is fine! Karl Berg sent me," said David Bauer. "He told me to tell you that he's sorry he couldn't meet you for your favorite hazelnut-flavored latte."

"Get off me," said Audra Bauer. "How dare you involve my husband!"

"He demanded to be here," said Munoz. "Are we good?"

"We're far from good," she said, still struggling.

"Honey, they're on our side. I've been with them for a few hours in a safe location," said her husband.

"Where the fuck is Karl?"

"Karl can't move right now," David answered. "He was severely beaten and tortured."

"Jesus," she muttered, all of the resistance melting away.

"Can I get off you now?" asked Munoz. "Without getting a straight arm across the face, that is?"

"We're good."

Munoz and Daly let her up, buckling her in between them. She started to talk, but he silenced her with a curt shake of his head.

"Echo One, how are we looking?" asked Munoz.

"No police units between your position and the interstate. Alpha units need to hustle. First responding unit is like twenty seconds out from the intersection," Graves responded.

"Oscar One moving. I don't think a pickup is advisable," said Melendez.

"Oscar Two concurs. We're almost back at the car, but I'd rather be moving away from the intersection when the police arrive," said Daniel. *"We didn't open fire, so our cover is still intact. We can circle back around to a busier street in the downtown area and grab Alpha One on our way to grab Alpha Three."*

"Sounds like a plan," said Munoz. "Echo One, help them out."

"My pleasure."

"Where are we headed?" Bauer asked.

"Safe house owned by a trusted friend," said Munoz. "A nice, secluded spot. Karl's waiting for us."

"Why didn't Karl give me a heads-up about your plan?" said Bauer. "That could have gone really badly for you if I had a knife with me. And who exactly are you?"

"Jeffrey Munoz. At your service," he said, smiling at her.

"No shit," she said, shaking her head. "Sanderson's people?"

"Recognize me?" said the driver, turning his face toward her for a moment.

"You gotta be kidding me!" she said. "Mazurov?"

"I go by Eric Freeman these days," he said.

"And you? You don't look like one of the original members," she said, nodding at Daly.

"I led the raid on Sanderson's compound in Argentina two years ago. Scott Daly."

"Who else is involved?" she asked.

"The Petroviches and a few others," said Munoz.

"And you all happened to be in the country at the same time when this Russian plot unfolded?"

"Not exactly," said Munoz, checking the street behind them.

"What does that mean?"

"I think it's better if Karl explains it," said Munoz. "Whatever happened here may not be the Russians."

Chapter 41

Falls Church, Virginia

Jessica Petrovich crouched behind a minivan, waiting for the signal from Graves. She'd arrived at the lot a few hours earlier in a car she'd stolen from the Tyson's Corner Galleria Mall parking garage. She'd parked in the middle of the lot and walked through the back door of the Freaky Bird Coffee Roasters.

Cappuccino and scone in hand, she walked around the quaint downtown area, ducking into shops and killing time. An hour before the never-to-happen rendezvous between Karl Berg and Audra Bauer, she strolled past the lot along West Maple Street, casually scanning the cars for any obvious signs of surveillance, taking a mental note of the empty spaces. Nothing appeared off.

Berg had asked Audra to park behind the coffee shop so she could slip into the place unobserved from the street. From an espionage field-craft perspective, the request made little sense, which was why he had suggested it. The shop had wide, floor-to-ceiling windows facing Broad Street, so it was ridiculous to suggest that they might remain unseen.

Their possible eavesdroppers would make the same observation, deducting that the parking lot request was a ruse to intercept Bauer and move her to a safe location. They'd station at least one team, if not two, in the immediate vicinity. Jessica predicted one team inside the parking lot and another inside the coffee shop to block that avenue of escape. A third team nearby on West Maple Street or the bank parking lot across the street was not out of the question.

Not detecting anything an hour before showtime, she walked to the next cross street and took a left on Park Avenue, finding a bench near the Falls Church municipal center. She waited about thirty minutes before heading back down Park Avenue and slipping between two businesses connected to the lot. From her new vantage point behind a full trash dumpster, she had scanned for newcomers, starting with the spaces that had been empty. After five minutes passed and nothing grabbed her attention, Jessica started to wonder if she'd made a bad assumption.

She was moments from leaving her position when the team sent to grab Bauer made a small mistake. A head poked up from the rear compartment of one of the SUVs. She barely caught it through the tinted windows, but a light across the street provided enough background illumination to see it. She'd low-crawled across the pavement to reach her current position, where she could accomplish her mission right now if she wanted.

All she had to do was attach a GPS tracking unit to the SUV, preferably somewhere hidden, though it wasn't required. Graves said she could throw the damn thing at the vehicle as it was pulling away if the situation required. Powerful magnets would do the rest.

She had a better idea. Infinitely more risky, but exponentially more rewarding, a combination Jessica couldn't resist. Daniel would not be happy with the revised plan. Not in the least.

"Alpha Three, Alpha One is moving to the transfer point. Get the GPS unit in place and get out of there," said Graves.

"Alpha Three copies."

Jessica waited, finally hearing a commotion in the SUV next to her. She slid behind the minivan and planted the GPS under the bumper, continuing to the driver's side of the vehicle in a low crouch. She paused, peeking around the corner. The rear driver's door slammed shut and revealed a man already pulling the driver's door open. He got in the driver's seat, too focused on the task at hand to see her moving down the side of the SUV.

She opened the rear driver's side door and methodically fired into the cabin, starting with the guy in the cargo compartment and finishing with a single shot into the back of the driver's neck after dispatching the man across from her. Jessica backed out and shut the door, headed for the back entrance to the coffee shop. She detected hurried movement through the clear glass door to the coffee shop and slowed her pace—to time everything perfectly.

The door flew open, and two men barreled in her direction. The first one barked orders into a handheld radio. She pretended to talk animatedly into a phone with her left hand, keeping the pistol hidden behind her right thigh. Neither of them noticed that the object in her hand clearly wasn't a phone.

Jessica let the first man soft-shoulder her aside, bringing the business end of the suppressed pistol under the second man's chin and firing. The leader abruptly stopped in his tracks. She flicked open the serrated blade in her left hand and stabbed him firmly, but not deeply in the upper left back. When his body automatically folded to the left in response to the pain, she slipped the arm over his lowered shoulder and placed the blade against his throat. The pistol went into the middle of his back.

"Drop the radio and keep walking," she said.

He dropped the handheld and took a few choppy steps forward, faltering.

"You have no idea how quick I am with this knife," she hissed in his ear. "I'll have your carotid slashed and a bullet in your lower spine before you realize you made a mistake. You'll bleed out in this parking lot, clawing your way across the pavement toward the coffee shop. You won't make it."

"What do you want?" he grunted.

"I want you to keep walking," she said, pressing the pistol into his back again.

He moved stiffly but steadily past the bloodstained windshield of his SUV.

"Don't look. Keep moving. We're headed toward that dumpster over there," she said.

Distant gunfire echoed off the buildings.

"Keep going. Don't make me carry you," she said.

They retraced the route she'd taken to arrive surreptitiously in the lot, stopping behind a two-story building on Park Street. Blue and red lights flashed off the building, the police officers both on and off duty at the Falls Church municipal center racing in their cars toward the reports of gunfire. She waited until the sirens faded and the street went quiet, prodding him forward onto Park Street.

"Alpha Three, I have a good signal on the tracker, but it hasn't moved. What are you seeing?"

She tightened her grip on the knife and stuffed the pistol behind the small of her back, activating her radio. "I made an adjustment to the plan," she said. "Will advise shortly. Tracker in place."

"Who are you talking to?" asked the man in front of her.

"Friends. Keep walking," she said, returning the pistol to his back.

"Copy that, Alpha Three."

"We're headed toward the police station," he noted.

"They'll be too busy cleaning up your friends to notice," she said. "See that park bench over there?"

"I see it. You're fucking crazy, you know that?"

"So I've been told."

Jessica stopped him directly in front of the far right side of the bench. With the knife fixed firmly to his throat, she turned his body left and pulled him into a seated position, sliding past the edge of the bench into the bushes behind. She rested comfortably on both knees, adjusting the knife so it wasn't so visible from the street. It took a few seconds to find the opening at the bottom of the bench's back and reestablish contact with the man's body, just to reinforce the obvious. She had two ways to kill him quickly if he tried to escape or draw attention.

"Now what?" he asked.

"We wait for my friends to finish their business."

"You're pretty confident in your friends' abilities."

"They've thwarted all of your little operations," said Jessica.

"Is that so?" he said, not sounding convinced.

"You don't know who I am, do you?"

"No idea," he said. "Enlighten me."

"Nicole Erak."

"Never heard of you," he said.

"Aka Jessica Petrovich."

The man stiffened. It wasn't the most obvious reaction, but she felt it. A dark cloud of dread settled over her. This man shouldn't know either of those names. She hadn't expected a reaction. In fact, she'd been hoping for zero response. This changed everything.

"My friends will be here shortly," she said. "And yes, I'm confident in that assessment."

Chapter 42

Vienna, Virginia

Audra Bauer peered between the vehicle's front seats at the well-lit European-style villa that materialized beyond the thick trees. She knew a few well-connected and wealthy people living in the D.C.'s Virginia suburbs, but she'd never seen something like this behind the private gates separating the Beltway elite from the government-subsidized hoi polloi that saturated the area.

The SUV pulled even with a wide wrought-iron gate set in the middle of a vine-covered half-wall that defined the front entrance courtyard. A long clay-tile-covered porch wrapped around each side of the house. Her husband turned his head in the front seat and met her gaze, a look of deep concern evident on his face. She could read his mind.

"Who owns this place?" she said.

"Ernesto Galenden," said Munoz. "He apparently owns several of these in the area."

"Must be nice," said Bauer, nodding imperceptibly at her husband.

"We're safe here," said Munoz.

"For how long?" said Bauer.

"The answer to that question is under constant reevaluation," said Munoz.

"Great," said her husband. "How many people do you have out here?"

"Right now, four inside," said Munoz. "The rest are in this SUV or en route."

"You don't have anybody walking the perimeter?" said David Bauer.

"This place is untraceable," said Munoz.

"Let's hope so," said David.

"Now I have your husband breaking my balls," said Munoz. "This deal keeps getting better."

"My husband spent eight years with the 75th Ranger Regiment. Got out in ninety-eight," said Bauer.

"And you didn't think to mention that earlier?" said Munoz.

"Must have slipped my mind," said David Bauer before opening the door and getting out of the vehicle.

"We had a shooter in the front seat the whole time and didn't even know it," said Daly, shaking his head.

"He's riding a desk now, so don't get any ideas," said Bauer.

"I heard that," yelled her husband while walking around the front of the SUV.

"Seriously. He's off-limits," said Bauer.

"Got it," said Munoz, hopping down from the SUV to let her out.

She walked with her husband to the arched mahogany entry doors and waited for Daly and Munoz to catch up. The SUV disappeared from sight behind a wide one-story stucco structure to the right of the house, which she assumed to be a garage. Munoz pressed the illuminated doorbell and stood with his hands behind his back.

"Seriously?" said Bauer.

"The door is locked," said Munoz before winking. "Best we can do without perimeter guards."

She shook her head. Staying here sounded less and less appealing by the moment. The door opened after a short delay, and an Indian-looking guy in his twenties appeared in the doorway.

"Look what the cat dragged in," he said. "Anish Gupta at your service, ma'am."

"What?" said Audra, turning to Munoz. "Is he part of the team?"

"Hell yeah. I work the electronic magic. I was out there on the streets when all of this went down. We just got back."

"That's right," she said. "I remember the name from before."

"You thought I was *the help*?" said Gupta, making air quotes with his fingers.

"No," said Audra. "I really didn't. I'm a little out of it right now. Sorry."

"Sorry doesn't make me feel better about my brown skin," said Gupta.

"I'm really—" started Bauer.

"Hey, just fucking with you! Seriously. Welcome to the sickest house you'll ever see," he said, gesturing for them to enter. "It's a pleasure to finally meet you."

"Likewise," said Audra, utterly confused.

"You'll have to excuse Gupta," said Munoz. "He wasn't held as a child."

"What the fuck, man?" said Gupta, with a hurt look. "I was in foster care my whole childhood. Some of us didn't have loving parents."

Munoz raised both hands. "Sorry, Anish. I really didn't know that."

"Gupta! Are you gonna make them stand out there all day?" said Graves, appearing behind Gupta.

The second man looked at least twice Gupta's age, with a balding head.

"What? No," said Gupta, stepping out of the way.

"Timothy Graves," said the man. "Welcome to our temporary humble abode. And by the way, Anish was raised in a very comfortable and loving home in a rich suburb on the north side of Indianapolis."

"Come on, dude! You're ruining my street cred," said Gupta.

"Trust me. You cashed in the last of your street cred when you graduated summa cum laude from MIT."

"Damn. You're a regular gangster," said Audra Bauer.

"Hey, that's not—" started Gupta.

"Just fucking with you, Anish," she said. "Thank you for working your magic today."

"Any time," said Gupta.

"Foster care," said Munoz. "Should have known better."

"Dude, that was the first time I've ever seen you look sorry. Classic."

Audra took in the grand two-story hallway, which ended at the back of the house, with a floor-to-ceiling bank of windows. "Very humble."

"It's kind of crazy," said Graves. "And the place is fully stocked for us. Whatever you need, it's here."

"Right now, I need to see Karl Berg," said Audra. "Try to make sense of this insanity."

"He'll be relieved to see you," said Graves. "He's been monitoring the situation very closely, against doctor's orders."

"I can't believe this happened," said Audra. "How is he doing?"

Darryl Jackson appeared from the shadows of the closest doorway in the two-story entry hallway.

"He'll survive," said Jackson. "But he's in bad fucking shape."

She detected resentment in Jackson's voice. "How bad?"

"Bad enough," said Jackson. "This shit got out of hand—real quick."

"Not by my choice," Audra said defensively.

"Nobody's blaming anybody, but he ain't good," said Jackson. "He wanted to see you right away."

Audra squeezed her husband's hand. "I'll be right back."

"I'll fix us something to eat," said David Bauer, kissing her cheek and letting go of her hand.

Her husband headed toward the back of the grand hallway with Munoz and Daly while she made her way toward Jackson.

"It's a pleasure to finally meet you," she said, offering her hand.

He glanced at her hand skeptically before shaking it. "Wish it was under different circumstances," said Jackson before guiding her through a dim hallway to a series of rooms that occupied the right half of the house.

"So do I," she said. "How did you know they'd come after me?"

"Karl pieced it together," said Jackson. "They grabbed him right out from under me last night. We'd just finished dinner."

"He was really looking forward to having dinner with you," said Bauer.

"Karl mentioned it?" said Jackson.

She nodded. "The day before. He stopped by with something."

"He came by your office?" said Jackson.

"He did," she said.

"Then all of this goes down," said Jackson. "Sounds like somebody over at the CIA didn't like this little something the two of you discussed."

"Apparently not."

Jackson stopped at a closed door, gripping the doorknob. "You sure you're ready to see this?" he said. "He's in bad shape."

"Yes."

He opened the door and nodded for her to enter. "I'll let the two of you catch up."

"Thank you, Darryl," she said, patting his shoulder. "For everything."

Jackson's cautious look softened. "I'd do anything for that fool, and he knows it."

"Then we have that in common. He can be persuasive."

"Audra?" said Berg.

"See you in a few," said Jackson before leaving.

She stepped into the massive room, immediately locating her friend. Berg lay on a patio lounger in front of the king bed, with a handheld radio gripped in his left hand. Even from the opposite side of the room, she could see that his face was badly bruised.

"Everyone got sick of you already?" she said, keeping the conversation humorous.

"Funny. I'm supposed to be resting. Out of the action," said Berg.

"Welcome to the recovery wing of Galenden's villa."

She approached the lounger, noting the small scattered red stains on the white sheet pulled up to his neck. He caught her staring at the spotted sheet.

"Seventy-six cuts," said Berg. "They didn't know what they were doing."

"Jesus. I'm sorry, Karl," she said. "Who did this to you? What did they want?"

"It's complicated," he said.

"How complicated?"

"I don't know."

"What do you mean?" said Bauer.

"I mean I truly don't know," said Berg. "Nothing makes sense, which is why we need to spend some time sorting through the facts—as a group. A lot has gone on over the past twenty-four hours."

"When do you want to start?" she said.

"As soon as they can wheel me into the main room," said Berg. "We can't afford to lose any time."

Bauer nodded, taking his hand. "Thank you, Karl. I have no idea what they had planned for me, but judging by this—"

"I don't think they had plans to kidnap you, Audra," said Berg. "They were looking to close the loop on this."

"On what?"

"All things Reznikov," said Berg.

"The gift that keeps on giving," she said. "I'll get everyone together."

Chapter 43

Vienna, Virginia

Berg felt somewhat embarrassed by his predicament. He lay in an admittedly plush lounge chair from the back patio, situated in the center of the home's two-story-ceilinged great room. Not a bad place to convalesce under normal circumstances, but nothing was normal about the current situation. He'd been transferred to the lounge chair from a bed and carted here like royalty so they didn't have to squeeze everyone into the bedroom to include him in the meeting.

On top of that, they needed quick access to Graves and Gupta's suite of electronics. It made far more sense to bring him to the party instead of the other way around despite the fact that he looked ridiculous and largely out of place among them. At least he wasn't in a hospital bed. That would have been the icing on the cake.

He caught Jackson shaking his head, trying to stifle a laugh. His friend glanced at him and looked away just as quickly, putting his head down to laugh into his hand.

"What?" said Berg.

"Nothing," said Jackson, breaking into more silent laughter.

"Seriously. What?"

"I'm sorry, man. You look like…I don't know what you look like."

"Like the mummy," said Melendez, pushing Jackson into a full laugh.

"Sorry, Karl," said Jackson. "I'm fucking slaphappy at this point, and you do look a little out of place lying where the coffee table used to be."

A few more laughs followed; then everyone settled down for the serious business at hand.

"First, this is not how I envisioned my next vacation. Just in case any of you were curious," said Berg, getting the last of the laughter out of their systems.

"I think we can all agree that none of what has happened over the past twenty-four hours is a jumble of coincidences. This is all connected somehow, and I'm still not fully convinced it's the Russians."

"Sanderson is pretty convinced," said Munoz.

"I want to go over what we know and expand our theory base if warranted," said Berg. "I'd like Audra Bauer to take over at this point, because she does this kind of thing for a living, and as the newest addition to the island of misfit operatives and intelligence officers, I think she's the least biased. Audra?"

Audra Bauer rose from the couch next to Berg and moved toward Graves and Gupta, who sat at a long Shaker-style table that supported all of their electronics gear. The table had been moved from the dining room and placed flush against a long bank of windows overlooking the pool and forested backyard. She stopped a few feet away from them and nodded at the group.

"Most of you don't know me personally, though our paths have crossed. I don't think it's any secret that I work at the CIA. I was deputy director of the National Clandestine Service when those paths crossed, so I know about the background events potentially contributing to this sudden outbreak of kidnapping events. I've always been both impressed by and thankful for your work, even if I cringed every time I heard Sanderson's name."

"You're not the only one," said Daniel.

"I'll second that shit," said Jackson, and the group shared an uneasy laugh.

"Seriously, I just want to set the record straight. I believe in Sanderson's work. Your work," said Bauer. "The fact that any of you are here is a testament to the program."

"Sanderson can be persuasive," said Daniel.

"He's a smart guy, with a solid knack for seeing the bigger picture," said Bauer, pointing at Berg. "Same with this guy."

"So how do we do this?" asked Jackson.

"Right now, we need to share what we know and piece things together. Here's how I'd like to do it," said Audra. "I ask directed, big-picture questions and get brief answers. If anyone disagrees they speak up. I'll gradually narrow the questions until we get as close to a consensus as possible. Sound good?"

Everyone nodded or mumbled agreement. Berg had made the right choice putting her in charge. Audra facilitated decisions faster and more accurately than any high-level CIA officer he'd ever worked for during his thirty-plus-year career. Until True America stepped into the White House, he was convinced she'd sit behind the director's desk one day.

"Let's start in Chicago, with the attempted Petrovich abduction-murder. What do we know about the attack's motivations?"

"Well justified in Srecko Hadzic's mind. No question about that," said Berg, glancing at Daniel, who nodded in agreement.

Jessica was missing from the group, which Berg still found to be highly unusual. She'd felt dizzy after planting the GPS tracker, according to Daniel. He didn't press for a better answer. Daniel looked pretty short on patience, and he'd given up trying to figure out the Petroviches. He barely had the mental energy to focus on the problem at hand.

"What stands out as odd?" said Audra. "Big picture."

Munoz answered, ostensibly as Sanderson. "Hadzic had been confirmed as killed in a botched attempt to rescue him from the United Nations Detention Unit at The Hague. There's no way this could be covered—"

"Hold on," said Bauer. "The shorter your answers, the better. Let's get to the heart of the matter. Did Hadzic have the money and contacts necessary to make this happen?"

"Unlikely," said Munoz.

"But not impossible," Berg countered. "He still had several million dollars floating around and a devoted group of followers."

"So we really can't move beyond theories regarding Chicago," said Bauer.

"I suppose not," said Daniel, clearly not happy with the assessment.

"Let's move on to Karl's abduction," said Audra. "What was different?"

"The team that kidnapped me was American. Military-style contractors, if I had to guess," said Berg, instantly realizing she'd correct him.

"Let's not guess," said Audra. "Mr. Graves?"

The flat-screen TV mounted above the fireplace mantel activated, displaying a face with a red hole in the center of its forehead.

"Jesus," said Audra's husband.

Audra nodded curtly. "Sanderson's people know how to shoot."

"Bottom of the stairs," said Munoz.

"Sorry. I would have done this in private, but there hasn't been a spare minute since I got back," said Audra. "Darryl, we'll go through these quickly, on the off chance you recognize one of them. Mr. Jackson works in this industry and has extensive contacts throughout."

"Sounds like a plan," said Jackson.

The grotesque slide show proceeded until the fifth image.

"Hold up," said Jackson.

Berg recognized the face. The man with two bullet holes in the upper forehead had been his chief torturer in the farmhouse cellar.

"You know him?" asked Berg.

"I don't know for sure," said Jackson, "but I swear I've seen him at Brown River. He's not a member of the Special Operations Division. I know that much."

"What do we know about this guy, Graves?"

"FRD identifies him as Samuel Harper. Staff sergeant in Force Recon, back when that was still a thing."

"FRD?" Jackson queried.

"Facial Recognition Database," said Graves. "Kind of like the federal fingerprint database, but for faces."

"I didn't know they had that kind of shit," said Jackson.

"It's part of the Next Gen Identification program. DNA, facial recognition, voice recognition, fingerprints. Big Brother stuff," said Graves.

"Back to Harper, please," Bauer prompted.

"Yep. Sorry. Harper got out of the Marine Corps in 2004 and worked for KBR in Iraq."

"We provided security for the vast majority of KBR installations and convoys in Iraq. Still do. That's it?" said Jackson.

"The trail stops with KBR, aside from a P.O. box in Fredericksburg, Virginia," stated Graves.

Berg met Jackson's eyes. This wasn't good news.

"Brown River is based in Fredericksburg," said Jackson. "What about the rest of the team?"

"All ex-military special forces, with P.O. boxes in—"

"Let me guess," Jackson cut in. "Fredericksburg, Virginia."

"We have possible employees of Brown River involved in Berg's kidnapping."

"Possible?" interrupted Graves.

"We'll get to that," said Bauer, cutting off Graves. "Karl, what did they want from you, beyond what we already discussed?"

Berg swallowed hard, thankful for her discretion. She understood the risks involved for his contact in Moscow.

"They wanted to know everything I knew about Reznikov's current whereabouts, which is nothing."

"So they sought very specific information to Reznikov?"

"Yes. A few days after I brought information about Reznikov to your attention."

"Noted," she said. "To recap, Berg's abduction has no apparent direct tie to Jessica Petrovich's, though the timing is suspicious. Berg's captors were extremely interested in Reznikov's current whereabouts, in addition to something I can't share with you."

Grumbling erupted from the group, which Berg expected. Secrets never sat well when people's lives were on the line.

"I know what she's referring to," said Munoz. "This is the kind of secret you take to your grave. Trust me on this."

"I couldn't have said it better myself," said Berg. "Did I really tell you?"

"And Jackson," said Munoz. "I think the painkillers were talking."

"Anything else related to Berg's abduction?" said Bauer, steering them back on course.

"We're still analyzing phone data," said Graves.

Bauer nodded. "From what I'm told, you'll find something if it's there."

"Damn skippy," said Gupta. "Sorry. I felt like I needed to say something."

"Don't," said Graves. "Please."

"That brings us to tonight," said Bauer. "Darryl, would you take over for me? I can't answer my own questions objectively."

"If you insist," said Jackson, standing up. "Not sure I can match your style, but I'll sure as shit try. First question is for Karl. How the fuck did you know they were all over her?"

Berg was thrown off by the question and the gruff tone. "Uhhhh…I didn't. It was a theory. If it didn't pan out, no harm, no foul."

"Aside from one very pissed-off Audra Bauer and her husband," said Jackson.

"Stick to questions," said Bauer. "Big picture. Actually, there's only one question you need to ask."

"That sounds like a challenge," said Jackson, appearing to think carefully. "All right. What was different about tonight?"

"Multiple vehicles following Bauer. A team set to grab her in the coffee shop parking lot. Itchy trigger fingers," said Melendez.

Jackson shook his head. "Wrong question."

"How did they know where Karl and Audra planned to meet?" Jackson probed.

Bauer nodded her approval while Berg refrained from answering. He needed the conclusion to be drawn from someone who hadn't initially resisted the Russian theory. Abraham Sayar gave the answer he was looking for.

"Bauer's phone is tapped."

Jackson knew where to go with the answer. "Karl, what phone did you use to pass the meeting location and time to Audra?"

"Can I answer?" said Gupta.

"Go ahead," said Jackson.

"On the most encrypted, secure-ass motherfucking satellite phone there is."

"Thanks for the colorful description," said Jackson. "Audra? How did you take Karl's call?"

"On the encrypted phone in my office."

"Karl, did you involve or inform anyone outside of this group about tonight's plan?"

"No."

"Has anyone else? Only answer if you have," said Jackson.

Everyone shook their heads, mumbling.

"What is the likelihood that the Russians have compromised your office phone, Audra?"

"Zero," she said.

"Bug planted in your bag? On your person somehow?"

She shook her head. "Unlikely. I'm screened for electronics upon entry to the building and again when I get to my floor."

The conclusion was inescapable.

"Then tonight's attempted abduction was an inside job," Jackson concluded. "Inside the CIA, or inside Sanderson's crew?"

A low discordance of disbelief and muttering started.

"Darryl is right. We can't individually discount everyone in here based on their word alone. Sorry," she said. "Graves?"

Sanderson's lead surveillance tech smirked, a rare show of emotion from the guy, based on what Berg had witnessed from him today.

"Assuming I didn't rig the game," said Graves, "I'm confident none of Sanderson's operatives sent any unauthorized transmissions."

"How can you be sure?" said David Bauer.

"Because Sanderson is a paranoid motherfucker, as my colleague might say, and insisted that I monitor all of your communications," said Graves. "Unless one of you is hiding a phone or tablet we didn't manage to detect and infiltrate, the team is clean."

"Even my phone?" asked Mazurov.

"Especially your phone," said Graves. "Anyone that's been out of the direct fold for a while got extra scrutiny."

"So what do we have?" said Jackson.

"Not much," admitted Bauer. "My office phone or the office itself is likely bugged. That indicates an internal problem."

"Shit," muttered Berg.

"What?"

"I was in your office talking about Reznikov a few days ago. They came for me first."

"And I passed on your request to monitor any and all channels for any information about Sokolov or Reznikov."

"Who's Sokolov?" asked Daniel.

"Possible accomplice in Reznikov's recent escape. Long story," said Berg.

"Escape?"

"The Russians received information that Reznikov was working at a clandestine bioweapons laboratory sponsored by the Solntsevskaya Bratva. The raid failed, but the circumstances surrounding Reznikov's truly miraculous last minute escape are suspect at best. Sokolov has been one of Reznikov's personal bodyguards for a few years. His body was not recovered at the site, but the rest of Reznikov's guards, along with a very high-ranking Bratva commander, were found dead a few miles downriver from the lab. We think Sokolov sold Reznikov to the highest bidder."

Daniel nodded. "And that bidder is now trying to tie up any loose ends connected to Reznikov."

"That would be my guess," Berg agreed.

"Wonderful," said Daniel. "Any idea who the highest bidder might be?"

Berg had to tread lightly here, because his latest theory sailed straight past conspiracy and landed in uncharted territory. They'd done it once. Why not again? He decided against sharing the theory.

"No. We need more information to start down that path," said Berg. "Right now, we need to figure out who we *can* and *cannot* trust."

"I don't trust anyone outside of this room," said Munoz. "Except for Sanderson."

"We obviously can't turn to the CIA," said Jackson. "I'd cross Brown River off the list too."

"FBI?" said David Bauer. "I have a few contacts there."

Berg had almost forgotten about his conversation with Ryan Sharpe.

"Sorry. I forgot something. It's been a long twenty-four hours," said Berg. "I called Ryan Sharpe right after I brought the Reznikov intelligence to Audra's attention, and asked him to facilitate adding Sokolov to as many international terrorist watch lists as he could wrangle. I didn't explain why I was interested in Sokolov, and I never mentioned Reznikov. I asked for this as a favor. Sharpe is a guy I trust."

"But we can't cross him off the list of suspected leaks," said Bauer.

"Then it looks like we're back to square one, unless your electronic wizards can conjure up some kind of answer by mixing all of the captured cell phones in a cauldron or something," said Jackson.

"I wish it worked like that. Be a lot easier than drinking ten cups of coffee between now until dawn," said Graves. "We're working on something, but it might take some time."

"Then we'll have to expedite the process," said Jessica.

Everyone turned toward her voice. Jessica stood in the wide, high-arched opening that connected the main hallway with the great room—holding a knife to a man's throat. The man in her grip had a black bag over his head.

"I guess the cat's out of the bag," said Graves.

"My guess is that this fucker can move things along nicely," she explained.

Berg glanced at Daniel. "Looks like your wife made a speedy recovery."

Daniel stood up. "We've been working on something."

"Jesus," stated Jackson, shaking his head in disbelief. "Now *we're* kidnapping people? Did you know about this, Karl?"

"I honestly had no idea," said Berg, looking to Audra. "Seriously."

Bauer sighed. "This is officially out of control."

Jessica wrangled the man into the room.

"The whole thing has been out of control since it started," said Daniel. "This might be the only way to get it back under control."

"Where did he come from?" asked Bauer.

"He was waiting for you in the parking lot behind the Freaky Bird," said Jessica. "I kind of couldn't help myself."

"Nice of you to finally unveil your little secret," Jackson smirked.

"To be honest, you've been the only thing holding it up," said Munoz.

"Me? Seriously?" said Jackson. "I'm the only motherfucker in this room that can get in his car and go back to a normal life. I'm here for one reason and one reason only. To make sure my best friend doesn't end up back where you guys found him this afternoon."

"Sorry if we couldn't just take your word for it," said Daniel.

"Who's we?"

"Everyone except Karl, Audra, and her husband," Munoz answered. "The possible connection established to Brown River earlier today made us a little nervous."

"And how exactly does this change things?" asked Bauer. "No offense, Darryl."

"None fucking taken, I guess," said Jackson.

Graves explained, "We did some deep digging—"

"That means hacking," Gupta interrupted.

"Thank you for the unnecessary clarification," said Graves. "We hacked into Brown River's payroll database and found Samuel Harper. He makes a lot of money for a contractor."

"How much?" asked Jackson.

"One hundred and fifty thousand. Salaried."

"Salaried? Security contractors aren't salaried."

"Definitely salaried. We also found a onetime payment of one hundred and fifty thousand dollars paid two months ago."

"Sounds like a onetime sign-up bonus, though we stopped those three years ago," said Jackson.

"Apparently not," said Daniel.

"Let's cut to the point here," said Jackson. "How does this supposedly clear me for your circle of trust?"

"You never left the circle," said Berg. "We just needed to find someone bigger than Harper involved at Brown River to fully convince Sanderson's people."

"This guy?" asked Jackson, pointing at the hooded man.

"Yes. We found our new guest on the payroll too," said Graves. "But his pay structure was a little higher."

"How much higher?" said Jackson.

"To the tune of three hundred thousand higher."

Jackson whistled. "Not many people at Brown River making that kind of money. Not anymore."

"Then maybe you'll recognize him," said Munoz, nodding toward Jessica.

She pulled the hood off, tossing it to the floor, pushing the man forward.

"Jack Wellins?" said Jackson. "He ran Brown River's Direct Action Group, a kind of off-the-books special missions roster. Left close to two years ago for another security firm. Ajax Global."

Berg noted the timing. Another link supporting a wild theory he was starting to believe more and more by the minute.

"Then Brown River has made a continuous and costly payroll error," said Graves. "He's received a monthly paycheck from them for the past seven years, uninterrupted, plus a three-hundred-thousand-dollar bonus six months ago."

"Damn, Jack! You hit the jackpot! Care to explain this peculiar discrepancy?" said Jackson. "Or maybe why you were waiting around a coffee shop to murder a senior CIA director."

"Good to see you again, Darryl," said Wellins.

"Wish I could say the same. Let's get a closer look."

Jessica manhandled him around one of the couches until he stood on the edge of the group, in easy view of everyone. He came across more defiant than intimidated.

"You look a little smug for your predicament," Berg noted.

"I know exactly what's going to happen here," said Wellins. "Why dwell on it?"

"Then why not sit down in a comfortable chair," Berg offered, motioning to an empty seat. "And enjoy a rare Scotch from the den while filling in the blanks for us. Beats the alternative."

Wellins swallowed hard, looking around the room; his defiant facade tempered. "You know that's not gonna happen. Hard to scare a dead man."

Daniel Petrovich started laughing, followed by Sayar. When Munoz and Melendez joined in, Berg looked around to see what was so funny. Most of them were focused on Wellins, shaking their heads.

"What's so funny?" said Wellins.

"I can't speak for anyone else in the room, but I'm not here to scare you," said Daniel. "I'm here to make you talk, by any means necessary.

We'll skip the beatings and move right into the cutting, of course. Seems like an appropriate place to start given what your team did to Mr. Berg. Then we'll move on to far more creative methods. If all that fails, a few of us will make the drive down to your house in Midlothian and set up an interactive teleconference with your wife and kids. Interactive in a 'you tell me what I want to know, and I don't poke a kid's eye' out kind of way."

Wellins struggled, held tightly in check by Jessica's forearm and the knife pressed against his neck.

"You will not touch my family," snarled Wellins. "They're off-limits."

"I don't have any limits," said Daniel.

"You can't let them do that," said Wellins, looking to Bauer. "We follow unwritten rulebooks governing these things. You know that."

"Maybe if I knew who you were working for, I could convince them to observe those rules," said Bauer. "Brown River doesn't count."

"They're off-limits," repeated Wellins. "You know that."

"I'm not the one you need to convince," said Audra.

The man's glance shifted to Berg.

"Don't look at me," said Berg. "I have seventy-six painful reminders why I don't give a fuck what they do to you *or* your family."

Chapter 44

Vienna, Virginia

Darryl Jackson strolled into the great room, sipping his coffee more out of habit than necessity at this point in the morning. The effects of caffeine long ago quit having any measurable impact on his system. Just a little longer, and he'd settle in for a long nap. His wife was on the road, headed up to Princeton to get their daughter Liz and disappear until this mess cleared up. *If* it cleared up. Their other daughter, Emily, would be a little harder to safeguard. She was in her first year of law school at the University of California at Berkeley, thousands of miles away. Convincing a first-year law student to ditch classes and "disappear" would take some finesse. He'd let his wife handle that one, backed by a sizable emergency nest egg. Whatever it took for them to disappear.

As soon as he could break free from this mess, he'd meet up with his wife and figure out a way to get Emily. Unfortunately, he couldn't give his wife a timeline for his departure. The more information they dug out of Wellins, which had been surprisingly scant so far, the stranger things sounded.

Audra Bauer walked into the great room and collapsed on the couch next to him. Karl Berg jarred awake and glanced over at them from the lounge chair. He'd been here all night, in and out of sleep based on the acquisition of new information.

"Well?" Berg prompted.

"I think the well is dry," said Bauer. "He mumbled Ajax a few more times then passed out."

"That's it?" asked Jackson.

"He's barely recognizable," she replied with a tired, vacant look. "I can't imagine they'll get anything else out of him. He's wrecked far beyond what they did to you, and I'm not letting them pay a visit to the man's family. That's nonnegotiable. I'll turn myself in before I let that happen."

Berg shook his head. "Sanderson's cyber team hasn't made any headway with Ajax. It doesn't exist."

"We scoured every possible public and government record for a company matching that name, involved in the same line of work," said Graves. "Nothing remotely related came to our attention."

"Well, you missed something," said Jackson, turning toward Graves. "No offense."

"I'm used to it," said Graves. "But we didn't miss anything."

"Your head was on the desk a few minutes ago," said Jackson.

"We're all tired."

"I distinctly recall a few managers and executives jumping ship for Ajax around the same time as Wellins. I checked out their website. Pretty slick compared to ours. I remember bringing that up with HR," said Jackson. "The place is real. Somewhere just outside of Petersburg, Virginia."

"Have you actually seen it?" asked Berg.

"You ever actually see Brown River?" Jackson shot back, slightly agitated.

"We're not questioning the existence of Brown River," said Berg.

"Fine. No, I've never seen the Ajax facility."

"Maybe we're not defining Ajax correctly? We know Wellins never technically left Brown River, right? He can say Ajax all day until he's blue in the face," said Berg. "But he's a Brown River employee. Same with Harper, which brings up another issue. Brown River has done a lot of hiring over the past six months, according to payroll. What was the total, Graves?"

"Three thousand six hundred and forty-three new hires, all former military or law enforcement. Pay scales are divided into three distinct categories. Three thousand and forty-two at seventy-five thousand dollars annually, plus a single one-hundred-thousand-dollar lump sum payment. Then it jumps to five hundred and fifty employees at the same level as Harper. All salaried. That leaves fifty-one coming in at the very generous Wellins level."

"This is all news to me. I was told we're in replace-only mode for hiring," said Jackson. "How much does all of this represent?"

"For fiscal year 2009, we're talking seven hundred and thirty-six million dollars, rounded up. Fixed salary costs moving forward will be three hundred and thirty-four million dollars. This isn't counting guys like Wellins, who joined Ajax beyond that six-month window."

"That's one hell of a capital expenditure," said Bauer.

"Like they're building an army," said Berg. "Called Ajax."

Jackson was stunned by the numbers. Nearly a billion in salary expenses alone for this year? He worked on the global operations side of the house, and their budgets had shrunk consistently over the past three years. Maybe Ajax was paying Brown River to piggyback on their payroll department? He knew that didn't make sense, but he had to ask.

"Any way Ajax is using Brown River's payroll division to process their own payroll?"

"Brown River is claiming these employees for tax purposes," said Graves. "And that would be one hell of an employee expansion for a company that doesn't exist."

"I don't know what to say or do at this point," said Jackson. "Seriously. We can't go to the FBI or CIA, and we might have a four-thousand-man death squad operating on U.S. soil, half of which is probably driving the streets, looking for us right now."

"Looking for us," Berg corrected. "Not you."

"I don't like the way that sounded," said Jackson. "It sounded an awful lot like I'm about to be asked to do something that scares the shit out of me."

"The cyber team has put together something they hope you can deliver to Brown River," said Bauer.

"Waltzing into Brown River with this discovery doesn't sound like a healthy idea right now. Or ever."

"Hear us out," said Berg.

"I knew I shouldn't have left the two of you alone earlier," Jackson grumbled.

"Graves wants you to log into your computer from a hardwire connection at your desk and insert a flash drive. Follow the directions on the screen, and the virus will take care of the rest. They think the Ajax information is on a network compartmentalized from the rest of Brown River's visible network, but might be able to find a way to access it internally."

"It's highly probable that someone 'officially' working at Brown River has full knowledge of Ajax. Possibly several or more. It's just too damn big of an operation to exist in a vacuum, and the fact that they're piggybacking it on the Brown River payroll suggests collusion. I'm guessing these are highly placed executives and managers, who would require access to the Ajax network."

"It's a long shot, Darryl, but that's all we have at this point. We need to keep pulling at threads until this unravels," said Bauer.

"All right. I'll do this, but after I deliver the virus and you guys confirm it's working, I need to take care of my family. Cheryl's on her way up to Princeton to get Liz, and I have no idea what's going on with my daughter in California."

"Does the timing work?" asked Berg. "I don't want to put you in danger. You've done enough already."

"I'm due back from my conference tomorrow, but it won't raise any eyebrows if I roll in later this morning. I've been known to bail on conferences early."

"Thank you, Darryl. If you sense anything is wrong at Brown River, you walk away. Promise me that."

"You can bet your ass on it."

And he wasn't kidding. One sign of trouble and Darryl Jackson was gone.

Chapter 45

FBI Headquarters
Washington, D.C.

Ryan Sharpe took the call, despite it originating from a satellite phone, as indicated by its prefix. He had news for Karl Berg and had previously left a message asking him to get in touch.

"Karl, this is Sharpe," he said. "I've been trying to get a hold of you. I have some information to pass related to the favor you requested."

Berg sounded flustered. "Yes. Sorry about that. My phone was stolen a few days ago. I was required to remotely deactivate it, for obvious reasons. You've found Sokolov?"

"I wouldn't say we found him, but a report out of Libreville fits the bill."

"As in Gabon? Africa?"

"Of all places, right?"

"Actually, it's not surprising, if this is him," said Berg.

"Here's what we have. A local organized crime informant reported the purchase of small arms with ammunition, a few sets of body armor, and an expensive four-wheel-drive vehicle by two Russians that flew into an airport on the outskirts of the city."

"This is unusual in Libreville?"

"Russians aren't uncommon in Libreville, but filthy ones flying into sketchy airports and liaising with Gabonese crime syndicates in the middle of the night are apparently very unusual. Enough for the informant to file a report."

"Filthy?"

"The two men smelled and looked like they had walked out of the jungle," said Sharpe. "That's right out of the report."

"Like they've been on the run."

"And headed somewhere in a hurry," said Sharpe. "I hope this helps."

"It does. Thank you," said Berg. "Is there any way for me to get more detailed information? Perhaps a place to start an investigation if we were to put some discreet assets in Libreville?"

"The Saint De Marquis market west of the city."

"Perfect. Thank you," said Berg, a long pause ensuing.

Sharpe could sense something else brewing and wasn't surprised at all when Berg continued.

"I stumbled onto something that…let's just say I have no idea how to present this without coming across as paranoid."

"Sounds promising."

"I know. Not exactly the best hook, so I'm just going to be blunt," said Berg. "Have you ever heard of a company called Ajax Global?"

"Sure," said Sharpe. "We've lost a number of agents to them over the past few years. They become law enforcement consultants, whatever that means. Same thing used to happen with Brown River, but that slowed down. Pretty much stopped, actually."

"Interesting. That fits what I uncovered."

Sharpe didn't really have time for CIA conspiracy theories, but he had to admit that Berg had him intrigued. If anything, he might be able to pass something on to the Human Resources Branch that could help them stem the tide of departing agents.

"What's on your mind, Karl?"

"Ajax doesn't exist," said Berg.

"Of course it does," said Sharpe.

"Just hear me out. Ajax exists in name, but not in substance. I have evidence directly suggesting that employees who left Brown River for jobs at Ajax have continued to be paid by Brown River, for up to two years in some cases. On top of that, Brown River payroll indicates close to four thousand new hires in the past six months, but a senior Brown River executive swears they've been in a hiring downswing for three years. The payroll numbers add up to nearly a billion dollars for fiscal year 2009, a big number for a company that has never been valued at more than a billion dollars."

"Sounds like a Treasury issue to me. IRS?" said Sharpe.

"I think they're raising a small army under the radar," said Berg. "Just look into this, discreetly, and get back to me if you want to hear the rest of the story."

"The rest of the story?"

"Be *very* discreet. I can attribute two domestic kidnapping attempts to employees on this mysterious Brown River payroll."

"That's sounding more like the FBI's jurisdiction," said Sharpe.

"You have no idea. I'm going to email you a file with the payroll information, all packaged for your consumption."

"I'm sure there's a federal warrant associated with the acquisition of that data."

"Sure. I'll send that along later today," said Berg. "Promise me you'll do a little digging and get back to me."

"I'll take a look," said Sharpe. "Is this a good number for you?"

"Let me give you a different number," said Berg. "It's a redirect. I'm serious about being discreet, Ryan."

"Understood."

"Be in touch shortly," said Berg, ending the call.

Sharpe stared at the phone. That was by far the most intriguing call he'd taken all year. He rubbed his chin. What to do with this one? Seriously. The side investigation into Sokolov hadn't uncovered any earth-shattering reason to explain why Shelby and Berg were keen to find him, other than what they knew from the start. Former Eastern Bloc commando turned mercenary. Dime a dozen, really. He'd turned up in an interesting location, but that was about the extent of it.

Now Berg was talking about "off the books" domestic paramilitary groups on a kidnapping spree? Cooked books, perhaps, at one of the largest international security corporations in the world? Why not? It wouldn't take Dana and her team long to substantiate enough of Berg's claim to decide whether to look further.

Sharpe got up from his desk and opened his office door, making his way toward Dana's office. He knocked on the door frame and stepped into the opening.

"Busy?"

"You know I'm not," she said. "Come in. What's up?"

He stepped inside, closing the door. "I just passed along the Sokolov news to Berg, and he hit me with something else."

"You were just talking to him?" she asked.

"Yeah. Why?"

"Probably nothing, but remember when we tied Sanderson's original Argentina location to various land holdings owned by Ernesto Galenden?"

The memory of that exciting moment came with a bitter taste. He paused a little too long. Hesterman had originally discovered Sanderson's headquarters.

"Sorry. I didn't even think of the connection," she said, touching her scar. "I kind of wear a constant reminder of Eric."

"It's not your fault. Sometimes it just hits me like a hammer," said Sharpe. "Usually when I'm least expecting it. Galenden?"

"Murdered yesterday in his Buenos Aires office."

"That's big. How did you come across that?"

"I activated every possible reporting protocol linked to Berg when you had me look into Sokolov. Same protocols that helped us narrow our search for Sanderson to Argentina, adding everything else we've ever connected to Sanderson. Came up in my feed this morning. I thought it might be something you'd want to pass on to Berg, to tell Sanderson. We know he played a major role in funding Sanderson at one point."

"Probably still does today. I'll give Berg a call when I get back to my office. Any suspects?"

"I didn't dig any deeper," she said. "I can call our liaison at the embassy."

"No. I have a direct line to a senior federal investigator there," said Sharpe. "I need you to look into something else." He explained Berg's call.

"Wow. That's one hell of a conspiracy theory," she said.

"It's probably nothing, but be discreet."

"This won't take long. You can't hide a company," said O'Reilly. "Especially one with four thousand new employees."

"Let's hope not," said Sharpe. "They don't sound like the kind of employees you want to vanish."

Chapter 46

Vienna, Virginia

Berg didn't have to wait long for Sanderson to answer his call. He imagined the general sitting around in the same kind of sleep-deprived stupor, racking his brain with conspiracy theories while the information trickled in at a painfully slow pace. The news he had to share would definitely wake him up.

"Karl, what are we looking at?" Sanderson asked.

"Good news and bad news. I just got off the phone with Ryan Sharpe. They have a lead on Sokolov. Sounds like Reznikov's with him."

"That's good news. How solid is the intelligence?"

"Not very," said Berg, explaining what Sharpe had passed along.

"Thin, but promising. Any chance of getting CIA support on this? Some money-pliable law enforcement contacts? Information on the organized crime scene players? We're going to attract a lot of attention there poking around the markets for Russians buying illegal weapons."

"This is where the bad news starts. Audra Bauer was my only conduit to get that kind of information, and she doesn't know who to trust."

"Right," said Sanderson.

Berg still sensed a lingering doubt about the CIA mole theory, despite having presented nearly incontrovertible evidence to support it.

"Terrence, someone listened to my conversation with Bauer from her end. That suggests a real problem at the CIA. Add the phantom army Brown River created for someone with deep pockets, and a disturbing picture emerges. A picture with True America written all over it."

"I'm analyzing every angle. Hear me out on this. Assuming the phantom Ajax group was behind your abduction—"

"There's no assuming. The team was on Brown River's payroll, and Wellins went to work for Ajax, whether it exists in writing or not."

"Fair enough. An off-the-books team paid by Brown River grabs you, looking for information about your contact in Moscow. A well-placed contact, from what I gather."

"One I'm willing to go to my grave protecting," said Berg.

"Apparently," said Sanderson.

"I don't think they had any practical experience with torture methods," said Berg.

"Sounds like they did a fair enough job," said Sanderson. "So. They grab you—interested in all things Russian."

"And Reznikov," said Berg. "True America has a vested interest in putting that story to bed."

"So do the Russians," said Sanderson.

"Fair enough."

"Then they lose you rather spectacularly. Right?"

"Right," admitted Berg.

"Less than six hours later, they try to grab Bauer out of desperation, who they could have easily followed out of Langley. The Russians know the two of you are connected. They do their homework."

"But they set up at the coffee shop before Bauer drove out of headquarters."

"One of her favorite stops on the way home. A shitty private investigator hired to find Bauer would stake that place out," said Sanderson. "And Wellins? He's part of this Ajax group. A very real, well-paid, under-the-radar part of Brown River that maybe doesn't discriminate against well-paying clients."

"The Russians," Berg stated.

"I wouldn't be surprised if you found a Russian-backed investor or two behind the sudden influx of capital at Brown River. I'm not saying this isn't a major fucking problem or that we ignore it. I just can't shake the strong feeling that the Russians are behind this. And now they have a small army inside the U.S. Wellins probably thinks he was running some kind of patriotic errand. Taking on a rogue cabal of conspirators within the CIA. Wouldn't be the first time contractors at Brown River have been misused this way. I seem to remember an enterprising CIA officer sending some contractors to kill an imminent threat to the United States back in 2005."

He was right. Berg had convinced Jackson to send a team up to D.C. to kill Petrovich under the guise of national security. Sanderson's case for Russian puppet masters was solid, possibly made stronger by the rest of the news he needed to share.

"There's something else you need to know, which I think tips the scale in favor of your theory. Ernesto Galenden was murdered sometime yesterday. I just received word from Sharpe, on the heels of the Reznikov tip. One of Sharpe's contacts in the Argentine Federal Police said Galenden was tortured extensively."

"When was the estimated time of death?"

"They think before midnight," said Berg. "His last appointment of the day was with two Russian executives from Gazprom."

"They weren't executives with Gazprom. More likely Zaslon. None of this is coincidence, Karl," said Sanderson. "Is there any doubt in your mind what's going on right now?"

"There's always doubt. But it sounds like we need to relocate."

"That's a good start. There's no telling how deep the Russians will dig into Galenden's holdings, and with an army ready at their disposal, there's no telling how quickly you might have uninvited guests. I'll do the same here, effective immediately."

"Our primary focus right now is to build an airtight case against Ajax, or whatever Brown River is hiding."

"Add *staying alive* to that to-do list," said Sanderson.

"We'll fit that in somewhere," said Berg. "Right now, we need to find new accommodations. I may need to break this group into smaller pieces to stay hidden."

"I don't advise that," said Sanderson. "Munoz and Melendez will stay with you, guaranteed. You're their mission right now. Same with Graves and Gupta. I can't say the same for Mazurov or Sayar, and I know the Petroviches will fade away if pulled too far away from the group's center of gravity. If the Petroviches split, you can definitely kiss the other two goodbye. That doesn't leave you with much if an opportunity arises."

"Any chance of reinforcements?"

"Everyone I have here is either tied up waiting for the Reznikov mission or tied up with our imminent evacuation. I have some assets in Europe, but given Russia's sudden interest in my organization, they'll need to lie low," said Sanderson.

"We'll figure something out."

"I know a secluded place about three hours out of D.C. It's a little rustic and hasn't been used in about three years, but I can guarantee its secrecy."

"How can you be sure?"

"Because you don't know about it, and neither does the FBI," said Sanderson. "I monitor it remotely. Nobody outside of the Black Flag family has entered the structure. You'll be safe there as long as you don't drag anything back with you."

"Does it have running water?"

"If you can start the site's generator. If not, a large off-the-shelf replacement will run everything you'll need for now."

"I'll take it," said Berg. "Send directions to Graves."

"No need. Munoz and the Petroviches know where to find it."

"That's where you rebooted the program," said Berg, with an air of reverence.

"I spent two good years there. Productive years. I'd love to see it again."

"One of these days."

"I'm not counting on it," said Sanderson.

The thought of turning into a permanent refugee like Sanderson depressed him. They needed to get to the bottom of this conspiracy fast so they could figure out who to trust or, more importantly, who *not* to trust. He'd already taken one giant leap of faith in that direction.

"I asked Sharpe to look into Ajax," said Berg. "Hopefully he'll have something by the time we get resettled in our new location."

"I was going to suggest trusting Sharpe," said Sanderson. "You might want to consider a few press sources. Blowing this wide open could put Brown River out of business at least. Also might come in handy as an insurance policy."

"I hadn't thought of that," said Berg. "I'll make sure Graves puts together a tidy, failsafe package."

"We'll get this sorted, Karl. Might be a little messy, but that's the nature of this business. It certainly wouldn't hurt if we got our hands on Reznikov. He's our ultimate bargaining chip with the Russians. I can't move my team to Libreville without better intelligence or local cooperation."

"I'm not sure how we can pull that off right now."

"What about Manning? Is there any way Audra can convince her boss to help with Libreville? Activate some ground assets to start asking questions? Liaison with my people on the ground? There's no way he's in on this conspiracy."

"I'll see what I can do," said Berg. "She doesn't want to get him killed."

"Give her some time to simmer down from last night," said Sanderson. "I need to get moving. I want to be long gone when they arrive."

After the call ended, Berg lay alone in the great room, replaying the conversation. Something nagged him, a stray thought washed away by relentless waves of exhaustion. It was probably nothing. He had bigger things to worry about right now, like their immediate departure. They'd have to figure out what to do with Wellins. Probably dump him in a shallow grave in the woods.

Same with Foley. He hated to do it to her, but they couldn't risk properly dealing with her body. It wasn't like they could leave her at the front door of a funeral parlor with a note. They'd deal with her later. Bauer walked in from the kitchen, interrupting his thoughts.

"We're almost packed up," she said.

"Good. Sanderson has a safe place we can use. It's about three hours from here."

"The further the better for now."

He suddenly remembered what was bothering him. "Audra…Thomas Manning," he started.

"I'm not getting him involved," she said forcefully.

"Have you spoken with Thomas this morning?"

"I called to let him know I wouldn't be in today. He's at the office. I bypassed him with the Sokolov request and went straight to Zane Abid, my replacement at NCS. There's no reason for Ajax to go after him."

"But he knows about Reznikov. Everything about Reznikov," said Berg. "Yet he wasn't targeted."

"He wasn't in the loop."

"The latest loop. Something about Reznikov's recent escape made someone nervous," said Berg. "Sanderson just had me ninety-nine percent convinced it's the Russians cleaning house, but Manning should be missing if that was the case."

"Three missing CIA officers at one time would raise some serious eyebrows," said Bauer. "Maybe they were showing a little restraint."

"Maybe," said Berg, not really convinced.

He needed a lot of rest and some time to think this through. The three-hour car ride ahead of them would be a start.

Chapter 47

The White House
Washington, D.C.

James Quinn stormed across the White House lobby, annoyed that he'd been pulled from the weekly Homeland Security meeting. It was hard enough to get everyone in one place with his or her undivided attention. By the time he got back, Jacob Remy would have command of the room, cheered on by that monkey on his shoulder, Gerald Simmons. How Crane had retained the two of them seriously perplexed Quinn.

Now he had Shelby on the line, insisting the call was critical. Normally he would have called Shelby back later, but the former director of the FBI had somehow curried serious favor with Beverly Stark, Crane's chief of staff. Shelby wouldn't hesitate to jump the chain of command and call her. Quinn had a good idea why Shelby had called, and didn't want to hear about it from Stark. He could envision her interrupting the meeting he'd just left with the news, which would make him look like an idiot.

The internal politics in this place made his head spin. Part of him wished the new administration had given him the boot, along with everyone else that seemed to have a clue. He entered his office in the northwest corner of the West Wing and thanked the unfortunate staffer tasked to drag him out of the meeting. After shutting the door firmly, Quinn took a seat at his desk and picked up the encrypted phone, pressing a button to connect the call.

"Sorry about the delay, Frederick," he said. "The staffer spent longer than usual fretting outside the Roosevelt Room."

"Nobody wants to drag the national security advisor out of an important meeting, especially the Homeland Security meeting. I apologize for insisting, but I have some time-sensitive information that I think you'll agree beats entertaining the likes of Jacob Remy and Gerald Simmons."

"You really don't like them, do you?" asked Quinn.

"No. And neither do you," said Shelby, bluntly getting to the point. "I just received some promising intelligence from the FBI regarding the possible location of Reznikov. Admittedly, the intelligence is a little light on substance, but it's worth investigating."

Quinn listened to the details, feeling less than enthused by what Shelby recounted.

"I'm not saying this doesn't have potential, but I don't think I can take this to the president, Frederick," said Quinn. "Seriously. Two Russians arrive in Libreville in the middle of the night to buy guns and an SUV on the black market? I'm not even sure who we'd send. I can't imagine General Gordon biting off on this unless he was forced."

"My next call was going to be Zane Abid. NCS should be able to lend a hand," said Shelby.

"I wouldn't get your hopes up too high," said Quinn. "The U.S. hasn't focused much attention on Gabon recently, or ever. Their embassy presence will be minimal."

"Somebody has to follow up on this intelligence," said Shelby. "I'd get on a plane myself and do it if I didn't look more fit to be on a luxury safari than a covert field operation. The CIA will have to figure something out. I'll call Abid and apply some pressure. You do the same on your end. Please. Sorry if it sounded like I tacked the please on as a formality. I didn't ask for things in my former job."

Shelby's last statement was the closest the man had come to *not* sounding like an asshole since he'd met him. Quinn had wondered if Shelby realized that going from the job of director of the FBI to principal deputy director of National Intelligence was a significant step down in authority. Even the director of National Intelligence was more of an administrative and advisory role than anything, exercising no authority to command any of the sixteen agencies comprising the United States intelligence community. It wasn't a bad place at all to land if one had higher ambitions in government, and Quinn was fairly certain Shelby had his eye on a bigger prize.

"Let me see what I can do," said Quinn, recalling a recent conversation with Raymond Burke, senior counsel to the president.

Burke had asked Quinn where things stood with Sanderson's people, specifically if they could be trusted to work on behalf of the new administration. President Crane had so far been reluctant to use any unconventional programs, waiting for the political dust to settle. Burke indicated that the president might soon be open to exploring these options, especially if they could solve problems without the public deployment of troops.

"There is another option. Something off the books we've used before. In fact, you have some experience with this option. Both good and bad."

"I think I know what you're talking about," said Shelby. "I'm not a big fan of using mercenaries, particularly the kind with a history of attacking federal agents and blackmailing the United States."

"I feel your pain, trust me, but they've proven themselves trustworthy time and time again since those days. If the CIA and DOD can't help, they may be our only option."

"Then we better hope the president can convince at least one of the vast public entities entrusted with protecting the United States to do their job," said Shelby.

"We'll work this from both ends. We can't afford to let this opportunity slip by. And very nice job wrangling this intelligence. The fact that it came from a nontraditional intelligence source will help sell it."

"I'll pass that along to my guy at the bureau."

After hanging up with Shelby, Quinn leaned back in his leather office chair and considered the options. The Homeland Security meeting would have to go on without him, not that it ever stopped. He'd take this to Beverly Stark immediately and get the ball rolling. Maybe NCS could put together a ground team here, augmented by a few area experts, and fly them into Libreville. If the decision was made within the next few hours, they could have a team on the ground and in place within twenty-four hours. How hard could it be to track two out-of-place Russians in the Gabon jungle?

Chapter 48

FSB Headquarters
Lubyanka Square, Moscow

Yuri Prerovsky walked up the stairs to his floor, egg salad sandwich and warm Styrofoam container of potato soup in hand. He was bummed about the sandwich. The seemingly endless string of meetings had pushed well past one o'clock, leaving him with the wretched choice between egg salad and the barely seasoned ground mystery meat. The decision came down to numbers. Two egg salad sandwiches remained in the stainless steel bin, dwarfed by a neighboring mountain of plastic-wrapped mystery-meat bombs. It wasn't a tough call.

Half of his section was empty, most of the agents and staff eating in the underground cafeteria. He usually took his lunch at his desk, catching up on emails or prioritizing reports. Mindless work while he took a few minutes to fill up on enough calories to keep him from buying crap at a vendor stall on the way back to his apartment, where he could cook a real meal from scratch, one of the few things he looked forward to on weekdays.

He reached his tiny office and squeezed between the wall and desk to his chair facing the door. Placing the desk in the middle of the office like this was one of the least optimal configurations to take advantage of the confined space, but Kaparov had taught him well.

"Why make it so easy for me to see that you've been staring at the same screen for the past hour?" he'd say. *"I can always find something for you to do, or stare at."* Truer words had never been spoken at headquarters.

Prerovsky settled into his chair and faced his most important decision of the day. Did he start with the soup or sandwich? He started to unwrap the sandwich. Better to get it out of the way. The potato soup wasn't half bad. With one hand holding the sandwich, he typed his password with the other, activating his home screen.

A quick scan of his email inbox revealed dozens of messages sent by other assistant deputy directors or their minions during the morning stretch of meetings. Several came from Gennadiy Yurievich, who'd sat right next to him all morning and never said a word to him! He was the second most junior assistant director in the organized crime division, a precarious position in the hierarchy to hold in a division that clearly had a few too many assistant directors. Prerovsky's presence could only be perceived as a constant threat to the man's job. If only Yurievich knew that he'd gladly trade this office for a field job at this point.

The sandwich had drifted close enough to his nose to remind him why he didn't like egg salad. Egg salad was something you made with eggs nobody would eat, and enough mayo to cover up the reason why. He'd almost taken a bite anyway when an "email alert" caught his eye. He didn't get many of those. Prerovsky lowered the sandwich after reading the subject line and clicked on the message. He skimmed it once and picked up his office phone, dialing a familiar extension.

"Deputy Director Kaparov," his friend answered.

"Why the formality?"

"Ah, Yuri. It's because they swept in a few weeks ago and installed that abysmal key-encrypted phone system. It doesn't give you any indication of who's calling. Could be the fucking director himself! You can't let it go to voicemail. Or shouldn't. I don't really give a shit."

"A few weeks?" said Prerovsky. "I'm surprised they haven't made the transition here already."

"I'd be surprised if they ever did. How else would the Bratva stay one step ahead of the FSB?" said Kaparov. "You didn't hear me say that."

"But everyone else did," said Prerovsky. "Have you taken lunch yet? There's a hotdog cart not too far away. I'm staring at an egg salad sandwich, or rather smelling it, and sincerely wishing it away. My treat."

"You know the way to my stomach, Yuri. I can eat Stardogs for lunch and dinner."

"Meet you downstairs in a few minutes," said Prerovsky.

He memorized the details of the message, shaking his head. If Sokolov and Reznikov were still connected at the hip like his friend suspected, this information could only mean one thing, and it changed everything.

Chapter 49

Salta, Argentina

Sanderson sat on the balcony of an apartment a few blocks west of Plaza 9 de Julio in Barrio Los Molles. The building had been renovated into luxury apartments close to a year ago, with one of Sanderson's shell companies as its earliest significant real estate investor. He'd purchased three adjoining units to use as a backup to their new headquarters in the hills north of the city. The shell company used for the transaction had no link to Ernesto Galenden, nor had it been used to purchase anything remotely traceable to the Black Flag program. It sat mostly dormant all of these years, maintained in electronic perpetuity by a Cayman Islands-based financial house.

He'd stay here with the organization's remaining skeleton crew until they found a new location safe from Russia's renewed interest in his operations. He'd strongly considered leaving Argentina altogether. With their connection to Galenden no longer a secret to the Russians, Argentina might prove to be a difficult place to stay hidden, no matter where they relocated.

When Farrington's team returned from Africa, he'd rent warehouse space and housing outside of Buenos Aires to accommodate the group until they came up with a permanent plan. It wasn't like they were busy. The operation in Gabon was the first full-scale deployment of Black Flag assets in several months, and it felt like more of a wild-goose chase than anything else.

Not that he was complaining. Even if they'd just thrown him a bone to keep him occupied, a professionally and discreetly executed mission would make an impression on somebody. Then they'd get another operation and another. Baby steps. If the Africa operation yielded Reznikov, he could get the Russians off his back in a hurry. Even if it didn't produce the scientist, he'd offer to deliver an unambiguous warning to the Russians about the price of kidnapping CIA officers. Everything hinged on Farrington's success, which was why he'd stacked the deck, sending most of his operatives.

The satellite phone attached to his belt chimed. He wasn't expecting to hear from Farrington for at least another hour, when they landed at the Royal Air Force airfield on Ascension Island to refuel for the continued trip to Libreville. He hoped the mission hadn't been scrapped. They really needed this one. The numbers indicated on the phone's digital screen eased his worry. He could think of no reason why they'd have Karl pass him the bad news.

The CIA officer wasn't in the operational loop on this one. Or in any official loop, it appeared. At this point, Berg was running solo, with Bauer pursuing a soon-to-be irrelevant angle, all from an isolated location three hours away from D.C. Out of respect for everything Berg had done for Sanderson in the past, he would keep him in the loop regarding the Africa mission. He owed him that much.

"Miss me already?" he answered. "The light switch for the back porch is in the pantry off the kitchen. Whoever wired—"

"We have a problem," Berg cut in.

Here we go.

Berg's mind was relentlessly spinning in circles around the evidence he'd gathered, unable to settle on the obvious conclusion.

"Now what?" he asked, unable to restrain his irritation.

"I just received word from my source in Moscow. Sokolov was spotted in Ciudad Juarez, Mexico, yesterday, accompanied by an unidentified Russian."

"He can't be in both places at the same time," said Sanderson. "What's the source?"

"Hard to say. An FSB surveillance operation in Mexico City logged the call, placing Sokolov and his Russian friend at a bar in a brothel within the city's red-light district. FSB surveillance confirmed that the Bratva has sent a team north to investigate."

"The source used the name Sokolov, but not Reznikov?"

"Yes. The Bratva placed a considerable bounty on Sokolov's head. I just learned that. They must have drawn the same conclusion I did about Reznikov's all too convenient escape."

"How significant of a bounty?"

"I know what you're thinking. Money makes people see things."

"In this case, conveniently at the source's favorite whorehouse."

"I have two problems with summarily dismissing this as a fake sighting. First, the source identified two Russians. The bounty was specific to Sokolov, making no mention of anyone else. Why would the source make up the sighting and add another Russian to the mix?"

"To make it more realistic?" Sanderson suggested.

"Maybe, but what's the point? When the Bratva arrives, you're stuck holding an empty bag, no matter how detailed you described its contents. Which underscores an even bigger problem. What does the source think is going to happen to him when the Bratva finds the bag empty and quickly determines it never held anything? You'd have to be suicidal to report a false sighting like this to the Russian mob."

"This information is a day old?" said Sanderson.

"At least."

"Then Sokolov and Reznikov are either dead or back in the Bratva's possession by now. Unless you can convince the powers that be to deploy a second task force to Ciudad Juarez, there's nothing we can do about it right now."

"Munoz and Melendez said they'd head south. This is exactly the kind of mission they've trained for," said Berg.

"Two men, without support?"

"If the report is true, we're looking at a game changer. There's only one reason I can think of to explain why they'd be on the U.S.-Mexico border."

"I can't think of any, which is why I'm ninety-nine point nine percent convinced it's a bogus report."

Sanderson's own statement triggered another thought. The surveillance report itself was fake. It made sense given the fact pattern. He couldn't believe he hadn't thought of this as soon as Karl described the report.

"Terrence, they're bringing him here," Berg stated flatly.

Of course they are. Just what they want you to think. They don't even have Reznikov, but they can wield him like a weapon. Brilliant.

"Who? The Russians?"

"What? No. Why would the Russians bring him here?"

"They wouldn't. The Russians don't have Reznikov. The whole thing is a ruse," said Sanderson.

"Dammit, Terrence!" said Berg. "Quit being obtuse. I'm talking about our government."

"I think you're obsessed with True America. Why would they bring Reznikov to the United States?"

"I don't know," said Berg. "To finish the job they started in 2007?"

"Karl, the Russians manufactured this intelligence. Think about it. They know you're looking for Sokolov. They know you have a source in Moscow. I'm not saying your source is compromised, but they conjure up some phony intelligence about Sokolov on the U.S.-Mexico border and dump it in the system. Instant panic."

"I don't—" started Berg, pausing for a long moment. "What's to say it's not the other way around?"

In his excitement, Sanderson had skipped right past that possibility. *Both* reports could be false. Could the Russians deploy a large enough force in the Gabonese jungle to ambush Farrington's team? Would they risk the political fallout from killing the Special Operations Command operators assigned to accompany the team?

"General?"

"Sorry. I was thinking about what you said. The Russians dragging us into Gabon—"

"Stop," said Berg. "Terrence, I'm not talking about the Russians. I'm talking about whoever is behind Ajax and the attacks here."

"True America," said Sanderson.

"I don't know yet, but tell Farrington to watch his back. I suspect we've just scratched the surface of this conspiracy, and you have most of your eggs in that C-17 basket."

"I confirmed the authenticity of this operation with General Frank Gordon, the head of SOCOM, and Bob Kearney, the president's Homeland Security advisor. I trust Bob with my life, and Frank Gordon is the most principled soldier I've ever met, even if he's the biggest pain in my ass. The op is real. Farrington didn't sense anything off when the aircraft picked them up. SOCOM assigned four operators from DEVGRU to keep an eye on us. Not exactly the kind of posse you send to round up twenty of my people."

"I'm just repeating some sound advice given to me a few days back, right before I was kidnapped. Watch your back."

Sanderson remembered the conversation and the scent of the Montecristo No. 2 in the air at the time.

"Words to live by," he said. "I'll warn Farrington. The team is about an hour out of Ascension by my calculation."

"That's an isolated place," said Berg. "What about Munoz and Melendez?"

"Let's see how things play out in Africa. I'll call you when they reach Libreville."

"Thanks for keeping me in the loop. I feel pretty damn useless right now. We all do."

"We'll get things back on track for all of us. This is the first step on that path. I never forget my friends," said Sanderson.

He ended the call and immediately dialed Farrington's satellite phone, not expecting to get through. Unless he wandered onto the flight deck and the phone caught a satellite signal through one of the windows, he would be unable to communicate with Farrington until they landed on Ascension Island. He waited to leave a message.

"Rich, we've had a few developments. Nothing critical, but keep a close eye on your escorts and check for stowaways. Call me as soon as you land on Ascension. Just being cautious."

He thumbed a text message, relaying an abbreviated version of the voicemail. Sanderson lowered the phone to his side, knowing he'd place a call every few minutes until he got through to Farrington on the runway. Berg's paranoia was like a contagious rash. Once you got it, scratching only made it worse, and he'd just scratched the hell out of this rash.

PART FOUR:

BLACK MARK

Chapter 50

Royal Air Force (RAF) Base
Ascension Island

The C-17 Globemaster's wheels bit into the runway and rumbled for a few seconds, before the massive aircraft rapidly and unnaturally slowed from the reverse thrust of its four over-powered turbofan engines. The sudden deceleration pushed Farrington into Dihya Castillo to his right. Jared Hoffman knocked into him from the left; a victim of the same, seemingly impossible physics prank played by the aircraft's engines.

The behemoth taxied smoothly for a few minutes before coming to a stop. Farrington looked forward to getting off this thing for however long it took to refuel. Despite its impressive size, the two-story, windowless cargo bay felt like a flying tomb. He might reconsider the flight crew's offer to sit on the flight-deck level, where he'd have a chance to see the sky. They had a long flight ahead of them to Africa, their destination still up in the air. Literally.

The Gabonese government had apparently been less than receptive to the idea of allowing a U.S. military transport to land at their air base in Libreville to "refuel." The current plan was to covertly parachute a small group into the farmlands southeast of the city along the aircraft's approved route to the United Nations Base at Entebbe International Airport. The group would link up with CIA-friendly assets and make arrangements to receive the rest of the team when they filtered into the area on private flights. The plan was far from ideal, but it got some of them on the ground in the target area as quickly as possible to start the search for Reznikov.

After the aircraft remained stationary for several seconds, the C-17's loadmaster, seated in a sturdy flight chair next to the flight deck stairwell, released his harness and gave them all a thumbs-up. Farrington unbuckled the far less serious-looking strap holding him into the jump seat. The loadmaster opened the crew door on the forward-most, port side of the cargo bay, close to his station.

The team milled about the section of the hold they had claimed, groggy from the eight-hour leg of the flight. Farrington could sense they were ready to press their feet on terra firma and breathe some fresh air before they were sealed up again. The DEVGRU operators stuck together toward the rear of the hold, like they had for most of the flight. The SEALs had neither been openly disdainful, nor subtly disrespectful toward Farrington's team, they merely stuck to themselves. He hadn't expected an ice cream social. They had been assigned to babysit Farrington's team, and it clearly wasn't a choice assignment.

"If your team wants to breathe some crisp middle-of-fucking-nowhere Atlantic air tinged with aviation fuel, they can stretch their legs on the runway!" the loadmaster yelled. "Just keep them near the stairs and out of the refueling crew's way so we can get out of here."

"Which side do they use to refuel?" asked Farrington.

"That side," said the loadmaster, pointing toward the starboard side of the cargo bay.

Farrington nodded at the U.S. Air Force technical sergeant, turning to face the bulk of his team nearby. "Stick close by. There's nothing to see out there anyway. This place is literally in the middle of nowhere."

The group mumbled and nodded, at least half of them immediately moving toward the hatch leading out of the aircraft. He stopped Aleem Fayed on the way by. "Make sure they don't wander."

"Got it," said Fayed. "How long do you think we'll be here?"

"They topped off in Buenos Aires, so I'm thinking twenty to thirty minutes. I'll meet you out there in a few. I need to update Sanderson."

"What's there to update?"

"That they didn't fly us to Guantanamo Bay."

The seasoned operative shook his head and laughed, heading over to organize the pack gathering at the door. Fayed led the Middle East Group, which comprised at least a third of the task force put together by Sanderson for this operation. Given the final destination, any skin tone naturally darker than Farrington's tan bought you a ticket on this flight. The entire South-Central America group, minus Munoz and Melendez, had also been sent.

Not that operatives from either group would blend right into the Libreville population. Far from it, in fact. The quick-fused mission exposed a significant weakness in the Black Flag structure. They had only two operatives who could walk through the main Libreville market without drawing immediate attention. Andre Luison, a French-Creole descended operative attached to the European Group, and Jon Holloman, a former Special Forces soldier with two years of intense German language training from the Defense Language Institute in Monterrey, California. Needless to say, they'd both parachute into Gabon tonight.

Castillo remained in her seat, rubbing her temples, an empty airsickness bag between her knees. Farrington patted her on the shoulder, nudging her forward.

"Get some air," he said.

"I don't feel like moving," Castillo groaned.

"You need to walk those rubbery legs. You're hitting the ground later tonight."

"Pain in the ass," she muttered, pushing off the seat.

Farrington grabbed her arm before she plopped right back down. She didn't look well, a slight film of perspiration visible on her face. He might have to reconsider sending her with the advanced party if she didn't come around.

"Sure you didn't eat something sketchy earlier?"

"I didn't eat for more than six hours before our scheduled departure. I get airsick. Every time. I'll be fine."

"I need you steady when you hit the ground," he said.

"I'll be fine," she said, shaking his hand off her arm.

Castillo headed for the door with most of the team, leaving him with Jared Hoffman, who would most definitely *not* be part of the parachute team. He was somehow whiter than Farrington. Hoffman, aka Gosha, was the Russian Group's sniper, and one of Farrington's most reliable operatives.

"She looks like shit," Gosha quietly commented.

"I don't have another sniper that doesn't glow like a fluorescent light."

Gosha smirked. "Funny. Never thought I'd be discriminated against for being too white."

"You can file a complaint with HR when we get back," said Farrington. "She says she'll be fine."

"Shaky hands make a useless sniper."

"There won't be any sniping when they land. Not right away. I need to make a call."

"I'll be here."

"Not going outside?"

"What for?"

"Good point."

Farrington walked toward the door, taking the satellite phone out of a cargo pocket. The loadmaster flipped switches at his station, looking up from his work and glancing past Farrington. A loud mechanical whine cut through the deep hum of the engines, drawing Farrington's attention toward the back of the cargo bay. He caught some movement behind the vertical ramp, which was immediately noticed by the SEALs.

"Any reason you need the ramp open!" one of them yelled over the noise.

The loadmaster either ignored the question or didn't hear it. The SEAL walked closer as the ramp started to descend.

"Hey! What's up with the ramp?"

"Fresh air! I get to sit here and balance fuel while everyone else takes a break," replied the loadmaster.

The SEAL shook his head. "At least dim the fucking lights! I don't need my picture on the cover of *Newsweek* magazine."

"Whatever," mumbled the sergeant. "It's not like anyone's watching."

The lighting scheme shifted to red, the best choice under the circumstances. Red light released less energy and was harder to detect from a distance.

"How long do we have until we take off?" asked Farrington.

"The pilot wants us rolling within thirty minutes," the loadmaster replied. "I'll give you a heads-up when it's time to gather the flock."

Farrington nodded and joined the last of his operatives waiting to get out, checking the satellite phone. No signal. Castillo stepped through the hatch, her deep red form bathed in silver moonlight. His phone buzzed twice, indicating he had a voice message. It buzzed again, once. A text. He read Sanderson's words twice, fighting the urge to immediately scan his surroundings. Fuck. Maybe they *had* landed in Guantanamo. How the hell would he know the difference?

Farrington poked his head through the hatch, scanning the moonlit tarmac and the buildings beyond. It didn't look like Guantanamo, even in the darkness. He saw nothing in the distance beyond the base. Facing the hangars in Guantanamo at night, you could see lights from the towns outside the base perimeter. He suspected nothing but Atlantic beyond these buildings. Headlights appeared in the fuel farm on the edge of the tarmac, followed by a long truck.

"Fuel's inbound. No smoking, obviously," said the loadmaster.

Something's inbound, he thought.

His paranoid mind was taking over after reading Sanderson's message. He glanced toward the SEALs, who now sat on top of the pallets of double-stacked Pelican cases, which contained the taskforce's primary weapons and gear. They talked and laughed quietly, appearing to have no interest in leaving the aircraft. Nothing felt off to him. The SEALs didn't have the numbers or weapons to take down his team. Everyone carried a pistol, a condition Sanderson had insisted on. Primary weapons would be removed from the cases and issued to the team infiltrating by parachute later in the flight.

The SEALs all carried rucksacks, which could contain a few surprises, but Farrington's team had a few spoilers hidden in their personal gear just in case. Satisfied that nothing was immediately amiss inside or outside the aircraft, he backed up and approached Gosha, who looked surprised to see him.

"Back so soon?"

Farrington lowered his voice. "Sanderson wants us alert during the refueling. Didn't say why. Any chance they hid another team on this thing?"

"We checked before takeoff in Buenos Aires. Lower deck and lavatory were empty. Flight deck had two pilots in the cockpit. The rest empty. If we have a problem, it's going to come from the outside."

"That's what I was thinking. What about our friends over there?" he asked, without glancing up at the SEALs.

"DEVGRU is good, but not that good. If something went down, my guess is they'll disappear right before it happens," said Gosha, cocking his ear. "Fuel truck?"

"I hope so."

"Maybe one of us should keep an eye on it," Gosha suggested.

"That doesn't sound like you're volunteering."

"Wouldn't it look suspicious if I suddenly developed an interest in leaving the aircraft?" said Gosha, smirking.

"Put your earpiece in. Primary tactical channel."

Before heading back, Farrington pulled a wired earpiece free from a Velcro hook hidden in his collar and pushed it into his left ear. On his way out the door, he heard Gosha joking about kosher MREs, the team's previously agreed upon code to watch their hosts very closely. When he got to the bottom of the stairs, he tapped a reply to Sanderson's message.

LANDED IN RIGHT PLACE. ALL KOSHER HERE.

The reply came instantly: MSG FROM FLT DECK WHEN UR BACK IN AIR.

He pressed K, followed by SEND.

"Aleem, Gosha said he's going to fight you over the kosher MREs," said Farrington.

"He's about as kosher as my Saudi grandmother," replied Fayed, pausing a few moments before walking a little further out onto the tarmac.

Nobody immediately reacted to Farrington's use of the code word, but over the next several seconds, the operatives casually spread out from the hatch.

Chapter 51

Royal Air Force (RAF) Base
Ascension Island

Jared Hoffman dug through his pack, removing what was indeed a kosher MRE from the depths. His hand brushed the pistol grip of his MP9 on the way out. He placed the tan plastic pouch on the seat next him and pretended to rearrange the contents of his pack, instead maneuvering the compact submachine gun into a readily accessible position. The weapon was loaded with a twenty-round magazine to keep it concealable. An additional thirty-round magazine lay flat along the left side of the weapon, kept in place by a magnetic strip attachment. A few more magazines had been hidden in various external pouches on the pack. It was one of their insurance policies. He had others.

The fuel truck arrived, its squeaky brakes audible through the aircraft hull behind him. The loadmaster slid out of his seat and peered through the window in the emergency exit hatch next to his station.

"Fuel's here!" he announced.

Hoffman nodded politely, and the loadmaster went to work on the switches.

"Gosha," said Ashraf Haddad, grabbing his attention.

Two of the SEALs headed in their direction, one of them stretching his arms and yawning while walking, the other yapping about a new rifle he'd fired. He resisted the urge to put his hand inside his pack, secure in the knowledge that all seven Black Flag operatives were thinking the same thing and were ready to respond in the blink of an eye. The de facto leader of the SEALs spoke to them for the first time since Sanderson's team boarded the aircraft.

"Headed up to the flight deck, gentlemen," said the leader. "Take a look at this dump from the cockpit so I can tell my kids I saw it. You're welcome to join us."

Hoffman held up the tan pouch. "I have a date with a kosher MRE. Maybe later."

"Not much to see up there anyway," said the commando.

They passed through the small knot of Sanderson's operatives and climbed the stairwell without saying a word to the loadmaster. Hoffman casually glanced at the red, monochromatic forms of the two remaining SEALs, not detecting any change to their behavior or posture. He relaxed a little, giving the MRE some thought. Chicken and black beans didn't sound so bad right now.

Hoffman reached for the MRE, and the cargo bay went dark. Before he got the MP9 out of his pack, suppressed gunfire rattled from the top of the stairwell, striking one of his teammates with a wet thud.

Hoffman launched backward, gripping the submachine gun and his pack, the next tightly spaced pattern of bullets zipping through the space he'd moments ago occupied. He hit the metal deck hard and rolled onto his left side to face the source of gunfire, his MP9 firing at the top of the stairwell a fraction of a moment later. A weapon clattered down the stairs, indicating his burst had been accurate, but it was immediately replaced by more gunfire from the same location.

A warm splash hit the back of his neck, followed by suppressed and unsuppressed gunfire from the rear of the aircraft. A body dropped behind him, momentarily shielding his back from the new threat. Deafening gunfire from the team's nearby pistols echoed off the cargo bay walls, the muzzle flashes lashing out toward the front and rear of the aircraft. Bullets struck the body behind him again. Someone was desperate to put his MP9 out of action. They couldn't win this fight. Not caught in a crossfire with nowhere to maneuver.

He reloaded the MP9 with the attached magazine and dug through his pack again, retrieving a flashlight. While the sharp reports of his team's pistols slackened, he unscrewed the top and shook a flash-bang grenade onto the deck, tossing the flashlight shell aside. The grenade's safety lever released automatically, the device's pin pulled before it was squeezed into the flashlight.

"Grenade out!" he yelled, tossing it toward the rear of the aircraft.

Chapter 52

Royal Air Force (RAF) Base
Ascension Island

Farrington dropped to the hard tarmac the moment the red light disappeared from the crew door next to him. His quick instinct was rewarded by the hollow metallic *thunk* of a bullet above him. Aleem Fayed spun and fired two quick shots toward the nose of the aircraft.

"Two targets! Front landing gear," said Fayed before his body crumpled to the ground like a rag doll.

Flashes erupted behind Farrington from the rear wheel housing, bullets cutting through the team from a third direction. This would be over in a few seconds if they remained exposed like this. There was only one place to go, and he had no idea if the situation would be better or worse when they got there. Holloman's head snapped back, a dark splotch appearing against the side of the gray aircraft. It couldn't be any worse than this.

"Go under! Get to the other side!" he yelled, rolling underneath the aircraft.

Bullets chased him across the concrete for half of the trip, the initial gunmen quickly losing their firing angles from positions best suited for catching them in an ambush along the port side of the aircraft. When he emerged on the opposite side of the C-17's belly, he caught two men in full tactical gear crouched in the open next to the refueling truck.

They either didn't see him or didn't expect him. It didn't matter. Farrington lined their dark forms up with his tritium sights and fired center mass. One of the men dropped into a seated position on the ground. The other spun against the truck's front wheel well and went to his knees. Knowing they weren't out of the fight, he closed the short distance, alternating bullets between them until he was close enough to shoot them in the face. He drilled the seated man in the nose; then the pistol's slide locked back.

"Shit," he muttered, ejecting the magazine while his free hand retrieved another.

He'd practiced swapping pistol magazines more than a thousand times, under every possible condition, but when the second commando unexpectedly twisted on his knees to face him, Farrington knew it wasn't going to happen. A thousand times? Two thousand times? When your time was up—your time was up.

He slammed the new magazine home anyway, staring down the barrel of a compact rifle. The man's head jerked backward against the tire well, the rest of his body going slack. Farrington crouched between the two dead men and searched for his savior. Dihya Castillo lay flat on the tarmac directly underneath the aircraft, her pistol extended in both hands. She was the only other member of the team that had made it under the C-17.

"Keep going!" he yelled.

She started to crawl, but fell flat on her stomach with an agonized groan. Farrington started forward, then froze. Castillo held her left hand out, telling him to stop, while the other rapidly fired her pistol at a dark form barely visible to him on the other side of the aircraft. The shadowy figure slumped to its hands and knees, head down. Farrington picked up the suppressed M4 carbine and fired twice. The shooter's body flattened. He started toward Castillo again.

"No! There's a sniper out there!" she yelled. "I'm done anyway."

"Fuck that," he muttered, determined to grab her.

Her body shuddered from a high-velocity impact, the supersonic crack startling him. Gunfire continued to rage inside the aircraft, but he could tell that battle was dying down. Farrington resolved to make this as painful as possible for whoever was behind this. He'd use the fuel truck to blow the whole fucking plane up before he was finished. He snatched three thirty-round magazines for the M4 from one of the vests and took off behind the fuel truck, stuffing the magazines in his pocket as he ran.

A shooter hidden behind the bulging wheel well fired at him when he poked his head around, striking the edge of the fuel tank. Scratch the fuel truck idea. He'd find another way. Farrington peeked again, drawing fire, one of the bullets creasing his hair. He dropped into a prone position behind the back wheels of the truck and leaned quickly into the open, finding his target in the rifle's holographic sight. A single trigger press sent a bullet straight into the shooter's chest before he could readjust his aim. The man staggered sideways, trying to recover from the hit to his body armor.

Farrington followed up with three shots to the upper chest and neck area, putting him down.

He searched the shadowy area around the massive landing gear, coming up empty, which didn't mean he was in the clear. His view was limited, and he knew it. The pistol fire inside the C-17 had nearly stopped, the sound of Hoffman's submachine gun conspicuously missing. Even the suppressed fire from the hostile rifles had slowed, replaced by more methodical bursts. They were mopping up the last survivors. He had to act.

Farrington burst into the open, sprinting for the rear cargo bay ramp. He'd almost reached the ramp when he heard a familiar voice.

"Grenade out!"

They were still in this.

Chapter 53

Royal Air Force (RAF) Base
Ascension Island

Hoffman's intentional use of the word grenade had the desired effect. Unable to see what he'd thrown into the rear of the cargo bay, the gunmen scrambled out of the aircraft, shouting panicked orders. Fragmentation grenades and fuel-laden aircraft didn't mix. The moment they scattered for the ramp, he rolled to the left, drawing fire from the top of the stairs.

A pistol low to the deck and across from him unleashed several shots at the elevated gunman before Hoffman pressed the MP9's trigger, adding to the sparks flying off the top of the metal staircase. A tightly spaced series of earsplitting explosions crunched his eardrums and lit the cargo bay, spurring him into action.

"Clear the front! Clear the front!" he screamed, barely able to hear his own words.

Hoffman leapt forward onto his feet and rapidly moved to the front of the cargo bay, firing short bursts up the stairwell and scanning for the loadmaster. Ashraf Haddad sprinted past him on the right, checking the loadmaster station before pressing himself against the side of the aircraft and aiming his pistol at the open crew door.

The loadmaster had disappeared, either out the door to help ambush the team outside or down the short passageway next to the stairwell to hide behind the stairs. Both scenarios presented a problem he needed to solve in the next few seconds before the confusion sowed by the flash-bang grenade dissipated.

With Haddad covering the door, he chose to clear the area behind the stairs. Another flash-bang would do nicely right about now, but he didn't have the time to dig through one of the packs behind him to retrieve one. Hoffman improvised, firing the rest of his MP9's magazine into the dark red space, igniting it with sparks before yelling, "Grenade out!" He tossed the spent submachine gun into the loadmaster's possible hiding space and dropped to the ground with his pistol drawn.

Much to his surprise, the ruse worked. A dark figure lurched into the dark red passageway and charged forward, firing a compact weapon on full automatic. The bullets zipped harmlessly over the Black Flag operative's head, the fusillade answered by several swiftly fired bullets from Haddad's and Hoffman's pistols. The loadmaster twitched from the repeated hits, careening into the stairway's handrail and sliding to the deck.

Hoffman picked up the rifle dropped earlier by one of the shooters at the top of the stairwell and signaled for Haddad to follow. They had to get off the cargo level. The sound of suppressed gunfire raged behind them. Without a moment to spare, he rushed up the stairs, sweeping the open space above and to the left with the compact rifle. The business end of a suppressor poked over the top of the stairs, a dark stain sprayed against the bullet-riddled wall beyond it. As he continued to climb, a facedown head appeared. Another body lay close by.

He quickly stepped over the body at the top of the stairs and triggered the rifle's flashlight, illuminating the entire space. Two rows of commercial-airline-style seats faced forward, taking up most of the room. A quick check confirmed they were alone. Haddad stopped at the top of the stairs and detangled the dead man's rifle, lowering himself into position to cover the inevitable counterattack. Hoffman would deal with the pilots if they were still alive. Judging by the number of holes in the wall behind Haddad, it was anyone's guess.

"What do you see?" he whispered to Haddad.

"Nothing," replied the operative with a surprised tone. "It's completely quiet."

"How far can you see?"

"About three-quarters of the way, with a blind spot on the left, all the way back."

"Something's wrong," said Hoffman, the rifle aimed at the cockpit door.

A suppressed crack echoed from below, but the bullet wasn't aimed at the stairwell.

"Are they shooting our wounded?" said Hoffman.

"I don't think so," Haddad answered. "I can see all of our people."

Another crack rang out, followed by a familiar voice. "Cargo bay is clear! Status update on the flight deck?"

"It's Farrington. Get down there," whispered Hoffman. "Tell him I'll have the cockpit clear in a second."

While Haddad descended, Hoffman repositioned himself, lying flat on the deck with his feet facing the cockpit door. He had no idea if the door on one of these had a lock like commercial airliners and had zero desire to test the handle. It was an easy way to get shot through the door. He nestled the rifle into his shoulder, the rifle pointing up at the space between the handle and the door frame. Hoffman gave his plan a second thought. This bird was likely their only way out of here. Shooting through the door should be his last resort. Instead of bullets, he hit the door twice with the bottom of his boot.

"Open the door!" he said.

He kicked again. "Open the fucking door, or I'll shoot it open!"

"Don't do that! You do any more damage to the cockpit controls, and I can't fly this thing," replied the voice.

"You're going to fly us out of here?" said Hoffman.

"If you promise not to kill me."

"What about the copilot?"

"Dead. The first bullets that passed through the bulkhead killed him," said the pilot. "We don't have a lot of time here. The base is on full alert. They have a small garrison."

"He's right about running out of time," said Farrington, appearing above the top of the stairwell. "I'd rather not get stuck here answering questions about this. He's willing to fly us?"

"That's what he claims," said Hoffman. "Good to see you, by the way. Who else made it?"

"We're it," said Farrington, climbing the rest of the stairs.

"Careful," said Hoffman, pointing at the bullet holes.

Farrington didn't seem to care. "Is the door unlocked?"

"Unlock the door and take a few steps back. Lace your fingers and place them in front of your face, covering your eyes," said Farrington. "If you shoot me, my colleague will shoot you. Understood?"

"Yes."

"Do it!"

A sturdy-sounding mechanism clunked.

"It's unlocked. I'm standing as you—"

Farrington opened the door and leaned inside, pulling the pilot by his flight vest through the opening and slamming him against the bullet-riddled bulkhead. Hoffman didn't need to be told what to do next. He slid into the surprisingly spacious cockpit and cleared it, finding the copilot exactly how the pilot described, slumped in his seat, half of his head splattered on the front and side windows.

"Clear! Were either of you armed?" said Hoffman as Farrington wrangled him back into the cockpit.

"They don't typically arm the pilots."

"Nothing typical about this flight," said Farrington, pushing him back into the pilot's seat. "Get us moving."

"I need confirmation that fuel truck didn't connect," said the pilot.

Farrington pushed the rifle barrel against the back of his head. "Don't fuck with me. This wasn't a refueling stop."

The pilot suddenly got defiant. "They might have hooked it up to keep you from getting suspicious. This flight will not get far connected to a tanker truck!"

"They didn't bother," said Farrington. "Saw it with my own eyes. Get us moving!"

"Someone needs to close the ramp. We can't take off with it open."

"Can you taxi with it open?" said Farrington.

"It's not ideal."

"If this aircraft isn't moving within the next few seconds, I'm going to kill you. I know the APU is running, and these engines don't need long to warm up."

"It will still take at least a minute for the APU to bring the engines back to idle. Maybe quicker," said the pilot, flipping a series of switches that created a mechanical humming.

Farrington pulled the copilot's body out of the adjacent seat and swung into the seat behind him. He sat down and pulled out his satellite phone. "I assume you're not U.S. Air Force?"

"I used to fly these in the Air Force," said the pilot.

"Who hired you to fly a U.S. Air Force C-17?" asked Farrington, keeping the rifle trained on the pilot.

"CIA. We work on a contract-to-contract basis."

"What about the SEALs?"

"We picked up four SOCOM operators and their gear at MacDill. Shortly after taking off, they rerouted us to the air base at Guantanamo. The teams swapped out during a brief stop there."

"Without SOCOM's knowledge, no doubt," muttered Farrington.

"Look, we just fly. They told us to lock the door; then the shooting started. We had no idea."

"Your loadmaster seemed to know what he was doing," said Hoffman.

"Not all of our contracts are the same."

The pilot flipped a few more switches, grasping the four-engine throttle on the center console and the control stick in front of him.

"We're ready," said the pilot, increasing the throttle.

The aircraft started to move forward. A loud pop filled the cockpit, blood splattering the window in front of the pilot. Farrington grabbed the man's collar to pull him out of the seat, but a second bullet snapped through the side of the aircraft and hit the pilot before he could yank him down. The pilot arched his back and slumped in the seat—dead. A third bullet hit the cockpit, puncturing the hull behind the pilot's seat and ricocheting off Hoffman's rifle. He dropped to the deck, in the row between the back seats, and inspected the weapon, finding a cracked handguard. The rifle was still functional.

Farrington slipped out of the copilot's seat and crouched behind the pilot, reaching over a long console of switches and electronics to pull the throttle back to idle. The aircraft lumbered to a stop. Another bullet passing through the cockpit's thin aluminum skin struck the copilot's headrest.

"Now what?" said Hoffman. "Fly it out ourselves?"

"How hard could it be to take off? There's a throttle and a joystick," said Farrington.

"Taking off sounds easy enough, but what about the rest?"

"We can worry about that later," said Farrington. "But we're not going anywhere with that sniper."

"How bad could it be if we surrendered to the base garrison? The sniper has to vanish once they arrive. Right?" said Hoffman. "Just saying."

"Sure. They'll put us on the next C-17 flight back to the States," said Farrington, smirking. "Everything will be fine."

Farrington was right. They had to take out the sniper. More accurately—Hoffman had to take out the sniper.

"I have an idea," said Hoffman.

Chapter 54

Royal Air Force (RAF) Base
Ascension Island

Dihya Castillo lay on the tarmac in a wide pool of her own blood, still alive. The second bullet fired by the sniper had struck the concealed ballistic plate she'd chosen to wear under her clothes, and ricocheted into the night. Castillo had played dead to keep Farrington from attempting a pointless rescue. She was as good as dead. No reason to get them both killed.

The first bullet had torn through her right thigh and exited her left pelvis, no doubt making a mess of everything in between. The pain had been excruciating at first, but started to fade quickly. She'd be gone in a few minutes, satisfied that she'd played a small part in turning the fight around. Castillo had no idea what went down behind the aircraft, her view of the ramp area blocked by the C-17's massive wheel wells, but she'd watched Farrington methodically fire one burst after another while moving toward the ramp until everything went quiet.

The engines whined louder. A few seconds later, the aircraft above her started to edge forward. She raised her head a few inches to calculate the path of the C-17's rear wheels. Even mortally wounded, the thought of getting crushed under those tires breathed a little life into her. Fuck. It didn't look good. She hadn't crawled far enough under the aircraft before she took the first bullet.

The supersonic crack of a bullet drew her attention away from the slowly approaching tires. If she had her rifle, she'd put an end to that fucker. She'd located the sniper's nest a few shots after the one that hit her body armor. The sniper wasn't in the air ops tower, the most obvious location to a non-sniper. He or she had set up on the roof of a two-story hangar building.

She watched the structure, catching a flash. A moment later, the crack echoed across the concrete. Another flash-crack immediately followed, and the engine whine lowered, returning to idle. The pilot was dead. She found herself with mixed emotions when the wheels ground to a halt several feet from her. She was glad not to be crushed to a pulp but bummed that Farrington and the survivors wouldn't escape. A few more gunshots echoed across the tarmac; then a long silence ensued.

She closed her eyes, thinking she'd let go and slip away when a hollow, metallic sound brought her back. Another clunk, and she opened her eyes. Two dark objects skittered to a stop about thirty feet away from the C-17's fuselage, exploding in a billow of thick smoke.

Interesting.

The chemical cloud expanded and drifted straight for the aircraft, following the gentle Atlantic breeze she'd first felt when she stepped onto the tarmac.

When it had thickened enough to obscure her view of the sniper's building, a figure descended the crew door stairs, carrying a scoped rifle. She recognized him through the haze.

"Jared," she said, barely able to raise her voice over the engines. "Hoffman!"

He crouched, scanning in her direction. She raised her right hand a few inches, catching his attention. Hoffman got to her quickly, kneeling down to grab her.

"No. No. I'm gone, Jared," she protested.

"I need to get you away from these wheels," said Hoffman. "Farrington is leaving. Somebody has to survive this mess."

He pulled her well past the stairwell, laying her on her back behind Andre Luison's bloodied body.

"You can keep me company," he said, lying down next to her with his rifle.

The aircraft rumbled to life behind them, once again moving.

"What are you doing?" she said.

"Taking care of the sniper," said Hoffman. "They'll be too busy trying to put that beast out of business to notice me."

The smoke grenades had already started to dissipate. They'd be exposed to the sniper again in a moment.

"How do you get out of here?" she asked, a bullet cracking overhead.

"I don't. I take my chances with the RAF," he said, opening his rifle's scope covers.

She knew what that meant. He'd be shipped back to the U.S. on another fake flight, his body dumped over the Atlantic.

"I know where the sniper is. I can take the shot," said Castillo. "Set me up behind your rifle and get out of here."

Hoffman stared at her through the thinning smoke, a thin smile barely visible. "I don't know. That's at least a thousand feet. Tough shot."

"I know it's an intimidating range for *you*," she said. "But *I* can handle it."

He laughed for a moment. "Hard to argue with you on this one."

"Then get moving," said Castillo. "Farrington doesn't look like he's waiting around."

Hoffman turned her on her stomach and set her up behind the rifle, which lay across Luison's back. He slid an extra ten-round 7.62mm magazine next to her left arm.

"I won't need that," she said.

"Of course you won't," he said, kissing her on the forehead.

"What was that for?" she said.

"Always wanted to do that," he said. "Thank you for this."

She turned her head to say something, but he was gone, his form scarcely visible running through the last of the smoke screen.

She refocused on her task.

The smoke had cleared enough for her to see the outline of the left corner of the two-story building. The sniper fired every several seconds, trying to put the C-17 out of commission. The muzzle flashes were drawing her right to the shooter. By the time the smoke thinned a little more, she had a good sight picture. Castillo centered the crosshairs on what little she could see of the well-concealed target, noticing a spotter to the right. Her second target.

She made a few quick calculations. The wind was coming directly at her, so she made no initial adjustments. She took Hoffman's word for the distance. He wouldn't have come out here without a reasonable idea. Castillo would use the scope's tick marks to compensate for the range.

With the crosshairs fixed on the sniper, she made an infinitesimally small adjustment to the rifle's position and started to take the slack out of the two-stage trigger. When the rifle bucked into her shoulder, she knew it was a hit without even seeing it.

She quickly reacquired the corner, the spotter fumbling to replace the sniper. When the spotter's dark figure stopped moving, she pressed the trigger again. The scope's field of vision wavered from the shot, but settled just in time to see the target jerk back out of sight.

Her focus came back to the tarmac and the screaming engines. She never looked back to see if Jared had made it. Instead, she expended every last bit of her energy to flip onto her back. Dihya Castillo stared skyward, seeing more stars in the last minute she remained alive than she'd seen in her entire life. Nearly two thousand miles from the nearest continent, Ascension Island was the ultimate "dark sky" location. Millions of stars appeared to her, then faded away.

Chapter 55

Royal Air Force (RAF) Base
Ascension Island

Farrington rose a little higher next to the pilot's seat, peering through the blood-smeared front window to guide the monstrous aircraft with the control stick. The sniper fire had completely ceased, which meant Hoffman had killed the sniper, or they were locked in a duel. Either way, it was too late for Hoffman to escape with them. The C-17 had reached the edge of the tarmac, headed for the runway. Once he made the right turn and pointed this thing down the runway, he'd increase the throttle and hope for the best. The aircraft would either reach for the sky or catapult into the Atlantic.

A hand rested squarely on his shoulder.

"You're clear for takeoff," said Hoffman. "The sniper's down."

Farrington looked over his shoulder. "How the fuck?"

"Castillo was still alive. She took the shot for me," said Hoffman.

"Alive?" He'd seen her take a second bullet. "Where is she?"

"She was on her way out. Bad hit," said Hoffman. "She did good."

Farrington shook his head. "She sure as hell did."

"Haddad's closing up below. What's the plan?" asked Hoffman.

Farrington climbed into the pilot's seat and wiped the bloody window with his sleeve, barely improving the situation.

"We take off and fly due west. When we reach Brazil, we fly for a while and point it back at the ocean, bailing out near the coast."

"Then what?"

"I don't know. We have about five hours to figure out something as long as we get off the ground. You ever fly a plane?"

Hoffman shook his head. "Nope."

"Me neither. But I've been steering with this joystick thing, and my guess is it's like a video game. Get to the right speed and pull back gently."

"What's the right speed?"

"I've heard like two hundred miles per hour for commercial aircraft," said Farrington.

"I'd go with, like, two-fifty, maybe. Just a hunch," said Hoffman.

The aircraft turned onto the long runway, which stood out from its moonlit surroundings as a dark line extending beyond Farrington's view. All he had to do was keep this thing in the middle of the unfolding black strip. Easier said than done. Just getting it to the runway had been difficult enough.

"You ready?" Farrington asked.

"What if I say no?"

Farrington laughed and pushed the throttle forward, the C-17 responding immediately. The aircraft accelerated down the runway faster than he'd anticipated.

"Take over the throttle and watch the airspeed. This stick thing is shaking," said Farrington.

"Where's the airspeed?"

Farrington pointed toward a bank of green glowing screens. "Somewhere there. Look for the one that's changing a lot."

"Jesus," said Hoffman, climbing into the copilot seat.

Hoffman took the throttle with his left hand, nudging it forward. The aircraft surged forward, racing past one hundred miles per hour.

"A little more," said Farrington.

Hoffman eased the throttle forward until it was a few inches forward of the straight-up position. The C-17 raced down the dark runway.

"Speed?"

"Passing one seventy. Rapidly increasing," said Hoffman.

"Tell me when it reaches two-twenty-five."

"Got it," said Hoffman.

A few seconds later, Hoffman announced the number. Farrington eased the stick back, feeling the aircraft leave the runway.

"No shit," said Farrington. "Is the altitude rising?"

"We're rising," said Hoffman. "I can tell you that much."

"Just find the altimeter. It'll be the one with the numbers going up. Hopefully."

By the time Hoffman found the digital altimeter display, they were five hundred feet and climbing over the Atlantic, headed almost due east. Now he had to figure out how to turn the craft around and head west. Given their miraculous escape, he was in no hurry to try.

Chapter 56

Allegheny Mountains, West Virginia

Karl Berg took Sanderson's call with trepidation. Deep down, he knew it was bad news. The timing was too close. The flight carrying his team had been an hour from landing at RAF Ascension, one of the most isolated islands on the planet. The perfect place to sweep your dirt under a deep blue rug. He and Bauer shared a concerned look as he put the phone to his ear.

"Terrence?" said Berg.

"You were right."

Sanderson sounded deflated.

"Can I put you on speakerphone?" Berg requested. "Audra Bauer is with me. The rest of the team is working on putting this place back together. Rustic was a bit of an oversell."

"Sure," said Sanderson.

Berg set the phone on the table next to them.

"General, what happened?" asked Bauer.

"It's not the Russians," Sanderson stated. "Not in a big-picture way. The team was ambushed at the RAF airfield. Farrington, Hoffman, and Haddad are the only survivors."

"Shit," muttered Berg, too stunned to conjure anything else.

Despite hinting to Sanderson that Ascension Island would be the perfect place for an ambush, he truly didn't think anything could happen there. It was a Royal Air Force base! An isolated one for sure, but still an official military installation. Berg had been far more concerned about what might happen when they reached Africa after splitting up on the ground into small groups.

"How many did you lose, General?" Bauer asked.

"That's what I like about you, Bauer. None of that phony 'sorry for your loss' crap. Straight shooter to the end," said Sanderson. "Seventeen. And you can call me Terrence."

"Well, I *am* sorry for the loss of your people, Terrence, and angered by their deaths," said Bauer. "I assume the survivors are hiding out on the island? Not in RAF custody, I hope."

"You may not believe this, but they're flying west toward Brazil," said Sanderson. "In the same aircraft."

"Who's flying?" asked Berg. "Not that it matters. I'm just glad they got out of there."

"It does kind of matter. Farrington is at the controls."

"Jesus," said Berg. "He knows how to fly a C-17 Globemaster?"

"He got it into the air and managed to turn it one hundred and eighty degrees. He's not really keen on trying anything else. They plan on bailing out over Brazil after pointing the aircraft back out to sea."

"What happened to the pilots?" asked Bauer. "And I'm not implying anything with that question."

"The copilot was killed by a stray bullet. The pilot was killed by a CIA sniper."

"CIA?" said Bauer, giving Berg an unconvinced look.

"I can't confirm that the sniper, the fake SEALs, or the phony refueling crew were CIA, but the pilot told me he was contracted by the CIA to fly the mission. The flight was diverted to Guantanamo Bay after leaving MacDill Air Force Base. The four DEVGRU SEALs confirmed by General Gordon from SOCOM were replaced by an assassination team that turned on my people. Does the National Clandestine Service hire pilots to do this?" Sanderson asked.

"We have a roster of pilots and crew for every type of aircraft," Bauer replied.

"And the Department of Defense just loans out aircraft when you ask?"

"No, we receive official DOD aircraft when the president and his national security advisors decide that the mission transport phase requires an extra degree of perceived legitimacy. A U.S. Air Force C-17 stopping in Argentina or Ascension Island to refuel doesn't draw attention. Neither does that same C-17 headed to the United Nations Base in Uganda. We don't do it often."

"How does this stay a secret?" asked Sanderson. "I assume a squadron somewhere is missing an unmistakably large aircraft?"

"A limited number of squadrons are on the short list to supply aircraft for these missions. It's very hush-hush. They provide a fully flight-checked aircraft, our contractors walk on board and fly them away, returning them later. Nothing is recorded."

"Fucking spooks," said Sanderson. "So now what?"

"We obviously can't trust the CIA," said Bauer. "They set up the flight."

"With the help of the White House," Sanderson chimed in.

"Maybe, maybe not. Someone high in the Department of Defense is definitely in on this, though," said Bauer.

"Let's cross the DOD, White House, and the National Security Council off the Christmas card list for now," said Sanderson. "Except for Bob Kearney."

"I don't know," said Berg. "He's pretty close to the president."

"Bob has been my man on the inside for a while now," said Sanderson. "He warned me about the raid against my compound back in 2007. This information obviously stays between the three of us."

"I always wondered," said Berg.

"I trust Bob with no reservations, but I don't trust that his office, house, car…all of it, is clear of bugs. He'll get in touch with me discreetly when he hears what happened."

"*If* he ever hears about it," said Bauer. "Ascension Island is in the middle of nowhere."

"We'll figure out a way that doesn't involve Farrington setting the autopilot for Cuban airspace before they bail out. They have three hours to figure it out."

"Don't cross the option off the list," said Berg.

"Wouldn't that be a fucking sight to see?" said Sanderson.

"We're better off if everyone involved in this conspiracy thinks they ran out of fuel and crashed at sea. When they get to Brazilian airspace, they should declare a fuel emergency and claim their navigational equipment malfunctioned. Point north before they bail out over land. That will send the aircraft into the middle of the North Atlantic. It'll run out of fuel at some point and crash. End of story."

"I'll pass that plan along," said Sanderson. "What else?"

"The Petroviches split," Berg informed him. "Snuck off without saying goodbye."

"That's disappointing, but it doesn't surprise me. They were on the brink of vanishing from my radar when you passed the news about her mother."

"I guess we were lucky to have them while we did," said Bauer.

"You mentioned still having a Russian problem?" Berg prompted.

"The Russians were behind Galenden's murder. There's no doubt about that. They just showed up in town," said Sanderson. "With a small army."

"Then get the hell out of there," said Berg.

"No, I need to put an end to this," said Sanderson. "Solve my Russian problem."

"That's not the kind of problem that goes away permanently," said Berg.

"Not usually, but I have something different in mind."

"Keep us posted," said Berg.

"If you don't hear from me again, you'll know it didn't work."

"In that case, while I still have you on the line, what about Munoz and Melendez?"

"Send them south to pick up Reznikov's trail."

"Could be bullshit, just like Africa," said Berg.

"We can't ignore the possibility that it's real. If Reznikov is in the United States, he's here by invitation, and we need to find out who invited him."

"I already know the answer. And so do you."

"I sincerely hope we're both wrong," said Sanderson.

Chapter 57

Salta, Argentina

Mihail Osin got into the beat-up rental sedan and glanced into the backseat at the two Spetsgruppa Omega snipers chosen for the reconnaissance mission. Their orders were simple: determine if Sanderson was at the location provided by Galenden and indicated by his records. Thermal satellite imagery confirmed the presence of a group at the site, consistent with the suspected size of his remaining force, but the thick tree cover prevented satellites from taking high-resolution daytime photos to prove Sanderson was among the group.

Sanderson was the primary target, and if the sniper team located him at the site and the shooting conditions were entirely favorable, they would be cleared to take him out. Ardankin much preferred the quiet use of two men to accomplish the mission rather than a direct assault by thirty. Colonel Levkin would set up an ambush on the isolated road leading out of the site, just in case the sniper team failed. A squad of Omega commandos hidden along that road, backed by anti-vehicle mines, would be more than adequate, according to Levkin. Satellite imagery showed no more than a dozen of Sanderson's people at the site.

He looked back at the darkened Quonset-hut-style warehouse serving as their base of operations. The rusty, neglected building cost them a small fortune to rent, most of the outrageous fee designed to buy them privacy and discretion.

"Let's go," said Osin. "Stay around the speed limit."

"Nobody drives the speed limit around here," said Vadim Dragunov, the only Zaslon operative assigned to the task force.

"Then drive like everyone else. Just don't get us pulled over," said Osin, a little bit annoyed.

Dragunov tore out of the dirt parking lot. He had soured after the

Galenden mess. They were supposed to have time to devise a discreet plan to grab the Argentine businessman. Follow him for a few days, determine his routine, map his routes, and analyze the man's security detail. They always found a weakness, but it took time. Time they didn't know would be snatched away at the last minute, forcing a different, unavoidably messy approach that burned their careers as covert operatives.

Once they walked through the front doors of Galenden International's glass and steel high-rise and announced themselves as Galenden's four-thirty appointment, they'd banished themselves to a career at headquarters. Osin wasn't happy about it either, but they still had a job to do.

They quickly connected with a smooth four-lane highway that circumvented the city to the west. In about twenty minutes, they'd be on Route 9, heading north out of the city toward the drop-off point roughly eight point nine miles away. Barring a flat tire or some other kind of unforeseen holdup, Osin and Dragunov should be headed back toward Salta in less than a half hour.

For all practical purposes, their mission ended after this drop-off. They would remain at the warehouse to coordinate the timely and rapid departure of Levkin's Spetsgruppa and possibly dispose of a body or two if Levkin's commandos ran into any overzealous or incorruptible police officers along their travel route to and from the target. Beyond that, they would be in sit-and-wait mode for however long it took to eliminate Sanderson. He really hoped the sniper team ended this quickly.

The mostly deserted highway wound north, turning abruptly east to connect with Route 9 in the northern part of the city. They drove along the quiet, sporadically lit outskirts of town until they broke out into the countryside north of Salta, where the highway became a winding, two-lane rural road.

Route 9 snaked through the hillside, the streetlamps becoming less and less frequent the further they drove from the city. The less light the better. Far too many houses dotted these hills. The last thing they needed was a nosy night owl observing the drop-off. Osin checked his handheld GPS unit. One point two miles to go. A minute and a half at most.

"About a minute," he said.

Levkin had picked the drop-off point, which gave his sniper team the shortest point of approach to the target area. Short being a relative term. They had a ten-mile hike through thick forest ahead of them. He didn't expect to hear from them until late tomorrow afternoon.

They passed a streetlight, which momentarily cast an orange glow through the sedan, followed by nothing but darkness for the next minute. Point two miles to the drop-off and not a hint of light ahead. Perfect.

"Point two miles. Slow down a little," he said.

The car decelerated in a controlled manner for a few seconds; then he was thrown against his seatbelt.

"Dammit, Dragunov!" he snapped when the car rumbled to a stop.

Dragunov was out the door before Osin could process what was happening. Masked figures rushed the car from both sides of the street. Dragunov raised his suppressed pistol, instantly dropping to the road in a crumpled heap as the darkly dressed figures moved past him without slowing down. They instantly enveloped the sedan, their weapons pointed at the vehicle's occupants.

Osin expected one of Levkin's commandos to panic, but a few seconds passed without gunfire, convincing him they grasped the situation. A light metallic rap sounded against his window. He turned his head and saw someone signaling for him to roll down the window. A quick nod and he moved his hand to the button. He was surprised to hear perfect street Russian.

"Hands on the dashboard. The two guys in the back put their hands on the headrests. You get out first, then the guy behind you, then the remaining passenger. We have no intention of killing you. Understood."

"Yes."

"Do it," said the Russian speaker.

They were herded out of sight of the road and lined up on their knees, hands above their heads. A quick pat down relieved Osin of a knife. The two Spetsgruppa commandos gave up nothing, their kits sitting useless in the trunk. One of their captors stepped forward and crouched in front of him, offering a hand.

"General Terrence Sanderson, retired, pleased to meet you."

Osin hesitated, not sure if this was a trick.

"Take the hand," said Sanderson. "If I wanted you dead, you'd be dead."

Osin shook the general's hand, placing his own back on his head. "How did you know?" he asked.

"This is my backyard, and news travels fast. Galenden, Russians at the airfield…it wasn't hard to connect the dots."

He remained silent, thinking he should have gone out like Dragunov.

Now he was a bargaining chip, along with the two Omega Spetsgruppa commandos.

"I don't expect you to say anything. In fact, I'd respect you far more if you didn't. And I'm not going to torture you to death like you did with Galenden," said Sanderson.

Osin swallowed hard.

"That's right. I saw a video of you and your friend visiting Galenden International the same day he was found mutilated and dead."

He wanted to say something. Even started to move his mouth.

"Don't," said Sanderson. "I don't hold that against you."

"What do you want, then?" asked Osin, genuinely unsure where this exchange was headed.

"I need to talk to the director of your Foreign Intelligence Service."

"That's not going to happen," said Osin, expecting a rifle butt to the head.

"I'll settle for Dmitry Ardankin for now, who I assume is your boss. Directorate S?"

Mention of Ardankin's name was unsettling, but hearing the words *Directorate S* bordered on disturbing. He wasn't naïve enough to think the Americans didn't know their structure, but it felt entirely different to actually hear it spoken by his enemy.

"That's not going to happen either," said Osin.

"Is that because you won't make the call, or because they won't take it?"

"Both, but mostly the latter," said Osin.

"I strongly suggest you try to get Ardankin on the line," said Sanderson. "The lives of about thirty of your comrades depend on it. Security is sloppy over at the warehouse. No sentries. Pretty much an open invitation to drive a truck bomb right into the place. Or place a ring of claymore mines aiming inward and starting a gunfight."

Osin kept a neutral face, or so he hoped. Sanderson's information about the warehouse was dead-on. They had decided against sentries to avoid drawing attention.

"Even better, I could wake up the police commander for the Salta Province and inform him that an army of Russian mercenaries are sitting in a warehouse close to the airport. Wouldn't take much convincing to shut down the airport. I'm sure the commander of the National Gendarmerie unit based in San Miguel de Tucuman would be interested in this information as well. Thanks to my late friend Ernesto Galenden, I have a direct line to both of them."

He quickly weighed his options, coming to the same conclusion Sanderson had obviously reached. Colonel Levkin's Spetsgruppa represented a devastating liability to Russia. Any course of action that pointed in the direction of their unhampered departure for Moscow was worth pursuing.

"I'll make the call."

Chapter 58

SVR Headquarters, Yasanevo Suburb
Moscow, Russian Federation

For the first time in his career as director of operations of Directorate S, Dmitry Ardankin sailed through the outer chambers of Director Pushnoy's office without the slightest pause. Doors opened as he entered, secretaries motioned for him to continue, security stepped swiftly aside. It was a horrible feeling. Even the smallest diversion would be welcome on the express train to Hell's gates. When he reached the inner sanctum, even the secretary he'd come to despise over the years had a look of pity on her face.

"The director will see you now," she announced as he continued forward without breaking stride.

"Thank you," he said, feeling small for judging her.

She sat at that desk, day in, day out, guarding a powerful man's time, completely oblivious to the dark secrets and life-altering decisions made beyond those thick mahogany doors. It had to gnaw at her. Returning home every day, with the full understanding that her job was so close to the epicenter of everything, yet utterly disconnected from any meaning. He returned her look, a moment of understanding passing between them before he stepped into Pushnoy's den of iniquity. The door closed quickly behind him.

"Let's get this over with," said Pushnoy, pointing to the chair he would occupy.

He didn't bother with apologies or any obsequious flattery. He moved immediately to the chair next to Pushnoy's desk and sat down. The director's light blue eyes burned a hole through him, but he maintained his quiet composure.

"The silent treatment, huh?" said Pushnoy. "Incompetent, maybe. Stupid? Definitely not."

The director pressed a button on his desk phone and placed both elbows on the desk, resting his chin on his hands.

"General Sanderson, it's a pleasure to finally meet you."

"Likewise, Director Pushnoy. I appreciate you taking my call."

"Yes, about that," said Pushnoy. "What do you propose?"

"Not much, in the grand scheme of things," said Sanderson. "I want a truce. Your word that I'm off whatever hit list you keep over there."

"And you're going to hang up your jacket and never interfere with Russian Federation affairs again?"

"It's hang up your hat, Director," said Sanderson. "And yes, I agree to that term, with a few conditions."

"And what might those be?"

"I need your help with something," said Sanderson. "Something that concerns us both."

"I can't wait to hear what this might be."

"It involves Reznikov," said Sanderson.

"How so?"

"First I need you to answer a question."

"That depends on the question."

"How did you find me?" asked Sanderson.

"You really want to know?" said Pushnoy. "Sometimes the truth hurts."

"I just lost most of my organization on a remote island in the middle of the Atlantic. People I've known for years. People I've trained personally. I can handle the truth."

Pushnoy briefly explained how they had acquired the information regarding Sanderson's presence in Argentina, and that it had been his idea to lure Sanderson's people away to Africa.

"You expect me to believe that you didn't know who you were talking to on the other side?" said Sanderson. "Just an anonymous email exchange?"

"What did it matter?" said Pushnoy. "We vetted the information provided to our satisfaction. They upheld their end of the bargain. Speaking of bargains. Reznikov?"

"Well, that's where this gets really interesting. I have reason to believe he's in the United States—by invitation."

"From whom?"

"From the same group that used the Russian Foreign Intelligence Service to cripple the only force capable and willing to rescind that invitation. A group with quite a stranglehold on things in my country right now."

A pause so long ensued Ardankin nearly broke the interminable silence himself.

"I'm listening," said Pushnoy.

Sanderson explained his theory and the early stages of a plan to track down the scientist. Pushnoy listened, his face never changing. When he finished, Pushnoy agreed to Sanderson's truce and gave him contact instructions to use if the American unearthed evidence to support his theory. The director replaced the handset and rubbed his chin while Ardankin waited patiently for instructions.

"Still silent?" said Pushnoy. "There's hope for you yet. Get Osin and Colonel Levkin's Spetsgruppa out of Argentina immediately."

"Yes, Director," said Ardankin, starting to get up.

"Did I say I was finished?"

"No, Director."

"Send part of Levkin's team to Ciudad Juarez. I don't care how you do it. I want them standing by to *assist* General Sanderson with the elimination of Anatoly Reznikov."

"You trust this Sanderson?"

"I trust he wants to find and kill Reznikov. That's all that matters to me."

Chapter 59

FBI Headquarters
Washington, D.C.

Ryan Sharpe pressed the microchipped ID attached to the lanyard around his neck against the card reader and waited for the adjacent fingerprint scanner to activate. A few seconds later the biometric security device confirmed his identity, permitting him to open the windowless metal door to the National Security Branch section of the J. Edgar Hoover Building.

He navigated the expansive maze of fluorescent-lit cubicles and dark conference rooms, glad to find it still empty. He had about a half hour before it started to fill, the sound of ringing phones, clacking keyboards, and voices rising to a crescendo shortly after that. Then Assistant Director Fred Carroll would arrive, and Sharpe wouldn't get a minute to himself until he left twelve hours later. He needed this hour to clear out any unfinished business from yesterday and make some progress on longer-term tasks that would undoubtedly get pushed further behind once the section rolled in.

When Sharpe rounded the corner that led directly into the cluster of cubicles and windowed offices that defined the National Security Branch's "executive suite," he was surprised to find Dana O'Reilly's office door open and brightly lit. Maybe she forgot to turn off her light last night. She had planned on staying another hour to tie up the quick investigation into Berg's mystery group. He hadn't wanted her putting any more time into it.

She'd quickly verified what Berg had passed along. While intriguing, it didn't warrant continued FBI attention. Brown River definitely had personnel and accounting problems, something that Treasury would find interesting given the billion-dollar scope of the issue. Then again, Sharpe wasn't sure how he could pass the information along to Treasury given that the files were obtained illegally. He could give them a nudge through one of his contacts and let them sort it out.

And what about Berg's phantom army? Ajax Global solely existed as a paper corporation based in Delaware, which wasn't uncommon. Delaware and Nevada had some of the most flexible business laws, plus no state corporate income tax. A publically available record search yielded a short list of corporate officers, all fictitious names from what O'Reilly could determine. Once again, not exactly a surprise, but more importantly, none of their business.

Berg had no doubt stumbled onto something strange. Sharpe just didn't see how or where the National Security Branch, or the FBI in general, could get involved. The two kidnapping attempts referenced were FBI business, but the FBI field office determined by regional jurisdiction would handle that. Sharpe could call over to check on the progress and stress the importance of the investigation to NSB, but that was pretty much the extent of his influence in that matter.

"That you, boss?" O'Reilly called out well before he reached her door.

"Yes. The evil boss," he said, poking his head inside. "Please tell me you didn't come in early to work on that project."

She had that look he had come to recognize over the years. Sharpe knew her next words before she spoke.

"I found something," she said. "Been here all night, actually. Take a look at this."

"All night?"

"I left to grab dinner and slept for a few hours on the couch in the break room."

He took off his jacket and threw it on a low filing cabinet next to the door. "What the hell did you find, O'Reilly? Things tend to get crazy when you find things."

Sharpe stood behind her desk and leaned against the windowsill, glancing at a digital map on a flat-screen monitor. The second screen immediately to the right displayed a detailed list, resembling the payroll file sent by Berg.

"Taking a few last glances at the payroll file, I noticed a pattern that Berg's people might have missed or perhaps they purposefully withheld. I almost missed it myself," said O'Reilly.

"Why would they withhold anything?"

"I don't know. Maybe they wanted us to find this on our own. Generate an *aha moment*. Or like I said, they just missed it, like I almost did."

"They've been poring over this for longer than you have," said Sharpe.

"Either way, it's interesting, if not disturbing. The addresses highlighted by Berg are all P.O. boxes, which we already knew, and that's not exactly unusual for people in the Brown River line of work. I do find it a bit odd that all of the employees suspected of being part of Berg's phantom army use P.O. boxes. I found that roughly seventy percent of Brown River's non-phantom army employees have personal addresses listed. Odd, but nothing earth-shattering."

"Let's move on to the earth-shattering part," said Sharpe.

"I started to see some repeat P.O. box locations, so I mapped a sample of two hundred mystery employees, finding this," she said, clicking her mouse button.

Tight clusters of icons appeared across the United States, centered on a few dozen major cities.

"People come from all around," said Sharpe, not fully vested in his counterargument.

"Then I mapped a thousand more. This takes time, by the way. We need a software upgrade," said O'Reilly.

"I'll get right on that," said Sharpe. "Well?"

She clicked the mouse, and the identical pattern remained, with another dozen clusters appearing in some less populated cities. If Sharpe had to roughly guess, the clusters appeared in forty to fifty cities. He could immediately see a direct relationship between the number of icons appearing in a city and its population, with a few notable exceptions like Fredericksburg, Virginia, which had a disproportionately high number compared to New York City or Los Angeles. The picture represented a purposeful distribution.

"What about now?" she said.

"I'll admit, that's pretty unusual."

"They don't all use the same postal building for their P.O. boxes, especially in the larger metro areas, but they're still tightly clustered," said O'Reilly.

"Could they be spreading this out for tax reasons or something corporate related?"

"Based on Brown River's latest quarterly statement, they shouldn't have a billion or so dollars to fund an expansion. They've barely kept the doors open as it is," said O'Reilly.

"Strange," said Sharpe.

"You want to see something even stranger?"

"Probably not."

She clicked the mouse again, the pattern remaining the same, but more concentrated. "This is all three thousand six hundred and forty-two phantom employees."

"Same exact pattern," muttered Sharpe.

"You haven't seen the strange part yet," she said. "I broke all of this down in a spreadsheet by city and metro area, salary, military or police specialty, years in service prior to joining this payroll, and a few other factors. I created a graphic with bar graphs, pie charts, and all kinds of bells and whistles."

"That's a lot of work," said Sharpe.

"I think you'll agree it was worth the time. There's nothing random about the distribution of this group. In fact, it's organized down to a level that suggests something more nefarious than corporate tax evasion. I identified forty-six geographical clusters, each with the same proportion of employees, based on salary. Six at the seventy-five-thousand-dollar level per one at the one-hundred-and-fifty-thousand level. Sounds like a team of grunts with a team leader. For every ten at the one-hundred-and-fifty-thousand level, you have one at the four-hundred-and-fifty-thousand level. Like an area coordinator. The grunt to team leader ratio never varies. The area coordinator to team leader number stays consistent until you start dissecting either the highest population metro areas or low population clusters. Makes sense. One area coordinator runs a few states out in the Great Plains, while the New York tri-state area requires a more intensive management approach."

"This holds up in every cluster?"

"Yes. It's structured like—"

"A sales organization," interrupted Sharpe.

"Or a paramilitary organization," O'Reilly countered. "I found something else, which doesn't exactly shed any light on the purpose of this structure, but I found it interesting. Ajax wasn't the only company recruiting military contractors. I ran a few search strings through the social-media tracking database—"

"Which doesn't officially exist anywhere at the FBI," said Sharpe.

"Yes. I used a system that doesn't yet exist to link names on the payroll list to Ares Global and Mars Global. Two more Delaware companies with bogus corporate officers. The matches I made corresponded geographically. Ajax is East Coast to the Ohio River, roughly. Ares is everything west of the Rocky Mountains. Mars is everything in the middle. Not sure what that means, but I wouldn't be surprised if some folks high up on the Brown River payroll had responsibility for these larger areas."

"It looks like a deliberate arrangement," said Sharpe. "Each a mythological name associated with warfare."

"Berg claims they're directly involved in two kidnapping attempts," said O'Reilly. "Should we take this to Carroll? I'll take the heat for it, say I was contacted by an anonymous source and stole some time away to investigate."

"First, you're not taking the heat for my problems, though I appreciate the offer," said Sharpe. "Second, Berg warned me to be discreet with this. He sounded a little paranoid."

"He's a career CIA officer," said O'Reilly.

"Right. Which also begs the question, why does he need to bring me into the fold? The CIA has resources," said Sharpe, standing up. "I need to hear the rest of this story he alluded to. We'll make a decision at that point."

"One more thing, since you'll have Berg on the line," said O'Reilly. "Maybe I should have started our conversation with this. Sanderson and his known associates are back on the FBI's most wanted list. Interpol. Europol. Everywhere."

"Jesus. That does shade your findings a different color."

"Or it's just an incredible coincidence."

Sharpe rubbed his face. "I know I'm going to seriously regret this call."

He walked to his adjacent office and closed the door, dropping into the guest chair facing his desk, staring at the deep red patches of horizon peeking between the buildings of the East End. Sharpe did the same thing every morning, taking a few minutes to stare out his office window at the waking city. He really had a bad feeling about this.

Mumbling a few obscenities, he turned the desk phone in his direction and dialed the number scribbled on a Post-it note stuck to the secure phone. As he expected, the CIA officer answered immediately.

"Good morning, Ryan," said Berg.

"That depends on one's perspective, I guess," said Sharpe. "Six men, one team leader, an area coordinator for every ten teams."

"Each coordinator has one team comprised solely of former Special Operations types. Los Angeles, Chicago, New York and Fredericksburg each have a team of former tier one special operators," said Berg. "This is an army on U.S. soil."

"Tell me more about these attempted kidnappings."

"What do you want to know?"

"Who was kidnapped, and how do you know it was this group?"

"Are you sure you want to know?" said Berg.

"Cut the theatrics, Karl. If this group is behind domestic kidnappings, what else are they into? I need to know what to do with this."

"Don't say I didn't give you a chance to sit this one out," said Berg.

"You reeled me in good," said Sharpe.

"Technically, only one of the kidnappings was attempted," Berg began. "I'll keep this short."

When he finished, Sharpe stared out at the buildings. He wasn't sure what to do with the information Berg just shared. All he could summon was a simple question.

"Who can I trust?"

"Inside the Beltway? I don't know yet," said Berg. "We're meeting to discuss this shortly."

"Be careful who you discuss this with. Sanderson and his crew just went back on every law enforcement watch list in existence."

"Son of a bitch. They had an immunity deal. Wide scope," said Berg. "I guess I shouldn't be surprised."

"I haven't read the corresponding write-up for the watch list. Could be something completely different."

"What are you doing this weekend?" Berg asked.

"This weekend? Why?"

"I'd like you to meet the people I know for a fact that we can trust."

"I don't know if that's a good idea."

"I can't see you walking away from this, Ryan," said Berg. "You're going to need a tight circle of trust. One you can call on at any time for help and that can rely on you for the same. If my suspicions prove anywhere even remotely correct, we won't get much help outside of that circle."

"I'll consider it," said Sharpe.

"Call me when you've decided," Berg said, and hung up.

Sharpe closed his eyes for several moments, wishing this nightmare away. When he opened them, the sun's deep orange rays skimmed the tops of a few buildings in the distance. He buzzed O'Reilly, who appeared almost instantly, shutting the door behind her.

"What did he say?"

"What are you doing this weekend?" said Sharpe.

"Are you and Mrs. Sharpe on the outs?"

"Funny," said Sharpe. "I think we need to meet with Berg's circle of trust. If we decide to pursue this, we're going to need a few friends to back us up. Friends that don't fuck around."

"As long as your wife doesn't have a problem with it," she said.

"Trust me. If this is what Berg thinks it is, I'm putting her on the first flight to New Zealand."

"Why don't you put me on the New Zealand flight, business class, and take your wife this weekend."

"Even funnier," said Sharpe. "Keep digging through the data. His people seem to be ahead of you."

"Is that a challenge?"

"Just saying," said Sharpe. "And Dana?"

"Yes."

"This has the potential to go sideways really fast, so—"

"I'd feel really insulted if you gave me an out or a pass on this one," she said.

He grinned. "Just letting you know it could get ugly."

Really fucking ugly.

Chapter 60

Number Seven Line
Moscow, Russian Federation

Alexei Kaparov held onto the metal horizontal rail next to the subway car's door, occasionally glaring at the youngster hooligans slouched in the plastic seats across from him. He was the oldest passenger on the train by twenty years, and these punks just sat there, earbuds inserted and stupid hats pulled over their unkempt hair. If they knew he was an FSB deputy director, it probably wouldn't make one bit of difference. Today's youth didn't care or scare easily. He could turn a bit more and show them his service pistol, and it wouldn't matter. Nothing was going to dislodge them from their seats. Especially not the sight of an older man hanging on for his life as the subway shook and rattled.

His phone buzzed in his suit coat pocket, barely audible over the Metro car racket. Now he got to pull out his flip phone and add to the agony. The kids were busy swiping screens larger than his first apartment's bathroom mirror. He flipped open his antique device and checked the caller ID. This couldn't be good. Karl Berg had been brief during their last call. Curt was a better word. Something had been wrong, but it wasn't information his friend intended to part with too easily.

"To what do I owe this pleasure?" asked Kaparov.

"Sorry about cutting you off the other day. I needed to pass on the information immediately," said Berg. "It made a difference. Thank you."

"How are things? You sounded surprised by the information."

"Things are not good over here. At all," said Berg. "Which is why I'm calling."

"I've never heard you like this."

"It's that bad, and I can't go into details on the phone. I know what my side can do to track phrases and words. Understand?"

"Yes. These capabilities are ripening here," said Kaparov.

"I need you to carefully cover your tracks regarding our most recent conversation. I'm not sure how much longer the name in question will remain off the radar," said Berg. "The next time we are in touch, it will be in person, over drinks and dinner—on me of course."

"That bad, huh?"

Berg laughed. "I'm not betting against that dinner, but there are factors working very strongly against it."

"Understood. Stay safe, my friend. Watch your back. Don't trust anyone. All that crap."

"Sage advice," said Berg. "If we don't speak again, thank you for everything. It's been an honor and a pleasure knowing you."

"I'd toast to that if I hadn't left my damn flask in the office," said Kaparov.

"Toast to it when you get back to your apartment. I'm sure there's no shortage of vodka there."

"You know me too well."

"Take care, old friend."

"You take better care. I look forward to our reunion," said Kaparov.

He closed his phone, fairly sure that he would never hear from Karl Berg again. The CIA officer hadn't sounded like himself. The confidence and energy was gone, replaced by uncertainty—and a stern warning about Sokolov.

Prerovsky had identified Sokolov through what could only be interpreted as a routine and logical follow-up into Zuyev's death. The "known-associates" list had contained hundreds of names. Their story started to fray when Prerovsky added a few dozen of the names to the FSB Intelligence Network watch list, conveniently including Sokolov.

Prerovsky had been clever enough with the watch-list stunt, openly suggesting it to his fellow directors. Since the Organized Crime division hadn't been given the details regarding Zuyev's death, he easily sold it as a background intelligence-gathering effort. Innocent enough from an FSB standpoint, but unlikely to withstand the paranoid scrutiny of a Foreign Intelligence Service inquiry.

He considered his options while the subway car continued its stop-and-go journey. A few stops later, he decided that the best course of action had to be an active one. He'd never reported his analysis of the raid directly to Greshnev, as the chief Counterterrorism director had asked. Tomorrow morning he would schedule an appointment to suggest the theory that

Kaparov had been taken by an insider—the fourth man in the boat. He'd then offer to liaison with Organized Crime, where an incredible coincidence would materialize.

Until then, he'd drink several toasts to his American friend tonight, until the memory of the conversation faded from his thoughts, along with his consciousness. Like so many others, the day had suddenly turned into one he wanted to forget.

Chapter 61

Tverskoy District
Moscow, Russian Federation

Matvey Penkin stole an impatient glance at his Patek Phillipe Nautilus before taking a sip of his cognac. 1:35 AM. He despised being out this late, especially in a strobe-light-filled, hip-hop-gyrating nightclub, but this was one of the prices he paid for keeping a girlfriend half his age. Alina loved to party, one of the few "skills" she excelled at beyond snorting cocaine, looking good and spending his money. Penkin really hoped she wasn't powdering her nose again. They'd be there for another hour, surrounded by her insufferable fan club.

At least once a week, she insisted they "be seen" together—usually at one of the most exclusive clubs in Moscow. Of course, in order to "be seen," her friends needed to be on the VIP list, which Penkin arranged. On top of that, he paid their exorbitant bar tab, which tended to skyrocket after he left. The only downside to leaving before the place shut down for the night. Alina was no doubt using him on every level, and he really didn't care. She was easy-to-maintain eye candy, which was all he really wanted in a relationship at this point.

Alina strutted through the crowd at the edge of the pulsating dance floor, two of his security staff clearing her way like Moses parting the Red Sea. She moved swiftly, Penkin sensing that the night had finally come to an end. Alina had a sensitive stomach, and the spicy tuna tartare she'd eaten a short while ago might have saved him from another two hours of headache-inducing sound and light. He stood up to offer her his arm when she reached the heavily guarded table.

"You should have your men talk with the chef," said Alina. "His tuna got me sick again. Let's go."

More like thank the chef. He'd have to remember this for next time and suggest ordering food as soon as they arrived. Anything spicy.

"I'll make sure they get the message," said Penkin. "Do you want to say goodbye to your friends?"

"No. I need to get back to my apartment," said Alina.

"Very well," said Penkin, holding her arm. "I'm sorry the night had to end like this for you."

"No, you're not," she said, pulling him away from the table. "And I'm not walking out the back door like a criminal."

He nodded at his security chief. "That's fine."

Sometimes he wondered if she was too stupid or oblivious to understand whom she was mixed up with right now. Maybe all of the oligarch types she'd snagged over the past several years had looked and felt the same to her, and Penkin was just another billionaire meal ticket. Except he wasn't a billionaire. Not even close.

He lived like an oligarch, but that lifestyle owed its existence to his position within the Bratva. Penkin could demand certain things from the private sector by creating uncomfortable leverage. He was obviously doing something right. Professional gold diggers like Alina didn't stick around too long when they smelled the low tide of bad fortune.

They left the main nightclub area, his security detail clearing a wide path on the way out. The lavish, dimly lit reception lounge had been emptied by the club's security ahead of their arrival.

"Ten seconds out," his security chief said before signaling a group of four men clustered in the entrance foyer.

The small team deployed through the double doors, securing the sidewalk immediately in front of the club. Penkin nodded his approval to Gennady Kuznetsov, who lingered discreetly in the alcove leading to the coatroom. The sharply dressed former Moscow police detective turned top nightclub manager returned the gesture, pausing at the end of the nod to emphasize his respect and loyalty. The man had been very accommodating and protective over the years, which Penkin had always rewarded generously. It paid to have reliable friends in this city, a cost of business one could ill afford to ignore.

"Ready, Mr. Penkin," said his chief, gesturing to the door.

They hit the wide sidewalk at a quick pace, sliding into the black Range Rover moments later. No sense in making it easy for rival gangs to take a quick shot at him or detonate a suicide vest while he was in the open. They'd been at the club long enough for word to spread around. Another reason he disliked these nights out.

The door next to Penkin slammed securely shut, the lock mechanisms immediately engaging with a solid *thunk*. Movement behind the second row of seats reminded him that a third security officer always rode concealed in the cargo compartment, ready to jump into action. He had the shittiest of all the jobs, often remaining in place for long periods of time when the SUV was parked in plain sight.

His security chief moved quickly along the curb to the front passenger seat, hopping inside and shutting the door. They were impervious to anything less potent than an antitank missile at this point, which unfortunately wasn't off the table in Moscow.

"Let's move," said his chief, and the three-vehicle convoy departed.

The ride to Alina's apartment proceeded smoothly despite the high volume of street traffic on the main roads. The convoy turned right onto Burdenko Street, moving out of the steady stream of cars on the Smolenskiy stretch of Moscow's "B-Ring." Alina's building was a few blocks away.

"We're almost there," he said, softly stroking her hand.

"Are you coming up?" she said.

"Not tonight. I need to get an early start tomorrow," he lied.

The prospect of hanging around her apartment while she complained about stomach pains, and eventually made good on their promise, held little appeal.

"Brunch tomorrow?" she said.

"If you're feeling better," said Penkin, feigning a concerned smile.

The SUV lurched to a stop, slamming him against the seatbelt. Alina let out a feeble yelp. Penkin didn't waste any time yelling at the driver or interrogating his security chief. He'd been around long enough to understand that they had come to an abrupt halt for a life-threatening reason. His driver would run over a dog or small child to keep them moving on an open road.

"Back up," said his security chief, turning in the front seat to look through the rear cargo window.

"No good," said the guard behind them. "We're boxed in."

The sound of rifles charging filled the cabin as the two non-driving security guys readied short-barreled AK-74s. Ahead of Penkin's lead Range Rover, three black luxury SUVs and a silver Tigr-2, the civilian version of the GAZ Tigr armored infantry vehicle, had boxed them into the center of the intersection. Shit. You didn't see many Tigr-2s around Moscow. This wasn't an attack.

"Stand down, Yury," he said, patting his security chief on the shoulder. "They're Maksimov's people."

"Are you sure, Mr. Penkin?" said Yury.

When Sergei Mirzoyev hopped down from the massive Tigr-2, there was no doubt in Penkin's mind. Mirzoyev was Dima Maksimov's right-hand man. One of "Two Spies" charged with maintaining order and loyalty within the organization. He ran an extensive intelligence network inside and outside of the brotherhood, paying off the right people to keep things running smoothly. Penkin had been ducking Mirzoyev for several days while trying to salvage something from the setback they'd experienced in India. It was time to face the music.

"I'm sure," said Penkin, opening his door. "Keep everyone inside their vehicles."

"Understood, Mr. Penkin," said Yury, repeating the order over the communications network.

"What are you doing?" said Alina, terrified. "Where are you going?"

She looked far more worried than he would have thought. Maybe she wasn't as dumb as she acted.

"I need to have a little talk with a business associate," said Penkin. "It shouldn't take long."

"I just live a block away," she said, pulling on her locked door handle. "I shouldn't be here."

"Don't let her out under any circumstances," said Penkin, shutting the door on her screams.

He walked past the lead Range Rover and met Mirzoyev alongside the imposing Tigr-2 SUV.

"No need to be so dramatic, Sergei," said Penkin, offering his hand.

The squat, crew-cut Russian contemplated Penkin's hand before shaking it. "Mr. Maksimov is not amused."

"I understand," said Penkin. "I really thought I'd have some good news to offer him by now."

"The two of you can discuss this in private," said Mirzoyev. "Somewhere else. He's waiting."

"Now?" said Penkin, looking at his watch. "I don't want to inconvenience him."

"He would have appreciated that courtesy earlier in the week," said Mirzoyev, gesturing for him to get in the Tigr-2.

Penkin didn't have a choice in the matter. If he didn't comply, they'd either grab him forcefully or shoot him dead on the street. Given the bad news he would deliver to Maksimov, he wondered if a quick death on the street might be the better option.

"I've always wanted to take a ride in one of these," said Penkin.

"Very good," said Mirzoyev. "Call Yury and tell him to dispose of the girl."

"What? Why?" said Penkin.

"Do I need to ask again?"

"No," said Penkin, shaking his head. "Message received."

And just like that, Alina Dudnik's life came to an abrupt end. Actually, it had been running on fumes since he'd decided to conceal the full scope of the India debacle from his *Pakhan*. He pressed send on his phone and gave the order, wondering what he could possibly say to Maksimov tonight to avoid the same fate.

Chapter 62

Allegheny Mountains
West Virginia

Karl Berg sat partially upright in the same patio lounge chair they had taken from the Virginia safe house. It was the best he could do under the circumstances and would have to suffice for this critical meeting. He no longer felt like his skin would come apart at the seams when he wasn't lying flat on his back, but he didn't want to push his luck.

The doctor had been crystal clear about the complicated nature of healing seventy-six separate and varying wounds. His body's repair system would be overtaxed for weeks, requiring constant care and significant rest. With limited medical support on-site, a runaway systemic infection would require hospitalization, where Berg's wounds would undoubtedly draw the wrong kind of attention, putting his life at risk in more than one way.

Playing the good patient once again made him feel ridiculous as the weekend's guests filtered into the modern, remarkably well-equipped conference room. Remarkable because the entire property had looked condemned when they arrived, which turned out to be a carefully maintained façade.

The oversized barn adjacent to the farmhouse looked ready to collapse. Faded red paint, splintered wood sides, and a buckled roof combined to portray decades of neglect. Inside the securely locked barn doors, a cage of steel beams and thick wooden planks enclosed the main floor, protecting the generous space from imminent collapse. Several four-wheel ATVs and three mint-condition SUVs sat under blue tarps on the immaculate concrete floor. The house hadn't looked promising either. Chipped white paint, missing porch spindles, and broken window lattices matched the exterior conditions of the barn.

Even the massively long, one-story cow shed behind the main house had looked sketchy, though it was clearly a more recent addition to the farm. Connected to the house by a breezeway, the worn sides and roof of the fully enclosed shed served as a shell to conceal the recently constructed barracks, armory, and briefing room, where they now gathered.

Berg eyed the odd collection seated in front of him, or in the case of Special Agents Ryan Sharpe and Dana O'Reilly, standing cautiously next to the exit. He didn't blame them. There was nothing normal about this meeting, particularly its attendees. In fact, he was surprised Sharpe had even agreed to attend, given the circumstances.

Graves caught his attention and nodded, indicating that Sanderson had joined via teleconference. Since everyone in the room had been introduced, he started the meeting.

"Looks like we have everyone," said Berg. "General Sanderson?"

"Still here, despite everyone's best efforts," said the general.

"You'll be pleased to know that the guests we discussed earlier have joined us," said Berg. "Though they don't look like they'll be straying too far from the exit anytime soon."

"I would be highly suspicious of them if they did," said Sanderson. "Welcome, and thank you for hearing us out. If you still think we're nuts by the end of this meeting, all I ask is that you give us a heads-up before revealing this location."

"Your secret is safe as long as you deal straight on this," said Sharpe. "The moment you stray from that path, I will shut you down."

"I'd expect nothing less," said Sanderson. "I have the highest respect for you and your colleague."

O'Reilly's face tightened, her mouth opening to respond, but Sharpe stopped her with a quick whisper. She glanced at Abraham Sayar, her angry look easing slightly. Sayar had played a key role on Sharpe's task force in 2007, nearly giving his life to stop the bioweapons plot against the United States.

"Now that we have the pleasantries out of the way," said Sharpe. "Every known or suspected member of your current or previous organization is once again wanted for terrorism against the United States. What are we looking at here?"

"We're looking at a coordinated effort to destroy my organization and anyone currently looking into the whereabouts of Anatoly Reznikov," said Sanderson. "I lost seventeen operatives in a double-cross ambush on Ascension Island. They were on their way to Gabon to pick up the scientist's trail, accompanied by a team of SEALs. Everything about this mission turned out to be fake, right down to the SEALs and U.S. Air Force flight crew. The entire operation was sanctioned by the National Security Council and confirmed by independent sources high up in the Department of Defense and White House chain of command."

"I assume you've contacted your sources since the ambush?" said Sharpe.

Sanderson shook his head. "General Frank Gordon at SOCOM won't take my call."

"That's not a good sign." Sharpe frowned.

"No, it's not. My other source, who will remain unnamed for now, shed some light on why Gordon wouldn't take my call."

"Let me guess," said Sharpe. "The official government story differs significantly."

"A one-hundred-and-eighty-degree flip. In their version, my team murdered the SEALs and aircrew during the refueling stop, stealing the aircraft. A C-17 Globemaster."

"Where are your survivors now?"

"They parachuted into eastern Brazil after starting the C-17 on a slow descent and pointing it toward the Atlantic," Sanderson explained.

"I'm sorry for the loss, General," said Sharpe. "This Reznikov business has killed a lot of good people. I had no idea the Sokolov intelligence was connected to any of this."

"That's what's so interesting about all of this," said Berg. "Grigor Sokolov wasn't on the CIA's radar."

"I ran his name through all of our databases before issuing a watch-list addendum with his information," Audra Bauer interjected. "He wasn't cited in any ongoing or previous intelligence-gathering effort. We had a short file, which had likely been compiled from Interpol data."

"The request from DNI mimicked yours," said Sharpe. "I got their call the morning you called."

"They called?" Bauer asked. "That's a little unusual."

"Not if you're working off the books," said Berg. "Like I was."

"Requests like this are usually electronically submitted, but the call came from my old boss. I didn't think anything of it. He checks in on me now and then."

"Frederick Shelby?" said Berg. "That's pretty high up the food chain for something like this, regardless of your relationship."

"Given the ultimate reason for the request, maybe it's not that unusual," said Sharpe. "Calling me directly was a not so subtle way of making sure it got prioritized."

"The timing is suspect," said Berg. "I talk to Audra, Audra submits the watch list addendum for Sokolov, and suddenly the deputy director of National Intelligence calls you, requesting an international law enforcement bulletin for Sokolov. Shelby was one of the most obvious beneficiaries of True America's sudden rise to power."

"You're sure Sokolov wasn't on the CIA's radar?" said Sharpe. "It seems to me that you guys do a pretty good job of keeping secrets from each other over there."

"It's remotely possible," said Bauer.

"I don't think so," said Berg. "The Sokolov connection originated from a unique source, based on information unlikely to be available to the CIA."

Sharpe shrugged. "We can theorize all day. The bottom line is that Sanderson's people were attacked on the way to Africa to investigate intelligence requested by and passed to DNI. Berg and Bauer were attacked after Bauer drew attention to Sokolov. The crew sent after Berg and Bauer is connected to Brown River, presumably paid through Brown River. And they appear to be part of a geographically distributed, structured organization, based on what my colleague determined and you already knew. Where do we go from here?"

"We were hoping you could help us with that," said Sanderson.

"We're two agents swimming against an incredibly strong tide," Sharpe replied.

Berg nodded ruefully. "More like a tidal wave."

"I appreciate your candor," said Sharpe. "What do you suggest?"

"Nearly a billion dollars is passing right through Brown River. Determining the source of that money would be a good start," said Bauer.

"I'm going to need my boss's approval to start opening some of those doors," Sharpe said.

Graves held up a USB thumb drive. "We can open those doors without his approval if you take this back to your office and plug it into your computer."

"Funny. Why don't you just upload the virus to one of our phones and have us carry it in?" asked Sharpe. "Like you did at the National Counterterrorism Center."

"I suspect you left your phones behind," said Graves. "You guys discovered that?"

"You know we left our phones behind, and yes, we did," said Sharpe, directing his attention back to Bauer. "We're talking about more than just digging through financial records, in the long run."

"Probably much sooner than later," said Berg.

"This is going to take a concentrated effort, requiring a task force of sorts, likely pulling agents from different branches. I'll need Fred Carroll's tacit approval to pull that off, which means Carroll will need to know the purpose of the task force, and I can't bullshit him. He can smell it coming through the door."

A short silence ensued, broken by Sanderson.

"Ryan, the men and women in your presence represent nearly all of the people left in the United States that I know I can trust. We're looking at a massive conspiracy. One in which Audra Bauer's office is bugged. One that can conjure an authentic-looking Department of Defense Special Operations mission on short notice. One that feels comfortable snatching senior CIA officers off public streets. One that commands an army four thousand strong."

"I get it," said Sharpe. "We need to thoroughly vet Carroll."

"That's the easy part," said Berg. "Then we need to convince him that a clear and present danger to the entire fabric of our nation's security exists, and convince him to take action."

"Sounds like an easy sell for someone like you, Karl," said Sanderson, getting a few laughs.

"Here's the thing," said Sharpe. "We're going to need more evidence than some cooked books and a paper mercenary army. The former is a Treasury issue. The latter is padded-cell territory."

"A lot more than that has transpired over the past several days," Berg said. "I'm living proof of that."

"Take a few steps back and look at this objectively," Sharpe suggested. "The kidnapping and torture of Karl Berg never happened."

Berg frowned. "Excuse me?"

"Where's the crime scene? Perpetrators? Probably cleaned up by now. The word of a disgruntled CIA officer, on the eve of retirement, might not go as far as you think. Have any big gambling debts? Strange financial activity?"

"No," Berg said defensively.

"Think again. If this conspiracy is as big as you think, you're either the proud owner of a shady offshore bank account or the subject of a lien against your home filed by an online casino. People who play with large sums of shady money tend to get hurt."

"That's crazy," said Berg.

"Not as crazy as the running gun battle in Falls Church a few nights ago. Gunmen snatched a woman matching Audra Bauer's description from her car, brazenly murdering her undercover protective detail in the process. A massive FBI and local police manhunt is underway as we speak," said Sharpe, feigning a concerned look. "I can't imagine anyone will rest until she is found and taken to a CIA safe house for her own protection."

"Shit," said Bauer.

"And we all know what General Terrence Sanderson did. Betrayed his country for the price of a C-17 Globemaster. Shameful. Did I miss anyone?"

"You made your point," said Bauer. "We need irrefutable evidence of a conspiracy."

"We have a long list of names," said Berg. "Broken down by pay grade and location."

"Wellins didn't tell us anything useful about the people pulling his strings, and he was in the top tier," Sayar added.

"Wellins?" said Sharpe, looking around the room.

Nobody seemed eager to offer an explanation, especially Berg. He could hear Sharpe's caustically objective version of the abduction and torture of a member of Bauer's "protective detail."

Sharpe grimaced. "That bad, huh?"

"Let's just say he turned out to be a dead end," said Berg.

"Wonderful. High tier? As in area coordinator?"

"Yes."

"Then we need to identify a conspirator outside of this phantom army structure," Sharpe concluded. "They're probably using cutouts for any interaction requiring face time, and one-way or dead-end electronic communications."

"Several numbers on his call list were dead-ended. Same with the other phones collected," Graves told him. "We scoured the data and found nothing."

"I bet any possible connection to his crew has been zapped. Same with the crew that took Berg," said Sharpe.

"So how the hell do we do this?" Berg asked.

"I honestly don't know," said Sharpe.

"I have an idea," Sanderson answered. "There's no diplomatic way to say this, but we could dangle some cheese in front of a mousetrap."

Audra Bauer's husband, David, launched up from his seat. "The general can shove that idea where the sun doesn't shine. That's up your ass, in case you're confused."

"I'm not, and for the record, I wasn't suggesting Audra," said Sanderson. "I'll be making my way north shortly. I'm sure I'd make an irresistible piece of cheese."

"How long?" asked Sharpe.

"A few weeks. Now that I'm back on the most wanted list, it won't be an easy trip."

"This will go cold by then," said Sharpe. "Completely evaporated."

"Then dangle me," Berg offered.

Bauer threw up her hands. "We're not dangling anyone as bait."

"Then this is over," said Sharpe. "Unless someone can cough up someone inside the core conspiracy."

The room went quiet, shoulders shrugging and heads mostly shaking. Berg noticed Timothy Graves and Anish Gupta whispering furiously back and forth in an apparent argument. Graves muttered an obscenity before standing up.

"There might be a development on that front," said Graves.

"What kind of development?" said Sharpe.

Graves hesitated.

"Tell them," said Gupta, nudging Graves.

"Tell us what?" said Berg.

"Dammit. I really wasn't supposed to say anything. It's not one hundred percent," said Graves.

"Spill it, Graves!" said Sanderson.

"Wellins might have mentioned a name at the end of his—ordeal," said Graves.

"And nobody thought to mention this?" said Berg.

"I didn't find out until several hours ago," said Graves. "We put together an intelligence package."

"Then let's get this ball rolling!" said Sanderson.

"It's already rolling," said Graves. "The Petroviches wanted to deliver a farewell gift."

"What kind of gift?" said Berg.

"The kind that dresses in an expensive suit and works at the White House."

Karl Berg felt a glimmer of hope.

Chapter 63

Sixteenth Street Northwest
Washington, D.C.

Daniel surveyed the crowded hotel bar from their cozy table in the corner. Happy hour had kicked into full swing about an hour ago, the room packed so tightly that their target drifted in and out of sight in the throng of well-dressed D.C. professionals. The man Wellins had traded for the guaranteed safety of his own family had entered the basement lounge twenty minutes ago, quietly occupying a saved seat at the bar. He'd shared words with several people since he arrived, but nobody had stopped for a long conversation.

"His second martini just arrived," said Jessica. "Time for work."

"You sure we want to go down this path?"

"We can't keep running. Not from this," she said, looking into his eyes. "Our work isn't done. That's been made painfully clear over the past few days."

Daniel took a small sip of the rye whiskey Manhattan he'd nursed to the bottom of his tumbler for the past hour. "I don't see how Berg and Sanderson can take this on."

"Somebody has to try," said Jessica.

He cracked a subdued smile. Jessica had changed since Chicago—for the better. He'd prepared for the worst after that traumatic experience, but she'd somehow emerged on the other side.

"What?" she said, raising an eyebrow.

"You're right, and I love you more than you know," he said before squeezing her hand. "You better get going."

Jessica got up from the table and stood next to him. She looked stunning in the low-cut black cocktail dress and matching high heels they'd purchased at an outlet mall in Leesburg, Virginia. He hadn't seen her dressed "to kill" like this in over a year. Sandals, sundresses and shorts had been her outfit du jour since they moved to Anguilla.

"Quit staring," she said.

"Kind of hard not to," said Daniel.

"That's the point," she said. "You better get out of here."

"Meet you on the corner of K Street and Sixteenth," he said.

"If he makes it that far."

Daniel swirled the remains of his drink and tossed it back before sliding through a polished-looking group of beltway acolytes to make his way out of the bar. A few steps up the wood-panel-finished stairway, he glanced back, catching a glimpse of Jessica from his elevated vantage point. She'd managed to wedge her way between their target, a brown-haired man with wire-rim glasses, and the woman next to him. The man slid his untouched martini in front of her and raised a finger to get the bartender's attention. Jessica touched his arm, leaning in to him to whisper. The guy cocked his head and turned in the chair toward her, a hungry look on his face. It was almost too easy for her.

Chapter 64

Office of the Director of National Intelligence
Tysons Corner, Virginia

Frederick Shelby's office phone buzzed, drawing his focus away from the computer screen and the endless stream of intelligence updates and analyst summaries that vied for his attention on the National Intelligence Fusion Network. He glanced at his office phone, an intra-office call from his secretary vying for his attention. It was a little early for the day's usual assortment of bureaucratic check-ins. Shelby lifted the handset and pressed the illuminated button connecting him to his secretary.

"Michael, can you hold any calls until after the eight-thirty morning briefing?" he asked.

"This isn't a call, sir," said the secretary. "You have a visitor. A rather important one. Raymond Burke."

Senior counselor to President Crane? At seven thirty in the morning? This couldn't be good.

"By all means, show him in."

Shelby stood up and moved around his desk, rapidly recounting the events of the past several days for any possible missteps that could lead back to him. Nothing came to mind. Shelby had just finished straightening his suit coat when the door opened. Raymond Burke, an average man in every aspect of his appearance, walked into his office and politely thanked his secretary, shutting the door.

"This is a pleasant surprise," said Shelby, offering his hand.

Burke shook his hand with a mostly official smile. "In my experience, and I assume yours as well, the words 'pleasant' and 'surprise' rarely yield anything positive."

"I usually reserve judgment," said Shelby. "But in this case, I felt comfortable going out on a limb."

Burke laughed, his smile coming closer to passing as genuine.

"Please. Have a seat. May I offer you some coffee?" asked Shelby, motioning toward a mahogany table used for private meetings.

"I can't stay long," said Burke, remaining solidly in place near the door. "I have good news and bad news."

Shelby's stomach tightened, waiting for Burke to continue.

"The bad news is that Gary Vincent died in his sleep last night. Suspected heart attack. News of his death has not been reported publicly," said Burke. "I presume you can guess the good news."

Shelby stood before him as the acting director of National Intelligence. Astonishing. "I wouldn't exactly call it good news under the circumstances," he said, forcing a solemn tone.

Burke eyed him cynically. "No need to pretend with me. You were promised the position. Now it's yours."

Shelby's vision narrowed for a brief moment, the full scope of the words sinking in. Burke was part of it. Quite possibly in charge of it.

"Frederick," said Burke, putting a hand on Shelby's shoulder, "you've served True America well over the past few years, but it's time to take this service and loyalty to the next level. We're going to rebuild this nation from the ground up, and we need your help."

All Shelby could manage was a nod.

"President Crane will immediately nominate you for the position of director, and the Senate will confirm the nomination after a brief hearing."

"You can count on my support," Shelby said. "I won't let our country down."

Burke's face deadpanned. "Changing our nation's current downward trajectory will be difficult. It'll require sacrifice."

"I'm willing to make any sacrifice to bring about the needed change."

"We're not talking about your sacrifice. Sometimes you have to burn down the forest to regrow it," said Burke. "This will not be an easy task or a job for the fainthearted, like Gary Vincent."

Did Burke just threaten him? It didn't matter. Shelby had sold his soul to True America when he held up the investigation into the attempted bioweapons attack and minimized the link between the fanatics responsible for the attack and the mainstream True America political party. The ink had long ago dried on that contract, and there was no going back.

"You don't have to worry about me," he said.

"I wasn't worried. I just needed to reemphasize the unwavering commitment required to be a part of the inner echelon."

"I'm fully committed," said Shelby, both thrilled and alarmed by Burke's statement.

"We'll make all of the necessary arrangements for your confirmation and call on you shortly," said Burke. "Until then, we need your help with something."

"Anything."

"A member of the outer echelon has gone missing. We'd like to find him immediately."

"Who?"

"Gerald Simmons. White House Counterterrorism director," said Burke.

Simmons? In the outer echelon? He didn't even know there were echelons. That explained how the weasel had landed a coveted position at the White House. Shelby hadn't thought the guy was worth a squirt of piss when he'd first met him.

"Do you suspect foul play?"

"I always suspect foul play," said Burke. "But in this case, I believe he was abducted. Gerry isn't the most stalwart guy, but he's fiercely loyal."

"When you say immediately, how immediately do you mean?"

"I didn't realize there were different shades of interpretation."

"Not interpretation, implementation," said Shelby. "How critical is Simmons?"

"He represents a dangerous nexus to the entire cause."

"I'll do everything in my power to find him," said Shelby.

"I appreciate the fact that you don't confuse authority with power," said Burke.

"I prefer not to limit myself."

Epilogue

80 to 90 miles northwest of Lubbock, Texas

Anatoly Reznikov bounced in his seat, the vastly oversized luxury SUV apparently jumping another fucking chasm. The seatbelt instantly locked into place against his chest and constricted his breathing. A sense of panic set in soon after that, no doubt a symptom of the goddamn hood over his head. His trembling hands scrambled to disengage the seatbelt, which required him to expel every bit of oxygen left in his lungs to create enough slack in the belt to set him free. Once again, his hands couldn't seem to figure it out, and he found himself clawing at the latch and whimpering in desperation. The tightness across his chest suddenly eased and the seatbelt released.

"There you go, my friend," said Sokolov.

Reznikov fumbled to grab the end of the seatbelt from Sokolov's hands, managing to click it back in place by himself. One of the Americans chuckled.

Under other circumstances, he might consider a simple *thank you*, but not with Sokolov. Helping him with the seatbelt wasn't an act of kindness on the mercenary's part. The fucker had sold him like cattle to the highest bidder. The mercenary was making sure that his payday didn't get damaged in transit.

The beast had dragged him from one dank shithole airport to another, spanning Southeast Asia, until they finally boarded a private jet that hopped the Pacific and landed in some Mexican city named after a dog. He feared that would be his last luxury for a long time.

Upon landing, the wide leather seats and unlimited food and booze transformed into dusty trunks and wooden crates that smelled like animal feces. This went on for a few days until they stopped at a border city, where Sokolov finally let his guard down. During one of Sokolov's frequent squabbles with the Mexicans hired to transport them, Reznikov slipped out of a dank garage into an equally squalid neighborhood and ran for the nearest sign of civilization. A distant gas station.

A quick taxi ride later, he found the dingiest-looking bar in the red-light district and somehow convinced the owner to pour him some vodka. Jet-fuel variety, but still welcome. He drank several shots, entertaining the grimy crowd with his Russian toasts, and patiently waited for Sokolov to find him, mostly so he could cover the bill. The easily amused group of locals looked like the types that would cut his throat at the first sign of insolvency.

True to form, the mercenary showed up while he was in the middle of deflecting an increasingly hostile string of questions in Spanish and English, aimed at determining if and how he intended on paying his bill. The bar's mood had turned dark enough that he wished he knew better Spanish. Or any Spanish.

He could have turned them on Sokolov in a heartbeat. A hint that the Russian carried lots of cash could easily buy a slit throat in this city. Reznikov saw his freedom in their murderous eyes, a fleeting glimpse he wasn't likely to catch again. The group that had taken possession of him at the border crossing was slick and well organized. They made the Bratva look like undisciplined rabble.

Americans without a doubt, and government from what he guessed, which perplexed him. His previous government-sponsored stay in the United States had nearly ended with his assassination at the hands of the CIA officer Karl Berg. They clearly didn't want him dead, or the men that met Sokolov on the banks of the jungle river in India would have put a bullet in his head. They went through a lot of trouble to get him here and to do it discreetly. The Americans needed something from him. Something they hadn't needed in 2007. He was intrigued despite the stifling hood over his head.

They drove for a brief amount of time before one of the Americans spoke.

"Unbag 'im. We're clear."

Reznikov squinted after the impenetrable hood was ripped from his head, despite the SUV's deeply tinted windows. He took a moment to reorient himself within the vehicle. Sokolov sat to his left, behind the driver. A look over his shoulder revealed two serious-looking gentlemen, one of them stuffing the black hood into a tan backpack. Reznikov noted the Taser pistols within easy reach of the men, certain that far more lethal options were hidden nearby.

Jumping out of the vehicle wasn't an option, even if he could somehow convince himself to take the risk. The doors next to Reznikov and Sokolov contained no handles or buttons, and a thick, clear glass shield separated the front seating area from the passengers. No viable escape option appeared to exist, and even if he somehow got out of the vehicle, where the hell would he go?

A featureless hardscrabble landscape extended as far as the eye could see in every direction. A constant low-grade rumble from the tires combined with the little he could see through the dust-caked windshield convinced him they were speeding down a dirt road toward a destination still too far away to see. The land reminded him of the vast Kazakh steppes, but drier and harder. Reznikov had no concept of where they had driven him or how long he'd been in the SUV. He had lost all track of time shortly after they started.

"We're getting close," said the man in the front passenger seat.

Reznikov leaned sideways and peered through the windshield. Getting close to what? Nothing had changed. He started to look away when the horizon subtly changed. It was still flat and barren, but something was different.

"What is it?" asked Sokolov.

"What do you care?" said Reznikov, keeping his eyes fixed on the vast emptiness ahead of them.

A few minutes later, the distant outline of an endless fence took shape, nearly blending with the environment. The SUV raced toward the barrier, thick coils of concertina wire topping the out-of-place barrier. The fence lazily parted ahead of them, and Reznikov started to wonder if the driver was paying attention. The vehicle barreled through the opening with less than a foot of space on each side. The fence shrank away behind them, the gate already returning to seal the gap. Now what? The landscape in front of them looked the same as before.

They drove past the fence for what felt like ten to fifteen minutes; then the SUV started to slow. Reznikov looked around. Still nothing. The vehicle decelerated rapidly, plunging down a ramp into a subterranean complex, where it came to a stop.

"Final destination, gentlemen," said the man in the front seat.

He didn't like the sound of that at all. Armed men met them at the bottom of the ramp, opening the doors on both sides of the SUV. Nobody grabbed Reznikov or pointed a weapon at him, but the message was clear. He hopped out of the vehicle and looked around, impressed by what he saw.

It was difficult to take in the full scope of the facility from where he stood, but he guessed they had descended into a man-made excavation the length and width of two soccer fields. Judging by the height of the SUV compared to the nearest wood-beam-reinforced earthen walls, Reznikov estimated the dig to be thirty feet deep, entirely covered by thick sections of camouflage-style netting supported by an expansive latticework of metal beams and supports. Two men worked swiftly to replace the section of netting at the top of the ramp they had just entered. Clever.

Underneath the canopy, several buildings filled the excavation. Two windowless, state-of-the-art structures drew his attention, their purpose unmistakable. The rest were forgettable prefabricated wooden assemblies, the word *MARS* painted in block letters on a few of them. The place was surprisingly quiet for a self-contained facility.

"Dr. Reznikov," said a tall man standing next to the set of guards that had opened his car door, "welcome to Site X."

He spoke fluent, academic Russian.

"Site X?" said Reznikov. "That's quite an original name."

"Site X felt appropriate given its purpose. Randolph Powers, Site X mission coordinator. It's my job to make sure you have everything you need and that your stay here is as pleasant as the circumstances allow."

"There's nothing pleasant about being a prisoner," said Reznikov, glaring at Sokolov, who stood in front of the SUV.

"Temporary guests. Your work is critical to our cause, and you'll be rewarded handsomely. Unfortunately, it's in our best interest to keep both of you out of the public's eye, so to speak, until a point in time when our cause has gained enough momentum to be self-sustaining."

"Sounds like a long time," said Reznikov.

"Not terribly long," said Powers. "Though time does have a way of dragging on down here, as you can imagine. Staying busy helps."

"I assume the samples are here?" said Reznikov.

"They arrived several days earlier," said Powers. "We've eagerly awaited your arrival."

"Of course you have," said Reznikov, nodding at Sokolov. "And him?"

"You're both our guests," said Powers.

"I'd prefer not to have to look at him while I'm here," said Reznikov.

"We presumed as much. His quarters are located on the opposite side of the site from you, with a separate recreation facility."

"That's very considerate of you," said Reznikov.

"My instructions are to keep you happy," said Powers, glancing around. "Within reason. You'll have twenty-four-hour access to gourmet food—"

"And drink?"

"As long as it doesn't impact your work," said Powers.

"Women?"

"We can make that happen, occasionally. Like I said, my instructions are to keep you happy."

"Within reason," Reznikov repeated.

"Exactly. You have a busy schedule."

"You know what would make me very happy?" said Reznikov.

"A few bottles of ice-cold Grey Goose and a few days to relax poolside? We have a pool, though you can't really work on your tan," said Powers, glancing upward at the canopy.

"That would certainly make me happy, but not *very* happy," said Reznikov.

Powers shrugged. "What would make Dr. Anatoly Reznikov *very* happy? It's your first day, and I'd like to make a good impression. Within reason."

Reznikov switched to English and nodded at Sokolov. "Is killing this piece of shit within reason?"

"I can't think of any reason why it wouldn't be," said Powers, turning to the group of heavily armed guards next to him and nodding.

Sokolov had already started backing up slowly, his English apparently a little better than Reznikov had guessed. Before the Russian mercenary could make a sudden move, the two guards raised their compact rifles and fired quick bursts into Sokolov, dropping him to his knees next to the SUV's front bumper.

Reznikov held an open hand toward the gunmen. "No more!"

Powers repeated the order, stopping the men from firing again.

"May I borrow your pistol? I promise to only use one bullet," said Reznikov.

Powers nodded and glanced at the guards, who shifted their rifles to cover Reznikov.

"The pistol is ready for action. Just pull the trigger," said Powers. "Once."

Reznikov walked up to Sokolov, who had braced himself against the vehicle by wedging his right elbow between the bumper and the grill. He spit blood onto the dusty ground and looked up at Reznikov, a grin on his filthy face.

"You're just as dead as I am, you pathetic fuck," said Sokolov.

"I've risen from the dead before," said Reznikov, nudging the pistol against Sokolov's forehead.

Reznikov pressed the trigger once, kicking the mercenary's limp body off the bumper. He held the pistol at shoulder height and pointed it toward the sky, his finger out of the trigger well. A hand snatched it from his loose grip a moment later. Turning to face his new captors, he smiled pleasantly at Powers.

"I believe you mentioned something about vodka and a pool?"

THE END

If you enjoyed the Black Flagged series, I have NO DOUBT that you will love my new FRACTURED STATE series. Set in the year 2035, FRACTURED STATE follows Nathan Fisher, the unwitting target of a black ops conspiracy, in a cat and mouse chase across a frighteningly recognizable, high-tech, dystopian southwest United States. YOU CAN ORDER FRACTURED STATE NOW FROM AMAZON.

To join my mailing list, GO HERE: http://eepurl.com/D2D1j

Periodically, you'll receive exclusive news, content and discounts regarding my work.

ORIGINS

A BLACK FLAGGED SHORT STORY
© Steven Konkoly 2017 All rights reserved

Foothills of Divjaka, Republic of Kosovo
August 1998

Marko Resja stood a few meters away from the raised dirt road leading into the crude village, swatting flies away from his grimy, sweat-covered face. August drew stifling heat and oppressive humidity to the Balkan Peninsula, which couldn't have been timed worse for the Yugoslav offensive. The heat seemed to incite the flies, which needed little encouragement in these hills. He wondered if these insects could sense their role in the impending tragedy. It would certainly explain their increased activity.

He raised his twenty-year-old M-76 sniper rifle and stared through the worn scope, scanning the road as far as possible. He was assigned to watch the most likely western approach for Kosovo Liberation Army (KLA) vehicles, sharing the duty with another relatively new member of Srecko Hadzic's Panthers. Satisfied that nothing threatened to approach from the outskirts of Divjaka, he lowered the rifle and shrugged at his partner, who then spoke a few hushed words into a cheap plastic handheld radio.

When Sava finished sending the report to their commander in the village, he rolled his eyes, before slapping the flies away from his head. Sava's dark green camouflage uniform was filthy; crusted with light brown mud up to the knees. Large sweat stains formed odd circular shapes under his armpits and across his chest. The only thing clean about Sava was his rifle, which was slung over his left shoulder—to free him to perform the occasional radio check-in and chain smoke cigarettes. Sava's face disappeared in a cloud of tobacco smoke and reappeared sporting a grin. His yellowed teeth stood out through the thin layer of unevenly applied green and black camouflage.

The camouflage greasepaint had nearly worn away over the past three days, as their unit moved through the hills mopping up "suspected" bands of KLA resistance. The designation "suspected" had always been a loose term among the Panthers, but after yesterday's gruesome discovery in Klecka, the word had taken on a new meaning. From what he understood, any ethnic Albanian Kosovar found in these hills was now classified as a "suspected" terrorist; the disturbing find outside of Klecka serving to "legitimize" an unofficial policy implemented by Milosevic's paramilitary nationalists for the past several years.

Regular Yugoslavian forces left behind to secure Klecka had been escorted to a makeshift crematorium, where evidence of scorched human remains were uncovered, along with several trenches filled with badly decomposing bodies in a nearby orchard. A young boy informed the soldiers that the KLA had killed a large group of kidnapped Serbians, ahead of the Yugoslavian offensive. Word of the discovery spread like wildfire through Serbian nationalist paramilitary units in the foothills, and Marko's platoon was roused from a deep sleep at three in the morning to prepare for an urgent operation.

Several armored vehicles arrived in the camp shortly after they mustered and provided the platoon with transportation to the outskirts of Divjaka, where a mortar team set up in a clearing to the west. Half of the thirty-man platoon drove to the eastern road on the other side of the village, along with a few of the M-80 armored personnel carriers. The entire platoon's focus was a cluster of homes and structures in northern Divjaka, isolated from the main town, and accessible by two roads, which were now blocked by a heavily armed Serbian paramilitary force.

They loitered in the western tree line until a crimson sun started to creep over the eastern hills of the tight valley, and fingers of deep orange light caught the tops of the trees around them. He could only imagine the terror spreading through the homes in front of them as residents helplessly listened to the distant rumble of idling engines beyond their sight—and waited for the inevitable.

Mortar tubes announced daybreak across the valley, firing a volley of 82mm high explosive rounds at the closest grouping of structures visible along the road. The shells sailed in a high arc and took an eternity to find earth again. When gravity finished its job, the ground behind one of the houses erupted skyward in a light brown cloud, followed by another geyser of dirt from the road. The sharp crunch of the impacts washed through the men, giving rise to a few cheers.

The mortar attack lasted five minutes, as the mortar crew haphazardly fired several more salvos into the village, adjusting their aim to walk the shells through the entire length of the community. Luckily for the inhabitants, the mortar team never focused on the buildings. Only once did they see a shell make a direct hit, sending large wooden chunks of a red roof flew skyward into the dust cloud obscuring the village. This led to a chorus of cheers from the men around him, which he pretended to eagerly join. He felt relieved that the mortar attack had done so little damage, but his solace would be short lived.

Without ceremony, the mortar teams disassembled their equipment and loaded it into the troop compartment of one of the M-80s. The entire detachment of regular army vehicles sped away, leaving his squad with their own odd assortment of AUZ jeeps and SUVs—and a ghastly task.

Nenad Sojic, the platoon's de facto leader, spoke to his radio operator, a lean, darker-skinned Serb named Goran, and waved the squad over. Through the radio handset, Goran relayed Sojic's orders to the men positioned on the eastern approach to the village. Without ceremony, Sojic told them that they would search house-to-house for KLA insurgents and weapons caches. Once a house was searched, the inhabitants would be sent to a centralized location for further questioning. Even the most naive members of the platoon knew what that meant.

They walked through the dew-covered fields down the road toward the simple concrete houses. Cool mountain valley air penetrated their thin uniforms, and most of the men still wore the black wool watch caps they had donned while shivering in the middle of the night. The caps would be ditched by mid-morning, as temperatures reached unbearable highs. The jeeps roared to life behind them and soon met up with the soldiers on foot.

When they reached the first set of homes, Marko and Sava were detached to serve as pickets at the western edge of the village. They were tasked to observe the same road the armored personnel carriers used to hastily separate themselves from Marko's paramilitary comrades—and report any incoming vehicles. They both quickly turned their attention to the road, as doors were forced open and the screaming started. He concentrated on the empty road, as the rest of the squad and the vehicles moved down the road, pushing hesitant villagers ahead of them. Neither of them wanted to look back and acknowledge what was happening.

Marko's thoughts shifted back into the present, as he tracked a crow flying through the air from the west. The large black bird landed on a crude wooden fence several yards back from the road, joining the several dozen already quietly arrayed along the fence. More crows were perched hidden among the nearby trees. They weren't intimidated by the soldiers' presence in Divjaka. They had as much right to be here as the flies, and they were here for the same reason.

"They know something we don't," Sava remarked, dragging on his cigarette.

The man had smoked non-stop since they left a Belgrade primary school soccer field three days ago, and he suspected that the young northern Serb must be close to exhausting his supply of cigarettes. All of them must be running low. Marko carried a pack of cheap Serbian smokes to fit in, but he generally never indulged, unless offered. He had always despised the habit, but his trainers at The Ranch had made it clear that he would smoke. Everyone smoked in Serbia, at least casually. He'd grown accustomed to the taste, and no longer minded the acrid smell of tobacco smoke in cramped spaces. Still, the habit did nothing for him, except help him blend into his environment.

Sava grinned nervously, and Marko wondered what he was thinking. He didn't look or sound too eager to head deeper into the village. He was young and didn't have the same brutal edge that was common among Hadzic's veteran Panthers. This thought brought another concern back into focus. His platoon was comprised of too many newbies, several of which had been swapped into the platoon just after last night's dinner. He was new to the Panther organization and had only been deployed to the field in a large-scale operation twice before, but this structure stuck him as odd.

Hadzic's field units typically overflowed with hardened paramilitary veterans of the Bosnia conflict, or former Yugoslav military. The process for integration of new recruits was brutal and discouraged most naive youth. Still, they had no shortage of volunteers, and in times of war, the training camps swelled with eager recruits—pushed through to augment roles left behind by combat hungry veterans. This platoon brimmed with newbies, and that concerned him. He wasn't sure why, but he knew something was off.

His concentration was shattered by the sudden crackle of automatic weapons fire in the distance, as hundreds of crows scattered, briefly drowning out the sound of the guns. Like the crows, Sava reacted instinctively and threw himself onto the ground next to the slightly raised dirt road. He flinched, but stood impassively in the middle of the road, as the volume of gunfire diminished, finally ending with an occasional shot. He hadn't felt or heard the familiar snap or hiss of bullets passing near him, so he kept his composure. He knew exactly what had happened, and turned his head lazily towards the center of the village. Occasional, single pistol shots started to fill the air, and Sava rose to his feet to rejoin him on the road.

He wore an expression that betrayed his true feelings, and Marko knew that the young Serb felt the same way that he did about the situation. They were both equally relieved to have been assigned to a deserted stretch of road, even if three hundred meters of separation didn't provide them with any absolution for their presence in the valley. Sava's radio crackled, and their respite from the madness was over. They had been recalled to the village center.

He slicked his thick, matted brown hair back with his left hand and wiped the sweat onto his camouflage pants. Sava looked terrified for the first time since they had piled into green, tarp-covered trucks in Belgrade. He patted the kid on the back and nodded.

"Let's get going."

The two of them started to jog down the road, careful not to twist an ankle in the shallow crater created by one of the mortar impacts. He spotted several AUZ jeeps in a clearing to the north of the village. All of the doors in the village had been left open, which gave the village a frightening aura. Almost like it had been abandoned. The first thing he heard was the crying, and it nearly stopped him in his tracks. He searched for the source and saw a group of women and children huddled under a tree, guarded by a soldier. As the scene started to unfold in front of him, he sensed that Sava had stopped altogether.

"Keep moving, or you'll end up in one of those trenches," Marko said, wondering if that was where they might end up anyway.

They were blocked by a group of Panthers and told to leave their weapons stacked against one of the vehicles. He saw several assault rifles leaned against a mud-covered chassis and walked over to the jeep to add his weapon to the collection. One his way, Marko scanned the scene to assess the situation. A shallow pit was visible, just beyond a dozen or so Panthers, who were staring down into it. A few of them shook their heads, while others spit at the earth. As he placed his sniper rifle against the jeep's rear tire, Sava joined him.

"Fucking burial duty. Wonderful," Sava said.

"It's typical for new guys," Marko lied.

He hadn't seen shovels among the men standing in front of the long pit. His stomach tensed, and he fought to remain calm. This would probably be his defining "critical point," as the Black Flag psychologists termed it. They had prepared him for these moments, characterizing the different types and their potential significance. This one looked like his "terminal critical point." He would either survive and emerge as a trusted member of the Panthers, or he would die in the pit along with the rest of the villagers. No aspect of General Sanderson's training program could truly prepare him for what would transpire in the next few moments. He had a choice to make.

If he lined up with the rest of the men, he would have to trust his chances to a gamble he had taken a few weeks ago. A little insurance policy that might save his life. His other option was to put his training to work and fight his way out of here. He might even be able to kill all of them. Half of the group was unarmed, standing unarmed like sheep, in front of their own grave. The twelve remaining men? He had several loaded assault rifles sitting right in front of him. He could sling two of them over his shoulder and start cutting down the armed Panthers with a third. The odds were in his favor, given his capabilities. It might even be blamed on KLA guerillas.

He glanced up at one of the men that had ordered him put his weapon against the jeep. The man's greasepaint camouflage had been recently reapplied, neutralizing his expression, but his eyes gave Marko pause. They were cold and alert. He would have to make his decision within the next fraction of a second. Taking his hand off the sniper rifle, he decided to gamble with his life. The payoff would secure his status among the Panthers, which was the ultimate purpose of his training as a Black Flag operative. He swallowed shallowly and followed Sava around the jeep, never taking his eyes off the hardened soldier escorting them.

As he approached the pit, a buzzing sound hit his ears, causing him to stop.

"Get with the rest of them," someone barked from behind, and he continued forward.

A few of the dirty soldiers ahead of him laughed and pointed down into the trench, which demonstrated exactly how clueless some of the new recruits could be, when confronted with the obvious.

Marko caught his first look into the shallow trench and fought the urge to gag. He betrayed no emotion as the full scope of the atrocity appeared before him. He no longer wondered about the buzzing sound. Thousands of flies swarmed over the freshly slaughtered corpses; fighting to land in bright red pools of blood, drawn to the stench of involuntarily voided bowels. As the smell started to overwhelm him, he decided to stop and turn around.

He faced the members of the same firing squad that had put all of the village's men into a hastily dug mass grave. A few of the executioners mingled with him in the doomed group, some complaining about being put on burial duty, others bragging about the accurate shots they had fired into the "terrorists." One of the loudest newbies called out to the platoon commander, who was talking into a radio headset.

"Hey, Nenad! How about the guys with the easy jobs guarding the road bury this garbage?" he said, pointing toward Marko and Sava.

"How about you shut the fuck up!" said a stocky Serb crouched near one of the jeeps.

The man's bravado instantly disappeared, and he started to melt back into the dozen or so men standing around in front of the trench. Marko took in the scene. Nobody was pointing weapons in their direction, but he could see the looks passing surreptitiously back and forth.

He located some shovels nearby, which were caked with dirt and had probably been recently used by the slaughtered Kosovars to dig their own grave. Nobody else glanced at the shovels. This was not a work detail. This was either some kind of sick initiation that might involve the surviving women and children, or something entirely different. Either way, he wondered if he had made a mistake.

His eyes found the nearest M-90 assault rifle, and he did the calculations, casually looking around. He could put a knife through the owner's throat and get the rifle, but his chances beyond that were now non-existent.

The sound of vehicles broke his concentration. Two black Range Rovers sped down the road from the east, kicking up a storm of dust behind them. The armed Panthers straightened up, and some of them even attempted to brush off some of the dirt and mud, in a futile effort.

Nenad Sojic and his radio operator, Goran, jogged to the road to meet the occupants. He recognized the SUVs, and suddenly it all made sense. He might survive the day, but only if Radovan Grahovac, Hadzic's security chief, decided to indulge in his patented sadism for a few minutes, before putting them all into the ditch. He was optimistic. The self-indulgent security chief didn't like to stray too far from Belgrade, without the promise of entertainment.

The Range Rover doors opened simultaneously, disgorging the Panther VIPs. Serious, brutal-looking men, dressed in pressed camouflage uniforms, formed a loose perimeter around the man who had emerged from the front passenger door of the lead vehicle. Radovan Grahovac stood in the middle of the heavily armed men, surveying the destroyed village and nodding in agreement with Nenad Sojic, who gestured toward the mass grave at Marko's feet.

Marko scoured Grahovac's face, looking for any indication he might survive what lie ahead in the next few minutes. As Radovan's group walked toward the pit, his heart sank, and he thought about the closest assault rifle. Maybe with this distraction he could pull it off. If he could get the rifle and find cover within a few seconds, he might be able to survive long enough to channel these overconfident simpletons into a few fatal funnels, which would give him easy targets until he developed a plan to escape.

He found too many flaws with the sudden idea. He carried the wrong ammunition magazines for an assault rifle, and would not have time to grab more if he wanted to survive the first few seconds. Plus, Radovan's entourage was comprised of special operations types that had worked together for years. He could handle them alone, with the element of surprise, but in this scenario, their presence would weigh heavily against his odds of survival.

Just as Marko finished his nearly instantaneous assessment, the group dispersed, and he spotted his only hope of surviving the day. Andrija Brujic was among Radovan's security team.

As Radovan approached, Nenad Sojic, de facto platoon commander, issued orders to Marko's group.

"Turn around and face the pit!"

Marko turned his body, along with most of the group. A few hesitated, possibly sensing what was in store for them, and one of the men, a particularly overzealous Nationalist named Vukasin Mokric, refused to follow Nenad's abrupt order. Vuk wasn't intelligent enough to realize the gravity of the situation, and Marko assumed his defiance had more to do with one of his many personality disorders than any sudden enlightenment regarding their fate.

Nenad issued an order directed at the platoon, and Marko heard the metallic sounds of several rifles put into an immediate ready state. Rounds chambered and safeties disengaged. He didn't have to look back to know that these rifles were now aimed at their backs, or in the case of Vuk, at his face.

"What the fuck is going on here? If this is some kind of initiation joke, I'm already fucking initiated. Get your rifles out of my face," Vukasin said.

The platoon commander ordered him to turn around, and Marko heard a few of the soldiers reinforce the command.

"Nenad, this is fucking bullshit. I joined this group to fuck and kill these pieces of shit. Not to be treated like a dog," he persisted.

"All thieves are dogs," a voice boomed, followed by two sudden pistol shots.

Marko heard Vuk's body hit the ground, and everyone in the line started mumbling prayers.

"Fuck with Mr. Hadzic's money, and you get treated like a rabid dog. No better than the scum rotting in the pit at your feet," the voice continued, and Marko now recognized it as Radovan Grahovac's.

"Just one week ago, a large sum of money disappeared from one of Mihail Kunac's safe houses. This money was on its way to Mr. Hadzic, when someone broke into the safe house, killing the guard responsible for watching the money," Radovan said.

"Evidence suggests that this was an inside job. Mr. Kunac had just stepped out when the money was stolen. I arrived with a small group to personally collect this money, no more than thirty minutes after the hit. The poor shit assigned to watch the money was still fucking warm when we got there. This is all too much of a coincidence for me, and you can only imagine my embarrassment. I'm ultimately responsible for this money, and having to explain to the loss of nearly fifty thousand dollars to Mr. Hadzic is not a pleasant experience!"

Fifty-three thousand, two hundred and eighty dollars to be exact.

"I had to front this fucking money to keep my own head from showing up at his feet! I haven't had a theft like this in over three years. So what's changed? We bring on a fresh batch of recruits, and I suddenly have a fucking major theft on my hands. I want this money back, and one of you pieces of shit knows exactly where to find it! Someone better start talking, or every one of you will end up in that pit…blamed for the worst massacre in recent history."

Time stood still, silent for several moments, until another gunshot broke the quiet, startling all of them. Marko felt a warm spray hit the left side of his face, and a large volume of thick, dark red fluid bathed the filthy corpses directly below him in the pit. Time slowed even further for Marko, as he registered the absolute insanity of the moment. He stood in a line of men about to be executed by a stark raving mad lunatic, and very little stood between death or salvation. His thoughts came quickly and clearly, as the man's body was kicked into the pit before it could even fall to the earth.

Marko gauged the moment and decided to let one more person die before making his play. He figured the odds were in his favor. Grahovac wasn't likely to shoot two people standing side by side. He knew the next bullet wouldn't be his. He figured the next one to be killed would be the first person to open their mouth.

"Mr. Grahovac, I wasn't even in Belgrade when this…"

He was right. A sudden gunshot completed the kid's sentence, and another body tumbled into the pit, momentarily disturbing the flies.

"I'll kill every one of you until I figure out who did this," he snarled, and started to walk back toward Marko.

At this point, Marko knew that Radovan had no intention of sparing any of them. He apparently had no idea who stole the money, and based on the fact that he had potentially killed three people who might have admitted the crime, it was clear that he didn't care. Radovan was deviously intelligent, and Marko figured this public stunt was designed to seal his legend as the most ruthless, unforgiving crime boss in Serbia.

If he couldn't punish the actual thief, he could send a clear message that stealing would result in random, murderous consequences. Sensing that his time was running short, Marko made a comment that he purposely intended to be undecipherable by Radovan. He made it quick, and there was an air of confidence to the statement that might have prevent his immediate execution.

"You have a traitor on your security detail. Someone with very expensive taste."

Radovan rushed up behind him and growled into his ear. "What did you say, thief?"

"One of your guard's is wearing a really expensive watch. I've seen similar watches, I think, in Berlin…while fucking around at a very expensive mall. I noticed it on him when you came by the assembly area two days ago. He was inspecting some of our weapons, and I got a close-up look," he whispered, and Grahovac remained silent for the longest few seconds of Marko's life.

"Which guard?" he demanded.

"Can I point to him?" Marko said.

"Yes, but if you fuck with me, I'll spill your guts all over the ground. Do it. I don't have all day," he said, and Marko sensed that he had taken a few steps back.

Marko turned purposefully, and quickly located Andrija Brujic, who looked amused by what appeared to be a new act in Radovan's travelling psycho performance. A few members of the platoon exchanged glances, and he could tell they were awaiting something horrific, yet enticingly different. Brujic adjusted the brim of his camouflage cap and touched his flattened nose. When Marko raised his hand and pointed at Brujic, the cocky smile vanished, and Marko detected a confused panic settle over the man.

"Andrija, roll up your sleeves," said Grahovac.

Brujic hesitated, glancing around as if it was a joke.

"Roll up your sleeves," he repeated calmly.

When Brujic didn't respond immediately, he lost his composure.

"Wrestle that fuck to the ground!" he screamed, spurring several members of the platoon to grab Brujic's arms and pin him to the dirt.

"Roll up his fucking sleeves!" Grahovac spat.

Without ripping the buttons, the camouflage sleeves only came up midway between the wrist and elbow, but it was enough to expose a thick, shiny watch. Very expensive looking.

"I want to see that watch," Grahovac said, taking a few steps away from Marko toward the messy tangle of men sprawled out on the ground.

One of the men stripped the watch from Brujic's wrist and tossed it to Grahovac, who took a several seconds to inspect it. Brujic broke the silence, which may or may not have made a difference in the outcome.

"He's the one that gave it to me! He said it was a fake that he stole from some shithead in the Zemun market. This is a fucking setup! Can't you see that?" he said.

Although he never actually said it, the tone suggested he meant to add "you stupid fuck" to the end of the sentence.

When several members of the platoon and Radovan's security detail chuckled at his comment, Marko knew the man was as good as dead. He still had no idea if he'd survive the next few minutes, but he now had a much better chance.

"Mr...?" he paused and looked to Marko to finish his sentence.

"Resja. Marko Resja, sir," he replied.

"Mr. Resja gave you this watch, in attempt to frame you?" he said, turning back to Brujic, who strained against the thick hands pressing him to the ground.

Now the laughter grew, as Radovan's tone implied that Brujic's story was nonsense.

"Yes! He gave it to me a few days ago. Out of the blue. He's trying to pull some shit on us. The watch is a fake. I don't have money to buy expensive watches," he said.

"But you have money to eat in expensive restaurants?"

"That's different. I wasn't paying. It was that whore from the—"

His comment was interrupted by a solid kick to the face by Grahovac's black, spit-polished combat boot, which momentarily silenced his desperate plea.

"Haul him up and shut him up," he said and turned around to Marko.

While the men struggled to get Brujic to his feet, Grahovac tossed the watch to Resja.

"That's a twenty-eight thousand dollar Rolex Cosmograph. I own two just like it. I could use a keen eye like yours on my security detail. Consider that a reward, and wear it as a reminder of what happens if you betray the cause," he said, in a more controlled tone.

Twenty-six thousand, eight hundred and ninety-five dollars to be precise. Arranged through an exclusive jeweler at the Potsdamer Platz Arkaden in Berlin. Paid for, in advance of pickup, by General Sanderson.

"What happens to him?" Marko asked, against Brujic's duct tape muffled screams.

"He goes into the pit with the rest of them, after Nenad's crew works him over," Grahovac replied, turning to the platoon leader.

"Give him the special treatment, reserved exclusively for the Kosovar whore queens…and get rid of that shit over there. What the fuck are you keeping them around for?" he demanded, pointing at the huddled women and children sitting off to the side, under armed guard.

"We wanted to save a few of them for you and your men," Nenad replied.

"Get rid of them, and get out of here. I want this wrapped up in thirty minutes."

"Grab your rifle, and hop in the rear vehicle. You smell like donkey shit," Grahovac uttered, still glaring at Brujic's battered, duct-taped face.

Marko ran off to grab his gear. When he returned, Radovan and his entourage were already on their way to the Range Rovers, forcing him to sprint to catch up with them. Radovan glanced his way.

"Sniper, eh? Any good?" he yelled.

Nenad, who stood a few feet away, answered the question for Marko.

"One of the best I've seen in a while, sir!" he said, then slapped Marko on the back. "Don't embarrass us, Resja,"

Marko nodded before climbing into the back seat of the rear SUV. The rich smell of leather penetrated the stench he had choked on for the entire three-day field operation, easing him into the vehicles luxurious interior.

"Fuck, man. You do smell like shit. Crack the windows," said the man directly in front of Marko.

"Bojan," said the burly guard next to Marko, extending his hand.

"Marko. What's going to happen to them?" he said.

"Your buddies in front of the pit?" said Bojan. "They're going into the pit…where they belong."

Marko stared out of the window at Sava, who looked slightly relaxed, despite the fact that they hadn't been allowed to face away from the pit. He was glad that the Range Rover's tinted windows hid his face. If Sava locked eyes with him for even a moment, the boy would know that he was as good as dead. He just hoped they made it quick for him. His thoughts of Sava faded, as the SUV started slowly moving away from the center of the village. Phase two of his mission had just begun.

He had just passed the most critical test for any covert field operative. What the psychologists and psychiatrists involved in Black Flag's mental readiness division program called a "permanent trust point," or "PTP." They had told his training class that most operatives will never reach a "permanent trust point" with any of the organizations they are attempting to penetrate, and among those operatives who do, even fewer will survive the circumstances surrounding it.

Marko had pulled off the impossible—but he still had a long way to go. Radovan Grahovac's personal security detail was a few tiers away from Srecko Hadzic's inner circle; the ultimate goal assigned to him by General Sanderson.

To be among the first to learn about new releases, exclusive content, future discounts, visit Steven's blog at:

StevenKonkoly.com

where you can join my mailing list and receive exclusive news, content and discounts regarding my work.

Work by Steven Konkoly

Fractured State Series—Near-future black ops thriller
"2035. A sinister conspiracy unravels. A state on the verge of secession. A man on the run with his family."
Fractured State (Book 1)
Rogue State (Book 2)

The Perseid Collapse Series—Post-apocalyptic/dystopian thrillers
"2019. Six years after the Jakarta Pandemic, life is back to normal for Alex Fletcher and most Americans. Not for long."
The Jakarta Pandemic (Prequel)
The Perseid Collapse (Book 1)
Event Horizon (Book 2)
Point of Crisis (Book 3)
Dispatches (Book 4)

The Black Flagged Series—Black Ops/Political thrillers
"Daniel Petrovich, the most lethal operative created by the Department of Defense's Black Flag Program, protects a secret buried in the deepest vaults of the Pentagon. A secret that is about to unravel his life."
Black Flagged Alpha (Book 1)
Black Flagged Redux (Book 2)
Black Flagged Apex (Book 3)
Black Flagged Vektor (Book 4)
Black Flagged Omega (Book 5)
JET BLACK (Novella)

Wayward Pines Kindle World:
GENESIS (Compilation of novellas set in Blake Crouch's Wayward Pines story)

About the Author

Steven graduated from the United States Naval Academy in 1993, receiving a bachelor of science in English literature. He served the next eight years on active duty, traveling the world as a naval officer assigned to various Navy and Marine Corps units. His extensive journey spanned the globe, including a two-year tour of duty in Japan and travel to more than twenty countries throughout Asia and the Middle East.

From enforcing United Nations sanctions against Iraq as a maritime boarding officer in the Arabian Gulf, to directing aircraft bombing runs and naval gunfire strikes as a Forward Air Controller (FAC) assigned to a specialized Marine Corps unit, Steven's "in-house" experience with a wide range of regular and elite military units brings a unique authenticity to his thrillers.

He lives with his family in central Indiana, where he still wakes up at "zero dark thirty" to write for most of the day. When "off duty," he spends as much time as possible outdoors or travelling with his family—and dog.

Steven is the bestselling author of ten novels and several novellas, including a commissioned trilogy of novellas based on the popular Wayward Pines series. His canon of work includes the popular Black Flagged Series, a gritty, no-holds barred covert operations and espionage saga; The Perseid Collapse series, a post-apocalyptic thriller epic chronicling the events surrounding an inconceivable attack on the United States; and The Fractured State series, a near-future, dystopian thriller trilogy set in the drought-ravaged Southwest.

He is an active member of the International Thriller Writers (ITW) and Science Fiction and Fantasy Writers of America (SFWA) organizations.

You can contact Steven directly by email (stevekonkoly@striblingmedia.com) or through his blog www.stevenkonkoly.com

Made in the USA
Columbia, SC
02 November 2018